RACHEL CAINE is the international bestselling author of over thirty novels, including the *New York Times* bestselling Morganville Vampires series. She was born at White Sands Missile Range, which people who know her say explains a lot. She has been an accountant, an insurance investigator and a professional musician, and has played with such musical legends as Henry Mancini, Peter Nero and John Williams. She and her husband, fantasy artist R. Cat Conrad, live in Texas with their iguana Pop-eye, a *mali uromastyx* named (appropriately) O'Malley, and a leopard tortoise named Shelley (for the poet, of course).

www.rachelcaine.com

By Rachel Caine

The Weather Warden series
Ill Wind
Heat Stroke
Chill Factor
Windfall
Firestorm
Thin Air
Gale Force
Cape Storm
Total Eclipse

The Morganville Vampires series
Glass Houses
The Dead Girls' Dance
Midnight Alley
Feast of Fools
Lord of Misrule
Carpe Corpus
Fade Out
Kiss of Death
Ghost Town
Bite Club

Morganville Vampires Omnibus:
Glass Houses, The Dead Girls' Dance, Midnight Alley

a&b

Gale Force

WEATHER WARDEN
BOOK SEVEN

RACHEL CAINE

This edition first published in 2011 by
Allison & Busby Limited
13 Charlotte Mews
London W1T 4EJ
www.allisonandbusby.com

A CIP catalogue record for this book is available from
the British Library.

First published in the US in 2008.

10 9 8 7 6 5 4 3 2 1

ISBN 978-0-7490-0989-2

Typeset in 11.5/16.25 pt Sabon by
Allison & Busby Ltd.

The paper used for this Allison & Busby publication
has been produced from trees that have been legally sourced
from well-managed and credibly certified forests.

Printed and bound in the UK by
CPI Bookmarque, Croydon, CR0 4TD

Gale Force

Prologue

'Honey!' I yelled. 'Get the phone, would you?' It was ringing off the hook, and I was a little busy trying to put out a fire – a wildfire, actually, blazing across Alligator Alley along the coast of Florida. It had been burning for three long days, sending choking black smoke our way.

Never off duty, that was me. Joanne Baldwin: Weather Warden by first choice – if a world-ending storm blew up without notice, I was the go-to girl. My secondary ability – and second choice – was to act as a Fire Warden, which was what was occupying me at the moment. Being an Earth Warden, helping living things heal and grow, and controlling things such as earthquakes and volcanoes, was also something I could do, though not nearly as reliably or as well. As far as being comfortable with the abilities, having Earth powers was still a distant, weird, cautious third.

I stood on the balcony of my apartment building, my eyes stinging from the whipping wind and drifting smoke, and worked magic. It didn't look like I was doing much of anything. Truthfully, I probably could have gone inside, picked up the phone, and talked to whatever cold-calling telemarketer was on the other end . . . but I was feeling frustrated, and I needed to do something positive, so I was concentrating, from a distance of several miles away, on rendering burnable underbrush less burnable. These changes would have to be undone later, for safety, but they made dandy firebreaks in the meantime.

Of course, I was interfering with Fire Wardens and Weather Wardens who were already doing their assigned jobs. Well, that was why I was the boss, right? That was what bosses did – interfere. (My bosses always had, anyway, although come to think of it, I hadn't liked it much when I'd been on the sticky end of the problem.)

The phone quit ringing. *Good,* I thought. Maybe they'd just given up.

The glass door behind me rumbled open on its track. I didn't turn away from the railing until a man's hand dangled the phone over my shoulder. I looked at the phone delivery service, eyebrows raised in silent question; David just raised his own in response.

David was always fantastic on the eyes, but

he was especially great just now, at sunset, when the red sky picked up bronze tints in his skin and highlighted supernatural sparks in his eyes. Oh, his eyes – currently the rich, dark color of old pennies – were taking on a brighter hue as I watched, because although David was currently wearing human form, and liked to wear it a lot, at a DNA level he was something completely different. We call them Djinn, because the old tales of those supernatural creatures able to do humans' dirty work were somewhat true.

Of course, these tales were also a whole lot *not* true, as I continued to learn every day.

David was only half dressed, in a pair of worn blue jeans riding low on his hips. There was a lot of tempting gold-dusted skin on display, and so much to admire, from broad shoulders to abs that would make a Greek statue cry with envy.

He usually had a shirt on, but then, David was actually more modest than I was. At least, in public. In private . . . well. Let's just say that when David played at being human, he brought his A game.

David waggled the phone again, significantly. I blinked and took it, thinking that the last thing in the world I wanted just now was to get distracted from enjoying the view. 'Hello?'

I wasn't prepared for the volume – or the tirade – that erupted out of the phone. 'Joanne, would you please *butt out* already? Jeez, woman, we *can* save the world without you! Just go relax! Do you even own a dictionary? *Vacation!* Look it up!'

The voice on the other end was Paul Giancarlo, one of the most powerful element-controlling Wardens in the country. He happened to specialize in weather work; he was also one of my oldest surviving friends. The tone was a strongly Jersey-accented bellow, barely contained by the phone's speaker. I held the phone farther from my ear, 'Oh, hey, Paul,' I said. 'So. How's that fire going?'

'The fire is going *fine,* and you need to quit screwing around. You are *not* on duty. I have coverage on the damn fire, and you need to stop—'

'Helping? Thought you needed it. Because three days is kind of a long time to be breathing smoke—'

'*Kid.* Stop already. We're on top of it!'

I doubted that. 'Let me talk to Lewis.' Lewis Levander Orwell, my old college buddy and part-time crush, was the only guy in the entire Wardens organisation who still had the right to tell me what to do, a fact that made me a little smug and – yes, I could admit it – a little insufferable.

'Lewis doesn't want to talk to you. Lewis wants me to tell you to *butt out.* Get it? You're on vacation. Vacate already.'

Before I could fire back, Paul hung up on me. I stared at the phone, surprised and a little wounded.

David took it from my fingers, put it on the patio table behind me, and said, 'I assume he told you that you aren't needed right now. No, actually I don't assume that. I overheard.'

'Eavesdropper.'

'People three doors down heard it,' he said. 'It wasn't a great feat of supernatural detection.'

I glared at him for a second, but honestly, I couldn't stay angry at David, especially when he gave me that *look*.

But I glanced toward the fire again anyway, and I heard him sigh. 'Jo. Let go. I know how hard it is for you, but you need to let other people handle their jobs. That's why they have them.'

'Three days!' I said, pointing an accusatory finger toward the smoke. 'Come on, you don't think they could have been a *little* more aggressive about it?'

'You know as well as I do that sometimes managing how a fire burns is more important than putting it out,' he said all too reasonably, and stepped between me and my view of the conflagration. Not that he wasn't, you know, burning hot himself. Because he definitely was, and I felt myself inevitably getting distracted.

'Stop that,' I said, not with a lot of strength.

'Stop what?' He reached for my hands, and I shivered as a breeze moved across my back, which was left mostly bare by my sky-blue halter top.

Florida had been kind to me, for a change, with lots of sun, lots of untroubled, cloud-free beaches. It was as if the Wardens themselves had conspired to make my vacation uneventful, at least on the weather front, until this fire thing had popped up.

And that had been OK for the first couple days. And then it had just kept on coming. I know it sounds crazy, but I'd gotten a little bit too rested.

Not that David couldn't make that haunting feeling of uselessness go away; he was promising to, just with the gentle pressure of his fingers moving up my bare arms.

'Stop making me want you,' I said. That got the eyebrows again, and a slightly wounded frown.

'*Making* you?'

'You know what I mean.'

'No, I don't, actually. You think I'm manipulating you?'

'You're Djinn,' I said. 'Manipulating people is basically built into your DNA. I'm not really sure you can help it. But – I didn't mean that. I'm just – I'm sorry. I don't know what I'm thinking. I just—'

'You want to be taking action,' he said. 'Yes. I know. You really do need to learn how to let go.'

'What I *don't* need is even more vacation.' I stepped back from David and dropped grumpily into a deck chair, stretching my long, bare legs out in front of me. The tan was coming along nicely. *Great accomplishment. Everybody else is saving the world; you're golden-browning.*

'Oh, I think you definitely do,' David said, and draped himself over the other chair, chin propped on his fist. 'I have never met anyone who needed to learn to relax more than you do.'

And that was saying a lot; he'd met a lot of people – millions, probably. I still didn't have any clear idea of how old David really was, only that his birth date was so far back in history that the idea of calendars had been newfangled. He'd been around, my lover. The fact that he was hanging around here, letting me be bitchy to him, was kind of amazing.

Before I could apologize to him, the phone rang again. I picked up the cordless extension, pressed the button, and said, 'Paul, I swear, I'm not—'

A businesslike voice on the other end said, 'May I speak with Joanne Baldwin?'

'Speaking.' I rolled my eyes at David. Another attempt to sell me flood insurance or steel hurricane shutters. I readied the I'm-in-an-apartment speech, which usually served to put a stop to these things.

'Ms Baldwin, hello, my name is Phil Garrett. I'm an investigative reporter with the *New York Times*. I'd like to speak with you about the organisation known as the Wardens. I believe you're one of its senior members. Could I have your title?'

I blinked, and my expression must have been

something to behold, because David slowly straightened up in his chair, leaning forward. 'You – sorry, what? What did you say?'

'Phil Garrett. *New York Times*. Calling about the Wardens. I have some questions for you.'

'I' – my voice locked tight in my throat – 'got another call, hold on.' In a panic, I hit the END CALL button and put the phone down on the table, staring at it as if it had grown eight legs and was about to scuttle off. 'Oh my God.'

'What?' David asked. He looked interested, not alarmed. Apparently, I was amusing when panicked.

The phone rang again. I didn't move to pick it up, David took it and said, pleasantly, 'Yes?' There was a pause while he listened. 'I see. Mr Garrett, I'm very sorry, but Ms Baldwin can't speak to you right now. What's your deadline?' His mouth compressed into a thin line, clearly trying not to smile at whatever my face was doing now. I could hardly breathe, I felt so cold. 'I see. That's fairly soon. Ms Baldwin is actually on vacation right now. Maybe there's someone else you can—' Another pause, and his gaze darted toward mine. 'You were given her number.'

I mouthed, blankly, *Shit!* David lifted one shoulder in a half shrug. This could not be happening. I mouthed, *By who?* David dutifully repeated the question.

'Not at liberty to divulge your sources,' he said, for my benefit. 'I see. If you want my opinion, I think you're being used, Mr Garrett. And you're wasting your time.'

He listened. I felt my heart hammer even faster. Mr Garrett wasn't going down easy.

'I'll have her call you back,' David said, hung up, and put the phone back on the table. He leant forward, watching me, hands folded. 'You're scared.'

I nodded, with way too much emphasis. 'Reporters. I *hate* reporters. I hate reporters from little weekly papers in One Horse, Wyoming, so how much do you think I'm going to hate somebody from the *New York Times*? Guess.'

'You don't even know him. Maybe this is a good thing. Good publicity.'

'Are you on crack? Of course it's not a good thing! He's a *reporter!* And we're a *secret organisation!* Who the hell gave him his info? And my number?'

'Jo, he's a reporter. He didn't have to get your number from anyone inside the Wardens. He could have gotten it through simple research. As to what put him on to the whole topic . . .' David shrugged. He was right. With all the disasters and potentially life-destroying events that we'd had the last few years, the Wardens had been a little more public than anyone liked.

And so had I.

I grabbed for the phone and dialed Lewis's cell. It rang to voicemail. 'Lewis, call me back. I've got reporter troubles. Look, if this is your idea of a joke and you staked me out as the sacrificial goat for the media, I am not going to be the only one on the altar when they get out the knives—'

David took the phone and hung it up, very calmly. 'That's enough of the metaphor,' he said. 'Look, you don't need to flail around. You know what to say. Deny everything. They won't have proof. They never do. And even if they do have something, refer them to the government and the UN. It'll go away.'

'What if it doesn't?' I chewed my lip in agitation, tasting tangerine gloss. Great. Now I was destroying my makeup, too, and the whole purpose of lip gloss was to stay interestingly kissable. 'Look, it's the *Times*. This is different. I'm worried.'

David cocked his head, looking bemused now. 'I've seen you face down monsters, hurricanes, and tornadoes, and you're scared of a phone call?'

'It's bigger than that.' I felt it in my gut. 'There was a reporter a few months ago. When I was on my way to Sedona with Venna. She knew things. It was just a matter of time, I guess, before word got around and people got to digging. Dammit! I should have known this was coming.'

He leant forward and took my hands. His felt warm, strong, calming. 'I have a question that will scare you even more, if you want to change the subject,' he said, after a long moment.

I frowned at him. 'No games.'

'No. This is a serious question.' He slipped off the deck chair, and one knee touched the concrete balcony floor. He never looked away from my face, and he never let go of my hands. 'This is a question that's going to need a serious answer.'

My heart froze, then skipped to catch up on its beats. 'I—' I couldn't begin to think of what to say. I just waited. I probably had it all wrong, anyway.

'Will you marry me?' he asked.

Oh. I didn't have it wrong at all.

My lips parted, and nothing, absolutely nothing, came out. Was he *serious*? He couldn't be serious. We were comfortable together; we had love, we had partnership, we had – everything.

Everything except . . . well, this – an official kind of commitment.

Not possible, some part of my brain reported briskly. David was a supernatural Djinn, only partly tied to the mortal world. I might have been a Warden, with extra powers over wind, water, air, earth, living things . . . but I was just human, when it came down to brass tacks. He was immortal; I wasn't, and I was achingly aware of that, every day that passed between us.

'David . . .' I came up against an absolute blank wall, inspirationally speaking. 'I – can we talk about this later?'

'Why? So you can come up with reasons to justify your fears about me leaving you?' He wasn't angry; he didn't mean it to hurt. It was matter-of-fact and strangely even gentle. 'Jo, I need to know that you feel as I do. I need to have you with me. And – it's mortal custom.' He was clearly reaching on that last one.

'Have you been married before?' There, I'd asked it. We didn't go into his past a lot, but I knew it was ancient, and there had been plenty of relationships – Djinn as well as human.

He raised my hands to his lips, and I shivered at the warm, intimate kiss. 'Yes,' he said. 'Ages ago. Before I knew what I was waiting to feel.'

I stared at him. 'And now you know.'

'Of course I know,' he said. His eyes had taken on the burning purity of newly minted copper. 'I was waiting for you.'

The phone rang. My gaze went to it; I was startled, but didn't move to pick up. One ring, and it cut off. I wasn't sure if the caller had thought better of it, or if David had severed the connection.

'If you say no, it's all right. I will stay with you as long as you want me to stay,' he said. 'You won't lose me. You don't have to agree if this doesn't feel right to you.'

'But it's important to you.'

'Yes. Or I wouldn't have brought it up.' David looked troubled for a second, as if he was unsure of how much – or little – to say. Then he plunged ahead. 'When humans make their vows to each other, it's the closest they can come to the depth of commitment a Djinn feels. You see? I just want – I'm afraid of losing you.'

And it had taken him a lot to risk the question – I knew that. David's feelings for me were fierce and constant; it was part of who the Djinn were. But human feelings were changeable, and I had no doubt he lived in fear that one day I'd wake up and be a different person, one he couldn't reach.

Being married wouldn't lessen that risk, but it was a symbol, a trust.

It all came down to trust. His, and mine.

'This is crazy,' I breathed. 'What the *hell* are the Djinn going to say?'

'Nothing, if they know what's good for them.' There was a glimmer of coldness to his tone. David was the leader of about half of the Djinn – the good half, in my opinion, although there were exceptions. The other half was led by a Djinn named Ashan, an icy bastard who didn't like me very much and wasn't especially warm toward David, either. 'If you're worrying what it will do to my standing among them, don't.'

But I had to think about that, didn't I? It wasn't just the two of us. The Wardens might have a thing or two to say about a human marrying a Djinn, too. And what minister was going to bless this union, anyway?

Aside from their religious beliefs, most ministers didn't believe in the supernatural, at least not in any good kind of way. And I knew David. He'd want complete honesty in this, no matter how difficult that would be.

The day was getting darker, the sky turning from denim to indigo. On the horizon, the sun was nearly down, pulling its glorious trailing rays with it.

Black, greasy smoke drifted into my eyes, and I blinked and coughed. David glanced at it, annoyed, and the smoke disappeared – moved elsewhere. The air around us was fresh and clear.

'Jo,' he said, 'you don't have to answer now. I just . . . had to ask the question.'

I ought to say no. I knew that. I just *knew*.

'Yes,' I said, and something in me broke loose with a wild, silent cry. I was off the cliff now, I realised, with a fierce joy, and that felt good. It felt free.

His eyes ignited into a color found only in the heart of the sun. 'Yes?'

'Yes, already. I'll marry you. Yes. Hell, yes. What am I, stupid?'

The phone rang again. David let go of my hands, picked up the extension, and thumbed it on without looking away from my face, 'Mr Garrett, I'm taking my lover to bed,' he said. 'If you know what's good for you, you'll reschedule your deadline.'

And he crushed the phone as if it were made of

marshmallow crème and dropped the smashed pieces on the patio table.

'Oh,' I said faintly. 'Problem solved. Good approach.'

On the horizon, the fire in Alligator Alley continued to glow. I discovered that I didn't care at all, as David's hand pulled me to my feet and into his arms.

I woke up hours later to the sound of screaming sirens. The Wardens had majorly screwed up – again. My apartment complex was on fire. We were being evacuated.

That was it. I was never going on vacation again.

Chapter One

Getting married was like planning a military invasion of a distant foreign country, only instead of moving soldiers and guns, you were organising bridesmaids and bouquets.

Of course, my bridesmaids were bound to be pretty tough chicks. I couldn't really be sure there wouldn't be guns.

'You know,' said my best friend, Cherise, staring thoughtfully into the mirror and smoothing her hands down the clinging lines of her dress, 'there's a math formula for wedding dresses.'

I blinked at her. I was trying to figure out if the layer cake of tulle and lace I had on constituted romantic excess, or if it looked like I'd fought off a demented pastry chef and barely escaped with my life. 'What?'

'The problem is, *this* dress looks totally fabulous

on me. And the better the bridesmaid's gown looks on her, the fuglier the bride's. I'm just pointing it out because I'm a kindhearted person, you know.'

She was right – she did look totally fabulous in the dress. The color was a dark rose, one that wildly complemented Cherise's blond hair and beautiful skin. It was a simple sheath dress, clinging in all the right places, and it ended at the right length for her, just below the knee, to display her perfectly sculpted calves to full advantage. No dyed generic pumps for Cherise; she'd scoured the stores and come up with a pair of Jimmy Choo shoes that made me pray to the fashion gods for something half as great to appear in my closet.

The first time I'd ever met Cherise, she'd looked fantastic. Cherise could look delicious wearing an oversized foam-rubber sun – I know, I've seen her do it, back in the days we both worked for the local bottom-of-the-barrel TV station as weather girls.

I, on the other hand, did *not* look delicious. I looked like a wedding cake that hadn't quite risen properly. And white really wasn't my color.

'You're a true friend,' I said, and unzipped my dress to let it slide into a confusion of frippery on the dressing room floor. The waiting dress wrangler rescued it, fussily dusted it, and put it back on a hanger and in a garment bag, the better to protect its doubtful charms. 'Right. Something in off-white? With less—' I made a vague, poofy gesture with my hands. The sales clerk, who must have seen brides make a thousand terrible decisions, looked relieved. She nodded and turned to Cherise.

'Ma'am?' she asked. 'Can I bring you some more selections?'

Cherise turned, hands on hips. 'You're kidding, right? Look, I gave her fair warning. I am *not* giving up this dress. I'll be maid of honor, but not *matronly* of honor.'

'Keep the dress,' I said hastily. 'It really does look great on you. So you're done. It's just me we're still working on.'

Cherise, mollified, unzipped and shimmied out of the dress. *She* was the one who fussed with it, getting it hung just so, and zipped it into the garment bag before handing it to the sales clerk. 'Be sure nothing happens to it,' she said. 'Put my name on it in giant letters: Cherise. In fact, if you've got a vault—'

'Cher,' I said, 'leave the poor lady alone. She's dealing with enough as it is. Your dress is safe.'

'Maybe I should take it with me.'

'Maybe you should put your clothes on. I'm feeling kind of outclassed, here.'

Cherise grinned, undermining her Playboy Bunny appeal but making herself real in a way most pretty women weren't. She looked after herself with care, but she also didn't put too much emphasis on it. Cherise liked to do things that the Genetically Chosen Few generally didn't, like read, geek out on TV shows, indulge in online gaming. Her most prominent body decoration, which showed plainly as she turned to gather up her jeans and tank top from the bench, was a Gray – a little gray alien tattoo waving hello from the small of her back, where most beautiful women would have put a rose as a tramp stamp.

That was Cherise, cheerfully mowing down the barriers.

I sat down on the other bench, legs crossed, feeling exposed and vulnerable in my lacy underthings. I had a huge list of things still to do for the wedding, and I was running out of time, and the last thing I needed to be doing was obsessing about the dress. I mean, I had good taste in clothes, right? I could usually walk into a store, grab something right off the rack, and get it right.

Today, I'd gone through more dresses than I'd worn in the last year. Maybe I ought to try the designer line again. Or get married in a garbage bag. Add a couple of frills, a nice bow – couldn't be worse than what I'd just seen myself in today. There was a fashion hell. I'd been there.

'You OK?' Cherise finished buttoning up her jeans, skimmed her top down to street-legal levels, flipped her hair, and voila, she was fantastic. She stepped out of the Jimmy Choo pumps and boxed them up with the care usually reserved for crown jewels or religious relics, and slid her perfectly pedicured toes into a pair of hot-pink flip-flops. 'Because you look a little bit—'

'Spooked,' I supplied sourly. 'Worried. Scared. Nuts. Insane. Completely, utterly—'

'I was going to say hungry. It's already two hours after we should have had lunch.'

Low blood sugar probably was impairing my impressive dress-choosing skills, and even though this was a full-service bridal store, I doubted that they catered. 'Oh,' I said. 'Right. Lunch.' Now that she mentioned it, my stomach growled impatiently, as if it had been trying to get my attention for a while and was ready to cannibalise another body part. I reached for my own jeans and top and began tugging them on. I wasn't as perfectly body-balanced as Cherise, but I had legs for days, and even in flats I topped her by several inches.

The hard-working clerk came back, sweating under a forklift's worth of alternate dress choices. I froze in the act of zipping up my pants. 'Um—'

Cherise, rightly identifying a moment when a maid of honor could take one for the bridal team, smiled winningly at the clerk and said, 'Sorry, but I've got a nail appointment. We'll have to come back later. Could you keep those out? I swear, it'll be an hour, tops.' She caught my look. 'Two, at the most.'

The clerk looked around the dressing room, which had far fewer hooks than she had dresses, sighed, and nodded.

I had just finished fastening the top button on my pants when I felt the whole store distinctly shake, as if a giant hand had grabbed the place and yanked. I froze, bracing myself on the wall, and saw Cherise do the same. The clerk froze under her load of thousand-dollar frocks.

And then all hell broke loose. The floor bucked, walls undulated, cracks ripped through plaster, and the air exploded with the sounds of glass crashing, things falling, and timbers snapping. The sales clerk screamed, dropped the gowns, and flung herself into the doorway, bracing herself with both hands.

I should have taken cover – Cherise sensibly did, curling instantly into a ball under the nearest cover, which was the bench on her side.

What did I do? I stood there. And I launched myself hard into the aetheric, rising out of the physical world and into a plane of existence where the lines of force were more clearly visible.

Not good. The entire area of Fort Lauderdale was a boiling confusion of forces, most erupting out of a fault line running directly under the store in which I stood. It looked as if somebody had dropped a bucket of red and black dye into a washing machine and set it on full churn.

We were so screwed.

I sensed other Wardens rising into the aetheric, responding to the crisis; there were two or three of them relatively close whose signatures I recognised – two were Weather, which wasn't much help, but one was an Earth Warden, and a powerful one.

I flung my still-new Earth Warden powers deep into the foundations of the building in which my physical form was still trapped, and began shoring up the structure. It was taking a beating, but the wood responded to me, healing itself and binding into an at least temporarily unbreakable frame. The metal was tougher, but it also fell within my powers, so I braced it up as I went, creating a lightning-fast shell of stability in a world that wouldn't hold together for long.

I reached out, in the aetheric, and connected with the other Earth Warden; together, we were able to blanket part of the rift with power, like pouring superglue on an open wound. Not a miracle, it was just a bandage, but enough. I didn't know enough about how to balance the forces of the Earth; it was different from the flashing, volatile energy of Fire or the massive, ponderous fury of Weather. It had all kinds of slow, unstoppable momentum, and I felt very fragile standing in its way.

Help, I said to the other Earth Warden – not that talking was really talking on the aetheric. It was crude communication, at best, but he got the message. I watched as he spread himself thin, and his aura settled deep into the heart of the boiling red of the disturbance.

Oh, hell no. No way was I going there.

Then again, if I didn't, I was leaving him alone to do the dirty work – the potentially fatal dirty work.

I took a deep metaphorical breath, steadied myself, and stepped off the cliff.

Sensations are different on the aetheric – properly, they're not sensations at all, because all the nerve endings are still firmly planted down on terra firma. But the mind processes stimuli, no matter how unpleasant or strange, and so what it felt like to me on my way down, following my Earth Warden colleague, was . . . pressure – being squeezed, lightly at first, then more intensely. It was like diving in the ocean and swimming deeper and deeper, but this didn't feel like liquid; it felt more like a metal vise, cranking inexorably tighter.

I faltered and nearly bugged out, but I caught a glimpse of the other Warden. He was below me, only a bit farther, and I decided that if he could do it, I had to. Down I went, and if I'd had an actual, physical mouth and lungs, I'd have been screaming and crying by the time I got there.

His aetheric form – which, I noticed, sported shadowy, shoulder-length hair and the ghost of a guitar slung across his back – was kneeling down, studying something. I joined him. He silently indicated what it was he was examining.

I'd never seen anything like it in the aetheric, but I didn't need a college course to tell it was very, very bad. It looked like some kind of black icy knife, sharp on all edges, wickedly pointed at the end. It was plunged deep into the ground, or what represented the ground up here.

The Earth Warden reached out and touched it, and from the way he jerked back, it was a very painful experience.

Well, I hadn't come all this way not to try.

The jolt that went through me when I tried to take hold of the thing felt like being on the receiving end of a live power cable, only not as much fun. I let go – couldn't do anything else – and looked wordlessly at my colleague.

He shook his head and pointed up, indicating we should rise. I nodded. Up we went, slowly, letting the pressure bleed off. I didn't suppose we'd get the bends in the aetheric, but it didn't seem prudent to push it, and besides, I was still trembling from the jolt that piece of black ice had sent through me.

Far above, in the softer regions of air, he made a gesture that was clear even in the aetheric – thumb toward his ear, little finger toward his mouth. And then he pointed from himself to me.

He was going to call me. I nodded and waved, and dropped out of the aetheric, back into my body.

The earthquake had stopped . . . temporarily, at least. The dress shop was a mess – plaster cracked, mirrors broken, racks toppled. Disaster with a designer label. Somebody was shaking me. Cherise. She had her hands fisted in my shirt and was trying to haul me up, but I was bigger and she was shaking too much to really be effective on leverage.

I helped her out by lurching to my feet and checking on the store's other occupants, including the clerk. Apart from being terrified, they were all miraculously unharmed, though hair, makeup, and wardrobe had been sacrificed to sweat, tears, and sifting plaster dust.

I made Cherise sit down on a bench and stood for a moment, letting my awareness spread through the structure, looking for major damage. A few cracked support beams, but nothing that couldn't be braced, and nothing that would come down unexpectedly, unless there was another hard jolt like the first one, which I couldn't guarantee wouldn't happen.

I pulled my cell phone out as it began to ring, and walked to the front, where plate glass windows had once been. They were now a glitter of broken fragments inside and outside the store. People were gathering out in the street, which was a hazard in itself, as drivers tried to navigate their way through to check on their families, their homes, their businesses. Nobody looked badly hurt, but everybody looked shell-shocked. Earthquakes in California came with the territory, but in Florida?

I answered the call. 'Joanne Baldwin.'

'Warden, it's Luis Rocha. Earth Warden. We met up top.' Meaning, up in the aetheric. I didn't know his voice, but I liked it – warm, brisk, efficient. No wasted words. 'Everybody OK there?'

'Looks like.' No wasted words here, either, apparently. 'Good work up there.'

'You too, but I'm worried. I don't know what the hell that thing is we saw, but whatever it is, it needs looking into.'

'You think it's the cause of what just happened?'

'Any place can have earthquakes, but not without some warning signs, and there weren't any. External cause, has to be. That thing – it seems to be the epicenter, and no way is that supposed to be there.'

I frowned. 'You think it could do more damage?'

'Don't know, but I wouldn't leave it there. We need to figure out what this thing is, fast.'

'My job,' I said. 'I'll get the Djinn on it. You do your thing, Warden Rocha, and thank you. Excellent job.'

I heard the grin in his voice. 'Yeah, well, put it on my bonus schedule. Adios, señora.'

'Adios,' I said, and hung up. I slipped the phone

into my pocket and wondered, for the first time, why David wasn't—

'I'm right here,' David said, appearing out of thin air in mid stride. He was dressed for business, not pleasure – sturdy blue jeans, a plain shirt, thick boots, and his long olive-drab coat. Glasses, too. They glittered like ice in the reflected shine from the broken glass. He didn't halt at a polite distance; he came right up and put his hands around my face, wordlessly smoothing away plaster dust, and placed a warm kiss on my forehead. I felt the various aches and pains melt away, and a mad jittering inside me go still and calm. I hadn't even realised how tense I was.

'What kept you?' My tone stayed dry, although I had a strange desire to burst into tears. 'Next time, don't stop for traffic lights, OK?'

He sighed and put his arms around me. 'Safe driving isn't just a good idea; it's the law,' he reminded me, in that mocking way that only Djinn can. He'd no more think of obeying traffic laws than I would that thing about not wearing white after Labor Day. 'Sorry. We were busy.'

'Yeah, no kidding. Busy here, too. What's—' My phone rang. I stepped back from him with an apologetic what-can-you-do lift of my hands, and answered, 'Baldwin.'

It was my friend and (technically) boss, Lewis,

and he was uncharacteristically angry. 'What the *hell* did you think you were doing?' he demanded. He was someplace close, or at least equally affected; I could hear the rising babble of confused voices and car alarms. 'We're going to be damn lucky if the whole eastern seaboard isn't in chaos by the end of the day!'

I stopped what I was about to say, frowned, and rewound what he'd said. I listened to it again in my head before saying, cautiously, 'Hang on a second. You think it's my fault?'

I felt, rather than heard, him coming to a complete stop wherever he was, as if I'd gotten his undivided attention. I hoped he wasn't standing in the middle of the street, like the idiots outside. And I thought he was replaying what *I'd* just said. 'Are you saying it isn't your fault?' he asked.

'I'm about ninety-nine percent sure I had nothing to do with it.'

'You were seen in the middle of the—'

'Yeah, trying to *fix it,* which is sort of my job!' I snapped, and looked at David. He was watching me with warm brown eyes, looking almost completely human. I wondered what kind of effort that was taking. 'If you don't believe me, ask the other Warden. Luis Rocha. He was there. He saw what I saw.'

'Rocha,' Lewis repeated thoughtfully. 'Yeah, I know him. Luis is solid. OK, let me talk to him, but meanwhile – sorry. I just thought, with you new to your Earth powers—'

'You thought I'd go yank around at force lines in the ground, because they were there? What am I, four? Come on, man.'

Ah, there was the Lewis I knew and loved, in that ironic lift in his voice. 'Jo, you know damn well that if you're standing at ground zero of trouble, I have to assume you've got something to do with it.'

'Convicted on prior bad acts?'

'Something like that.' He was moving again. I heard the shrilling call of a siren as it ripped by him and dopplered away, and then heard it coming into audio range on my end – same siren, or very similar. 'Where are you?'

'Delvia's Bridal. Um, it *was* Delvia's Bridal, anyway. I think it's Super Discount Gowns now. At the very least, there's going to be a whole lot of discounting going on.'

'And you say you didn't have a motive,' Lewis replied. 'Right. I'm heading that way. Stay put.'

He hung up before I could assure him I wasn't going anywhere. I looked around. The clerk was making sad attempts to right sales racks and rehang gowns. Cherise exchanged a look with me, nodded, and went to help. David, of course, could have waved a magic hand and put it all back to rights, but that wasn't the way things were done, at least not out here

in the open, where it could be witnessed by the general
public. We'd do most of our helping out later, when
people weren't looking.

At least, I hoped so. The old days of the Wardens
leaving messes behind them were over – or so I'd been
assured. This would, I thought, be a good test of their
resolve to do the right thing, and if they didn't . . . well,
I could always take names, kick asses.

'Not normal,' I said aloud. 'This shouldn't have
happened.'

I didn't need confirmation, but David gave it to me
anyway. 'Someone caused it,' he said.

'A Warden?'

He was silent. When I glanced his way, I saw that
his eyes were growing lighter in color and brighter in
power . . . but then they cooled again, and he shook
his head. 'Unknown.'

'What? How can it be unknown? How can *you*
not know?' Because David, after all, was sort of the
running definition of *omniscient* these days. Imagine
those surveillance cameras you see on every street
corner, only for the Djinn, every single object in the
world, living or inert, has a history and a path through
time that they can follow. David was capable of
unspooling that carpet back and following the threads
to . . . nothing, apparently.

That was unsettling to me – to him, too, because he
shot me a frown and said nothing in his own defense.

He turned away to pace, head down, and I was reminded for all the world of a tracking dog trying to pick up a scent.

Vainly.

I felt a slight bump of power on the aetheric level – it took concentration to detect it – and knew that someone had arrived. Someone of the Djinn variety. Could be a good thing; could be a bad thing . . . Either way, it would be unpredictable.

I turned, a determined smile on my face, and was relieved to see the Djinn Rahel lounging in the cracked doorway, arms folded, surveying the damage with amused, lambently glittering eyes. She was a tall creature, elegant as a heron, but her nature always put me in mind of a hunting hawk – predatory, alert, always on the verge of striking.

Today she wore a bright lavender pantsuit in what looked like (and probably was) the softest of peach skin. It was tailored within an inch of its life, clinging to her long legs and her sculpted torso. Purple was a relaxed color for her, as it was for me. In a less conciliatory mood, she'd have been wearing neon yellow.

'So,' she said, in a low voice as rich as spilt syrup, 'does this mean the wedding is off?'

'You wish,' I said. 'Thanks for the help. Oh, wait . . .'

Her smile widened, revealing white, even teeth. My, she *was* in a good mood. She didn't even bother with sharpening them to freak me out. 'Did you need help, little sister? All you had to do was ask.'

Like I'd had time to pretty-please. She tilted her head, still focused on me, and the hundreds of tiny, meticulous braids in her ebony hair shifted and hissed together, and the tiny beads clacked. Snakes and bones. I resisted the urge to shiver. I liked Rahel, and I thought she liked me, as much as that kind of thing could happen, but I was never really . . . sure. You never could be, with the Djinn.

And once again, she surprised me by saying, 'What do you need?'

Djinn didn't *offer*. But she did, and I gaped at her for a long, unflattering few seconds before I got control and composed myself into a grateful expression. 'If you could check and let me know if you find anybody wounded, anybody in trouble—'

She flipped a negligent hand – perfectly manicured, with opal polish on the sharp nails – and misted away. I looked around. David hadn't bothered to turn, and the humans in the store and on the street had been too preoccupied with their own trauma to recognise a truly strange thing when they saw it.

Two seconds later, more or less, a shadow darkened the doorway, and Lewis edged in past the sagging, glassless metal frame. He looked first to David and nodded; David had turned to face him, which said something about how Lewis rated on the whole threat-level scale as compared to Rahel. Not that Lewis *was* a threat, except in the sense that David probably never forgot (or could forget) that Lewis and I had once been . . . close. Not for ages, but still. It hadn't been the kind of one-night stand you forget.

Even so, the two of them were friends, if cautious friends. And they respected one another.

'Everybody OK here?' Lewis asked. I gave him a silent thumbs-up, not quite daring myself to speak. He looked – well, like Lewis. Drop him in the middle of Manhattan or in a forest in the Great Northwest, and he basically remained unchanged. Blue jeans, hiking boots that had seen miles of hard use, brown hair that shagged a bit too much, a three-day growth of beard on a long, angular face. Almond-shaped, secretive dark eyes. 'Jo. We're setting up a staging area. I'm on my way there now. If you're done here—'

'Yeah, I'll come with,' I said. I'd had a purse at some point, and I went back into the changing room to hunt for it. Good thing it was a hobo bag. I felt as if I matched it nicely, what with the rumpled clothes, sweat, and plaster dust.

When I turned, David was right behind me. He steadied me with big strong hands, looking into my eyes, and I couldn't resist an audible gulp. He just had that effect on me.

'Be careful,' he said, and kissed me. It was probably meant to be one of those gentle little pecks one partner gives another casually, but it turned into something else as our lips warmed and parted and made pledges to each other we couldn't really keep at the moment.

When we parted, I felt significantly more alone, and I could see he did, too. David tapped me on the end of my nose with one finger, an unexpectedly human sort of gesture, and gave me a heartbreaking smile.

'I almost lost you,' he said. 'I hate it when that happens.'

He'd really, truly lost me a couple of times. Once, he'd broken the laws of the Djinn and the universe itself to bring me back. I was well aware how much he'd risked for me, and how much he'd risk again if he had to.

I had to be more careful. Losing myself was one thing. Losing David was an unacceptable something else.

Cherise was still in the main room, hanging up gowns and dusting them off, shaking them out. The clerk, who looked pissed now rather than shattered, was muttering under her breath as she checked each dress for damage. I gave Cherise the high *call-me* sign, and she flashed me a grin and mouthed, *You owe me lunch, bitch!*

Cherise was the fastest rebounding human I'd ever seen. And that was only part of the reason I loved her like a sister.

Considering my actual bitchy, whiny, double-crossy, drug-addicted sister . . . *better* than my sister.

Lewis had a Hummer. I hated Hummers, but I had to admit, it suited him – and he was probably one of the few Hummer drivers who actually used it as God and Jeep intended, to be driven over hard terrain. It looked it, too – muddy, dented, cheerfully well used.

I came to a halt, staring up at the passenger door. 'I swear,' I said, 'if I split these jeans climbing into your damn truck—'

'Need a boost?' Lewis asked from behind me. And I had a terrifically tactile premonition of his big hands going around my waist and lifting me up . . .

Bad for my discipline.

'As if,' I said, and, with a mighty effort, levered myself up to the step and into the cab of the truck. It was like an eighteen-wheeler, only with better upholstery. As I got myself strapped in, Lewis swung in on the opposite side with the ease of long practice, and longer legs. I sniffed. The truck smelt like mud, leaves, wood smoke, and mildew. 'You ever get this thing detailed?'

'What would be the point?' Lewis put it in gear, and

the tank began to roll. He drove slowly, negotiating around stopped cars and people still standing in the middle of the street. Normal life was starting to reassert itself. As we got farther from the dress shop, I saw that the damage appeared limited to broken windows and overturned shelves in the stores. It looked like New Orleans after a really rocky night of Mardi Gras. 'OK,' Lewis said, drawing my attention, 'so give me the bullet points.'

I ticked them off, a finger at a time. 'One, I was minding my own damn business, trying on wedding dresses when it hit. Two, I worked with Luis Rocha to try to figure out what was causing it and lessen the damage. Three—' Number three was my middle finger, unaccompanied by the other two.

'Classy,' Lewis said. 'I'm sure the Wardens Council would be impressed with the summary.'

I repeated the gesture for the missing Wardens Council. Because I didn't much like most of them, anyway.

'When you and Rocha went up on the aetheric, what happened?'

I described it for him – the red boil of forces out of control; Rocha diving down toward the source; me following; the ice black shard of – something – driven into the skin of the planet.

'You touched it,' Lewis said, 'and it knocked you away.'

'Like it was Sammy Sosa and I was the baseball.'

'Nice sports reference. You do that because I'm a guy?'

'No, I do it because I like baseball. Back to the subject. I couldn't hold on to it, and if *I* couldn't—' The only Warden walking around who was stronger than me was currently driving the Hummer. 'You want to give it a shot?'

'I'd like to see it,' he said. We came to a stop light; he turned right, found a deserted parking lot, and parked. 'Show me.'

I took his hand. It wasn't strictly necessary, but it made me feel better. We launched up together, out of our bodies and into the aetheric, and I was, as always, interested to see that Lewis didn't really look all that different on the astral planes than he did back home. Most people tended to reflect the person they wanted to be – prettier, fancier, stronger, taller, skinnier. Hell, our friend Paul manifested as a kind of King Arthur-era knight, although I was pretty sure he didn't know that.

I had no idea how I looked up top. Did I want to ask? Yeah. But it just Wasn't Done. Warden protocol.

The aetheric was abuzz with Warden activity. Lewis and I stayed out of it, floating high and looking down on the teeming, busy swirl of light that was the city of Fort Lauderdale. I pointed to a cluster of Warden activity, and tugged on his hand. Down we went, hurtling fast, flashing past startled colleagues I didn't even vaguely recognise.

We headed down into the disturbance, which, though still roiling, was contained in a tight, glassy shell of power. It looked fragile – the shell, not the disturbance.

Lewis touched the surface, and it took on a milky swirl; then his hand passed through it. He went inside, pulling me after, and when I looked back I saw the bubble sealing itself behind us. Pressure closed in on me, real and intense, and I was glad I didn't have blood vessels to rupture, because there would definitely be rupturing going on, followed by copious hemorrhaging.

Down we went, sliding through what felt like molten glass, and then I saw the black otherworldly glitter below and pulled on Lewis's hand to let him know. He nodded, and we touched down on something that wasn't ground, wasn't surface, wasn't anything really except a shadow of reality.

And there it was: the black thorn of glass, driven deep.

Lewis mimed that he was going to grab it. I shook my head. He mimed again. I shook my head again.

Fat lot of good that did. He grabbed it anyway.

Lewis held on for longer than I had – long enough that I began to think he was actually going to manage to yank the damn thing out – but then was thrown back, just as I'd been. Well, more violently. And he hit and bounced and drifted, seemingly unaware of anything until I grabbed on and began hauling him upward, away from that . . . thing. I couldn't explain why, but it gave me the serious creeps. It *glittered*. It looked deadly sharp, no matter what angle you looked at it; there was a sense of purpose to it that made my skin crawl.

It meant to be there. And it meant to defend itself.

Lewis came awake again, thrashing, and broke free of my hold. I fumbled for him, but he was already swimming away from me, heading back down.

Crap. This wasn't going well.

I couldn't yell on the aetheric, but I damn well felt like shouting. I pushed after him, feeling sick from the pressure, and grabbed hold of his ankle. He shook free of my grip and kept going, arriving back in front of the black shard. He didn't touch it this time; he just drifted slowly around it, taking in every detail.

And then he went up, into another aetheric plane higher than this one. I tried to follow, but I slammed into a glass ceiling that no amount of trying would get me past. I was anchored in the real world, and that line stretched only so far.

I had no idea how Lewis was able to do it, but then that was why he was at the top of the Warden food chain, and I wasn't.

I waited impatiently, and in a matter of minutes he was back, falling back down. He grabbed my hand and we plunged through the aetheric levels, back down to the real world . . . into our bodies.

I coughed, gasped, and felt my head pound in time with my rapid heartbeat. I was covered in sticky, cold sweat. In fact, I felt downright sick.

So did Lewis, clearly. He looked just as bad as I felt, if not worse, and when I touched him, his skin was ice-cold.

Worse, his hands looked . . . burnt, flushed bright red on the palms. He wiped them on his jeans in a convulsive movement, as if there were something horrible on them that he wanted to get off, but it was clear from the way he was shaking that it went deeper than surface slime.

'Christ,' he said, and leant his head back against the whiplash rest. 'What the *hell*?'

'And here I was hoping you'd have some bright, easy answer,' I said. 'Because I've got no clue, man. I've never seen anything like it before.'

'Have you shown it to David?'

I hadn't, and as he mentioned it, I wondered *why* I hadn't. And why he hadn't immediately sensed it. Strange.

'No,' I said slowly. 'And I – don't think I should. Don't you think?'

Lewis nodded, not looking at me. His face had

gone the color of old newspaper, and his lips looked gray. 'I don't, either,' he said softly. 'Why is that?'

'What?'

'Why do we think that? Wouldn't we usually ask the Djinn to take a look?'

Usually, but this time . . . it just didn't feel . . .

I had no answer. I just stared at him, then shrugged. Lewis took a deep breath, started the Hummer's engine, and pulled back out onto the road.

The rest of the trip was spent in silence.

'You're kidding,' I said as Lewis negotiated the Hummer into a parking space built for a Hyundai. 'We're meeting at *Denny's*? Was Chuck E. Cheese already booked for the president?'

'Emergency meeting,' he said. 'This was the closest place we could find where we could have some privacy. Besides, I could use some food – how about you?'

Well, I supposed I could use a Grand Slam or a Moon Over My Hammy or something.

Getting out of the truck in the narrow space between two other vehicles proved to require moves illegal in some Southern states. I managed not to scratch the other car, which was good, because it was a Ferrari. Bright red.

Denny's had suffered little or no damage, as far as I could tell. Maybe they'd been outside of the shake zone. Plate glass windows were intact; diners still sat at tables; waitstaff circulated with trays and plates. Lewis and I walked in, out of the cloying humidity and into the frigid embrace of air-conditioning. I shivered a little – still fighting off the chill I'd gotten on the aetheric, I guessed.

Lewis led me back to a private room, one with sliding doors. Inside were four of the most powerful people in the Southeast, never mind Florida, and they were all digging in to breakfast.

I half recognised Luis Rocha from his signature on the aetheric; he was medium height, medium build, a bit broad in the shoulders. His skin was a dark, warm bronze color, and his eyes and hair were black. The hair was long, trailing down around his face and past his collar. His sleeveless gray muscle T-shirt revealed strong, defined arms inked up with flames and intimidation, but his smile was warm and rather sweet.

He was the only Earth Warden in the room. Two of the others – Sheryl Brewer and Nicholas Mancini – were both Weather Wardens, solid technicians, if not spectacular. Usually, trouble in Florida came from weather, after all – it wasn't known as Hurricane Central for nothing.

The fourth was, of course, a Fire Warden. Nobody I wanted to see. She no doubt went with the red Ferrari out front, and her name was Janette de Winter. Good at her job, but my God, didn't she know it. We exchanged narrow smiles. She was eating a delicate little fruit cocktail thingy. Even now, in the midst of crisis, she was perfectly put together – a tailored white suit, long tanned legs, open-toed pumps showing a perfect pedicure. Her makeup had that airbrushed quality of having been put on in layers, until she looked more like an animated magazine cover than a human being.

Maybe I was just feeling catty because I was sweaty, bruised, and covered in dust.

She raised an eyebrow at my appearance, looking coolly amused. Nope. It wasn't because I looked like crap. I felt catty because I just plain disliked the woman.

Lewis and I took seats at the table. He slid in next to the Weather Wardens, leaving me stuck next to de Winter, but also next to Rocha, who winked at me as he shoveled syrup-drenched waffles into his mouth.

The server appeared, and Lewis and I gave our orders – I went for waffles, after seeing Rocha's evident happiness with his. Also, just so I could see de Winter look pained. Waffles were clearly déclassé. Hooray for waffles.

'First of all,' I said as the waitress closed our doors, 'and just to get it out in the open, this is not my fault. Ask Lewis.'

All eyes turned to him, if they weren't already there.

He sipped coffee and nodded. 'She's in the clear,' he said. 'Whatever's going on, I don't think any Warden is behind it.'

Luis Rocha put down his fork. 'It wasn't natural. No way in hell. Did you see it?'

'We saw,' Lewis said. 'And I agree. It wasn't natural. But it's nothing a Warden could be powerful enough to do alone, either.'

There was a moment of silence. Brewer said, softly, 'Djinn?' It was the question we were all dreading and the reason, on some level, that Lewis and I hadn't wanted to go to David about what we'd found. Because either he knew, which was bad, or he didn't know, which was worse.

Either way, it put him, as the leader of the New Djinn, in an impossible position.

'That's certainly a possibility,' Lewis said. I knew what he was thinking: Ashan, and the other half of the Djinn. The old, arrogant half. But the truth was, I didn't believe even for a second that Ashan would have driven that evil black thorn into the skin of Mother Earth. In a curious sort of way, he cared more for her than for himself, his people, and certainly humanity. He wouldn't have done it, and he wouldn't have allowed it to be done, not by any of his people. *Or David's,* I thought suddenly. *There'd have been war first.*

Nothing scarier than a war between the Djinn. Been there. Had scars.

'Did you try to get it out?' Rocha asked Lewis. Lewis nodded and held up his hands. They were *blistered*. *'Madre de Dios.* That happened on the *aetheric*?'

'Yeah.' Lewis studied his palms with a frown.

'Shouldn't have.' I knew that self-healing was one of the toughest things for Earth Wardens, and so did Luis Rocha; he gestured to Lewis, and the two of them went off to a side table to sit close together, backs to us. Healing was, sometimes, kind of a private thing. Intimate. I sipped coffee and tried to ignore the fact that I'd been left on my other side with Janette de Winter, who was shooting me looks that could kill.

'Any report on injuries?' I asked the table at large. They all glanced at each other, and then Sheryl Brewer took on the job.

'Minor stuff so far,' she said. 'We've got some superficial cuts and a couple of broken bones, but nobody dead or seriously injured. The damage was contained pretty quickly. Whatever you guys did—'

'Wasn't much,' I said, 'at least on my part. Rocha deserves the credit for containment, definitely.'

Credit for more than containing the earthquake, apparently, because when he and Lewis rejoined us – coincidentally, the same time my waffles arrived, all fluffy and begging to be drowned in syrup – Lewis's palms were smooth and blister-free again. 'Surface damage,' he said to our questioning looks. 'Looks like the thing's hot.'

'Hot hot, or radioactive hot?' Brewer asked. It was an excellent question, and not the one Lewis had been hoping to answer.

'Radioactive,' he said reluctantly. 'We need to find this thing in the real world and contain it. Fast. Jo, I want you to talk to Paul, figure out if we've got anybody who specializes in radioactivity. We're going to need somebody who knows what they're getting into.'

I nodded and dipped my first bite of waffle into syrup. It never made it to my mouth, because my phone rang. I stepped away from the table to answer it – it was a number that didn't pop up with a name, but it was a New York City area code.

'Ms Baldwin? Phil Garrett here, *New York Times*. I hope you weren't injured in the disturbance down there?'

I was surprised first of all that he'd gotten a cell signal through; the Wardens had priority on connections in a crisis, along with various emergency services and governmental agencies, and I was pretty sure reporters weren't on that list. After that surprise wore off, though, a big, ugly ball of black stress formed in my stomach where my waffle was going to go, and my knees went a little weak. I felt light in the head for a second, and braced myself against the wall. *So not cut out for this.*

'No, Mr Garrett, I'm fine,' I lied, and was pleased

that my voice sounded steady and almost welcoming. 'What can I do for you?'

'Well, I don't know if you remember, but a couple of days ago I tried to reach you when you were on vacation . . . I wanted to talk about the Wardens organisation that you're part of.'

My heart trip-hammered, thanks to a sudden dump of adrenaline into my bloodstream. I supposed as an Earth Warden I ought to be able to take care of that stuff, but no, not happening. I struggled to keep my voice calm and light. 'Mr Garrett, I'm ashamed of you. A journalist, ending a sentence in a preposition?'

He laughed. *He* sounded at ease. I supposed this was fun for him. All in a day's work, terrifying the people on the other end of the phone. 'Ms Baldwin, if dozens of English teachers and journalism professors couldn't beat it out of me, I think you've got a lost cause on your hands.' The amusement fell away like a discarded carnival mask. 'Let's talk about the Wardens. What would you say if I told you I had a credible source telling me that not only are the Wardens real, and acknowledged by every government on Earth, at least in secret, but they also function as a kind of shadow governmental agency? One that fundamentally affects and controls the lives of ordinary people?'

'I'd say you need to call Spielberg,' I said. 'Bet it would make a great movie. Your source is a mental case, Mr Garrett. If you actually have one. Which I notice you didn't actually say. So, in theory, I didn't actually answer the question, either.'

He ignored that, although it at least deserved a chuckle, I thought. 'This is serious stuff,' he said. 'I take it seriously. I'm not convinced about all this talk of paranormal events and controlling the weather, but there's got to be something behind it. Maybe you guys have technology we're not aware of, something classified; we can get into the details later. What I want to know is the structure of your organisation. I understand it's worldwide. Do you report up through the US government?'

'I'm not having this conversation.' I kept it simple this time. Garrett waited for me to blurt out something else; silence was pressure. I held on to my tongue and turned to see the entire table of Wardens watching me. Lewis put down his fork and got up, walking toward me. Whatever he saw in my expression, it couldn't have been reassuring.

'So the organisation is independent of national interests? A shadow government of its own?'

'No!' One-word answers were going to land me in trouble; he'd box me neatly in. 'I'm afraid I can't confirm any information for you, Mr Garrett. I really have no idea what kind of fiction you've been fed by your source, but—'

'I have videotape,' he said. 'Television footage of a woman stopping a tornado in the Midwest last week.

The more I searched, the more I came up with – strange events caught on tape here, surveillance camera video there. Put it all together, and it confirms everything my source has told me.'

I took a deep breath, covered the speaker of the phone, and whispered to Lewis, 'We're screwed. The *New York Times* has the scent on the Wardens. I don't think he's going away. He sounds serious.'

'He's looking for independent confirmation,' Lewis said. 'Print reporters have to prove a story before publication. He's fishing.'

'He's got really big bait. Whale-sized.'

Lewis shook his head. 'Then we'd better handle it. If we don't, he'll catch us at a weak moment and get somebody to admit to something. Tell him we'll meet with him.'

'We will?'

'Both of us,' he said, and grinned. 'Tell him to pick a dark, smoky bar. They love that kind of spy shit. Besides, we need anonymity.'

'And scotch,' I muttered. 'Lots of scotch.'

Due to the excuse of the emergency, our appointment with Mr Garrett was in a week, in New York City. He'd offered to come to Florida, but the last thing I wanted was for him to run into some busy, annoyed Warden who blurted out the truth just to get him off their backs. We were working here.

A week. I had a week, in conjunction with the other Wardens, to come up with a good fiction to feed the hungry reporter – one that would induce him to back off. Alternatively, we could go for the big hammer – get someone in the UN or the US government to tell him to back off; but that would pretty much prove his whole case for him. I felt an itch between my shoulder blades, as though somebody had drawn target crosshairs right below my neck.

As it happened, there wasn't a lot for the Wardens to do about the earthquake; on the surface, it quickly became one of those weird leading-this-hour stories on the major news networks for half a day, then slipped into obscurity. It was all over but for the insurance claims, which were going to be considerable. No fatalities, only light casualties.

We'd been damned lucky.

I never finished my breakfast. By the time I felt composed enough to eat, the waffles were cold, tasteless hunks of dough, and I needed to lose a couple of pounds, anyway. Considering how nervous I already felt about facing Phil Garrett in a week, that wasn't going to be a challenge.

In the interest of having a comfortable place to work, I went home. Well . . . *comfortable* was a stretch right now, since half the complex had burnt to the ground, and the half left standing had sustained smoke and water damage.

Curiously, my apartment was perfectly fine. Not a water stain, not a smoke smudge. It even smelt newly cleaned.

David had done me a favor. Again.

I had a secure phone setup in my office area, and VPN access to the Warden's database systems back in New York; I logged in and began reviewing files. Earth Wardens who specialized in detecting and handling radioactivity were few and far between, and a lot of them were dead, missing, or had quit over the last few years. It had been tough on everybody. First we'd had internal strife within the organisation, and then the Djinn had found a way to destroy the rule book that bound them to servitude, and launched their own high-body-count conflict.

We were lucky to have as many Wardens as we did, but we weren't exactly spoilt for choice these days.

My best bet was a naval officer named Peterson, but he was on a carrier in the Persian Gulf. Second best choice was an ex-army guy named Silverton. No address listed, just a cell phone. He was shown as NFA – no fixed address. In other words, Ex-Sergeant Silverton was either homeless or liked living out of a suitcase and hotels. Since he could afford a cell phone, I supposed it was the latter.

The phone call with Silverton revealed nothing much, other than he was available and could be on the ground in Fort Lauderdale in eighteen hours. I authorised his travel – paperwork was going to survive the nuclear winter, along with cockroaches – and set about typing up my incident reports on the earthquake. When that got old – which I admit, it did quickly – I began surfing the Net for bridal information. I had a wedding to plan, after all. These things don't run themselves, unless you're so famous you can not only get your wedding services for free, but have people pay for the exclusive coverage.

Hmmm, now *that* was an idea . . .

I was looking at wedding cakes when the phone rang – the secured line. Paul Giancarlo's raspy, Jersey-spiced voice said, 'We've got a fuckin' note taking responsibility for the earthquake down there.'

'You've *what*?'

'Let me read it to you.'

> *To the Wardens,*
> *Your time is up. You've been given warnings, but you've ignored them. Either cut off contact with the Djinn, or face the consequences. Today's earthquake in Fort Lauderdale is proof that we can do what we say. The Djinn must be stopped.*

Paul paused and cleared his throat. 'It's signed, "the Sentinels."'

'The Sentinels? You're kidding me. Aren't they

some football team?' It was almost laughable. Almost. 'Seriously, man, I've heard rumors, but – wasn't it just talk?'

'Not according to this. Not according to what I've been hearing. Look, we've got ourselves a real, live splinter group,' he said. 'One not afraid of using terror tactics.'

'And they sent a note? How . . . 1980s of them.'

'Email, actually. And yes, we tried tracing it. No luck. We put the NSA on it, but nobody seems real positive about the prospects. This thing in the ground you and Rocha saw, you think it's some kind of device?'

'Maybe,' I said. 'But . . . it didn't seem man-made. Didn't register like that on the aetheric at all. I don't know. This is deeply weird, Paul.'

'Yeah, but what worries me a hell of a lot more is that what I've been hearing about the Sentinels makes sense.'

'I – what?'

'We all know the Djinn are unpredictable,' he said. 'We've seen it, all right? So is it all that surprising that the ones who got hurt the most – the Wardens who survived that whole bloody mess of a civil war – want to see the Djinn stay out of the way?'

I didn't know quite what to say. 'You sound like you agree with them.'

'Not entirely,' he said, which wasn't, I noticed,

exactly a denial. 'But I don't like the idea of putting our people at risk for no good reason, either. Maybe the Sentinels have the right idea, wrong tactics.'

'You're telling me you don't trust *David*?'

'Kid—' Paul sighed. 'I can't have this conversation with you. You're not exactly rational on the subject. But I was in the New York offices that day. I saw what happens when the Djinn go off the leash. I fought for my *life;* I saw friends ripped apart in front of me. You got any idea what kind of impression that makes?'

I couldn't think of any way to respond to that. He'd caught me off guard. I knew that Paul still had bitterness about the Djinn revolt, and he was right; bad things had happened, mostly to Wardens. But he was discounting – or ignoring – all the thousands of years of suffering the Djinn had endured on their side.

Most Wardens wanted to ignore that.

'Right, moving on,' Paul said into the silence. 'I'm getting the team together here for analysis. We're going to count heads, see who's not answering the pings for roll call. I want a line on anybody who's missing, just in case. I don't suspect my own, but it's useful knowing if somebody's in trouble.'

That, I thought, would be a full-time job. Following the Djinn problems of the past year, a lot of Wardens had simply . . . vanished. Most of them were dead, killed in the fighting, but some had slipped away, knowing that we didn't have time to track down every name on the list. It'd take years to round up any rogue agents out there.

'I'm pulling in Silverton,' I said. 'He's our best option for handling this thing, if it's radioactive. If I need anybody else, I'll let you know.'

'Yeah, you do that. And kid?'

'Yeah, Paul?'

'You sure about this wedding thing? Really sure?'

I knew that Paul, once upon a time, had harbored ambitions in the direction of me in his bed, and I'd been kind of willing to contemplate it. But all that had changed, and he was gentleman enough to acknowledge it. Under the exterior of a badass Mafia scion beat the heart of a very sweet man – if you could overlook all the cursing.

'I'm sure,' I said softly. 'I love him, Paul.'

He didn't sound impressed. 'You know what he is.'

There it was again, that thread of darkness, that almost-prejudice. 'Yes, I know what he is. He's someone who's saved my life more times than I can count. He's someone who's put his own life on the line not just for me but for the Wardens and all of humanity. I know *exactly* what he is. And who he is.'

Awkward silence, and then, 'Fuck, babe, I've gotta run. We're good, right?'

'We're good,' I said. 'Kisses.'

I said it to a humming disconnected signal. Paul

GALE FORCE   63

was already gone, off to the next crisis. I finished up at
my desk, closed the laptop, and sat back to think.

The Sentinels. That had an amateurish ring to it,
but who was I to judge? Lewis had started the Ma'at,
a separate Warden-like organisation, when he'd been
just out of college, and that had turned out to be a useful
thing – the Ma'at took in people without enough talent
to be Wardens, but more than the average human, and
paired them up with Djinn volunteers. They worked
on the theory of additive power – forming chains of
people and Djinn in order to amplify and direct power
that otherwise wouldn't be strong enough to make a
difference.

The Sentinels didn't sound like they had a new
idea, just a difference of political opinion. They
were anti-Djinn. Well, that shouldn't have come as
a shock; enough Wardens had been hurt or killed in
the troubles with the Djinn to make some kind of
backlash inevitable. I just hadn't thought it would
be so fast, or so decisive. I'd never thought that it
would come down to reasonable, responsible people
doing something like causing unnecessary loss of
life.

One thing was certain: whether it was a good idea
or not for David to be involved in this investigation
about the black knife, it was going to have to happen.
I needed him to know about the anti-Djinn movement,
and I needed a Djinn to try to analyze the history of

the black knife and tell me where it came from, who made it, who planted it, and how to remove it.

It was logical, all right.

I just had a sinking feeling that it was exactly the wrong thing to do.

Chapter Two

According to the checklist I'd downloaded from the Internet, I was already running about six months behind on planning any decent kind of wedding that didn't involve shotguns and pissed-off dads. As I waited in the Fort Lauderdale airport for Warden Silverton's plane, I read over the printed bridal list and anxiously jotted notes in the margins. Some things I just marked out. I wasn't fooling with wedding advisors, wedding consultants, or wedding planners; none of them would be equipped to deal with the complexities of the wedding of a Warden and a Djinn, anyway. And if they were, they'd be way, way too expensive.

Clergy. Now that was something I did have to think about. Unless we went for a civil ceremony . . . Hmmm. Maybe one of the pagan faiths would be willing to do it. And then there were the caterers. Photographers. Musicians for the reception. Florists.

The whole thing was obscenely complicated. I suspected the wedding ritual was designed to make absolutely sure you really *wanted* to get married. God knew that if you were on the fence about it, the organising would put you over the edge into permanent bachelorette-hood.

I was settled in an uncomfortable hard plastic seat in the baggage claim area, watching the arriving passengers. I had a sign propped next to me with the stylized sun symbol of the Wardens on it in gold and glitter – unmistakable, to anyone who knew what it meant, although I'd put SILVERTON below it in block letters, just in case.

I spotted a likely candidate – a tall African American man with erect military bearing who snagged an olive-drab duffel bag from the baggage belt. Sure enough, as his eyes scanned the waiting crowd, he fixed right on me and headed in my direction.

I stood up, claimed the sign, and waited for him to stride over. He got taller and taller the closer he came, very imposing. His handshake was firm and businesslike, and I realised he was older than I'd thought – probably in his early fifties, with a light dusting of gray in his close-cropped black hair, lines around his eyes. 'Mr Silverton,' I said. 'Joanne Baldwin.'

'Heard of you, ma'am,' he said. No hint of whether

the advance notice had been good or bad. 'Call me Jerome, please. No point in formality if we're going to be working together.'

'Right. Jerome, my car's outside. How was your flight?'

'Food-free,' he said. 'Could I impose on you to discuss this assignment over dinner?'

'Sure,' I said. 'Anything in particular?'

'Fish,' he said. 'Hate to miss the fish when I come to the coast.'

He liked my car. In fact, Jerome liked my car more than most people, walking all the way around it, asking questions about the engine, the performance, the mileage. I was betting that he'd ask to drive it, but he didn't; he stowed his gear in the trunk and took the passenger side. I made sure to drive extra fast, just to give him a demonstration, which he seemed to appreciate.

'So,' I said, as we whipped down North Ocean Boulevard, enjoying the sea breeze and late afternoon sun, 'I noticed you were NFA in the system. Travel a lot?'

'Prefer it that way,' he said. 'Not really interested in being tied down.'

'And that sound you hear is the hearts of women breaking from coast to coast.'

I got a low chuckle out of him. 'Not likely, ma'am.'

'Joanne.'

'Joanne.' He flashed me a million-dollar smile. 'Pretty women make me nervous.'

I doubted that. 'No Mrs Silverton, then?'

The smile disappeared. 'No. There was, but she's gone now.' The way he said it didn't invite mining that particular subject. 'Tell me about the earthquake.'

I did, sparing no details; no telling what was relevant. When I got to a description of the black glass thorn stuck into the aetheric, he frowned and turned toward me, intense and focused.

'That's why you called me,' he said. 'Because of the radiation problem.'

'That's one reason, but you're supposed to be a very good Earth Warden as well. One of the most sensitive to things not being right before things go to hell. That might really be an asset around here right now.'

I took a right turn into the parking lot of a seafood restaurant I particularly liked, parked, and turned off the engine. Silverton made no move to get out, so neither did I.

'I'm going to need some things,' he said. 'A handheld GPS device. A Geiger counter. Couple of other things.'

'Anything you need, I'll get,' I said. 'Make me a list.'

He was still studying me, in a way that made me feel like I should have something more to say. I followed a burst of inspiration and asked, 'Have you seen something like this before?'

With that, Silverton opened his door and put one long leg outside. Before he levered himself up, he met my eyes and said, 'I sure as hell hope not.'

It took the rest of the day to get Silverton's shopping list together, which included a detailed map and geological survey of the area, and a whole bunch of equipment whose names and purposes I didn't even recognise. 'What are you expecting to find, Jimmy Hoffa?' I muttered, loading the last of it into the backseat of the Mustang. I didn't like using the car as a packhorse. It was a thoroughbred. Besides, I didn't want dings in the upholstery.

Silverton didn't answer me. It was getting dark, and I'd proposed waiting until the next morning, but Silverton seemed anxious to get started, so we started driving, cruising slowly – just two people in a fast car, slumming it on a leisurely sightseeing trip.

Silverton kept his eyes glued alternately on the Geiger counter and the maps, and I could tell that he was also maintaining part of his awareness, searching the aetheric. It took a lot of control to do that. He steered me with terse commands to go right or left – once, he had me back up and turn around. I heard the Geiger counter begin to click, and Silverton nodded once.

The sun was going down in the west, layers of stacked colors trailing behind like vast silk scarves. A few cirrus clouds skidded toward the horizon, but it was a calm sea with fair winds.

And inside the car, the Geiger counter stopped clicking and started chattering. I instinctively slowed down. 'Here?'

'Not yet. Keep going.'

Not good. The clicking was already frantic. What did that mean for all those people driving by? Were they sick? Dying?

'Pull in up ahead,' Silverton said, and pointed off to the right. I bumped up a ramp into a deserted parking area – some kind of office building, marked as condemned. I barely paid attention. My gaze was fixed on Silverton as he compared maps, looked at the GPS, and used colored pens to mark our position. He shut off the Geiger counter, which was a storm of constant, nervous clicking, and got out of the car. I unbuckled my safety belt and hurried after him, grabbing the heavy duffel bag from the back. He paced the parking lot, prowling like a cat, and finally headed off across the asphalt toward the building.

It didn't look like much: three stories, mostly built of concrete slabs, with a few cheerless windows. The style looked vaguely 1970s, one of those designs of the future that had never really caught on. I'd always wondered why, in the future, people never seemed to appreciate things like plants, carpet, and comfortably padded furniture. I just knew that the offices inside this building would have hard plastic chairs and concrete floors and earth-toned macramé wall hangings.

Well, it would have, except that this building was long abandoned. Some of the higher windows were broken out; the lower ones were boarded up with warping plywood. A sign on the door announced NO TRESPASSING, in uneven Day-Glo letters.

Silverton, however, wasn't about to be warned off. He walked up to the double-glass doors and, without hesitation, yanked. Nothing happened. They were locked.

I cleared my throat. 'Maybe we should—'

Apparently, the end of that sentence was *break in,* because Silverton exerted a pulse of Earth power, and the lock made a little metallic snapping sound, and the glass doors shivered and sagged open. He shot me a look. 'You were saying?'

'Just wondering if we ought to alert the bail bondsman now, or wait until they let us have our one phone call,' I said. 'Don't mind me. I'm fine.' Well, I wasn't, really. 'Are we radioactive?'

Silverton raised his eyebrows. 'Well, yes. Did the clicking not tip you off?' He didn't wait for my answer, which would not have been helpful anyway; he swung the door open, and a wave of *eau-de-abandoned-building* swarmed over me. Old paper, turning to dust.

Mold. Stale, still air. A faintly unpleasant undertone of sewer problems, too.

Oh *man*. This was looking less like a good plan all the time. I had *not* worn the right shoes for tramping through sewer water. In fact, I didn't own the right shoes for that, and hoped I never would. Still, not cool to abandon the contractor you've hired to solve the problem.

So when Silverton strode on, into a dim entry hall, I followed.

Silverton was much better prepped than I'd thought; that even extended to flashlights, big heavy ones that would double as clubs in an emergency. I was glad, because I could hear scuttling somewhere upstairs. I know – big, bad Earth Warden afraid of things that scuttle. But it's all context. I'm fine with Nature's way, as long as Nature keeps it out of *my* way.

I cautiously split my attention between the real world – which was full of hazardous broken furniture, moldering carpet, and dangling wires – and the aetheric. The spirit world was tinted blood red here, and it felt hot . . . oven-hot. I didn't like it. Things had happened in this place, bad things. Their ghosts still hung around, joyless and draining. Workplace shooting, maybe. Or something equally horrible. Emotion stained this place, even over and above whatever our radioactive target might prove to be.

Silverton reached the end of the hallway and turned

a slow circle, then pointed at a dented metal door that said MAINTENANCE ONLY. It was locked. He did the trick again, and beyond was a pitch darkness that made my skin crawl. The flashlights weren't making a dent, really.

'Allow me,' I said, and twisted a small thread of Fire into a wick, then set it alight inside a bubble of air. I levitated it into the room ahead of us and turned up the brightness until the flickering magic lantern revealed rusted metal steps, going down, and mold-streaked concrete walls. 'You're sure about this?'

'You want to get to it; we go down there,' Silverton said. 'Tell you what – makes you feel any better, I'll let you go first.'

It didn't, but I was probably the best equipped to deal with any hostile force that popped up out of the darkness. Damn, I *hated* being competent sometimes. 'How radioactive are we, exactly?'

'On a scale from one to ten?' Silverton asked cheerily. 'Dead, ma'am. Or we would be, if we weren't Earth Wardens. Got some natural immunity against that kind of thing.'

'Some?'

'The longer we stay, the worse off we are,' he pointed out. Right. I was taking the lead. Fantastic.

I stepped onto the rusting metal, heard something creak, and hastily pushed my awareness down through the stairs, checking for structural integrity. They'd hold, thankfully, but just to be sure I added a little stiffener at the welded joints.

Twenty-two steps later, I arrived at the basement level, where the building's power plant was contained. At least that was what I assumed it was: a huge block of metal, dented and rusted, with inert panels of darkened indicators. I summoned the floating light closer as I walked around it.

'Should be close,' Silverton said. In the dark, his voice sounded like the whisper of a ghost. And there were ghosts down here; I could feel their presence on the aetheric. People had definitely died hard in this place. Enough of them could have spawned a New Djinn. Nobody knew where the Old Djinn, the ones from the dawn of time, had come from, but the newer ones were born out of enough energy being set free at the same time. Disasters and mass killings were particularly prone to it.

I kept looking into Oversight and templated it across the real world as I eased around the generator. Whatever this thing was, it ought to be right there . . . and it was.

It was a severed head.

I screamed and recoiled – reflex – and slammed into Silverton's hard chest. He steadied me, moved me out of the way, and crouched down to stare at the dead, still face.

'That's a Djinn,' he said softly.

'Can't be.' I was getting *control* of myself again, willing myself back to some kind of mental balance. My heart was still thumping like a speed-metal drummer, but my hands were only shaking a little. 'Djinn don't die. Not like that. And they don't leave corpses when they do.'

'This one did,' Silverton said. 'Recognise him?'

I didn't. I didn't want to, either. 'How can you cut the head off a *Djinn*?'

'You can't.' Silverton reached out and touched the head. It wobbled backward a little, but didn't roll. 'He's buried in the concrete up to the neck.'

OK, that was – if possible – even creepier. 'What about the black thing? Is it him?'

'No,' Silverton said. 'It's inside him. We have to get him out.'

He put both hands flat on the floor, on either side of the Djinn's head, and the concrete began to liquefy. Silverton reached into the wet concrete and gave me a glance. 'Grab his other arm.'

Last thing I wanted to do, but I did it. I reached down into the cool, wet cement and found something that felt more like flesh than liquid, and pulled. Silverton matched me, and we stood and walked backward, still pulling.

The Djinn's body slipped free, covered from the neck down in a gray, dripping mass. He was naked, and he looked very, very . . . human. The only way I could tell that he wasn't entirely human was the gauzy signature on the aetheric, barely perceptible now that we had him free of the ground.

Silverton was right. The black knife was inside him, driven in like a spike. This close on the aetheric it looked even deadlier than before. Glittering, sharp, lethal.

Silverton took a deep breath. 'We're going to have to open him up.'

I ran through all the reflexive denials and arguments in my head, and finally said, 'You tell me what to do.'

Silverton reached in his backpack and pulled out two pairs of thick, black rubberised gloves. He handed me one and donned the other pair, then took out a long, wicked-looking knife.

'You going to be OK?' he asked me. I must have looked pale. I nodded, poured on the power to the light drifting overhead, and swooped it closer to give Silverton as much visibility as possible. 'Quick and dirty. We're not doing an appendectomy here. This is an autopsy.'

I had no idea what a Djinn looked like beneath the skin. Human, I supposed – full of organs and blood and nerves and all the things that sustained us.

I was wrong about that. Maybe this Djinn had only assumed a human shape, or maybe the black thing inside him had corrupted him from within.

In any case, as soon as Silverton's knife pierced the

graying skin, what poured out wasn't blood . . . It was a toxic black liquid, like oil. It didn't leak; it *pumped* – as if some part of him was still alive. God, I hoped that wasn't true.

Silverton didn't pause, but his face went tense and still. He ripped the knife from neck to groin in one fast motion, put it aside, and yanked the cavity open. 'Hold it,' he snapped at me. Before I could come up with the very good reasons why I didn't want to do that, my gloved hands moved, grabbed the slick edges, and braced it open for him.

Silverton reached inside the Djinn, got both hands around the thing inside him, and *pulled*. It resisted, but then he rocked backward, as if something had broken free, and the top of the black shard swam up out of the black liquid and caught the light.

It flared into a galaxy of stars, glittering, and I gasped and looked away from it. There was something deeply wrong about it. Deeply alien.

'Oh God,' I whispered. Silverton's face had gone an unhealthy shade of gray, and his hands shook as he pulled the thing out. 'Drop it. Jerome, *drop it!*'

He got it free of the Djinn's corpse and let go. It fell to the concrete floor – not like the glass it resembled, not at all. It fell with a thick, metallic *clunk*. Drops of oily black dripped from its sharp edges, and both Silverton and I stared at it without saying a word for a few moments.

Then Silverton said, 'This shouldn't be here. This can't be here.'

I licked my lips and tasted sweat. 'What is it?'

He met my eyes, and I saw real fear in him, the big tough military guy. 'I don't know. If I had to apply some kind of scientific principle to it, I'd say it was antimatter. Antimatter in suspension, made stable in the real world.'

I knew the theory of antimatter, of course. Back in the 1970s, a scientist named Dirac had been trying to figure out an explanation for the way matter behaved in certain circumstances, and he came up with a theory about something called the Dirac Sea – a kind of negative energy that exists underneath the positively charged matter in a vacuum. That led to scientists talking about contraterrene matter, and antiparticles.

Human scientists had actually managed to artificially create antimatter – in fact, they regularly did it, in places like CERN and Fermilab. Of course, their antimatter was unstable – it had to be, considering that it was manifesting and interacting with the matter-based world. The longest antimatter had ever lasted, even with all their technology sustaining it, was about fifteen seconds before it annihilated itself.

But if *this* was some kind of bottled, stable antimatter, that was bad. Very, very bad. When matter and antimatter collided, gamma rays were one side effect, which would explain the radiation. Even this container, whatever it was, wasn't able to completely contain the antimatter, so there was a continuous stream of radioactive energy pouring off it.

'Antimatter collisions are about ten times more powerful than chemically based energy,' Silverton said, and wiped his sweating forehead with his sleeve. 'One kilogram of antimatter annihilating itself is supposed to produce about 180 petajoules of energy.'

'Which is . . .'

'Catastrophic would be charitable.'

'And how much do you think is in there?'

We both looked at the thing lying on the concrete floor, alien and deadly enough to destroy a Djinn even without being released.

'I think,' Silverton said slowly, 'that we're looking at about two kilograms.'

In other words, double the worst-case scenario he'd just described.

'We need the Djinn,' I said. 'At the very least, they need to know about what happened to him.' I nodded toward the dead Djinn.

Silverton nodded. 'I think we're going to need more than the Djinn,' he said.

'Like who?'

'God.'

Chapter Three

There was no way we could safely remove the black antimatter shard by ourselves. Touching it had damaged Silverton already; he was trying to hide it, but I could see the pain in his face, the way his gloved hands were trembling. I remembered Lewis's blistered hands – and that had been on the aetheric.

'Let's get out of here,' I said. Silverton didn't argue. He had trouble getting to his feet. I dumped the equipment, stripped off his pack, and supported him on the way up the stairs. He made it about halfway before his knees gave out. He was a big guy, and I had to work hard to get him up the rest of the way and out into the hallway.

'Leave,' he said. In the light from my floating lantern, he looked drawn and sick. 'You need to get the Djinn here, fast. Go.'

'I don't need to go anywhere to do that,' I told him, and concentrated on the invisible thread that linked me with David. It was thin here, but still a connection. I pulled, and distantly felt his attention shift toward me. I couldn't communicate with him over the aetheric, at least not from this spot, but he knew I was looking for him.

I put my back into pulling Silverton down the hallway, trying to avoid the worst of the debris. It seemed like a very long way, and I had to superoxygenate my lungs to keep spots from dancing in front of my eyes. I'd pay for it later, but for now, I just wanted *out*.

My heels hit an inconveniently placed broken computer monitor, and I tipped backward.

David caught me. 'What the hell is going on?' he asked. 'What are you doing?'

I whirled to face him. I can only imagine how I must have looked – wild-eyed, sweating, scared. He took a step back. 'Help me get him outside,' I panted. Without comment, he scooped up Silverton in his arms and walked down the hall, olive-drab coat belling behind him. I hustled after, feeling a shake in my knees that definitely hadn't been there before. In fact, I felt distinctly sick now, wobbly, light-headed, but I was determined not to show it. We had enough problems to talk about.

David simply blew the glass doors off their hinges at the entrance – effective, if a little showy. The resulting hail of broken glass melted away in midair and formed a soft mound of sand, which served as a bed on which he placed Silverton. 'Now,' he said, and turned to me, 'what the *hell*—'

He caught me as I collapsed. Which actually came as a surprise to me – the collapse, not that he caught me. I hadn't felt it coming on; I'd thought I was coping just fine. David pressed his warm hand to my forehead as he lowered me to the sand beside Silverton. 'Jo?' He muttered under his breath, something about stupid Weather Wardens and their foolish sense of invulnerability, which really wasn't fair because I didn't feel at all invulnerable at the moment. I felt scared.

David's magical touch poured warmth into me, but it was like pouring it into a black hole. Whatever was affecting me, it was wrong in ways I couldn't even begin to realise.

'Wait,' I said, and held his gaze with all the determination I had left. 'David, I need you to go into the basement. There's a dead Djinn there, and a thing – a thing we think is antimatter. Don't go alone. Be careful—'

I had more to say, but it got lost somewhere, and the light was too bright in my eyes, and then it was dark and still and quiet, and I was all alone, floating.

Well, dying always had been kind of peaceful for me.

*   *   *

I woke up in a hospital, hooked up to tubes, and I was alone. No David by my bedside. No Lewis loitering in a chair. No Cherise, even.

All alone.

I pressed the call button, wondering if I was in a Warden hospital. Pressing the call button seemed like an Olympic event, and one I wasn't likely to medal in at that. I was unreasonably exhausted, considering I'd just woken up. While I waited for attention, I looked over the room I was in. Typical hospital issue – an adjustable bed, with rails that were up. Machines that beeped. A silently playing TV high in the corner, tuned to the Weather Channel, which led me to believe that at the very least I'd had Warden visitors.

Nobody was responding to my call. I pressed the button again, sweating with effort. My mouth tasted like metal, and it was sticky and dry. Everything smelt wrong. My whole body ached, the kind of nasty, all-over body aches you get with high fever, and there were some white-hot spots of pain in various joints. I'd been hurt worse, but somehow, being all alone, hooked up to machines and left ignored, made this seem worse.

I gulped down a breath and pressed the button again, convulsively.

The door banged open, admitting a nurse wearing the latest scrub fashions – floral print, with a predominantly red color. She didn't look familiar, and she didn't look happy. 'Ms Baldwin,' she said. 'Awake, I see.'

I tried to nod. Appallingly, I couldn't seem to get my throat to produce sounds. I gestured at the water pitcher; she poured me a glass and held it for me. I gulped. Water had never tasted quite so good . . . until I realised that it was taking on a red tinge. I was bleeding into it. I pulled back, gasping, and wiped my lips. Blood on my fingers. It was coming from my gums, which were seeping red.

'Relax, honey,' the nurse said, unbending a little bit when she saw the obvious distress in my face. 'You had a pretty high dose of radiation. You're getting treatment, though.'

The water had lubricated my vocal cords. 'Where am I?'

'Extension Hospital Fourteen,' she said, which meant I was in the Warden system, not general human health care. Thank God. 'I'm sorry we didn't have anybody with you, but you've been out for a while, and we had other patients. Do you have a lot of pain?'

I managed to keep my nod to a measured sort of response, not a frantic oh-my-God-yes-give-me-drugs sort of gesture. She got the point, though, and showed me the meds button, which I pushed for all it was worth. Liquid gold painkillers slid through my veins, and I breathed a deep sigh of relief. Even tasting blood didn't seem that disturbing, suddenly.

'David?' I asked. My voice sounded horribly weak.

The nurse hesitated and didn't quite meet my eyes. 'Your friend and Lewis Orwell brought you in, but they had to leave. Some kind of emergency.'

'Haven't been back?'

'No, not yet. But I'm sure they'll be back as soon as they can.'

Not good. That meant something had happened. She'd said it had been days . . .

Someone else hip-bumped open the door, and came in carrying two tall coffees. It was Cherise. She looked tired, but still glamorously tousled, and the smile she gave me was pure relief. 'I *knew* a mocha would get you up,' she said, and flopped into a chair next to me. 'You are so predictable. So. How are you?'

'Sick,' I said. 'What the hell happened?'

The nurse cautioned her about hot liquids and my invalid state, which both of us ignored, and left the room. Cherise leant forward and helped me manage the mocha. It was warm, not scalding, and the caffeine/sugar/fat combo made me feel much steadier inside. 'Well,' Cherise said, 'you pretty much freaked everybody the hell out. Including people I've never heard of, who flew over from Switzerland and Australia and places like that.'

'Wardens?'

'Some of them, yeah. There's some kind of big

meeting going on. That's where everybody is.' Cherise's big blue eyes focused on mine, and I saw an internal debate going on for a few seconds before she said, 'Your friend's dead.'

'I – what?'

'Your friend Mr Silverton. He didn't make it, Jo. They tried, but he was too far gone. David and Lewis both tried, but nothing worked. They were scared about you, too.' Cherise's expression told me everything I didn't want to know about how bad off I really was. Bleeding gums were the least of my problems. 'You're going to have to rest up this time. Seriously.'

'But . . . did they say anything about the Djinn? The dead one? And the—'

'They said that under no circumstances was Joanne Baldwin supposed to jump out of bed and charge to anybody's rescue. Seriously, Jo. Not your problem. Not anymore.' She reached out and smoothed hair back from my face. 'You look like crap, by the way.'

'Gee, thanks. So glad you're my affirmation girl.' I actually was glad, but I couldn't let her know that. There was love, real and soothing, in the touch of her fingers. It lulled as much as the morphine. I felt sharp grief at the death of Jerome Silverton, and guilt. We'd gotten in over our heads, and that was the last thing we'd intended. I'd counted on Jerome, as the expert, to know when to back off. Instead, he'd continued though he'd known it was likely a suicide run. I guessed he thought it was necessary.

'He wrote you a note,' Cherise said. 'While he could still write. Do you want it?'

Cherise was a better mind reader than most of my magic-gifted colleagues. I sighed and nodded, feeling the hot prickle of tears in my eyes. She dug paper from the front pocket of her jeans, unfolded it, and handed it over.

Jerome's handwriting was messy. I couldn't tell if that was normal for him, or if the damage was taking its toll. It took me a while to work out what the note said, but when I did, it hit me hard.

It said, *I was wrong. Thought I could control it. Not your fault.*

And, on a separate line, *Hope you're OK*.

I folded it up, closed my eyes, and fought back wave after wave of useless tears. When I'd managed to get control again, I handed the note back to Cherise, who exchanged it for a box of tissues.

'The dead Djinn?' I asked.

'Well, that's the weird thing,' Cherise said. 'I mean, I wasn't there, obviously, but I heard people talking. According to David, the Djinn wasn't there.'

'What?' He most certainly had been there. I could still remember Silverton's knife slicing his body open, remember the elastic tension of holding open the edges of the incision so Silverton could pull out the black glass shard.

'Well, the Wardens say he's there. The Djinn say he's not. They say there's a body, but it's not Djinn. They can't see the black thingy, either. Nothing.'

I opened my mouth and shut it again, thinking hard. 'David, too?' I finally asked.

'Yup. None of them can see it, sense it, whatever. It's just not there for them.'

Oh, *man*. Not good. 'So what are the Wardens doing about it?'

'They're "containing the situation."' Cherise made air quotes around the phrase, and rolled her eyes. 'Some of them are talking about encasing it in a big block of lead. Some are talking about shooting it into space. Nobody knows what the hell to do, but everybody agrees, it's way too dangerous where it is.'

'Everybody except the Djinn.' I couldn't leave that alone. 'Seriously, they *can't see it*? How can they not see it?'

'No clue.'

'What does Lewis say?'

'*He* can see it, and yeah, he knows it's a problem. The Djinn think the Wardens have some kind of psychosis. They say that if the thing was there, they'd be able to sense it.'

Great. 'How do they explain Silverton? Me?'

Cherise looked grim. 'They think one of you screwed up, accessed something you shouldn't have. They can't explain it, but they don't believe the Wardens' explanation, either.'

'Not even David?'

'No,' she said softly. 'Not even David. Sorry, babe.'

Wow. That was . . . strange. And I was too tired and too sick to do anything about it. Cherise didn't need to worry about me going all heroic and crazy on her; all I wanted to do was hide under my blankets and pretend it was all just a bad dream.

And for a while, that was exactly what I did, as the morphine dragged me off to a dream-rich sleep.

Two days later, I was interrogated by a panel of Warden elders: Guillard from Switzerland, Jones from Australia, and Lewis representing the US. I felt a little better, and they'd let me walk to the shower and wash my hair, which made a difference in both body and soul.

There was also a Djinn in the mix – a short, round little thing with that indefinable glimmer to her skin and eyes. She was introduced as Zenaya, and gave me a slight nod but no other indication of how she stood on the subject of me.

No David. That was deeply troubling.

I went through things, step by step, detailing what I'd seen and experienced. Zenaya said nothing, but her eyes flashed an eerie green when I talked about the dead Djinn, and the manner of his death. I addressed a question to her. 'Wouldn't you know if one of your people disappeared?' I asked. She shrugged slightly. 'Wouldn't *David* know?'

'Yes,' she said. 'But he says he finds no one missing.'

'Ashan?'

Another green flash to her eyes. She folded her arms. 'Ashan says his Djinn are all well. He says nothing more.'

Which might or might not mean anything. Ashan wasn't chatty at the best of times. 'But I *saw* him. And trust me, he was a Djinn.'

'How could you tell?' Zenaya asked me, very reasonably. I started to answer, then hesitated.

Because I really wasn't sure how I knew. I just . . . *knew.* 'His aetheric signature,' I finally said. 'Only the Djinn look like that.'

'Leaving aside that point,' Guillard said, in his rich, dark chocolate voice, 'clearly you came into contact with something highly dangerous. Earth Wardens have not been able to correct some of the damage you sustained. We are dependent on simple human methods, which is why we've had to hospitalize you for so long.'

Lewis nodded. He wasn't looking at me; he kept his gaze focused on the window, on the rain outside. 'Sometimes damage just surpasses our ability,' he said. 'That could have been the case this time.'

'No,' I said. 'David tried to heal me, and you know he should have been able to. He has before.'

Lewis had no answer to that. Whatever he was thinking, he was keeping it close to the vest, and he wouldn't damn well *look* at me. I wondered why. Was he angry about Silverton? He had every right to be, I supposed. I'd screwed up, big time, and a Warden had paid with his life.

Guillard asked more questions about the black shard, things to which I had no real answers except to give a recitation of my conversation with Silverton in the basement. And then the whole thing was over; Jones and Guillard wished me well and departed, and Zenaya left without a backward glance.

Lewis stayed. He still wouldn't look at me. Out of sheer stubbornness, I refused to speak first. I sipped water and tugged irritably at my drying hair, trying to get it to stop poodle-curling around my face. I used to have straight hair. I liked my old straight hair.

When I finally turned my attention back to my guest, Lewis was staring at me, and what was in his eyes wasn't anger at all. Or even disappointment. It was something neither one of us could ever really acknowledge, and it was big and powerful and breathtaking.

He cleared his throat and looked down, and said, 'You scared the shit out of me.'

'Yeah. Sorry, I had no idea it was going to be that dangerous, or I'd have done more, taken better precautions—'

He waved that aside. 'Silverton was your expert; you were listening to him. So if there's blame, it's his, and he's beyond all that now, poor bastard. Even if you'd pulled back as soon as you found the dead Djinn, it would have been too late to keep you from getting sick. This stuff is badly toxic. We couldn't have left it there. As it is, we've had to inform NEST, and they're following up with radiation treatments for anyone who reports in sick to the hospitals.' NEST was the Nuclear Emergency Support Team, out of Homeland Security. I didn't want to imagine how *that* conversation had gone.

'But by taking it out of the Djinn's body—'

'The Djinn's body must have been containing it, to a certain extent. You exposed yourselves to a massive dose,' he said. 'Silverton more than you, because he actually touched it, even with protective gloves.'

It could have just as easily been me. Maybe Silverton had known the risks when he'd reached into that cavity to grab the thing; maybe he'd just been unlucky. No way to know. I'd come close to dying lots of times – I'd actually gone over the edge, once or twice – but this felt different.

This left me shaky and deeply unsettled.

'Is it true? That the Djinn really can't sense it at all?'

'The Djinn think we're all suffering from some kind of mass hallucination,' Lewis said. 'David's being kind about it, but it's a blind spot for them. A big one. I don't know how we're going to convince them.'

'If me lying in this hospital bed doesn't—' I felt light-headed, short of breath. 'David has to believe me. He has to.'

Lewis gazed at me, expressionless. 'I hope he does,' he finally said. He leant over and kissed me chastely on the forehead. 'About your wedding—'

Oh, man. I'd known we'd have to have this conversation sometime, but I really wasn't ready for it. 'Lewis, I'm sorry—'

'Don't,' he said. 'Trust me. It won't make things any better. I'm OK. And I'm happy for you. I'm just worried. This thing – the Sentinels. They already didn't like you. I can't imagine they'll be sending any congratulations about the ultimate mixed marriage.'

He left before I could say anything else.

I closed my eyes and floated in a morphine cloud, trying to figure out who, outside of the Djinn, could create the black shard that I'd seen. Who was capable of that kind of lethal, subtle action?

I didn't know.

I had dreams of distorted, screaming Djinn, of people being destroyed one by one, of the city in flames, of myself, walking through the rubble in a beautiful, perfect wedding gown.

Of David lying in the street, dead, with a black shard driven entirely through his body.

I woke up shaking.

Chapter Four

So . . . I healed.

David came to visit, of course, and he stayed as long as his duties would allow – longer than he should have, by the expressions of the Djinn sent to remind him of other duties at hand. But despite what I'd confidently said to Lewis, I could tell that David didn't wholly believe me about the black shard, or the dead Djinn. He couldn't. There was some kind of selective blindness that he couldn't control, and that was weird and scary. It didn't matter, though. The Wardens figured it out without the help of the Djinn.

Somehow – I don't know how – Lewis and a few other top-level Wardens managed to remove the black shard and take it to a containment facility, where experts, brought in under high-level security clearances, agreed that in fact it was, as Silverton had said, antimatter. Antimatter in some kind of stabilising matrix. When I asked where the stuff was, and how it was being contained, I was told it was need-to-know, and I didn't. Frankly, I was a little bit relieved. I was busy recovering, trying to get my strength back. My muscles seemed loose and weak, and once the doctors let me out of bed I spent my time mostly in the physical therapy room, working hard to get myself back in shape again. The pain went away. After a few weeks of natural healing, they tried Earth Wardens on me again, and, this time, it worked; burns and scars smoothed out and disappeared, and I was left with glossy skin badly in need of a tanning session.

Of course, I could always count on Cherise for that kind of therapy. She showed up one day toting a blue beach bag and told me to get dressed. *Undressed* was more to the point. She'd brought my favorite swimsuit, a skimpy little turquoise number that showed off as much skin as the law allowed. I changed, assuming we were going to the hydro pool for some swim therapy, but instead, she got me in the elevator, stripped off her white camp shirt and shorts, and revealed her own bathing suit choice: even less than I had on, though technically I supposed it could be considered clothing. It was a couple of scraps of tangerine orange, and she looked spectacular in it.

'Tell me we're not going to the cafeteria,' I said. 'They're having meat loaf. Again.' Cherise winked at me and pressed the button for the roof. It was restricted access, but she had a key card, which she used with the kind of triumphant flourish usually reserved for magicians with hat-dwelling rabbits.

'I know you're not up to a trip to the beach,' she said, 'so we brought the beach to you.'

They really had. It wasn't just Cherise; it was Kevin – her sometimes boyfriend, despite a five-year age difference – a Fire Warden with a deep-seated attitude problem. He was sitting in the shade of a beach umbrella, wearing camouflage baggy shorts and a death's head muscle T-shirt. He was, at eighteen and change, growing into his height; he was looking less like the underfed, awkward teen I'd first met, and more like the tall, strong man he would become.

Across from him sat Lewis, wearing khaki shorts and a ratty T-shirt advertising that Virginia was the place for lovers. They were both wearing slick sunglasses, and I had to admit, they looked pleased with themselves.

'Hey,' Kevin said. Too cool for any kind of more enthusiastic greeting. I nodded back. We kept our dignity. 'Heard you screwed up. Way to go.'

'Isn't this great?' Cherise didn't much care about things like dignity, if they got in the way of enthusiasm, but then, that was something I loved about her. Something I suspected Kevin loved, too. 'Check it out, we've even got waves!'

They'd outdone themselves. God only knew how they'd managed it, but they'd cordoned off part of the roof and put up patio tables, beach umbrellas, spread sand several inches deep, and put in a pool. Not a big one – more of a landscaping kind of thing – but sure enough, Lewis obligingly generated some rolling miniature surf. It was very cute.

There were two lounge chairs. I settled myself on one, already relaxing in the warm glow of the afternoon sun, and stretched my long legs out as Cherise kissed Kevin and took the other lounger. We debated the merits of coconut-scented oils over banana sunscreens. I went with sunscreen, figuring that I'd had enough dangerous radiation for a lifetime.

As I rubbed it into my legs, a male hand reached over my shoulder and took the bottle away. I looked up, pulled down my sunglasses, and squinted.

David gave me a slow, wicked smile. 'I'll do it,' he said. 'Lie still.'

I licked my lips, tasted sweat, and returned his smile. I settled back against the cushions. David came around to the side of the lounge chair, perched on the edge, and squeezed some sunscreen out into his palms.

'You guys aren't going to make this X-rated, are you?' Cherise asked. 'Because if you are, I need a barf bag. Or a video camera.'

David didn't glance toward Lewis, and I had to

fight not to. 'Nothing that couldn't air on the nightly news,' he said. 'Word of honor.' He held up his glistening hands. 'Ready?'

'Oh, yes.'

I closed my eyes in total, animal satisfaction as his fingers massaged sunscreen into every inch of my feet, then worked their way slowly up my legs, my knees, up my thighs, seeking out every ounce of tension in every muscle. He skipped areas that might have led to excessive moaning (not that I wasn't moaning already) and moved on to my hips, my stomach. What he did to my shoulders should have been in the *Kama Sutra*. It felt . . . healing. And yes, sexy as hell.

'Turn over,' he said, low in his throat, and I glanced up to see that wicked, lovely spark in his eyes. 'Time to do your back.'

Oh, and he did me. Thoroughly. I was a boneless, purring heap by the time he'd finished. David pulled up another lounge chair and parked himself next to me. When I looked at him, he was showing more skin than I could remember seeing from him before in public; he had on a simple black pair of swim trunks, and nothing else, and it was *spectacular*. I let my gaze wander down the clean sculptural lines of his chest, bump over his taut abs, and found myself staring none too subtly at his swim trunks.

'Jo,' he said. I heard the curl of soft reproach in his voice.

'Sorry,' I said. 'But you're worth a rude stare or two, you know.'

He smiled. I couldn't tell if he found me amusing or arousing, or both. He took in a deep, slow breath without replying and turned his face up toward the sun. I remembered how it felt for a Djinn, that almost sexual pulse of warmth and energy. Gave new meaning to the term *hot*.

It was a long, lovely afternoon. Lewis read a book. Kevin and Cherise played cards. There were cold beers, and all in all, it was just . . . perfect. Peaceful. There was weather out over the Gulf, but it held politely off, stacking up its clouds at the boundaries of the low-pressure system in neat storage ranks.

I wished it would never end, but of course eventually it did. As the afternoon cooled, and the clouds began to move in, David kissed my fingers and murmured, 'I have to go.'

'I know,' I said, and opened my eyes. His were brown, almost completely human in color as well as in the emotion they contained. I wondered from time to time what Djinn really thought about us, about the tedious nature of human existence, but David really seemed to delight in participating when the opportunity presented itself. 'You're being careful, right?'

That got me an ironic tilt of his eyebrows. 'Look who's talking.'

'Exactly. You're consulting an expert here. Nobody

better at getting into trouble than me.' I rolled up to a sitting position, facing him. 'I mean it, David. I dreamt—' No, I didn't want to talk about that. The image of him lying broken in the street, pierced by that black *thing* . . . no. 'I mean, I'm just worried you're not taking this seriously. About the antimatter.'

That earned me a trace of a frown. 'It's not that I don't take it seriously. It's that for the Djinn, it's invisible. We can't see it, touch it, measure it. It doesn't exist to us. How can I possibly watch out for it?'

'If it doesn't exist, how did it end up inside a dead Djinn?' I demanded. He kissed my fingers again.

'Jo, I already told you, there is no dead Djinn,' he said. 'Believe me, we'd know. We always know. None of us is missing.'

He kissed me again, an apologetic goodbye, and that was it. He misted away, off about his business, and I felt a sudden chill. Cherise had thrown a couple of wraparound robes in the beach bag, and I donned one, shivering in its terry cloth embrace.

Lewis noticed. I suspected he noticed a hell of a lot. 'Let's get you back in bed,' he said. 'You're checking out tomorrow. Don't want you relapsing.'

Not that there was much chance of it; with Lewis's Earth Warden treatments, and David's Djinn-powered supplemental healing, I'd have to be damn stubborn to screw up that badly.

But I felt cold – cold and scared, for no reason I

could really put a name to. Once I was back in my room, even piles of blankets didn't seem to thaw the ice. I wanted David. I wanted him here, with me.

I wanted him safe.

And I was desperately afraid that he wasn't.

When I tried to follow up and find out more about the dead Djinn, the antimatter black shard . . . I was told it was none of my business. Officially. This came in a curt email message from Warden HQ, courtesy of my good friend Paul, who had evidently decided that the only kind of ball I was going to play was hardball, and therefore he'd better play to win.

I couldn't really resent this, because he was right; I was recovering, I was weak, and it was being handled by competent people. So I needed to stay out of it

Naturally, I couldn't stay out of it.

Not really my thing, being sensible. Instead, I did my work quietly, hidden in between the obvious tasks of drafting the guest list for the wedding (everybody wanted to attend, and no, I wasn't going to feed the entire North American Warden contingent with lobster tails and open bar). I researched caterers, florists, and ministers.

Where we were having the actual ceremony, thankfully, was a foregone conclusion. There was a chapel in Sedona, one of the places where the Oracles reside . . . this one was the home of the Earth Oracle, a kind of super-Djinn who was an avatar of the Earth herself. I wasn't entirely sure what the Oracles *did*, exactly, except that they were the direct conduits from the Djinn to Mother Earth. If you wanted to talk to her, you went through them.

This particular Oracle was also my kid. Long story, but she'd been born in the Djinn way, from power – David's, and mine. Half-Djinn, half-human, and not strong enough to survive the Djinn civil war that had erupted around her literally on the day of her birth.

I'd thought I'd lost her forever, but she was alive, in a sense, if beyond my reach. Oracles didn't have as much contact with humans, and they couldn't reach us in the way that Djinn did.

If I wanted my daughter, Imara, to be at the wedding of her parents, then I had to bring the ceremony to her. Super-Djinn badass avatar or not, I didn't think she could actually leave the chapel, at least on the physical plane. Besides, it was a gorgeous place. I couldn't think of a better, more sanctified spot to exchange vows.

However, at most, it would hold only a couple dozen people, not nearly enough for the rapidly spawning guest list. That would be like trying to fit Mardi Gras into a two-room split-level. Maybe, I decided, we ought to have two ceremonies. A party in Fort Lauderdale, an all-access blowout to make the rank and file of the Wardens happy. And then a private ceremony in Sedona.

Maybe I could get the Wardens to kick in for the party as a morale builder.

I was working out the costs, and trying to persuade myself that I felt weak because I was tired, not because anything above four figures was unacceptable, when the telephone rang. I picked it up, had a bad reporter flashback, and checked the number. It was blocked, which meant it was probably a telemarketer. Annoying, but not nearly as stressful. 'Hello?'

The sound of breathing on the other end made my hackles go up. Couldn't really say why; breathing was not, in and of itself, a threatening sort of sound. But I knew something else was coming, and so I wasn't surprised when a rough male voice said, 'You don't care, do you? You don't give a shit about the dead. The ones who stood up and died for you.'

I flinched, remembering Jerome Silverton, and forced myself to stay still and listen. 'What are you talking about? Who is this?'

'You didn't even warn them it was coming. You didn't warn your own friends that the Djinn they trusted, the ones they *liked,* could turn around and rip them in half.' The hatred in that voice was chilling. 'Now you're screwing one of *them.* One of the enemy.'

'The Djinn aren't the enemy. Who are you?'

'You're already on the list,' the voice said. 'Fair warning, Baldwin. You're a traitor, and we don't want you in charge. Quit now, before it's too late.'

He hung up. I sat frozen for a few seconds, staring at the phone, then called Warden HQ and asked for a trace of the last call.

I got nothing. It would take a Fire Warden to disrupt the sort of trace we used, but clearly, our enemies were ourselves. That didn't bode well for a long-term solution.

I was trying to decide how much of this – if any of it – to tell David, when the doorbell rang. It took me a few long seconds to lever myself out of the chair, put my laptop aside, and go to answer it. The apartment was cool and quiet, except for the distant, constant sound of construction on the other side of the complex, where they were repairing fire damage.

When I got to the door, there was nobody outside. I looked right and left, frowning, and remembered to look down.

It was a delivery service package, plastered with labels. I didn't remember having ordered anything, but maybe someone had sent me a get-well present. I reached down for it, but as I did, David came up the steps at the end of the hallway and turned toward me with his luminous, lovely smile.

Now *that* was the best present ever.

'What are you doing up?' he asked as he came closer. He was tossing newly minted apartment keys in his hand; I'd insisted that if he was going to marry me, he'd have to start doing more mundane, human things, too, such as unlocking doors the standard way, and knocking before entry. He'd found it funny, of course. But he humored me.

'Just getting the package,' I said, and bent down again to pick it up.

As my fingers closed around it, David asked, in pure puzzlement, 'What package?' and it hit me like a speeding express train – I was already feeling worse. Woozy. Something was wrong here.

And he couldn't see the package.

Oh God.

'Get Lewis,' I said, and backed away, into the apartment. 'Get him *fast,* David. Go!'

He didn't waste time asking what I was on about; he just blipped away, moving faster than light could follow. I slammed the door and kept on moving, as far back as I could. I ran into the plate glass window, slid along to the opening, and stepped onto the balcony, where I braced myself against the far railing and slowly lowered myself into a deck chair. I was short of breath and sweating, and it wasn't all just nerves.

That box. *Dammit.* How many people had been exposed? The driver, for sure. People at the distribution center . . . I grabbed a pad of paper, threw away the lists of florists I'd compiled, and began to frantically scribble down anyone I could think of who might have touched the package during the shipping process. They all needed to be examined and treated.

I was only halfway through the list when the phone rang, and I grabbed the extension sitting next to the pad. 'Lewis?' It was. 'Get a disposal team over here, right now. There's a package outside my door. I think it's the same stuff as in the office building. Antimatter. David can't see the package at all. Get a team on tracing the package back through the system. People who came in contact with this thing—'

'Got it,' he said. 'Look after yourself. Get the hell out of there.'

'I don't want to go near it, and I'd have to if I leave by the door. I'll have to climb down—' I didn't feel up to the acrobatics, not at the moment.

I didn't need to. David came out of thin air, moving fast. He picked me up, out of the chair, stepped up on the balcony railing, and off into open space without a second of hesitation. I didn't even have time to gasp before his feet hit the ground, and then he was carrying me across the parking lot at breakneck speed. He dumped me in the passenger seat of my car, took the driver's seat, and started it up with a touch of his finger to the ignition.

'David—'

He wasn't listening. His eyes were focused and distant. He had a mission, and that mission was to get me out of danger. I didn't have anything to say about it.

I realised I was still holding the phone. Lewis's voice was a faint buzz on the other end. 'Right, I'm out of the apartment,' I said to him. 'And we're about to lose the connection. Hurry up with the disposal team. I don't want that thing lying around where anybody can pick it up. My God, Lewis, there are *people* here. *Innocent people!*'

David put the Mustang in gear, and we screeched out of the parking place, cornered hard, and accelerated out of the apartment complex and onto the street.

The phone went dead, of course. I tossed it in the backseat and rested my head against the cushions as David put the Mustang through its paces, driving way too fast for a human's reactions. He must have screened us out of other people's perceptions, because we blew past a police squad car doing about 120, and there was no reaction at all from the two protecting and serving in the front seat.

'I thought you didn't believe in this stuff,' I said to David. 'You're acting like you do.'

'I'm trusting you,' he said. 'If you say it's there, and you say it made you sick, I'm not taking chances. But Jo – I can't see it. I can't sense it. It's just not *there!*'

'Look, there are things that exist that are invisible to humans—'

'But not to Djinn,' he interrupted. 'Nothing is

invisible to Djinn. Nothing that belongs on this earth.'

This was kind of the point. He must have realised it, too. He was quiet for a moment, and when I looked over, I saw that his eyes had taken on a fierce orange color, like the heart of a fire.

'This isn't something being done by the Djinn,' he said. 'Not mine, and not Ashan's. Whether I personally believe in it or not is beside the point. If an enemy, is sending these things to you, personally, it's someone human. Someone who wishes you harm.'

No kidding. I remembered the angry phone call. 'Maybe it's a Demon,' I said. 'They seem to like to drop in for regular visits.'

'Not funny, Jo.'

'Yeah, not from this side, either. Do you think it is? A Demon?'

He seemed to consider it seriously. 'Demons aren't so . . . strategic in their approach. Their goals are simple and straightforward – consume, kill, escape. Whatever this is, there's no *sense* to what you described before. The dead creature—'

'Djinn, David. He was Djinn. We're sure.'

He let that pass, but I could tell he was far from convinced. 'And the black thing inside him. Who would do such a thing? Why?'

'Maybe,' I said slowly, 'it was a test.'

'A test of what?'

'Of the Djinn,' I said. 'A test that you failed.'

He took his gaze away from the road, which was eerie and alarming, though I knew he didn't need to be staring straight ahead to drive. 'Failed how?'

'Failed to sense the danger. Look, that *was* a Djinn we found—'

'It wasn't.'

'Argument's sake, if it was, why can't you admit it? It's as if you just can't bring yourself to—'

'There's nothing to admit!' he said, and I heard the unmistakable vibration of anger underneath the words. *'I would know if a Djinn had died!'*

'Except you don't, and one did,' I said, and closed my eyes. 'So what does that mean?'

'It means—' David took in a deep breath, and I could see him struggle to get his temper under control. 'It doesn't mean anything. Because all this is an illusion, Jo. Just an illusion. There's no dead Djinn; there's no such thing as your antimatter.'

Whoa. The blind spot the Djinn had was big enough to swallow the sun, and it was starting to really scare me. And there didn't seem to be any point at all to trying to debate it, because he simply wasn't going to listen.

I turned face forward as he steered the Mustang through traffic at speeds that would have made NASCAR drivers weep and flinch. 'Glad we got that all straightened out.'

Sarcasm was wasted on him, right at the moment. He sent me a heartbreaking smile of relief, and I realised he actually thought we *had* straightened it out.

Oh dear *God*.

We finished the drive in silence. Once the traffic cleared, David pulled off the road at a beachfront area, one loaded up with pleasure-seeking, bikini-wearing sunbathers, all one tequila short of a *Girls Gone Wild* video. He turned off the engine, and we sat for a while watching the waves crash and roll, and the tanners sizzle and flirt.

'I need my cell phone,' I said. David . . . *flickered*. Like a bad signal, or a hologram. And then he reached in his coat pocket and handed over my cell phone, which I knew perfectly well I'd left back on the table in the apartment. 'Hey. Don't do that, OK?'

He looked puzzled. 'Don't do what?'

'Don't go back there. Promise me.'

'Why?'

I swear, when I closed my eyes, I saw red. I counted to ten, deliberately, and tried to pry my fingernails out of my palms. 'Because even if you don't believe it's there, that stuff is toxic to me, and it could be fatal to you. All right?'

He shook his head. 'There's no danger. If there was, I'd know.'

Which was just *crazy*. But he earnestly seemed to think he was telling me the truth.

I took the cell phone and called Lewis. 'Where are you?'

'Just got here,' he said. I heard his breath huffing; he and what sounded like an elephant herd of people were jogging up the stairs. 'OK, I see it. Box in front of the door.'

'That's it,' I said. 'Be careful.'

'I'm not going anywhere near it, trust me. We're using a bomb robot.'

'We've got bomb robots now? Cool.'

'It's on loan from Homeland Security,' Lewis said. 'They're not going to like it if I get it blown up, though. I'll call you back.'

Homeland Security was loaning us gear? Wow. When had we actually come up in the world like that? Apparently, while I'd been unconscious in a hospital bed for something or other, or on the run. I wasn't sure if I liked it. Part of the reason the Wardens had existed for so long in secrecy had been the low profile. The more we 'cooperated' with other governmental agencies, the more likely it was that we'd get attention, and any attention was bad.

I remembered the reporters, and shivered. They had a job to do, and although they'd grant me some sick time, they'd be back.

'Let's change the subject,' David said. 'The wedding. Where do you want to have it? At the chapel?'

There was only one chapel for us – Imara's home,

the Chapel of the Holy Cross. I nodded slowly. 'But we'd have to have it in secret,' I said. 'After hours. They don't do official weddings there.'

'I could work it out,' he said. I was sure that was true, actually. 'It won't hold too many.'

'Small ceremony,' I said. 'Big reception. It works.'

He nodded, staring straight ahead into the rolling surf, the eternal sky. 'Are you all right?'

'Me? Sure.' I dredged up a laugh. 'Why wouldn't I be? Just because some crazy is sending me antimatter through the mail . . .'

'We changed the subject,' he reminded me gently. 'If you're worried about the wedding, you can still change your mind.'

I draped an elbow over my seat and curled around to face him, resting my chin on my forearm. 'I really don't think I can,' I said. 'And I really don't think I want to.' I felt a cold breath of . . . something. 'Unless . . . you're having doubts about us—'

'No,' David said immediately. 'I'm just concerned for you. You seem . . . unreasonably upset. I just can't understand how you can be so convinced and upset about something that has no evidence.'

Well, that was rich. He thought *I* was crazy. 'David,' I said, 'we're not going to convince each other on this stuff. Are we?'

He shook his head ruefully.

'Then let's stop trying.' I reached out. He took

my hand, and some of the fluttering in my stomach quieted. 'So if we can have only twenty people at the ceremony, who are we picking?'

He smiled. 'You go first.'

'All right. One name at a time.' I took a deep breath. 'Cherise.' Safe. He nodded.

'Lewis,' he said, which surprised me, but I supposed it shouldn't have. He and Lewis had known each other long before I ever set eyes on David.

'Um – Paul.'

'Rahel.' He gave me a quick, apologetic smile. 'I can hardly leave her out of the invitation. She'd only show up if we didn't invite her.'

She would, just to be a pain in the ass. Djinn. What can you do? 'Fine,' I said. 'How many is that?'

'Counting us? Six.' He studied me for a second, eyes going gentle again. 'Seven with a minister. Do you want to invite your sister?'

'Oh hell no,' I said. 'Psycho sister Sarah is *not* welcome. She's caused me plenty of trouble without this. I'll go with . . . Venna.'

David's eyebrows twitched, either in surprise or amusement, or maybe some of both. Venna was a Djinn, but she was on Ashan's side of the fence; she'd done both of us favors, but as with most Djinn, I couldn't peg her as good or bad, really. Still, she was always . . . interesting. 'She might attend,' he said. 'It might interest her. But she wouldn't come alone.'

'You are *not* inviting Ashan.'

That got an actual laugh. 'It would be politically wise.'

'And personally *stupid* because if I see him again, I swear I'll rip off whatever passes for his—'

He kissed me. It was meant to be a shut-me-up kiss, quick and sweet, but it turned warmer, richer, and I melted against him like chocolate on a hot plate. 'I'm asking Ashan,' he said when he let me up for breath. 'And you're going to play nice if he shows up. Which he won't. But it will be wise to ask him.'

I made a noise that brides-to-be probably shouldn't make, according to Miss Manners. He kissed me again.

We had so much to talk about – flowers, cakes, catering, dresses, tuxedos . . . We didn't talk about any of it. Instead, David pressed his lips to the pulse at my neck and murmured, 'I'm bored with planning the wedding. Let's plan the honeymoon. Better yet, let's rehearse.'

I'd been recovering for weeks, and my libido had taken a serious beating along with my body, but when he said that, I felt a fast, hot flush of desire. Aside from some gentle play, he'd been careful with me, knowing I was fragile.

Now he sent waves of energy flowing into me, curing the lingering aches and exhaustion, and I caught my breath in true, deep pleasure.

'Right here?' I asked. 'In the car?'

'I think I said before, the seats do recline.' Being a Djinn, he didn't even have to crook a finger to make it happen. My seat slipped back, nearly level, and I made a sound low in my throat as his warm hands moved over me, sliding the strap of my top down my arm, folding back fabric . . .

'Wait,' I said, and sat up again. 'There's a motel half a mile back.'

He looked surprised, and a little disappointed. I kissed him again.

'I'm not saying no,' I promised. 'I'm saying . . . I want lots of time, and a bed. If it's a rehearsal, let's make it a full undress rehearsal.'

'Oh,' David murmured. 'That's all right, then.'

Chapter Five

The rain hit while we were lying twined together, sweaty and completely satisfied, on the motel bed. It was a nice motel, nothing sleazy, and the rooms were actually quite lovely. Big ocean views. We'd drawn the curtains, though, for privacy. No matter how much fun it is, some things really aren't meant to be shared with strangers on the beach.

I listened to the patter of drops on glass and rested my head against his bare chest. He had a heartbeat, and his lungs worked just like any man's. In fact, he was all the way human in every way that I could sense, including his postcoital drowsiness. His fingers combed lazily through my hair, leaving it smooth and shining, the way it had been when he'd first seen me.

'How'd we do?' I asked, and his hand left my hair to

softly stroke my arm, skim my side, wrap possessively around me.

'I think we need more practice,' he said. 'I don't think I quite had that last part right.'

'The Russian judge gave it a nine point five,' I said. 'And you nailed the dismount.'

I loved it when he laughed. Djinn didn't laugh enough, and they had little enough to laugh about, in general. His happiness was contagious, like fever, and I basked in its warmth. We kissed, long and slow, and I heard the low vibration in the back of his throat. Still hungry. Still wanting.

I knew how he felt. The passion between us wasn't fading; if anything, it was strengthening as time went on, as we learnt each other and found new ways to please. I loved surprising him, loved the mixture of shock and wicked delight in his eyes.

When my cell phone rang, I flailed for it and switched off the ringer, but I couldn't resist taking a quick glance at the lit-up display. Lewis, of course. And I had to answer. Otherwise, he'd do something stupid, such as send the cavalry to bust down the door and catch me doing something morally questionable.

David groaned, deep in his throat, and buried his face against my neck. 'You have to get it,' he said. 'Right?'

'Afraid so,' I said. 'Put the porno movie on pause for a second.' I caught my breath, tried to pretend I was fully clothed and businesslike, and answered the phone. 'Lewis?'

'Took you long enough,' he said. He sounded tense, which wasn't good. Lewis was one of the most relaxed people I'd ever known, in general. 'OK, we've got the package in containment. Jo – there was also a card.'

'A *card*? Like, a greeting card?'

'You're not going to like it,' he said. 'It's a congratulations card. On your wedding. It had a message inside.'

I went short of breath, and it wasn't for any of the reasons that it would have been a minute before. 'What kind of message?'

He ignored that question, which didn't bode well. 'Who knows you're getting married?'

'I – not that many people. We haven't officially – I don't know. I didn't think it was a state secret! My God, I was about to order *invitations!*'

'I think we'd better talk,' Lewis said. 'All of us. Warden HQ in New York. There are some things you need to see.'

'Now?'

'Tomorrow. Let David drive if you're taking the car.'

I bit my lip. Not that I didn't love being in the car with David, but even at the speeds he was likely to travel it would be at least a fifteen-hour trip. Then again, it kept us mobile, and Weather Wardens generally didn't do too well in airplanes. We draw storms the way a bug zapper draws moths.

'See you there,' I said, and hung up. I dropped the cell phone back on the nightstand and rolled back toward David. 'Where were we?'

His fingers slowly stroked the column of my throat, down the valley between my breasts, and across to circle the hard cap of my nipple. 'That depends,' he said, low in his throat. 'How much time do we have?'

'How fast can you drive?'

He laughed. 'You wouldn't believe how fast I can drive if I'm properly motivated.'

'Any particular thing you find motivational?'

He put his lips close to my ear. 'Your mouth.' His tongue traced the folds of my ear, drawing shivers, 'I love the way you use it.'

'I'm guessing you aren't talking about pleasant travel conversation.'

I couldn't see his smile, but I felt its dark power. 'Don't want to give it a try?'

'Dude, there are *laws*, you know.'

'Laws against driving above the speed limit, too, but I don't notice you objecting to breaking them.'

'You are a very bad' – I caught my breath convulsively and pressed against his fingers, which had wandered lower – 'man. And we should get dressed and on the road.'

'In a while,' he said, watching me, and his hand

began to move. My mind went white and smooth with pleasure. His eyes were lazy and still somehow fiercely intent. 'Let me see if I can ease your mind first.'

I decided not to protest, unless *don't stop* counted.

Driving with a Djinn isn't really like normal driving. For one thing, nobody really sees your car; they have an *awareness* of it, for traffic safety, but even the most vigilant of peace officers can look right at you breaking the speed limit (and nearly the sound barrier) and not feel moved to react.

The downside? No bathroom breaks. Djinn just don't think of things like that. I know they eat, so they must have the other human-type functions at least when maintaining human form . . . but you'd never know it. They're better masters of their bodies than we are.

After six hours on the road, I was squirming in the seat and ready to die for a bush by the side of the road, never mind a bathroom.

'Comfort break,' I said to David. 'Sorry. Nature calls.'

He sent me a lazy, amused glance, entirely relaxed and at ease behind the wheel of my car. I'd learnt not to look out the windows; the constant smear of color reminded me of science fiction movie concepts of travel past light speed. Instead, I'd asked for a laptop, which David had obligingly provided, and an Internet connection. Bingo, I was back to research.

Only this time, I was tracking down suspects instead of china patterns.

'What are you doing?' David asked, leaning over. I nudged him back with one shoulder.

'Drive.'

'I am.' He stayed where he was, eyes off the road.

'You know that makes me crazy, right?'

His lips threatened to smile. 'Not the right kind of crazy. So?'

I sighed. 'I'm searching all my correspondence, trying to figure out how many people I've told about the wedding.'

'And?'

'Dozens.' I stared gloomily at the screen. 'Not only that, I didn't exactly think to make it eyes-only clearance. Those dozens told more dozens, who told their friends, who posted it in the Wardens chat room . . .'

'So it's a dead end.'

Yeah, and we might be the ones dead at the end of it. Wasn't sure I liked that symbolism.

I was on the verge of logging off the computer, but a word caught my eye on the Warden chat board. I frowned and scrolled back up, looking for it, and finally saw, in the message thread of people offering congratulations on the upcoming wedding, a single entry. You had to be registered for the Warden chat board, of course, and authenticated, but somehow, this particular entry had no name or IP address associated with it. What it said was, simply, *It'll never happen.*

I shivered. The Sentinels were at work.

'Bathroom,' David announced, and I closed up the laptop and was unhooked before he'd screeched the Mustang to a stop in front of the gas pump of the BP station. I barely noticed the convenience store, except that as I frantically scanned the interior walls, the bored clerk took pity on me and pointed toward the rear of the store. Clearly, he knew the look.

I found the bathroom; it was unlocked and relatively clean, and all that mattered was the sweet, sweet relief. When I finished, I went to the sink and washed, studying my face in the mirror. I looked OK – a little thinner than usual, more angular, but not as haggard as I'd feared. Stress looked good on me; it always had. Lucky me. As a beauty treatment, though, it sucked.

Hmmm. Maybe some cold cream. And Ding Dongs.

I was gathering up sweet, snack-treat goodness and heading for the register when I felt . . . something. Not exactly trouble, but . . . something. It was subtle, but I'd definitely felt something shift, and not on a natural real-world level.

I put the food down on the counter, smiled meaninglessly, and wandered back toward the cold-drink case to give myself time to think. Time to track what was happening. The clerk must have thought I was giving the Pepsi-Coke debate serious consideration. I glanced over my shoulder and saw that David was gassing up the Mustang, eyes scanning the horizon but without any sign of worry or alarm.

So maybe this sudden foreboding was just my imagination working overtime. Maybe I was tired, on edge, and still recovering from my near miss.

A big semitruck eased into the parking lot. It was a tight fit; the place wasn't exactly a truck stop, and I wondered what he was doing. Maybe he needed a bathroom, too, or Ding Dongs. Everybody needed Ding Dongs, right? But no driver emerged from the shiny red cab; it just sat, shimmering in the overhead lights, idling.

I felt a chill. I grabbed a drink at random from the case and went back to the counter, threw money at the clerk, and continued to stare at the truck without blinking or looking away. *Something. Something wrong.*

David didn't seem alert to anything at all. He replaced the gas cap and stood next to the car, leaning on it, waiting for me to reappear.

'Your change,' the clerk said, and pressed coins into my hand. I shoved it into my pocket without looking, grabbed the sack he handed over, and hurried outside. There was a cool breeze blowing in from the ocean.

Couldn't see the shore from here, but the sound of the surf was a distant, low murmur.

I stopped, staring at the red truck, which continued to idle where it sat. Nothing intimidating about it, other than its size. But then again . . .

'Let's go,' I said, and climbed into the passenger seat. David raised his eyebrows at my tone, which was fairly tense for somebody who'd achieved the desperately needed pit stop, but he got in the car and started it up. We pulled out onto the road in a smooth growl of acceleration, the tires biting and cornering perfectly.

Behind us, the semitruck lurched into gear and followed.

'Crap,' I whispered, and turned in my seat to look behind us. 'That truck—'

David glanced in the rearview mirror. 'What about it?'

'Don't you think there's anything strange about it?'

'I think you're tired,' he said. 'And you're worried. Let me worry about keeping us safe.'

'But—' I stopped myself, somehow, and managed a nod. 'OK. Just . . . keep an eye on it, would you?'

'Sure.' He sounded indulgent and amused.

'David, I'm not kidding.'

He gave me a strange look. 'I know,' he said. 'I'll watch.'

That was said with a good deal more seriousness. I nodded and turned again, looking behind us.

The truck was still there, but rapidly falling behind as the Mustang's engine opened up with its throaty growl. I frowned. The truck didn't seem at all intimidated by my scowl. *You've seen* Duel *one too many times,* I told myself, but I couldn't shake the feeling that there was something . . . something wrong. Something dangerous.

But despite all that, the steady blur of passing scenery, David's impeccable (nay, uncanny) driving, and the soft, lulling roar of road beneath tires took its toll. Before too long, I was leaning against the passenger-side window, sleepily contemplating the headlights visible in the far distance behind us, and slipping over the edge into sleep.

Or almost, anyway. I jerked myself awake with a start, banging my head against the glass, and blurted, 'How are they still there? The truck? How fast are you going?'

David didn't even need to glance at the speedometer to say, 'About one-fifty.'

No semitruck on the planet was going to do more than eighty on these roads, and that was if they were asking for trouble, especially at night. So at half our speed, more or less, he should have been far behind us by now.

Invisibly far.

I checked the headlights again. They were still visible, and if anything, they were closer. 'How fast is that truck going?'

It no longer mattered, because I felt a sudden snap of power out at sea, as if someone had pulled a steel wire taut in front of us, and I had time to see a wall of water rise up, glistening and glass-brick thick in the moonlight, beautiful and deadly . . .

David let out an almost inaudible hiss and reacted instantly, faster than any human could have.

It was almost fast enough.

Plowing into a puddle of water three inches deep in a car going a hundred miles an hour creates an incredibly strange set of physical problems. Forces shear in unpredictable directions, and as the driver, if you don't get it right in that first second, you're out of control. Spinning, skidding, flipping . . .

If only it had been that easy. But this was a *wall* of water, not just a puddle. It was at least a foot thick, probably more than that, a huge amount of mass.

If we'd hit it head-on, the car would have been crushed. Instead, David's reactions were just fast enough to throw us into a skid, which burnt off some of the kinetic energy. In that extra quarter second, he and I both reached out to snap apart the wall of water.

Again, we almost succeeded. It was evaporating into mist even as we hit it, but part of it was still inevitably solid.

The impact was like being slapped by God. I heard crumpling metal and I was jerked violently from side to side. The glass next to me shivered and cracked into a frosted geometric mess. I heard David's voice but couldn't sort it out; there was too much to process, and my body couldn't decide what to complain about first.

'I'm fine,' I said, although I probably wasn't. David did something to the car, swore quietly, and I heard metal grinding in the engine. Well, he could fix it. He was Djinn, after all. That was what they did; they fixed things. They were nature's great handymen.

'Hold on,' he said, and his hand closed over mine. I turned toward him. Mist leaked in through the window cracks. The water we'd vaporized had formed a thick, heavy, creamy fog that swallowed us up. 'I love you. Hold on. I'm sorry I didn't believe you, I'm sorry—'

The fog was getting lighter. It wasn't anywhere near dawn. David was still talking, low and quietly.

'I can't get us out,' he said. 'I can get myself out, but not you. If I try to pull you out, I'll kill you. So hold on. I'll protect you. Jo, I love you. I love—'

The semitruck burst out of the fog like the red fist of a vengeful god, and I felt the surge of power around us as David pulled together a bubble of protection just before the world came to a sudden, sharp end.

* * *

'Hey.'

I jerked awake, sweating and trembling. The sun was coming up, a hot blur on the horizon, and I wasn't dead – we weren't dead, and there wasn't any truck. There hadn't been any truck for hours, since we'd left it behind at the gas station.

We were alive. It had been a dream . . . no, not a dream, a goddamn nightmare, so real it still ached in every muscle. My heart was thumping so fast it felt as if it were on the verge of needing a shock to bring it back to normal rhythm. I was damp with cold sweat.

David was looking at me with worry in his eyes. His hand was on mine, just as it had been in the dream. *Exactly* as it had been. I twisted around, sure I was about to see the specter of the truck rising up behind us, but no.

Nothing but road, and early-morning mist, and the traffic of another normal, busy day. I recognised the road. I'd traveled it before I'd met David, driving nonstop through the night, heading for Lewis's last-known address in a desperate bid to save myself from a death sentence.

Why did it feel as though I were still on the run?

David chose not to ask about my all-too-obvious freak-out, for which I was extremely grateful. He downshifted the Mustang and blended smoothly into the traffic as he reached down between the seats and came up with a smoking hot cup of coffee. Not a word spoken. I cried out in relief, grabbed it, and found it was exactly right – just hot enough, not one degree over, although I would have gladly chugged it if it had been the same mean temperature as lava, damn the burns and blisters. I felt badly off balance and unsteady.

When I'd taken enough in that I felt part of the world again, I sighed, tilted my head back against the seat, and asked, 'So how far do we have to go?'

'Couple of hours,' he said. 'We'll be there on time. Do you need a comfort stop?'

Of course I did. We found a small roadside diner with clean facilities and a pretty spectacular breakfast. Probably not too smart to order the Heart Attack Special, given my earlier cardiac fibrillations, but damn, eggs, biscuits, and gravy all sounded like heaven. If heaven came with a side of bacon.

David watched me consume with a lazy sort of pleasure in his expression as he nursed a cup of coffee and a bowl of mixed fruit. If he noticed that the waitresses kept whispering and looking him over, he didn't mention it. 'That was some dream,' he said. 'What happened?'

I didn't want to talk about it. Unlike most dreams, this one remained vivid and terrifying. 'We died,' I said. No explanations. His eyebrows climbed, and I saw him think about asking for details, and then think better. 'That truck. Did you ever see—'

He was already shaking his head. 'There was nothing weird about the truck, Jo,' he said. 'It turned off and went its own way a little after you fell asleep. It was a Peterbilt, carrying a load of television sets. The driver was a Haitian immigrant. Want to know his name?'

I paused, studying him. A forkful of eggs cooled on my upraised fork. 'You really did pay attention.'

'Of course I did. He has six kids, a wife, and an elderly mother. I know everything about him, everything about the truck, everything about its cargo. I wasn't taking any chances. Not with your life. I've nearly lost you too many times.' He said it without any emphasis, but it went straight to my heart. I lowered my fork and put it down, and fought to catch my breath. He leant forward, cup cradled in both hands with exquisite care. 'Nothing will happen. You have to trust me on that.'

I held his gaze. 'And you have to trust me that everything may not be as simple as you think it is.'

'You're talking about the package.' I nodded. 'Jo, I promise, I'll try to keep an open mind. No matter how . . . unlikely all this seems to me.'

He really was trying. More than that, I knew it wasn't easy for him to devote so much time to me; there were constant demands in the Djinn world, just as in the human one. He had a day job, after all.

'I love you,' I said. 'More than chocolate. And you know how much that means to me.'

'Eat your eggs,' he said, and gave me that slightly off-kilter smile, with an intriguing tilt of his head. 'Wouldn't want you to faint like a girl later and blame it on low blood sugar. Again.'

'Hey, buster! When have I *ever* fainted like a girl?'

He picked up the spoon from his fruit bowl and licked it, slowly and contemplatively, tongue moving very deliberately around the sleek curves. 'I can think of one or two times.'

'That,' I said severely, 'is totally unfair.'

'What is?' He dipped the spoon into the little pot the waitress had left out for my coffee, and then licked *that* off, tongue curving lovingly into the bowl of the spoon. 'Mmmm. Fresh cream.'

I think one of the waitresses dropped a water glass. I distinctly heard one of the other ones murmur something that sounded like *Thank you, Jesus*.

'Stop it. Not even *you* can make me faint with desire,' I said. I was trying for stern, but it was coming out more indecisive than anything else. It wasn't that I was weak-willed; it was that nobody was immune to David when he really put effort into it. Especially me.

'Oh, I don't know,' he said, and even his voice was pure seduction. 'Five minutes from now, when I do this thing I was just thinking about—'

'Is it that thing with your little finger? Because I'm ready for that one this time.'

'Oh no,' he said, very earnestly. 'I was thinking of the thing with my tongue, actually.'

'What thing with your tongue?'

His smile deepened, and sparks flew in the darkness of his eyes. 'You sure you really want me to demonstrate? Right here?'

I was pretty sure that if he did, there'd be a lot of women asking to order what I was having. I took a deep, slow, determined breath, and said, 'Play nice, David.'

'I'm always nice.'

Oh, I didn't think so. That was part of his dark, chocolate-rich charm, and as I'd already noted to him . . . I really couldn't resist chocolate.

He ate the rest of the fruit, nibbling on the moist bites with such suggestiveness that I think every waitress in the diner made sure to come by and ask if there was anything at all she could do for him. He never noticed. He was having too much fun making me squirm.

But when I glanced down involuntarily at my watch, he sighed, ate the last bite of cantaloupe, and nodded. 'Right,' he said. 'Let's get going.'

'As soon as this is over—'

'Don't think I won't hold you to it.'

Chapter Six

When we came out of the diner, there was a van pulled up behind the car, neatly blocking us in. I felt my nerves tighten up and shiver, but I silently told them to stand down; I'd already made a fool of myself over the semitruck, and this would turn out to be just another idiot picking up, dropping off, or parking badly. In fact, it even looked like a delivery van – battered, a bit weather-faded.

The sunlight caught a glitter on the door, and I paused, blinked, and tried to convince myself it was nothing but random metallic paint flecks. Tried hard, but got nothing. I gave it up and took a quick look in Oversight.

The van took on the dimensions and solidarity of one of those military Humvees, wickedly armored and decorated with spikes. Tough and badass – that was its essential character, interpreted for me visually by whatever processing filter the Wardens had that others didn't. The aetheric showed truth, but it was a subtle and strange kind of truth.

One thing was unequivocal about the truck, though: on the door panel blazed the stylized sun emblem of the Wardens.

I opened my mouth to warn David, but he already knew, of course. He stopped, studying without expression the van and whatever occupants it held. All the playfulness was gone, and he reminded me of a hunting leopard, lean and powerful. His eyes had gone a color that should have been a warning, and probably would have been to anybody with sense.

Unfortunately, the Warden who got out of the van was Lee Antonelli, and he had less sense than a pet rock. He was a big guy, and a gifted Fire Warden, but when it came to subtleties, he was likely to crush them under his big steel-toed boots and never notice. How he'd survived the Warden/Djinn conflicts was anybody's guess, but the fact that he hadn't had a Djinn issued to him in the first place was enough to keep him off the initial hit list, and I strongly suspected he'd spent most of the conflict hiding out.

I said Lee was big. Not brave. Hence, of course, the unreasonably tough shell of attitude on his van, not on his person.

He leant against the passenger side of the van and

crossed his arms; they were impressively muscled, and he'd invested a small fortune in body art. It should have made him look intimidating. Instead, I thought it made him look like someone doing hard-ass by the numbers, especially when coupled with the shaved head. 'Warden,' Lee said to me. He didn't so much as glance at David. I wondered why, and then I realised that Lee couldn't see him: David had made himself invisible, although he was still there to my eyes.

'Warden,' I replied to Antonelli coolly, 'who taught you how to park? I'd say Sears, but really, they do a much better job. Maybe you were absent the day they explained what those parallel lines in the lot are for—'

'Shut up, Baldwin. I'm supposed to pick you up and escort you in,' he said. 'Since whatever you've got going on is so damn important, I guess I'm riding shotgun.'

This was weird, and it wasn't normal. Lewis knew I was coming; he knew David was traveling with me. Why send *Antonelli,* of all people, whom he knew I couldn't stand? Lewis might work in mysterious ways, but that was downright impenetrable. I bought time to think by digging a pair of big sunglasses out of my purse and putting them on. There. Without a clear view of my eyes, Antonelli was going to have a tougher time figuring out what I'd do. 'Shotgun,' I repeated, 'so you're the bodyguard. Flattering.'

Antonelli ran one hand over his bullet-shaped shaved head and gave me a grim-looking smile. 'Most ladies would say so.'

'Save the smarm, I'm not in the mood.'

He shrugged. Flirting was reflexive for him; he didn't fancy me, except in the abstract way that somebody like Antonelli fancied anyone with internal sex organs. If I stood still long enough, he'd gladly take a turn, but other than that, I was furniture. 'Playtime's over, then. Let's move. In the van.'

I stayed right where I was, next to the door of the Mustang. 'I'm driving my own car.' Technically, David was driving, but Antonelli might not know that. In fact, he didn't look nearly worried enough, so I doubted he had any idea there was an angry Djinn standing a couple of feet away, eyes lit up like Halloween lanterns.

'Look, I don't know the plan; I'm just following orders. Lewis says take the van; we take the van,' Antonelli said. 'I don't ask no questions; neither do you. Come on, sister, let's go. I've got things to do.'

There was a ring of sweat around the high neck of his muscle shirt, and dark streaks under the arms. Unless Antonelli had come straight from the gym, something was up. He was nervous.

'We can sort that out,' I said, and pulled my cell phone from my pocket. 'Let me just call—'

The circuitry inside the phone fried, boiled into

vapor in an instant. I dropped the red-hot case and blew on my blistered fingers. Antonelli hadn't moved, but something about him had changed. I could almost smell it: the burnt-metal bite of desperation, mingled with a coppery odor of fear.

'Get in the fucking van,' he said. 'I'm not playing, bitch. Don't make this a showdown; there are too many people around. Kids. I don't want to do that, and neither do you. Let's keep this calm.'

Oh God, he was serious. I could tell it from the sweat on his skin, the dark shadows in his eyes. He was a whole lot more scared of someone else than he was of me.

That needed to change, right now.

I dropped my purse to the ground, glad I'd donned the sunglasses. I made sure my feet were firmly planted, shoulder-width apart, the right slightly forward to give me a more stable base.

'You're right,' I said quietly. 'I don't want to do this. *You* don't want to do this. But somehow, I think it's going to happen anyway, because I can't get in that van, Lee. Whatever's going on, I can't take the chance. Let's think this through before we both start something that will end badly.'

David had not moved. Hadn't spoken. Still, I was feeling the vibration of menace from him like the subsonic pulses from a volcano about to blow; this was going to go south, very badly, very fast.

'Who is it?' I asked. 'Lee, tell me who's making you do this. It's not Lewis. It's not the Wardens. Somebody's forcing you to take me out of circulation. Come on, man, we don't have to make this a throw down. We can talk about it, work it out.' While I talked, I used my Earth powers, subtly sending calming vibrations to him, lulling him into a state in which he might be more inclined to listen. To trust.

Antonelli shook himself, as if he were throwing off a wrestling hold, and I knew my brief second of opportunity was gone. 'Save it,' he snapped. 'I'm not some wet-behind-the-ears trainee. You can't con me.'

And then Lee Antonelli, one of the best natural Fire Wardens I had ever seen, declared war.

I'll give him credit; it was a strategic strike, not just a general firestorm. He formed a fireball and lobbed it not at me, but at my car. Clearly, he did *not* understand my relationship with cars. He'd have gotten off easier if he'd gone ahead and set my hair on fire. I'd have taken it less personally.

I formed an invisible cricket bat of hardened air, swung, lined up, and hit a solid line drive, sending the fireball right back into Antonelli's midsection. It hit him hard enough to drive him against the body of the van, which rocked and creaked on its springs, and his muscle tee caught fire. He glanced down, annoyed, and brushed a hand over it. The fire went out, but there was a nice round hole with scorched edges baring his carefully developed abs. He'd had a tattoo put around his navel – a woman's face, with the navel representing her open mouth. Classy. 'Bitch!' he snarled.

'Repeating yourself already? We just started,' I said. I didn't alter my stance, and I didn't go after him. 'Walk away. Just get in your van and go. We'll all be happier.'

Only it wasn't going to happen. He was scared, and he clearly didn't think walking away from this was an option. Instead, he pointed his finger at me, and from the tip of it blazed a pinpoint of red light, hot as the sun. Coherent light, concentrated a thousand times stronger than the brightest earth-based laser developed by men.

Air wouldn't slow it down. Neither would water, although it would bend the beam and eat up some of its energy in steam. Both options were sure to fail, and I knew from experience that if he could break my concentration, he could hurt me badly enough that I'd have a hard time defending myself at all.

Instead of defense, I went for offense. I had to end this fast, before some innocent bystander traipsed out of the diner and into the line of – literally – fire.

First, I summoned up a gale-force wind that slammed into his chest and pinned him against the van. Then I took away his air.

It's damn hard to concentrate when you feel like you're suffocating. I started with the air going in, filtering out the oxygen as he gasped. Then I focused on the oxygen inside Antonelli's body – in his lungs, in his blood. I knew what I wanted to see, and it glowed bright blue for me.

I separated the hydrogen and oxygen atoms, took away an atom from the oxygen molecule, and within seconds, he was shaking in desperation, nearly out. I let him continue to breathe, because if anything it increased his panic, but I destroyed the oxygen before he could metabolize it.

There was a side effect of this, of course. Destruction creates energy, and I burnt off the excess in sharp blue sparks that danced on the antenna of the van, the metal rims of the wheels, even Antonelli's showy belt buckle.

It *felt* as though I were killing him, in a cruel and inhumane way, and that was exactly what I wanted him to feel. I wanted him to know that I wasn't going to give in, and I wasn't going to screw around. If he wanted to play hardball, he was going to have to live through the opening innings, and I'd taken the game to the professional level.

'Think about it,' I said. 'I could just as easily put water in your lungs. Drowning on dry land. Sound good to you, tough guy?'

Antonelli sank to his knees, eyes wide and desperate. I hadn't noticed before, but he had brown eyes, big and somehow childlike despite all the 'roided-up muscles.

I felt oddly detached about what I was doing, but there was no way I was going to let go until I sensed he was more afraid of me than of the theoretical bad guys.

'Jo.' David's soft voice. His hand touched my shoulder. 'You don't have to kill him.'

'Maybe not,' I said. 'But if he's one of *them*, it'd be a damn sight safer in the long run.'

He didn't say anything. I could tell he'd dropped the veil concealing him from Antonelli, because Antonelli's mouth stretched wide, and he tried to croak out something that was probably a plea. His lips had gone the color of iron, and his skin looked dead and pale and rubbery.

He was about to lose consciousness, so I let him have a torturous, cruel gasp of air, loaded with 02. He gagged and pitched forward, openly weeping; he wasn't coming after me, that much was certain. He just wanted to live to get away.

But I didn't *want* him to get away. I let him have just enough oxygen to survive, not enough to get his arms and legs in any kind of working order. Then I picked up my purse and walked over to him, crouched down to where he was sitting against the wheel of the van, and pulled down my sunglasses to look into his eyes.

'What were you going to do to me, Lee?' I asked him. 'Don't lie. It'll only make me angry, and you won't like what happens when I lose my temper.'

I let him have more oxygen, just enough. I'd scared him, all right. I'd terrified him almost more than was strategically necessary, and I knew – again, in a detached, academic sort of way – that it might bother me later. Maybe it would bother me a lot.

Or – and this was a lot more worrisome – maybe it wouldn't bother me at all.

It took Lee six breaths before he was able to decide to choke out, 'Going to kill you.'

'Meaning, you're *still* going to kill me, or you were *supposed* to kill me?'

'Supposed to.' His face contorted with effort, and he bared his teeth. 'Going to.'

I'd known that was a possibility, but somehow, it was very different hearing it. I glanced up at David. He was standing over us, quiet, but his expression . . . Antonelli was lucky not to be relying on his mercy. I might have developed a nasty streak, but I was the kinder choice between the two options.

'I guess I should give up on the friendship bracelets,' I said. 'Good, I suck at crafts. So, I'm guessing all this wasn't your own brilliant idea. You haven't had an original one since you set your cat on fire in the second grade. Who sent you? Think hard, Lee. We're going into the final lightning round. If I don't believe you, the next breath you take could be water. Or cyanide. I just love chemistry.'

He didn't want to talk, but self-preservation is a damn fine motivator. No matter how badass his bosses might be, they weren't here. I was. Like anyone else, Antonelli wanted his next breath to be sweet and life-giving, not foul and toxic. He knew better than to question whether or not I could do it.

'Sentinels,' he croaked. 'Want you dead. Paying cash.'

'Hmmm. How much?' He looked at me as if I were totally crazy. I wasn't so sure he was wrong. 'I'd like to know how much it was worth, stabbing me in the back.'

'Five million.'

I sat back, surprised. 'Five million *dollars!*'

'I'd kill you for free,' Antonelli muttered. 'Bitch.'

'Is that any way to talk to the person holding your oxygen tank?' I asked, and cut off the flow into his lungs. He choked and thrashed. 'Oh, OK, I see your point. Five million is a lot of temptation. But I don't think it was the money. You might like me to think it was, but I think whoever sent you scared the crap out of you.' I let him have an entire ten breaths of sweet, sweet air. He shook his head. 'Come on, Lee. Please. I don't want to hurt you anymore. Just tell me who sent—'

I had no warning. Neither did Antonelli.

Some tremendous force slammed into me, throwing me facedown to the gravel path. I rolled, tossed my

auto damage than anything else. Someone caught sight of me on my knees, with Lee's body cradled in my arms, and the tenor of the babble changed and grew louder as people converged around me in a forest of heads and shadows.

'What happened?' one of them asked. 'Is he OK?'

'No,' I said. I sounded *calm*. That was odd. 'I think he had a heart attack.' Stupid thing to say; there was blood on his shirt, on me, still dripping from his gaping mouth. 'Maybe a hemorrhage.'

'That's sad; he's so young,' someone else murmured. I heard a cell phone being dialed, and a voice asking for an ambulance. After a pause, they also asked for the police. Well, I *couldn't* blame them. Big dude dead on the ground, with a burn mark in his shirt and blood all over his face.

And me, with blood on my hands.

I couldn't explain, so I didn't try. I just sat next to Lee's body, and by the time I realised that I was uncontrollably trembling, it was too late to claim I was too badass to care about what had just happened.

I was crying by the time the sirens approached.

I should have realised that where the police went, the scavengers would follow. In this case, it was the local news crews, two different species by the plumage of their satellite trucks. The reporters had a certain sleek, predatory look to them that identified them clearly from the casually dressed videographers and sloppy, Earth-shoe-wearing boom guys.

I watched them approach as I was giving my story to the police, and it was like a flock of vultures circling, waiting for my last breath.

'Ma'am?'

I blinked. The police officer facing me was tall, beefy, ginger-haired, and excruciatingly polite. Despite that, he wasn't the kind to take any crap, and I heard the warning in his oh-so-polite question.

'Sorry, sir. I was just coming out of the diner with my – my fiancé, and we saw this gentleman get out of his van. He looked like he was in some trouble. I think he might have been having some kind of seizure.'

'Seizure,' the cop said, and noted it down. 'Uh-huh. Was his shirt like that when he got out?'

Oh. The burns. 'I didn't notice right away. I didn't see him with a cigarette or anything,' I said, which was the absolute truth. 'Is it important?'

'Probably not. He damn sure didn't burn to death. So, you didn't know him, ma'am?'

I was lucky that nobody appeared to have noticed our little confrontation in the parking lot – then again, it probably wasn't luck so much as David, taking care of business. Everybody remembered me and David inside the diner, but nobody appeared to have been paying attention when we left and went out

to the car. The glamour had held until the windows
blew out.

'No, I didn't know him,' I said. It was my first
real lie, and I had to make sure he bought it. I tried
not to hold myself too still or keep his gaze too long.
A good Earth Warden could have exerted some
mental pressure to make him overlook anything that
tripped his suspicions, but I'd never been that good,
and I wasn't about to try something like that at my
current level of emotional trauma. 'Sorry. I think he
didn't really know what was going on. Maybe he was
high . . . ?' Slandering the dead, Joanne. Good one.
I felt an uncomfortable roll of guilt, but then again,
Antonelli had been willing to abduct and murder me.
A little slander might have been appropriate.

'Where's your boyfriend?' the cop asked.

'Fiancé,' I automatically corrected him, and smiled
nervously. 'I think he went to the bathroom. It was –
this was awful. Really awful.'

The cop nodded, probably thinking of all the much
more awful things he'd no doubt seen in his career.
Probably thinking I was a lightweight ditz. That was
fine, because in some senses I was, and besides, I didn't
want him to take me too seriously. That would be a
very bad thing.

'OK,' he said. 'If you'll wait over there, Ms. Baldwin,
it'll be a little while. You said you were on your way
to New York?'

'Yes,' I said. 'I have a business meeting. Look, can I call—?'

'Sure,' he said. 'Just don't go anywhere.'

I walked away, *not* in the direction of the reporters, and headed for the pay phone. How long had it been since I'd had to use a public phone? Years. I missed my crispy-fried cell phone, especially when I saw the grime and dried spit on the telephone receiver. *You're an Earth Warden,* I reminded myself. *You laugh at public phone germs.*

Still, I fished a tissue out of my purse and wiped the plastic down before I started dialing.

Lewis answered on the third ring. 'Somebody tried to kill me,' I said. 'No, don't interrupt, and don't joke. It was Lee Antonelli. I had things under control, but somebody took him out at a distance. He said something about the Sentinels putting out a contract on my life.'

There was a silence on the other end that stretched on for longer than I would have liked. 'How'd they kill him?' Lewis asked.

'Some kind of aetheric attack, nothing I've ever seen before. Lewis, they just reached out and *destroyed* him. What the hell is going on?'

'Just get here,' he said. 'The faster the better.' He hesitated for a second, and then his voice softened. 'You OK?'

'Yeah. No damage.'

'That's not what I meant.'

'You mean, am I OK with the concept that somebody's capable of hiring marginally loyal Wardens as hit men to take me out, and killing them if they fail? No, not really.'

I went cold inside when Lewis said, 'If it makes you feel better, you're not the only target.'

'You?'

'Among others.' He didn't elaborate, and I didn't think it was a good time to ask. 'Watch your back. If they can kill Antonelli from a distance—'

'I've got David,' I said. 'And we'll both be watching for it now. You be careful.'

'Always. Call when you get back on the road.'

'Can't. Cell phone had a fatal issue during the fight.'

'Get David to fix it,' Lewis said. 'I don't want you out of contact for a second.'

And that was it. Sentimental, it wasn't, but then we understood each other too well for that most of the time. Not that we couldn't be friends, but business was business, and staying alive was serious business these days. I'd fought beside him, and he knew that when the situation got dire, I'd be there.

Still. A *little* verbal hug might have been . . . nice.

I replaced the receiver, listened to the machine swallow my quarter deeper into its gear guts, and peered around the corner of the scratched plastic bubble. The reporters were still there, trying to solicit comments from uncooperative cops. They were also talking to diner patrons. I hoped nobody had any creative explanations that involved magic.

David came out of the diner, hands in the pockets of his long olive-drab coat. He didn't look happy. Wind caught the tail of the coat as he strode toward me, giving him an almost princely magnificence, but I doubted anybody but me noticed except for some of the waitresses, who were still acutely David-oriented.

'I didn't find anything,' he said as he reached me. 'Are you all right?' He knew I wasn't. It was a pro forma question, but I especially liked that it was accompanied by a gentle brush of his fingertips along the line of my cheek.

'Fine,' I said. He held my gaze.

'Really?'

'No.' I gave him a very small smile that felt crooked and unsteady on my lips. 'That was – unpleasant.'

'I know,' he said, and looked down at my hands. They were clean – the cops had allowed me to wash up – but I still felt the psychic imprint of blood on them. 'It could just as easily have been you.'

'Maybe,' I said. 'I don't think so, though. There was something that made him vulnerable to them, maybe a link they'd created to keep track of him through the aetheric. It pushed us out of the way and went straight for him. If they'd been able to take me out the same way, don't you think they would have done it?'

I couldn't tell if it had occurred to him or not; David was being extraordinarily secretive at the moment. He gazed at me for a couple of seconds, then turned his attention to the reporters. 'We should get out of here,' he said.

'Do you know who was behind it?' I asked.

'If I did, would I tell you right now?' he asked, all too reasonably. 'But I think you already know.'

'If we can believe Lee, it was the Sentinels,' I said. 'How come I'm on their hit list when I barely know their oh-so-pretentious name?'

'Because of me,' he said. 'Let's get out of here. I'd like it if you were a less stationary target.'

'Cops want to talk to you.'

David took my arm, a sweet gentlemanly gesture that didn't exactly fool me. He walked me in the direction of the Mustang, which was currently an awkward bastard stepchild of a convertible, what with all the glass scattered in glittering square pieces on the ground. 'I don't want to talk to them,' he said. He opened the drivers-side door. 'I'll let you drive.'

'Bribery, pure and simple. You're bribing me to do something illegal.'

'What's illegal about it? It's your car. You already talked to the police. You're not guilty of anything.'

Well, he did have a point. But I still felt uneasy, driving away under the noses of cops and television cameras. 'We'll be seen,' I said, and nodded toward the news crews. David didn't bother to glance their way.

'We won't.' Only a Djinn could sound that confident. Or arrogant. I supposed if I didn't love him so much it would have been just a shade more on the arrogant side. 'If we get entangled here, more lives are at risk. We need to be moving, Jo.'

Djinn were nothing if not ruthlessly logical. And they weren't above hitting the pressure points, even on those they cared about.

I silently got behind the wheel of the Mustang. It started up with a low rumble. Nobody looked in our direction. 'Repairs,' I reminded David. The broken remains of our windshields and windows rose up in a glittering curtain from the pavement, liquefied into a pool in each open area, and then solidified into clean, clear safety glass. I checked that the driver's-side window rolled down, and it functioned perfectly.

'I'm disappointed in you,' David said. 'You believe I'd do it wrong?'

'I think that you have enough to think about already,' I said. 'His van's still in the way.'

Moving a working crime scene would have been a puzzle even to one of the most powerful Djinn on Earth, but David was a lateral thinker; he didn't bother to move the van, or the cops, or anyone else.

'Hold on,' he said, and our car lurched slightly and then began to float above the road. It rose at a steady pace, carefully level, then moved forward over the gabled roof of the diner. Nobody looked up to follow our progress. I held on to the wheel in a white-knuckled death grip; flying had never been my favorite method of transportation, and far less so when the vehicle wasn't actually designed for flight. Shades of *Chitty Chitty Bang Bang*.

'What are they seeing?' I asked. My voice was a half octave higher than I wanted it to be.

'Nothing of any significance. To them, the car hasn't moved from where it's parked. They see the two of us standing at the phone booth. Oh, and a flock of birds overhead, just in case someone has some rudimentary sense of the aetheric.' Some people did; the ones with a strong sense of it generally put out shingles as psychics or became wildly successful investors or gamblers. If they had more than that, they probably would have ended up in the Ma'at, where they were taught to combine their powers with colleagues, and work in concert, if their abilities weren't enough to qualify them as Wardens.

I had to rely wholly on David to keep me off the Warden radar. I would remain mostly difficult to find until I had to draw on my powers, but at that moment, I'd light up the aetheric like a spotlight in a cave.

My brain was babbling to distract itself from the impossibility of a ton of metal hanging in midair, gliding at an angle away from the diner and toward a very busy road. 'Landing will be tricky,' David said. 'Are you ready? When we touch down, you'll have to really accelerate to make the merge.'

Great. Now freeway merging was taking on a whole new dimension of complexity. I nodded, and got ready to put my foot down and shift as David brought the car in at a gliding angle, moving us faster and faster as the road blurred on approach . . . It was like landing a jet, only way scarier, from my point of view.

The tires hit pavement with a lurch, and I instantly clutched, shifted, and accelerated, leaving a rubber scratch where we'd hit. The Mustang bounced but recovered nicely, and when I checked the rearview mirror, the car behind us was still a few feet away. Not quite heart-attack distance, at least not on my end. I could only imagine that on the other driver's end, having a car just appear in front of him might have been . . . unsettling. Maybe when people said *he came out of nowhere* after an accident, they really were telling the truth.

I got the inevitable honk and New Jersey salute, returned the favor, and settled into the drive. David relaxed – but not all the way. I could translate his body language pretty well, and he was still tense. Trying hard not to let me know it, but tense.

'You're starting to believe me,' I said, 'that things aren't quite as straightforward as they seemed.'

'They never are with you. I've always taken you seriously,' he said. 'But now I'm taking your enemies seriously as well.'

Not a good sign for them, and that cheered me up as much as the food back at the diner. I was tired, and achy from the stress and the drive, but there was something restful and strangely comforting about having the wheel beneath my hands and my feet on the pedals. And David at my side, which happened far less than I'd always craved. Which reminded me . . . 'You're hanging round,' I said. 'Do Djinn get vacations from the day job?'

'Since I'm the boss, I can take vacation whenever I want,' he said, and took off his glasses to needlessly polish them. It was so cute that Djinn had poker tells, just like humans; I knew instantly that he was fibbing. 'I can take the time.'

David's job wasn't exactly low-key. He served as the Conduit for half of the Djinn, a link between them and the raw power of Mother Earth. Without that link, the Djinn were reliant on Wardens and their relatively feeble draw of power from the aetheric. His job was different from that of the Oracles, but even more crucial, and it didn't have time off.

The Djinn didn't like being reliant on humans. Ever. I supposed that if I'd been one of them, ancient beings who'd been forced into the worst kind of slavery imaginable for centuries at a time, I wouldn't be all that fond of relying on others, either.

What *else* David did besides managing that power flow for his people, though, was a mystery to me. I knew he had to leave me on a fairly frequent basis to attend to business; I knew some of that business had to do with Djinn stepping out of line and needing correction. In a sense, David had become the court of last supernatural resort, a role I instinctively knew he didn't want and wasn't comfortable in playing. His friend Jonathan had been a great leader, one who'd held the Djinn together despite all the infighting for thousands of years; he'd had a certain ruthless wisdom that everyone respected.

David, however, was crippled by two things: one, he wasn't Jonathan; two, he had me to worry about. I was his Achilles' heel, at least when it came to his fellow elementals. Most of them didn't understand why he spent so much time in human form, and they'd never understand why he had offered marriage to a mere bug like me. They'd forgive him for it, those who liked him; after all, pledging to stay at my side would only last a human lifetime, barely a blink to the Djinn.

But it was a worry. He'd become kind of a Crazy Cat Lady among the elementals, far too attached to humanity for his own good. It was a sign, faint but definite, that he wasn't destined for the same long-term status that Jonathan had held.

It made David vulnerable in ways I could only dimly imagine.

'What are you thinking about?' David asked. His eyes were closed, and his head was back against the cushion.

'Whether I want purple roses or yellow ones. I think purple might be a nice touch for the wedding bouquet.'

'That's not what you were thinking about.'

'How do you know?'

He smiled, but didn't open his eyes. 'Because I know when you're happy, and you're not. Thinking about wedding bouquets is something you do when you're happy.'

'You make me happy,' I said, and that wasn't at all a lie. I took his hand in mine. 'And that's all that counts.'

He lifted my fingers to his lips and pressed a warm kiss against them. 'Yes,' he said. 'It is.'

Chapter Seven

The rest of the drive was full of the normal annoyances of traffic, construction, and generally idiotic behavior by other motor vehicle operators. David didn't have to ward off any supernatural assaults, and all that the day required of me was moderately offensive driving to avoid the unexpected lane changes and people failing to check their blind spots.

We rolled into the Warden parking garage, checked through the extensive security procedures, and got our passes for the headquarters floor. It had been remodeled, again; somebody had kindly seen to taking my name off the Memorial Wall, where they'd hastily had it added when I'd been thought to be dead. That was what I thought, anyway, but then I looked closer. They'd really just put some kind of filler into the engraving, a clear indication that they expected me to get clobbered at any time. This way, they could rinse it out and voila, I'd be memorialized all over again. At a bargain.

I cannot even begin to say how much that bugged me, but I bit my lip and smiled when I noticed, and ignored David's slightly alarmed look. He was picking up vibrations, all right, and I tried hard to keep myself under better control.

Lewis was waiting for us in the big round conference room, the main one, and there was a crowd with him. Most of them I knew by sight, and some I counted as closer friends. There wasn't a single unfriendly face, which was something of a relief.

Unless you counted Kevin.

Kevin Prentiss was seated at the table like an equal member of the war council, and next to him sat Cherise. My best friend wasn't a Warden; she was way cool of course, but controlling the elements wasn't her bag. So I had to wonder what she was doing in such a high-powered inner circle.

She caught my look, raised her eyebrows, and shrugged. 'Don't ask me,' she said. 'Lewis wanted everybody here. Kevin was with me, and he said I could come along.' The subtext was that nobody had wanted to piss Kevin off by demanding his ride-along girlfriend step outside. He was maturing, but I suspected he'd always have more than a little of the sullen, aggressive attitude he was known for. He was at that startling age when the changes come fast and furious; his weedy physique was filling out, developing into a fairly impressive chest under that battered black T-shirt. He avoided my eyes, but then, he always did. We had shared some very unpleasant, even embarrassing, moments, and neither of us wanted to get too cozy. It had been a big step for him to spend time with Cherise (and coincidentally with me) on the roof of the hospital; he'd made up for it by ignoring me the rest of the day. I'd returned the favor.

Kevin was here because he was a seriously talented young man. Not trained, not restrained, but . . . talented.

And maybe he cared about me. A little.

I was surprised to recognise that there was a Djinn in the room as well. She sat in the far corner of the room, long, elegant legs stretched out and crossed at the ankles, displaying lethally gorgeous shoes. I hadn't seen Rahel since the earthquake in Fort Lauderdale, so it struck me how much better she was looking these days. She'd taken a beating at the hands of a Demon, not too long ago; for a while, we'd been worried she wouldn't recover.

When she turned her head slightly, I could see the scars on the right side of her sharp-featured face — etched grooves, as if she'd been clawed. I nodded to her. She inclined her head, and her thousands of tiny black braids slithered over her shoulders with a dark rustling sound like old paper on stone.

She was sticking with purple again for her outfit. It looked good on her.

Lewis got me and David seated at the table, and didn't waste any more time. He hit a control inset in the table, and a projector beamed a picture onto a screen at the far end of the room. It was grainy surveillance video, and it took me a few seconds to recognise that it was my parking lot, in front of my apartment. I started to ask what was going on, but then I got my answer . . . a delivery person got out of a dark-colored panel van and jogged up the steps toward the second floor. Lewis froze the picture. 'Ring any bells?' he asked me. I studied the face of the man on the screen, but it was an awful picture. I shook my head. Lewis released the freeze frame, and I watched the deliveryman disappear into the hallway with a familiar-looking box in his hands. When he came back ten seconds later, no box. Surveillance showed him getting into his van and driving away. It was the kind of thing that happened a dozen times a day at any apartment complex, nothing that would alert anyone to potential trouble. 'License plates?' I asked.

'Covered with mud,' said one of the Power Rangers down the table – Sasha, his name was, a nice-looking guy with a ready smile. I called him a Power Ranger because he worked with Marion Bearheart and was part of the unofficial police force of the Wardens. When someone broke the codes, Sasha and those like him took it on. I didn't much care for the system – it bothered me to have so much power in the hands of so few – but most of them were honest. More of them were honest than the rank and file of the Wardens, to be fair. 'We've been in contact with every delivery service. None of them had drop-offs at your apartment that day.'

'Which leaves us with . . . ?' Lewis asked. For reply, Sasha appropriated the controls, bringing up another video on the screen. This one was better defined but at an odd angle. One of the traffic cameras maybe.

'We tracked the delivery van back, but we lost it in the warehouse district. They were damn careful. It took hours to trace them this far, but I don't think we'll get much farther, not with these methods. If they're smart – and I think they are – they'd have had Earth Wardens ready to reduce the entire truck to slag and spare parts in a few minutes.' Sasha blanked the screen. 'If I had to guess, I'd say we ought to be looking for warehouses rented out in the last two months.'

'Put somebody on it,' Lewis said.

Sasha folded his arms and sat back with a cocky smile. 'Already done.'

Lewis turned his attention to another Earth Warden, young but sharp. Heather something or other; I'd heard good things. 'What about the package itself?' Lewis asked her.

Heather ducked her head shyly and studied her interlaced fingers. 'Still analyzing,' she said, so softly I could hardly hear her. 'But there is definitely a high decay rate to what's inside. It's dangerous, most certainly.'

'But not a bomb.'

She looked up at him, then at us, wide-eyed. 'Oh yes,' she said. 'It had a delivery system and a trigger. If you'd opened the package, it would have gone off and spread the contents.'

'And the contents are . . . ?' David asked, in that cool, controlled voice so at odds with the look in his eyes.

'Antimatter,' Heather said. 'Antimatter colliding with any kind of matter will produce a violently energetic reaction. The by-products are—'

'There was a trigger?' I asked. 'What kind of trigger?'

Her gaze slid away from mine, toward Lewis, and then back, as if she'd been seeking approval. 'It looked as if it was adapted from a more traditional bomb-making approach. Timer and a small charge designed to crack the shell holding in the antimatter, spilling it out into the world.'

'Not a skill you pick up at your local community college,' Paul grunted.

'Unfortunately, it's not exactly rare, either. And with the Internet so helpfully offering tutorials for this kind of thing, it will be hard to track.'

'The paper?' Lewis got us back on track. 'The wrapping, the card?'

Heather brightened immediately. 'That's a possibility,' she said. 'If the Djinn can help us, we may be able to trace the card's history back and find out who came in contact with it.'

But that experiment failed. I could have told them it would. When they brought in the card – in a heavily shielded container, since it was saturated with radiation – and presented it to Rahel, she just shook her head. 'Nothing,' she said. 'I see nothing at all.'

It was the same with David, and I could see his frustration and growing alarm. He'd dismissed all this at first, but there were too many of us now, and we were too credible. The Djinn *had* to believe us – but believing us meant accepting half a dozen impossible things. Heather, disheartened, reclaimed the thing and began to have it carted back to the lab for more tests.

I stopped her. 'Can I see it?' I asked. She looked surprised. 'Well, it was addressed to me. It stands to reason that I might see something others don't.'

I doubted she bought that theory, but I really did want to see it. It had been meant for me. So had the bomb – for me and David. I supposed the first explosion would have killed me, and the antimatter would have done the job for David . . .

Heather handed me a pair of protective gloves, draped a heavy shielding vest around my chest, and put a protective hood on me before she allowed me to reach into the container and pull out the card. It was, as Lewis had told me, a greeting card – a fairly nice one, actually, with a graphic of a wedding cake, a bride, a groom. Inside, cursive preprinted script read, *Congratulations to the happy couple!*

But when I saw what was underneath, I felt cold, clammy, and sick. It said, in plain block letters pressed deep into the paper, *Sleep with the enemy, pay the price.*

Beneath it was sketched a symbol, kind of a torch. The kind that peasants carry to attack the castle-dwelling monster.

I cleared my throat and turned the card over. 'Was there anything else?' My voice was muffled by the helmet, but clear enough. I distinctly saw Heather shoot another of those looks toward Lewis. 'Well?'

'Give it to her,' Lewis said. He sounded grim and calm. 'No point in hiding anything.'

Heather brought out another container. This one had several sheets of paper that had been folded in half – probably to fit inside the card or its envelope.

Plain white paper, no watermarking. Cheap quality. On it was printed in very small type a – I hesitated to call it a letter, because there was no hint of communication to it. A manifesto, maybe.

The Sentinels were declaring war on the Wardens and they'd felt compelled to give us all their reasons. It was quite a list, starting with a detailed analysis of why the Wardens could no longer be trusted to put the interests of the human race first. Seems we'd been corrupted not by our own greed or weakness, but by contact with the Djinn.

Most of the manifesto was about the Djinn, and the crazy paranoia gave me the creeps. Sure, the Djinn could be capricious, even cruel; they certainly didn't forgive those who trespassed against them, and turning the other cheek had never been a high priority for them. Added to that, they had millennia of pent-up anger against the Wardens.

But even so, the Sentinels' position wasn't that Djinn ought to be treated with care and caution – it was that none of them deserved to live. That every single Djinn in existence had to be hunted down and destroyed for the human race to survive.

That they had to be *punished* for their crimes before they were allowed to die.

I felt sick, and I'd barely skimmed the thing. David hadn't been able to, saturated as it was with antimatter radiation that rendered it effectively invisible to him, but he could read my expression and mood like flashing neon. He stood up and said, 'Enough. Jo, enough.'

I nodded and put the manifesto back into the container. Heather sealed it and took back her protective equipment. 'They intended that to be found,' I said. 'So they really didn't intend the bomb to go off, did they?'

Lewis and Heather once again exchanged that *look*. I was starting to really hate that look. 'These weren't in the box with the antimatter,' Lewis said. 'They were in your mailbox, where they'd be found later. But they're still saturated with radiation, enough to sicken anybody who touched them.'

No question, this was serious. If they'd succeeded with the bomb in the package, I'd be dead or badly injured, and David . . . David would be, too. Putting tainted, taunting letters in my mailbox was worse yet. It reminded me of the crudest of terrorists, who detonated one explosion and waited for rescue workers to arrive before detonating another. My friends would have been the ones to suffer.

I tried to lighten my own mood. 'Special Delivery Guy delivers the mail, too,' I said. 'Give him credit, at least he's a full-service assassin. Maybe we can get him to throw in a pizza and hot wings next time.' All my attempt at humor did was give everybody the opportunity to stare at me with faintly worried looks, as if they were afraid that I was going to scream, faint, or grow a second head.

At length, Heather said, 'We're following up on

anyone who goes into the hospitals for treatment of radiation sickness or burns, but I have the feeling that a well-trained Earth Warden could have handled these letters without lasting damage, if he was careful. Or she, of course. And we have to proceed on the idea that whatever the Sentinels are, they're well organized and well protected.'

Lewis nodded, acknowledging the point. He wasn't watching Heather, though; he was scanning the faces around the table. I didn't know what he was looking for, but he stopped and focused on Kevin. 'You've got something to say,' he told the kid. It wasn't a question.

Kevin, who'd been staring at the table, looked up, and his face flushed red along the line of his jaw, bringing a few pimples into sharp relief. His eyes were almost hidden by the messy fall of his hair, but I had no problem reading his body language. *Busted*.

'Yeah,' he said reluctantly. 'So, I got this message about a week ago.'

'About?' Lewis's voice was calm and even, but I wasn't fooled. Neither was Kevin, who looked down again at his clenched hands.

'About joining the Sentinels,' he said. 'They told me they could use my talents.'

There was a long, ringing silence. I instinctively put out a hand to touch David's, telling him without words to hold his temper.

'What did you say?'

Kevin cleared his throat. 'I told them I'd think about it. I figured maybe keeping the bait out there would help.'

'Good thinking,' I said. 'Thanks, Kev.'

He shot me a frown. 'Didn't do it for you.'

'I know. But as it seems that they're after me, I still appreciate it. Did they say they'd be getting back to you? Give you any way to approach them?'

'Yeah. They gave me a phone number.'

Lewis let out a slow, quiet breath. 'Let me have the number.'

'No.'

'What?'

'No. It's my lead. I get to follow it.'

'This isn't a goddamn *game!*' I'd never seen Lewis lose his temper, but that was a sharp crack of anger in his shell of Zen. He stood up, leaning both fists on the table. 'You can't screw with these people, Kevin. And you'd better not screw with me, either. They want Jo and David dead, but I don't think they really care how many people they have to take out along the way.'

It was a mistake, a big one, and I knew it the second Lewis raised his voice. Kevin had been raised by an abusive parent, and he didn't react well to things that dredged up that bitter past.

He said, without looking up, 'Fuck you, Lewis. I'm not your bitch. I don't have to do what you say.'

Lewis started to reply, but I grabbed him by the shoulder and squeezed hard enough to get my point across. I used fingernails. He flinched and looked at me, and I saw the light dawn in his eyes and clear away the fog of anger. He took a deep breath and walked away from the table, heading for the far corner of the room where Rahel sat in silent witness. Kevin's narrow gaze followed him, just aching for a confrontation.

I said, very softly, 'Would you be willing to join the Sentinels? Go undercover?'

That brought Kevin's attention back to me with a snap, and for a second he looked his age – far too young to be so angry and defensive. 'What?' he asked. On the far side of the room, Lewis turned and made a move, but then he checked himself with a real physical effort.

'You'd be credible,' I continued. 'You're strong, you've never really liked the Wardens, and you're on record as being one of my biggest nonsupporters. They're recruiting you already. Why not join up? You could be our inside man.'

David touched the back of my hand, just a light stroke of fingers, and I heard him whisper, so softly it could have been my imagination, 'Are you sure about this?' I wasn't, but it was the best chance we were probably going to have to send someone inside the Sentinels quickly.

Kevin abruptly sank back in his chair in a trademark

teenage slump, round-shouldered and boneless. His eyes drifted half closed. 'Yeah,' he said. 'Why not? They'll probably be better company than the old farts around here. The Sentinels may be assholes, but at least they have some backbone.'

A few eyebrows went up around the table, but nobody said anything. They were leaving it up to me, and I knew – *knew* – that I was about to make a decision that could cost a young man his life.

I said, 'Do it. And Kevin?' He cocked his head to one side. 'If they ask you to kill me, demand at least five million. That's the current market price. Wouldn't want you getting shorted on the deal.'

He smiled, and I have to admit, it wasn't a comforting smile at all. 'Maybe I'll do it at a discount,' he said, 'because we're such good friends.'

And then he flipped me off.

That ended the first official war meeting of the Wardens.

'I'm putting a stop to it,' Lewis said an hour later. He'd been pacing for at least forty-five minutes, with occasional stops at the window to twitch back the blinds and stare out at the city street. He looked off balance, and it was odd seeing him so out of control. Lewis had always, by definition, been the guy who held it together in a crisis. 'He's *a kid,* Jo. You can't send him in there by himself.'

'I wasn't planning to,' I said. 'Cherise is going with him.'

He spun and looked at me as if I'd lost what was left of my mind. I didn't blame him; if I'd meant exactly what I said, he'd have every right to order me a padded jacket in designer fall colors.

I raised my voice. 'Cherise?' And sure enough, my cute blond friend poked her head around the edge of Lewis's office door and gave me a tentative wave. 'Come in. Explain it to Lewis.'

She eased inside, gave Lewis a charming dimpled smile that didn't seem to make him feel any less unhappy about my idea, and shut the office door behind her. That didn't leave much room. Typical Lewis: give him a job as the head of the entire Wardens organisation around the world, and he'll do something goofy like take the smallest office available, even if he has to kick a junior analyst out to do it. There was a battered desk that still bore scars from the Great Djinn Rampage that Ashan had led through this place, and a couple of slightly-less-than-new chairs, and paperwork. And a sleek new computer that I doubted he turned on much.

With the four of us, it was crowded. I say four, even though David was, to all intents and purposes, a shadow; he hadn't said a word, and he'd taken up a post leaning in the corner, arms folded, watching us with an expression I could only think of as bemused.

Cherise spread her arms and dimpled even more. 'You rang?' she asked.

'You have any objection to going with Kevin when he joins the Sentinels? It could be dangerous, you know.'

'Ooooh, I live for danger! But do you think they'll believe I won't run back to squeal to you about what's going on?'

'I think just the opposite,' I said. 'I think they'll keep you as a hostage for Kevin's good behavior, and that also ensures you don't rat them out to me. It puts you squarely in the hot seat. It also makes you the one person they won't be thinking of as a threat. What do you think?'

Her blue eyes widened; she seemed lost in thought for a second, then nodded. 'Could work,' she said. 'Could definitely work.'

Lewis lost his cool. 'What the hell are you talking about, *could work*? Look, Jo, I'm iffy about sending a kid in, and I'm damn sure not allowing *her* to go. She's not even a Warden—'

'Exactly,' I said. 'She's not even a Warden. If they're going to underestimate anyone, they'll underestimate Cherise. Not that she really *is* Cherise.'

I gave Cherise the nod, and her form shifted, growing taller, darker, the sweetly rounded figure of the beach bunny taking on sharper edges and angles.

Rahel sighed, stretched, and looked down at her

clothes as they shifted to her traditional neon-yellow pantsuit. She flicked an imaginary mite of dust from the cloth, and cocked a sassy eyebrow at Lewis.

He closed his mouth with a snap, then opened it again to say, 'I didn't know you could do that.'

Rahel smiled. 'I'm sure, my love, there are many things I can do that you haven't even begun to imagine.' She winked, to top it off.

'Are you sure you're strong enough?' Lewis asked. He was trying very hard to ignore the somewhat intimidating charm she was sending his way.

'Strong enough to impersonate a *human*?' Rahel flicked her taloned, glossy fingers impatiently. 'Please. You insult me if you think otherwise. You are nothing like difficult to imitate.'

I thought Lewis found that as profoundly disturbing as I had. I'd known the Djinn could do it, of course; David had pulled it off with me when we'd met, and there was no doubt that he could, when he chose, take on other forms. But he'd told me that Rahel was the master of that sort of disguise, able to perfectly match whatever template she was given – something I hadn't known any more than Lewis had, evidently. I wondered whose form she'd taken on before, and for what purposes.

'You're sure you know what to do?' Lewis asked.

'I will watch out for the boy, and gather information for you. I will deliver it to David as often as I dare to, without exposing the boy to danger. Is that not what you want from me?' Rahel recited it like a laundry list, inspecting her nails for flaws. 'Don't worry, Lewis. It will hardly be the first time we have hidden among you, discovering your secrets.'

Well, if *that* didn't make us all paranoid . . . Lewis didn't look happy, but he'd lost some of the stiff, angry body language. 'You're sure you can do this,' he said. 'I'm putting Kevin's life in your hands, Rahel. And in some ways, I'm putting you in more danger than him – these guys don't like Djinn. In fact, it's safe to say they'd just as soon destroy you as look at you. And I'm really not so sure they can't, if they try.'

She let a slow, contemplative smile slip across her lips, and even I shivered. 'How would they then be any different from most of my so-called friends and allies?' she asked softly. Her eyes had taken on an unnatural gold glow, and there was no mistaking her for anything but what she was: Djinn, through and through. 'We have survived the Wardens. We will survive the Sentinels. You may count on it.'

There was no arguing with the Djinn once they got that look, and Lewis knew it. He put up his hands in surrender, came around the desk, and stood just a couple of feet away from her. They were almost of a height; he had an inch on her, maybe. 'Take care,' Lewis said, and leant in to kiss her lightly on the lips. 'Come back safely.'

I felt my eyebrows pull up, but I wasn't really surprised, not deep down. Lewis had a lot of secrets, but he'd always been intrigued by Rahel, and she was drawn to his power, if nothing else. Maybe it wasn't the world's great love affair; maybe it was just casual, but it eased some anxious part of me to see that Lewis wasn't still pining after me.

OK, it vexed that part of me, too, but that's a personal problem.

Rahel effortlessly folded her shape back into Cherise's cute, compact little body, tossed her blond hair with a flair so familiar it would have fooled even me, and winked at him. We all stared after her as she left, Cherise's trademark little gray alien tattoo waving at the small of her back.

I didn't even notice what she was wearing as Cherise; that was how much she'd thrown me off stride, and after all, I'd *known* who she really was.

Lewis turned his attention to David, still standing silently in the corner. David cleared his throat and pushed his shoulders away from the wall. 'She'll be all right,' he said. 'No, she's not full strength, but that could play well, considering what she's doing. There's no danger, Rahel can always leave if things get too hard.'

He sounded too casual about it. I felt an uneasy lurch; there it was, again, that strange blind spot, as if the Djinn just couldn't see the threat when it was right in front of them. What was it about these Sentinels? How could they have that kind of power – or were they just taking advantage of a weakness I'd never really seen before? I'd always thought the Djinn were invulnerable, except when they took on each other, or a Demon.

I'd been feeling good about my plan, but the good feeling was going away fast. 'But we're going to give her backup, right? Just in case?'

'Of course,' David said. 'What's next?'

As far as he was concerned, it was settled. I exchanged a look with my boss, and Lewis raised both hands and shrugged. 'It's your show. Go run it.'

'Then it's time for us to do some distracting, to keep them focused on their main targets. You get to live the dream, my love,' I said. 'You get to take me shopping.'

David and I began to make sure we were seen often in public – usually hand in hand. It was nice in one way, and nerve-racking in another, as, waiting for trouble, we both kept half our attention on the world around us.

Ominously, it didn't come. I'd been hoping to lure the Sentinels into more threats or attacks, and I'd especially wanted to keep their focus extended out toward us, instead of turning toward the all-too-vulnerable undercover operatives we'd sent to them.

To bring things to a head, and present the Sentinels

with even more of a target, Lewis called a mass meeting of the Wardens. Even on short notice he got about a third of the total membership – an impressive number. Not quite as robust as the UN General Assembly, but with nearly as many languages, nations, and attitudes represented. The lecture hall had seen better days, and still hadn't fully recovered from the devastation of the last Djinn assault, but it was still impressive, paneled in teak with mahogany trim, opulently chaired, with an illuminated sun symbol of the Wardens on the ceiling that served as a massive light fixture. I'd always liked the room.

Today, I kept looking for the exits.

Ostensibly, the program was a half-day presentation from various National Wardens on threat assessments in their fields of specialty – all of which were true and timely indeed, and much needed. We'd had far too many changeovers in staff, and too many crises for comfort. A little training and communication was positive, and desperately needed.

But really, the main point of the meeting was pure theater, and I was the starring act.

It came toward the end of the meeting, as Lewis was making his closing statement. He paused, glanced over his shoulder toward where I sat behind him, and said, 'I have one last item of business, and I think you'll all be pleased to know that it's a positive one. Joanne Baldwin has an announcement.'

My palms were damp, my knees were weak, and my heart raced as if it were trying to use up its entire quota of lifetime beats in the next ten minutes. I hoped I didn't look as nervous as I felt. Scratch that; I hoped I didn't look as *panicked* as I felt.

At least I'd dressed for it. If I couldn't be self-confident wearing a kicky Carmen Marc Valvo dress and a pair of honest-to-God Manolo Blahniks in matching tangerine, I needed to turn in my fashion police badge. My hair looked good – wavy and glossy and glamorous. My makeup was fine, even though I was fairly sure I could use another touch-up on the powder to get rid of the shiny spots.

All I had to do was sell as good as I looked.

I stepped up to the podium as Lewis gracefully relinquished it, and the spotlight found me, and all of a sudden it was time. No more thinking, no more nerves. You leap, and hope for the net.

'Hello,' I said. 'I'd like to thank Lewis for allowing me to make this announcement today, because I think it's an important one. The Wardens have been through so much over the past few years; we've lost great colleagues to unavoidable accidents, and worse, to each other. We were drawn into a conflict with the Djinn that nobody wanted, and we suffered for it. So many lives were lost, and none of us can ever forget that.'

There was utter silence in the lecture hall – not

even a nervous cough. I knew that many people in the audience – probably most – had lost friends, lovers, family. They'd survived, but many still held on to the pain, and the bitterness. Those were the prime recruiting ground for the Sentinels.

The ones who hurt the most.

'That's why this is important,' I continued. 'You all know me. You all know that I owe my life to a particular Djinn who's been my friend and my protector through all of this. What you may not know is that it's more than gratitude; I love David, and he loves me. And we know it's not easy, and it may not be popular, but I'm here to announce that we're going to do something no Warden and no Djinn have ever done in history.' I felt short of breath now, elated, scared, exhilarated. 'We're going to pledge ourselves to each other in marriage, and I hope that you'll all join us in the next couple of months for a great celebration of our wedding. We believe that in making this vow, we'll bring the Wardens and the Djinn together again, in friendship, respect, and cooperation.' I swallowed hard, suddenly feeling very exposed. 'Thank you all.'

For a heart-stopping second, there was still nothing – no sound at all. And then a lone pair of hands clapped, somewhere in the darkness, and then a few more, and then it turned into a round of applause. Not cheers and champagne, but it seemed positive enough.

Lewis reclaimed the podium and I went back to my chair and sank into it, feeling relieved and a little sick with adrenaline.

The next bit of theater belonged to Kevin, who was standing at the back of the hall, looking surly and militant, as only Kevin could do. When a lull came after the applause, Kevin said, clearly enough to carry throughout the room, 'I thought screwing a Djinn was off-limits. What, you're special?'

There was an audible intake of breath, and heads turned. Somebody laughed, but it was quickly smothered. Lewis, who'd been about to speak, seemed thrown off balance. He focused on Kevin with a baleful stare, and said, 'If you want to offer your congratulations, Warden, do it to her face. I'm sure Joanne will be glad to take them personally.'

That got general laughter. People knew me all too well. I stood up slowly, making sure that everybody saw my expression.

Kevin pushed away from the wall. 'Yeah? Well, I'm just saying what everybody in here is thinking. We just got done burying people who were killed by these bastards, and now she's going to marry one? Not just a Djinn, but the Big Kahuna? What's the matter, Jo? Blowing off the Warden rules wasn't enough of a thrill anymore?'

'Shut up, Kevin.' We'd worked this out, but I was still taken aback by the venom in his voice. Kevin had a huge backlog of hate stored up, and some of it was meant for me; it was an officially approved opportunity for him to vent some of it, and I was going to have to be the one to control my reactions. *He's a kid,* I reminded myself. *He's a kid who's been wounded, over and over. Cut him some slack.*

My slack-cutting hand was getting tired.

'Shut up? In your dreams, bitch.' He stepped up again, this time addressing the entire hall. 'Look, you can see where this is going, right? You think the Djinn are just going to forgive and forget all the time we spent sticking them in little bottles, making them do our shit work? You think they don't hate us for that? Don't kid yourselves. *She* thinks this is some kind of peace process. It's not. It's obscene. Believe me, I know *all about* obscene. Especially when it comes to people using the Djinn for sex.'

'That's *enough*,' I said, and moved to the edge of the stage. 'Enough, Kevin.'

'Don't think so. Bad enough the two of you popped out some kind of mutant kid—'

I saw red, and fury burnt up from around the base of my spine and jolted into my head like a physical shock. *Son of a bitch.* He'd never said he was going to drag Imara into this, and while I was prepared to overlook personal insults to myself, my kid wasn't part of the deal. Some of the audience agreed with me; they were shouting him down. But a significant portion was either silent or nodding in agreement, shooting me frowns and dark looks.

'We need to move away from the Djinn, not get all cozy all over again,' Kevin continued. 'She just wants everything to go back to normal. What the hell was so great about that, anyway? What about the rest of you? You think we should just rip up the bloodstained carpet, remodel, and get over it? Or should we figure out what the Wardens are *supposed* to be? Not depending on Djinn, not letting them into our heads or our homes or our *beds*—'

'What's the matter, Kevin?' I asked. 'Some hot Djinn chick turn you down?'

We'd scripted this part. I hadn't wanted to do it – had argued against it, in fact – but now I took just a tiny bit of satisfaction in seeing him visibly flinch. The pallor that set into his face, followed by a vivid flush, wasn't acting. I was bringing up old demons, opening old wounds.

'No,' he said. 'I turned *them* down. But it didn't matter. They had their orders, and the Djinn always follow their orders, don't they? My *mother* made sure of that.'

Rumors had floated around over the past year about Kevin, about his stepmother, Yvette, who was truly one of the most morally grotesque people I'd ever met. About her illicit use of Djinn for personal gratification, and for other, even less savory, purposes.

Kevin had suffered at her hands. I didn't know whether or not she'd turned her Djinn on him in a sexual sense, but I didn't doubt it. It would have been a tragedy for the Djinn as well as Kevin, but Kevin wouldn't necessarily feel that.

The worst part of it was that for at least some period of time, Yvette had owned *David*. I'd never asked him what his history was with Kevin, and neither he nor Kevin had ever really come clean about it.

I hoped I wasn't hearing the truth of it, right now, but the pain and rage in Kevin couldn't possibly be mistaken for anything else but honesty.

'I hope you get what's coming to you. Both of you,' he spat, and turned to leave.

'Wait a minute,' I said. 'You think you just get to make a dramatic exit?' I sent a gust of wind past him and blew the doors shut with a heavy thud. 'Sit your ass down, Kevin.'

'Bite me.' He whirled back toward me, and there were tears glittering in his eyes, real and agonising, and I almost stopped it there, almost went to him and put my arms around him and told him he didn't have to do this.

Lewis got in my way. 'Sit,' he said flatly. 'I'm not telling you again, Kevin. If you can't control yourself, I'll do it for you.'

In answer, Kevin formed a fireball in both hands, glared at both of us through the unholy orange glow, and then turned and threw the fireball straight at the doors. It hit and detonated with enough force to blow the doors open and off their hinges.

He walked out.

'No,' I said, and put out a hand to stop the guards who started after him. 'No, let him go. If he wants to leave, let him leave. This isn't over, but there's no point in destroying the place. Again.'

That got a weak wave of nervous chuckles. Some of the Wardens out there looked as if they were suffering a PTSD moment; I completely sympathised. This was turning out to be less theatrical and more gut-wrenching than I'd ever intended, but I supposed that was a good thing, ultimately. *It's for his own protection,* I reminded myself. *If the Sentinels can't buy his defection after that, it can't be done.*

But I was going to have a hell of a lot of fence-mending to do. And I felt filthy inside, as if I'd dragged my soul through a sewer.

Lewis took my hand, out of sight behind the podium, and squeezed. He knew what I was feeling. I moved back to let him get to the microphone, and he said something to close the meeting . . . I wasn't really listening. I was staring at the smoking, destroyed doorway where Kevin had made his grand exit.

God, please, watch out for him, I thought. *If anything happens to him . . .*

Lewis must have finished, because in the next

moment people were getting up in the auditorium, chattering excitedly, making their way toward the exits. And Lewis put his hand at the small of my back, guiding me off into the shadows at the back of the stage, where he whispered, 'I think it was all right.'

'Brutal,' I said. My voice sounded strange. 'I didn't want to put him through that.'

'He signed up, Jo. It's something he wants to do. Let him be a hero for once.'

'Yeah, well, it's hard to just stand by and watch.'

'No kidding,' he said, and smiled a narrow, bitter smile. 'How the hell do you think the rest of us feel about watching you?'

I got a lot of 'That was uncalled for!' supportive comments on the way out, but not quite as many as I'd expected; the majority of Wardens seemed to want to stay out of the line of fire. Couldn't really blame them for that; most of them had reason to be gun-shy.

What bothered me was the significant number who seemed to be huddled together whispering in the halls, who fell silent when I came near. I felt stares on me all the time. A few nodded, but it didn't feel like support. None of them were my friends, and most of them were people I knew only by reputation. Were they Sentinels? Potential recruits? No way I could tell, but it made the back of my neck itch.

Lewis escorted me to the elevators, staying

protectively close. We'd agreed that David should stay away for this part; it would have been harder with him in the room. So Lewis was taking his bodyguarding duties seriously, even in the relatively secure confines of the Warden's own halls.

'You really think somebody's going to try to take me out here, with all these Wardens around?' I asked, as we waited for the elevator to arrive. He had his hand on my arm, and he didn't smile.

'Let's just say I'm not counting on anything right now. Where's David meeting you?'

'Downstairs in the parking garage.' I shook free of Lewis's grip. 'Honestly, back off, would you? I'm not glass, and I can take care of myself. I'd have thought I'd proven it by now. I'm a big girl. I can ride the elevator all by myself.'

I could tell he was just itching to go all macho and protective on me again, but he managed to hold himself back, raising both hands in surrender and stepping away. 'Fine. Just don't come crying to me if you end up dead. Again.'

The elevator's arrival saved me from having to make a snappy reply. I got in, a few other Wardens crowded after, and I saw Lewis make a visible effort to stay where he was. *I'll be fine,* I mouthed as the door slid closed.

I wished I were as confident as I appeared to be.

Still, nobody tried to kill me on the way down,

although a few unfriendly looks were thrown my way by one or two of my fellow vertical travelers. One made up for it by delivering a cordial congratulations on the upcoming wedding, although he politely called it a 'celebration,' as if he wasn't quite sure of the legality of the whole event. Well, neither was I, actually.

We made a couple of stops, including one at the lobby level, where half the passengers disembarked.

Next stop was the secured parking area, and as the doors opened, I was relieved to see the familiar form of David leaning against a support pillar, looking deceptively casual. He was wearing his full-on normal guy disguise – jeans, checked shirt, slightly mussed hair. Glasses to distract from his eyes, although at the moment they were solidly unremarkable. And the coat, of course. He hardly ever showed up without the coat, even in the humidly close heat of late summer in New York City.

'You know, you're going to have to start learning how to dress for the seasons,' I said without preamble, taking his offered arm as we headed for the car. 'No more of this one-outfit-fits-all thing.'

He smiled. 'Are you threatening to take me shopping again?'

'Threatening? No. It's an absolute certainty. Besides, we're supposed to stay public, aren't we? Present a distraction?'

'Shopping is a distraction?'

'It is the way I do it,' I said. 'By the way – what's my new last name?'

'Excuse me?'

'Well, I'd like to know how I'll be signing checks in the future. Mrs Joanne . . . ?'

'What's wrong with Baldwin?'

'Nothing. In fact, I may hang on to it, but if you're planning to do the normal-life thing, you need to have an identity other than David, King of All Djinn.'

He shot me one of those amused half smiles. 'Seriously, King of All Djinn? That's funny.'

'Answer the question. What's your last name?'

'Whatever you want it to be.'

I remembered that he'd used a credit card at a hotel early on in our relationship. 'What about David Prince?'

He sighed. 'If you like.'

'You don't?'

'Jo, I don't *care*. Even when I was actually built to care about those kinds of things, I didn't have a family name. It was always David, son of—' He stopped, and something indefinable flashed across his expression. I waited. 'Son of Cyrus.'

'Cyrus? Your father's name was Cyrus?'

'It was a very honored name at the time.'

'Then your name ought to be David Cyrus.'

He looked thoughtful. There was something going on behind his eyes, something I couldn't guess and probably had no context to understand even if I could. He'd never mentioned his human father, or his human mother, or anything about that period of his life before it had come to a cataclysmic end on a battlefield, with thousands of men pouring out their life energy. His best friend, Jonathan, had been like Lewis, a Warden with all three powers, and deeply beloved of Mother Earth; David hadn't been able to let go when Jonathan had passed over and been reborn as a Djinn. David had been reborn as well.

I wondered how much real memory he had of those early, fragile years of his human life. Of his birth parents, before that rebirth. He'd seemed surprised that he'd remembered his father's name . . . and seemed affected by it, too.

At length, as we passed rows of parked cars, David said, 'Cyrus sounds . . . fine.'

We arrived at the parked, sleek form of the Mustang, which was in perfect, gleaming condition, for having had its windows blown out less than a day before. David opened the passenger door and gracefully handed me in, like a princess into a carriage. He shut the door and headed around to the driver's side, and we didn't speak again until we'd exited the garage and were already on the road, heading for the bridge.

'You haven't said how it went,' he said.

'It was harder than I'd thought,' I confessed. 'Not

the we're-getting-married part. The Kevin part.'

David nodded. 'I was concerned about that. He's fragile, in some ways. And he has good reason for a lot of his anger. Putting him in this kind of position is a risk, at best.'

'He said – David, he said that his mother used Djinn against him.' I couldn't even really bring myself to articulate the implications. 'Did she?'

He was silent for a moment, apparently focused on steering around the traffic and increasing speed as the road opened up in front of us. The steel structure of the bridge flashed past in a blur, and I wondered if the speed wasn't more about David channeling anxiety than wanting us to get back home quickly. 'You know she did,' he said. His face was smooth, expressionless, and he'd changed his glasses now, darkened them to hide his eyes. 'In many different ways.'

I couldn't ask. I knew I should; I knew he'd tell me and it would be a relief if he did, maybe for us both, but I just . . . couldn't. I closed my eyes, rested my head against the window, and tried not to imagine David as Yvette Prentiss's slave.

As her weapon.

'Sleep,' he murmured, and whether it was his influence or my own weariness, the steady roar of the tires and throb of the engine lured me down into the dark.

*   *   *

When I woke up, David was carrying me in his arms. I hadn't been carried like that by him, except when I was in danger or injured, in a long time, and it felt . . . wonderful. Hard not to appreciate the strength and surety of his body against mine, and his smile was gentle and deadly at such close range. 'Good nap?' He set me down, and my feet sank into sand. I hastily stripped off the Manolos. Sacrilege, to walk on the beach in those. Also, awkward. It was night, and the surf curled in from the horizon in sweetly regular silver lines. It broke into lace and foam on the beach, and we were close enough to the water to feel the breath of spray.

'Where are we?' It wasn't Fort Lauderdale. The beach was too quiet, too secluded. It felt as if it had never been touched by humanity.

'Nowhere,' he said. 'In a sense, anyway. It's a place I come sometimes to be alone, when I'm troubled.'

He was telling me something. I looked around. No lights on the horizon, no roads, no airplanes buzzing overhead. Just the beach, the surf, the breeze, the moon bright as a star overhead.

'This isn't real,' I said.

'It's as real as we want it to be. Like Jonathan's house, beyond the aetheric.' David shrugged slightly. 'One of the benefits of being the Conduit is you can create your own realities if you feel the need.'

'And . . . you feel the need.'

He took my hand, and we walked a bit in the moonlight. It felt as if we were the first people to walk here, and I supposed we were. I didn't ask. He didn't volunteer. After a while, we rounded an irregular curve and I saw a low-burning fire ahead, warm and inviting. I knew, without a word being said, that we were supposed to sit down, and I settled into the cool sand without complaining about the damage to my dress. Besides, my dress was still on my sleeping body, somewhere out there.

David took a seat beside me. The fire snapped and popped and flared like a real flame, and it warmed like one, too. I stretched out my hands toward it. *As real as we want it to be,* he'd said.

Like the two of us, together.

'The question you won't ask me is, did Yvette ever force me to abuse her stepson,' David said. 'The answer is no. Not in the way you're thinking.'

I have to admit, a weight of dread rolled away, and I must have given an audible sigh of relief. But David wasn't finished.

'What she did force me to do was to bring him to her, and watch,' he said. 'Yvette always did like an audience. Kevin avoids me because I'm part of those memories. I'm bound up with all the sex and pain and horror of it. So yes, I was part of it, even though I never – I never hurt him. I wanted to destroy her for it. I wanted to rip her apart into so many pieces not even God could find a trace.'

I heard the ring of hate in his voice, real as what I'd heard from Kevin. He meant it, and I ached for him, too.

'But you didn't, because you couldn't. You were as powerless as Kevin to stop her.'

He said nothing to that. The Djinn were not comfortable with the idea of powerlessness; in a sense, it was worse now than ever, because they had thousands of years of slavery to try to put into some kind of context. He hurt, and I couldn't help him. Not with that.

'I'm telling you this because Kevin doesn't trust me,' he said. 'And that's part of the reason I sent Rahel with him. He's a bit fascinated with her, like most humans seem to be, and she's got no history for him to fix on. If he can trust any Djinn, he'll trust her. But he'll never truly trust me.'

This felt so intimate that it frightened me. He came here to face his fears, face his history, and there was a lot of that to get through – more than I'd ever be able to understand. He could read my life at a glance, if he chose, and that more than anything else made me feel disadvantaged.

David put his arm around me, and I leant against him. We both stared at the fire for a long time before he said, 'My birth mother was like you. Strong, like you. Beautiful. Willful, which gave my father plenty of heartaches; it was a time when women were more constrained by society, or at least had fewer choices in how to misbehave. She taught me many things, but one of the things she gave me was a love of learning, and that was rare then. Not even the sons of kings were learned; it wasn't considered manly.'

I closed my eyes and breathed in the night, the peace. Maybe this wasn't real, but it had a kind of solemnity to it that we couldn't get out there, in the daily whirl of life.

'Tell me about her,' I said, and snuggled closer to his warmth. 'Tell me everything.'

And he did.

Chapter Eight

When I actually did wake up, we were still driving, and I wasn't sure that I hadn't dreamt the whole thing until David looked over at me. He had an expression, open and vulnerable, unlike any he'd ever really shown me before. I'd never even realised how armored he was before, until the armor was removed.

'I wanted to tell you all that,' he said. 'I'm sorry I didn't before, but there never seemed to be time. Always something happening with you. And it usually involves explosions.'

'That's an exaggeration,' I replied with great dignity. 'Things hardly ever explode. They burn, they shake, and occasionally they break, but explosions aren't my thing.'

'Point taken.' He gave me an assessing look, and took the next exit. 'You need a break.'

'Buster, you need to learn how to take them, too. If you intend—'

'To live like a human, yes, I know. I'll start tomorrow. First thing. For tonight, I just want to get you safely home.'

Home. I imagined the soft bed, imagined waking up with him, and imagined that it would be like that every day for the rest of my life.

It seemed too precious to be true.

The truck stop where we pulled off the freeway was one of those open-all-night places that specialized in everything, from deli sandwiches to wind chimes. After investigating the facilities, which were scrupulously clean, I browsed the snack aisles and stocked up on road food, looked over the DVDs, rummaged through the books, thought about purchasing those wind chimes, and finally ended up with nothing but a bag of chips and a cold soft drink at the register. No sign of David. I wondered where he'd gone off to; maybe he was still in the car.

I collected my purchases and went outside. No, the Mustang was empty. I went back inside, strolled the aisles, saw nobody I recognised. Somewhere inside, a slight tightening started in the vicinity of my stomach. I walked faster, looked harder.

Nothing.

'Excuse me,' I said to the guy behind the counter. 'I

came in with a guy, a little taller than you, brownish hair, kind of long—'

'He left,' the guy said. 'Said he'd be right back. I figured he'd just gone out to the car or something. He's not out there?'

I checked again. No sign of David anywhere. I waited out in the darkness, indecisive, and paced. Manolo Blahniks weren't meant to be paced in, but I wasn't taking off my shoes on the stained concrete of Moe's All-Niter, either.

I finally stopped and said, 'David?' Just in case he was there and watching, though why he'd do that I couldn't imagine.

Someone answered me, but it wasn't David. 'He's gone,' said a little girl, standing in the shadows at the edge of the building. She didn't move, but she emerged from the darkness, as though the lights had brightened around her, and I saw that it was Venna. Venna was one of the most puzzling Djinn I'd ever met, and that was saying a lot; she was the only one I'd ever seen who preferred the form of a child, and she usually liked to dress in Alice in Wonderland-style blue, with a white pinafore. Long blond hair, held back by a simple band, and big china-blue eyes.

There was absolutely nothing human about her right now. The clothes – the body – were a disguise.

I took a long step toward her. 'What the hell did you do to him?' I blurted. 'Where is he?' Showing aggression probably wasn't the smartest thing to do in this situation; Venna could be deadly, although she'd also been my friend more often than not, and saved my life a few times. Putting her on my bad side wasn't a good career move.

But I couldn't stop myself.

She didn't react. Her hands stayed folded, but her eyes flashed a more intense blue, just for a second, and I found myself unable to advance. My heart raced, and I shuddered in every muscle, trying to fight, but it was useless. She had me shut down.

'Ready to listen now?' she asked mildly. 'I'm sorry, but you're angry. I'm just trying to be sure you don't hurt yourself.'

I hadn't known Venna was capable of doing this. I hadn't known *any* Djinn could do this, not so easily. Not against someone of my strength level.

As if she were reading my mind, too, she smiled. 'Don't be scared,' she said. 'It's only because you have so much power, so many ways to get inside you. If you were any other Warden, I couldn't do it at all.'

'Except for Lewis,' I managed to say, and her smile took on dimples.

'I'd never do this to Lewis. Lewis would never make me.'

As always, there was this subtle tone in her voice when she mentioned his name – all the Djinn had it, a kind of puzzlement, or awe. I'd gotten to my current status as a triple-threat Warden, controlling weather, fire, and earth, through a series of circumstances – died, reborn as a Djinn, then reconstituted as a human, *then* granted Earth powers by my half-Djinn daughter turned Earth Oracle.

Lewis had just been born that way. One in a thousand years, I'd been told, and nobody since the original – Jonathan, later leader of the Djinn – had displayed so much raw power from the outset.

If I were Lewis, that comparison alone would make me very, very nervous about my future.

Venna studied me for a moment, then nodded. I felt the force gripping my muscles let go. I lurched forward, then got control and glared at her. It had all the impact of an ant glaring at a galaxy a few billion miles away.

'David has been summoned,' she said. 'He'll return to you as soon as he can.'

'Summoned? Who summoned him?'

That earned me a pitying look. 'Who can?'

Oh. Mother Earth. I couldn't fight that, and neither could he, whatever his original intentions. 'Why would she do that?'

'Her reasons are her own. Perhaps she wants to keep him away from you for a while.'

'Why?'

Venna shrugged. 'Some say you're corrupting him.'

'You're sure Ashan doesn't have some ulterior

motive here?' Because for better or worse, Venna had gone with Ashan when the Djinn had split between Old and New; I didn't think she belonged there, because she seemed genuinely curious about humanity, if not exactly caring. 'What's going on?'

Venna shrugged. Not her business to wonder such things. 'I was just dispatched to reassure you.'

'You're doing a great job so far.'

She cocked her head, her gaze growing sharper. 'Is it true? That David intends to pretend to be human for the rest of your life?'

I cleared my throat. 'We're getting married, if that's what you mean.'

It obviously was. Her cute little-girl face scrunched into a frown. 'Why?'

'If you have to ask, there's no way I can explain it.'

'Are your sexual encounters not currently satisfying?'

'Venna! I know you're not a child, but really, that's just creepy. And personal.'

She looked surprised, then thoughtful. 'So many rules,' she sighed. 'All right. I accept that I will not understand your reasons. But do you understand the risks? There are many of your people who won't approve. Many who don't like the Djinn at all, and want us to leave you alone.'

'Can't imagine why,' I said dryly. 'You're all just so darned nice.'

There was that smile again, mischievous and dimpled. I thought she must have copied it from a young Shirley Temple, but for all I knew, it could have been a young Cleopatra. She didn't take the bait.

'How long is he going to be gone?' I asked. She shrugged. 'Well, should I wait?' Another tiny shrug, as if it didn't even matter enough to her to waste the energy on a gesture of indifference. 'Let me say it another way: Can I go?'

Venna rolled her eyes, a shockingly human gesture for her. 'Please,' she said. 'Go. I do have better things to do.'

And she misted away, just like that. I was on my own.

I felt alone, driving away from the truck stop; I'd entered it feeling peaceful and excited and happy, and now I was back to living on the edge. All because Mommy Earth had yanked David's leash. That could happen any time, and I'd forgotten about it, or wanted to. The car felt empty without him, and I felt exposed. *So much for my 24/7 protection,* I thought, but then I felt guilty. Was that why I wanted him? To make myself feel safe? Boo. Boo on me.

Sunrise dawned warm and clear, and by the time the heat grew oppressive I was upstairs in my apartment, eating a small container of yogurt. Exhaustion was blurring my eyes, and I didn't care much about eating

– hence the yogurt, which wasn't really eating, per se. All I wanted to do was take a shower and nap. *Can't do anything until David comes back,* I reasoned. *Might as well rest up.*

Instead, after my shower (which was every bit as wonderful as I'd anticipated) I ended up, phone book and phone next to me, parked in front of the Internet, obsessively researching so I could cross off items on my wedding checklist. I was puzzling over the catering problem – $18.95 per plate for a meal that was going to be served on *plastic*? Really? – when the phone rang. I picked it up immediately, thinking it would be a callback from the florist.

Instead, it was Cherise, and man, was she *pissed.* 'You don't trust me,' she said. 'I can't believe you!'

'Where are you?' I asked in alarm, because I'd left strict instructions that Cherise could not be seen or heard from, under any circumstances, until this charade with Kevin and Rahel was over with. 'Cher—'

'Oh, relax, this is a secured line. My buddies from the Wardens and Homeland Security all say so, plus my own personal Djinn bodyguard. So I'm being a good little convict,' she said. 'By the way, thanks for booking me at a nice hotel. Lewis said I could order room service any time I wanted, but no bonking the waiters, no matter how hot they are. Oh, I'm ordering movies, too, and you guys are paying. Even if I order porn.'

If that was the worst of it, I'd gladly pony up the

cost of pay-per-view. 'You need anything? Clothes?'

'What's the point? Not going anywhere. I'm just lounging around in a T-shirt. It's like a pajama party, except I'm going to get really bored with painting my own toenails. So I'm going to call you and take it out on you.' She paused for a second, and her tone grew more serious. 'Is this really dangerous? You know, for Kevin?'

'Maybe.' I couldn't be dishonest with her, not Cherise. 'But he wanted to do it. In fact, he kind of insisted.'

'He would. Rahel's doing me, though, right? So he's covered?' She made it a question, painfully eager for reassurance. I swallowed hard.

'He's covered,' I said. 'Rahel's smart, and she's strong. If anything goes wrong, she can get him out.'

Not if she can't see the danger. But I'd fought that battle with David, and lost. All I could do was hope that Kevin, whom I'd properly prepared with all the information I had about the antimatter, would be able to recognise trouble coming and help her avoid it.

'These Sentinel people. Do you know who any of them are?'

'No,' I said. 'Well, one, but he's dead now.'

'Then how do you know who you can trust?'

'I trust you,' I said. 'I trust Lewis. For this, I trust Kevin. I always trust David. But believe me, my trust circle's getting smaller, all the time.'

'Good. Maybe you won't get yourself hurt quite as often.' I heard the TV come on in the background, and the bed creak. 'OK, I'm going to my happy place. Russell Crowe movie festival, baby. Sorry you can't be there, but if you decide to come over—'

'I'm not in New York,' I said, 'and even if I was, going to see you would blow our whole operation.'

'I guess.' She sighed. 'OK, Mr Dreamypants is on. Call you later?'

'Yes,' I said. 'Hey, Cher?'

'Yeah?'

'Do you know any good caterers?'

Cherise's question about the Sentinels stayed with me the rest of the day, as I went about my so-called normal life. If anybody had turned up likely suspects for the Sentinels list, they weren't sharing it with me. No sign of David, and no messages from beyond. I got calls from various Wardens either congratulating me about the upcoming marriage, or fishing for gossip about the confrontation with Kevin. I answered honestly to both, so far as it went. I didn't try to hide my frustration with Kevin, but I told them it was Lewis's problem, not mine.

None of the phone calls had seemed overly strange, but my paranoia dials were all on high. I couldn't rule anyone out.

Hearing my doorbell ring only made my self-preservation alarms go off. I was boiling pasta. I took the precaution of turning off the burner – in case I died, no sense in burning the building down again – and went to look through the peephole.

It was David. Oh. I *had* told him to start acting like a human, hadn't I? I needed to get him his own key. I unbolted the door and swung it wide—

David lunged forward, grabbed me by the throat, and drove me back to the wall as he kicked the door shut. It was a real threat; his grip was bruising my neck, making parts of me panic in fear of imminent strangulation. I grabbed for his wrist, which was stupid, and tried to get a scream past his hand.

No good.

He smiled, and I recognised the expression. It wasn't David's, although he was wearing David's face. I croaked out, 'Don't you fucking pretend to be him!' and David's body shrugged, and the Djinn morphed into his more usual form.

It was Ashan, leader of the Old Djinn. Venna's brother and boss, and the least likeable creature I'd ever met, including the ones who'd tried to kill me. Ashan was a cool, smooth, handsome bastard, all chilly grays and ice whites, and he didn't care for people at all. He liked me a good deal less than that. 'I've come for a purpose,' he said, 'but I don't need to hear your prattle.'

I made some incoherent noises, which got the point

across that his grip on my throat was impairing my ability to curse, and he finally let up enough to allow breath in, profanity out. After the profanity, I got my pulse rate dialed back from Going to Die to Total Panic, and said, 'What the *hell* are you talking about?'

'You brought this on yourself,' Ashan said. He emphasised that by slamming me back against the wall with painful force. 'I was content to let you live, but you, you push, you always *push*.'

'*Let go!*' I snarled. He must have sensed I meant business, because although he didn't obey instantly, he finally released his grip and stepped back. Not far back, though, and the cold fury in his eyes stayed in place. 'Where is David? What have you done to him?'

He slapped me. A solid man-slap, one that I was not prepared for; it burnt and I felt a wave of total rage crest at the top of my head and flow down every nerve ending. Somehow, I held myself back, but my hands clutched into convulsive fists. 'You will destroy him,' Ashan said flatly. 'I care nothing for you, but I *do not want* another war among the Djinn, and you will bring it on. It is best if you disappear from this world before you can rain destruction on all of us.'

Word had gotten around fast, even on the outer reaches of the aetheric. I hadn't expected the Djinn to approve, but I hadn't expected *this*. 'All because we're getting married?' Venna was right about one thing: the two of us engaging in a little sexual adventure hadn't bothered too many people. It was the wedding that was pissing them off.

'It is a vow,' Ashan said. 'And a vow is, for us, unbreakable. Do you understand? You will bind him to humanity, and he is the Conduit.'

All at once, I got it, and it was like a second, harder slap, only this one was directly to the surface of my brain. 'Oh crap,' I breathed, suddenly not angry at all. 'You mean that by taking vows to love and cherish in sickness and in health—'

'Through him, all of the New Djinn could also be bound,' Ashan said. 'Conduits to the Mother must *not* make such vows. We became slaves the last time such was made. I will not allow it to happen again, not for such small gain as your personal happiness.'

And another thing came crystal clear to me. Ashan wasn't screwing around this time.

I read it in his expression: he was going to kill me. Problem solved.

And I think he would have, except that right at that moment, somebody *else* tried to kill me.

I thought it was Ashan who'd attacked for an instant, as I felt the force slam into me and pin me back to the wall, sink past my skin, and close around my heart like an iron hand. But I could see that in fact it wasn't him, because he'd been forced back from me by the attack, and he was off balance and confused.

I remembered David at the diner, blown back by the aetheric attack that had taken out Lee Antonelli.

They were coming for me. No warning, no quarter, I was under attack by the Sentinels.

Dark shadows flew out of the walls and coalesced into Djinn – Ashan's bodyguards, who'd been keeping their distance until they were summoned. A threat to their boss brought them running, but once they were on the ground, the next step wasn't exactly clear, since Ashan wasn't the target. I was.

And one more coalesced out of the air, a blur of motion, burning copper-bright. *David*. He was coming, and coming very fast, heading straight for me, blind to everything else around him.

The Djinn bodyguards stopped him, but only for a few seconds. He was too strong for them, even collectively, but the instant he broke free, Ashan lunged like a white tiger. The two of them fell, rolling, a blur of motion that somehow still conveyed the fury and power of the conflict.

As David tried to fight his way to me, I drew all my power inside, fighting the invisible fist that was trying to contract and squeeze my heart into red jam. I felt my distant, powerful daughter's flow in to augment mine; she couldn't act directly, but she could help.

It was enough – barely – to keep me alive. For now.

I opened my eyes. The fight between the two most powerful Djinn was already over.

David was on his knees, held fast with Ashan's arm around his throat and his hands twisted behind his back, and the look on his face nearly made me cry out. It was shattered. Horrified. *Betrayed.*

'Oh, God, no. Jo, hold on,' he said, his voice rough and trembling. 'Ashan, let go, damn you. *Let me help her!*'

The Djinn stood silently, watching. Waiting to see what would happen. Probably waiting to see how fast I was going to drop dead. This was nothing but a gift to Ashan – I'd die, and his hands would be clean. There was no reason for David to come after him.

I held against the assault, somehow pushing back the squeezing hand around my heart, and I didn't dare speak to David. I couldn't. No breath and no strength left over, and I knew it wouldn't do any good, no matter what I said. He couldn't act, not with Ashan in the way. If he could have, he'd have already done it.

'Ashan, you can't stand by and see her murdered!' David screamed. 'Let me *go!*'

Ashan said, in a soft but deadly cool voice, 'It's the business of humans. *She* told you that. I'm only enforcing what you know are the rules.'

My vision was eroding, black spots appearing at the edges. Maybe that was why I didn't immediately recognise that one of the Djinn standing next to Ashan was Venna, dressed not in her Alice pinafore outfit, but in plain black. I focused on her. Her blue eyes were blazing hot, the color of a gas flame.

She said nothing. She didn't try to help either one of us, not even David, whom I knew she loved. She loved Ashan more.

No help was coming.

The Sentinels can't keep this up, not at this level of power, I told myself, trembling. Only maybe they could. The assault continued on the aetheric, furious and unrelenting, and it required every bit of concentration I possessed to keep myself from folding. Power was counteracting power, and the resulting forces were out of control; I couldn't do anything to reduce the damage, or I'd be instantly dead.

Around us, sparks began to crawl on every available metallic surface, zipping and popping. Lightbulbs blew out. The Sentinels – if that was indeed who was behind this – pressed me harder, and I had to respond.

Windows shattered. I heard the plate glass patio door break with a catastrophic crash. One of the curtains caught fire from the constant sparking. It burnt slowly, but it burnt, giving off acrid black smoke.

'Stop this! They'll destroy her!' David screamed, and writhed to get free. Ashan held him, but just barely. Venna looked visibly upset, and turned away from them. She brushed her hand across the flame on the curtains and transferred it to her palm, then rubbed it contemplatively between her fingers, frowning, and looked at Ashan. Something passed between the two of them, something I couldn't understand.

The whole world was narrowing, darkness closing in on me. I could feel it all around me, eating away, sinking into every nerve, every muscle.

And the hand around my heart tightened, and every labored thump seemed likely to be my last on this earth.

David's face was taut, pallid, and desperate. He was still trying to twist free, but his strength, like mine, wasn't up to the task.

The odds were too high this time.

'Ashan, give me your leave,' Venna said. Her brother frowned, and nodded sharply, once. Venna disappeared so suddenly there was a small thunderclap of air left in her wake. I couldn't even spare the breath to curse, or to cry out. The pressure was throbbing in every nerve of my body, a constant, grinding pain that grew sharper with every heartbeat. The Sentinels weren't going to let up. They were going to slaughter me one inexorable inch at a time, and the Djinn – the Old Djinn – wouldn't lift a finger to stop it.

And they were going to make David watch, to make it that much more horrible.

I felt something new in the attack – a tremor. Just a flicker, but somewhere, someone was weakening. If it was a combined attack, and I thought it must be, then at least one and maybe more were faltering, running out of power. *Hang on,* I told myself. I felt sweat dripping from my chin onto my shirt front. *A little longer.*

It was an eerie way to face the end of your life. If it had just been the Old Djinn, standing there impassively, that would have been bad enough, but David – the dread and anguish in his eyes was too much. I squeezed my eyes shut and concentrated harder.

Hold. You have to hold.

I felt another element of the attacking force weaken and drop away, leaving a purer signature to it. If I could only outlast the rest, I might be able to trace it back to one source . . . at least get the name of the bus that was going to run me down.

Even that cold comfort didn't seem too likely. I felt myself shaking harder now, as I pulled all the power out of my muscles, out of my flesh, pouring my last vital resources into defending the stronghold of my heart. I couldn't hold out for long; my reserves had gone shockingly fast, and without David's help, even Imara's contributions weren't going to be enough . . .

I felt something in me give way, and my next breath felt wet and labored. Pain flared through me. I tasted blood, coughed, and felt warmth spray out of my mouth.

'No,' David whispered. 'Ashan . . . please . . .'

Ashan didn't speak, not even to refuse.

Another element of the attack against me broke with an almost physical shock. I could count them now: three. Three of them left, but one was unbelievably strong, much stronger than I was. Stronger than I could ever hope to be.

My legs gave out. I fell to my knees, hardly felt the impact. Part of the carpet was on fire now, and none of the Djinn were reacting to the emergency. I heard the shriek of the smoke alarm going off, and knew that I was on the verge of creating yet another disaster, one that could claim the lives of the innocent people living around me.

I closed my eyes and found one last tiny pool of strength. With that last drop of power, I pushed back. Two of the three attackers dropped away, surprised by my sudden aggression, and I saw the last one clearly.

On the aetheric, he burnt a brilliant white, less a person than a star bound in human form. I couldn't see his features, but I could see *where* he was, in the instant before he cut off his attack and disappeared into the boiling mass of confusion stirred up by the attack like the smoke in the apartment.

I'd won.

I pitched forward to my hands and knees, gasping in thick, tainted breaths, coughing and wheezing. My mouth was full of blood, and my coughs brought up more of it. I was hemorrhaging from my lungs, too weak to save myself, too weak to control the fire taking hold around me, or cleanse the air I was breathing. *No. You can't die now. You won!*

Winning isn't everything. You need to have something left, in the end, to move on. This was the very definition of a Pyrrhic victory.

I realised that I was staring at David, still on his knees, held pinned and helpless by Ashan. His face was the color of ashes, and his eyes an unholy, almost demonic red, consumed with pain and pent-up fury.

'She survived,' Ashan said, and I heard a note of pure surprise in his voice. I felt a surge of power move through the apartment. The siren cut off; the air turned sweet again. No more sparks. Before my watering eyes, the curtain knitted itself into its original un-burnt form, and the carpet healed itself.

That wasn't David's doing. I could tell that he was blocked by Ashan here, completely cut off. Helpless. The bodyguards wouldn't have dared take that kind of initiative, which left only the last person I'd have ever expected to do me a kindness.

Ashan was staring at me with half-closed, thoughtful eyes. I couldn't read his expression. I was too tired to even try.

'Go on and finish me off,' I said hoarsely. 'I can't stop you.'

'I know,' he said. It was the first time I'd heard him speak with such a level tone, no trace of hate or contempt. 'You fought well. Almost like a Djinn. But you're not a Djinn anymore, and you never will be again.' After another pause, I thought I heard him say, very quietly, 'Pity.'

He let David go and stepped back. David didn't hesitate. Ashan ceased to exist for him the instant the barriers fell, and he lunged to me and gathered me in his arms. I felt healing power cascade through me in burning, almost painful urgency, and I shuddered and buried my face against his neck.

'Jo?' He whispered it with his lips against my skin. His hands were everywhere on me, frantic, protective. 'I'm sorry. I'm so sorry.'

I felt tears welling up, and whether they were shock or relief or the delayed effects of fear, I couldn't tell. I didn't have any defenses left, not even against myself. I wanted to lie down on my side, curl up, and weep myself into unconsciousness in his embrace, but instead, I lifted my head – which felt as if it weighed about a hundred pounds – and focused on Ashan. His expression was closed and still, but I thought I saw something in it that hadn't been there before.

'It was necessary, you know,' he said. 'Necessary you stop before it's too late.' Which wasn't an apology, but the fact that he felt compelled to explain himself was an enormous change.

David growled, deep in his throat, and I stilled him with a hand on his cheek, still looking at Ashan.

'Thank you. I won't expect it again,' I said. I saw a flash in his cool eyes, and he bent his head a fraction of an inch.

And then he misted away, and his bodyguards followed, giving me a range of stares from curiosity to anger.

One faded in. Venna, still in black. I curled closer to David, taking comfort in the heat of his body, the strength of his embrace. I was shaking all over, and couldn't seem to stop. It wasn't just physical injury. I'd come close, so desperately close – in some indefinable way, I felt more fragile now than I ever had, despite the fact that I'd won.

I wouldn't have wanted to show so much vulnerability to Ashan, but it was different with Venna. She'd seen me crying, filthy, beaten, broken. She'd never made judgments, not in the way that Ashan would.

I felt the soft touch of her hand stroking my hair.

'You had to win alone,' Venna said. 'I am sorry. I couldn't help. It was a human matter, not for the Djinn.'

I gulped air and nodded. David wasn't so understanding. He let out that low, vicious growl again, and Venna sat back on her heels, clearly taking the warning very seriously. I couldn't tell if it angered her, but I doubted it. She seemed to understand his desperation.

She studied the two of us with a sorrowful and composed expression, like a graveyard angel. 'Your enemies are much worse than you are. You should be prepared for the fight.'

I croaked, 'Who? Who are they?'

'You know,' she said, and stood up. 'You knew before, and you will again. You saw him. You just won't allow yourself to *see*.'

I reached out and grabbed her hand. She looked down, frowning a little, and pulled free without any difficulty – but she did it gently. 'I hope you survive. And I hope – I hope you are happy.'

I laughed hollowly. 'I hope so, too. I don't suppose we can count on you for a little help along those lines?'

Venna raised her eyebrows. 'What do you expect?'

Nothing, I supposed.

Which was, as Venna performed her dramatic Djinn exit, exactly what we got.

David picked me up and carried me into the bathroom. I might have passed out for a while; when I woke, I was naked, and the two of us were in the bathtub, stretched out and facing each other. He was gently sluicing hot water over my chest, and when he saw I was awake, he switched to a washcloth, which he used to sponge blood from my face and mouth. There was a lot of it, which was alarming in a distant sort of way. I was too weak to really feel panic.

He pressed his lips to my forehead.

'I'm sorry,' he whispered. 'I'm sorry I left you. I won't leave you again.'

'Not even for—'

'No. Not even for the Mother.'

It had the feeling not of seduction, but of ritual, and the heat of the water eased something cold and small and terrified inside of me. We stayed in the bath until I felt sleep overtaking me, and then he carried me to bed, where I fell into a black, dreamless pit.

Sleep wasn't without its horrors. I woke a few times feeling phantom fingers scrabbling for my heart, but it wasn't an attack, just raw unfiltered panic. David was there to drive it away. *Hush,* he told me, and soothed the fear with gentle strokes of his fingers. *I won't leave you. You are safe in my arms.*

When the phone rang, he answered, and I drifted back to a dark, quiet sleep for the rest of the night.

In the morning, I woke up stronger than I'd felt through the night – though that really wasn't much of an improvement, since I'd started from a baseline of near death. I found out from David, who was up bright and early fixing coffee and eggs, that the phone call had been from Lewis. The aetheric dust-up had been witnessed by hundreds of Wardens, though nobody could tell what had been going on or who had been the target. Lewis had decided to check in, just in

case. A team of Wardens had been put on smoothing
out the effects of the fight, which was good, because it
was well beyond me. Sitting up for more than an hour
was beyond me.

David poured me a cup of coffee and slid into the
chair beside me. 'How do you feel?' he asked.

'Like I survived. Barely,' I said. 'You want the truth?
I feel fragile. And glad to be alive.' I sipped without
really tasting the nutty brown richness, though the
smell of the coffee warmed me. 'Why did Ashan make
you watch?'

His hands went still on the table. He didn't look
up. 'Punishment,' he said. 'I didn't have permission
to leave the Mother. She wasn't pleased. She – she can
cut me off from her, and she did it, to prove the point.
That's why I didn't have the power to stop him.'

He'd disobeyed the Mother for me. I almost dropped
the china cup, and it rattled when I managed to get it
back to the saucer. 'David—'

'If you're about to tell me that it was stupid, I
already know,' he said. 'But don't ask me to promise
not to do it again.'

'But – what did she *want*?'

'Djinn business.' His tone made it clear that it
wasn't any of mine. 'You wouldn't understand even if
I tried to explain.'

Because of me, David had already lost his status
as the sole conduit for the Djinn; Ashan had taken

on responsibility for the Old Djinn. Now, if he wasn't careful, he'd lose everything. I felt that knowledge stab deep, and lodge like a dagger of ice somewhere near my heart. 'I don't think I'm worth it,' I said slowly.

He raised his head, and the look in his eyes broke me. 'I think you are,' he said. 'I think you're worth far more. You've proven it to me so many times.'

I had to take a deep breath, or I'd have burst into tears. As it was, my voice trembled. 'David – Ashan told me the risks. If we exchange vows, it could bind the New Djinn the way that Jonathan's vow bound the Djinn in the first place. I could be responsible for enslaving you again. All of you.' I swallowed hard. 'I can't take that chance.'

'No?' He smiled, but it was a bitter, dark thing, and it made me shiver. 'I can.'

'David—'

'I warned you. When Djinn fall in love, there's no middle ground. Our love is deep, and total, and merciless.' He regarded me for a long moment, and his hand closed around mine, far gentler than the look in his eyes. 'You think I did this without considering the consequences? Without considering the cost to my own people, and my responsibilities?'

'I—' I finally shook my head. 'I don't know. I don't know how it is for Djinn, but where love is involved, humans aren't usually that strong on logic.'

That made his smile warmer, more genuine. 'True

enough for us as well. However, I believe that the New Djinn need to stay close to humanity, and I believe this is an important step to ensure that happens. You see? Logical. It also happens to be what I *want* to do. It's a risk, yes, but it's a risk I think is acceptable. In addition, it's a way to force the Sentinels out in the open, by forcing them to counter our move.' He lifted my fingers to his mouth and kissed them, just a light brush of lips. 'If you decide we can't go through with it, I'll abide by your decision.'

'But . . . what about the others?'

'The other New Djinn? I won't say there aren't a few who are doubtful, but by and large, they're interested. Intrigued. It's possible that if we exchange vows, the Djinn could regain some measure of the additional power they had under the old agreement with the Wardens – but still retain their autonomy. As I said, we all consider it worth a try.'

'Especially since it's temporary,' I said. 'Right? Till death do us part. Once I'm gone, the vow is broken.'

Sadness softened the metallic glitter of his eyes. 'Yes,' he said. 'Exactly. Unlike the agreement Jonathan made, which was to a group, this is to an individual. But the Old Djinn still don't want to take the risk. They're the more conservative force, and they worry about consequences. About precedence.'

He was describing a lot more to me about Djinn politics than he ever had before, and I had to admit,

I was intrigued. 'The Mother said to let me fight my own battles, didn't she? That was why she summoned you both in, you and Ashan. To lay down the law.'

'Yes.'

'Which you promptly broke by racing to my side.'

'Ashan broke it first,' David pointed out. 'He came to kill you, and I have no doubt he'd have done it. He didn't see you as worthy, not in any way, of what I'm offering.'

'Flattering.'

David shrugged. 'Ashan's not known for being overly fond of mortals, but if he was going to be impressed by any human, it would probably be you.'

'Why? Because I didn't whimper and die?' I shoved eggs around on my plate. I needed food, but everything seemed distant, lacking any kind of attraction or urgency.

'Because he saw what I saw. He saw your strength, your power, your beauty.' David paused, studying me with an expression so tender that it melted my heart and gave me shivers. 'He saw what I saw in your core, and it shook him. It shook all of them. You have a peculiar gift to make Djinn *feel*. In a way, that makes you more dangerous than anyone they've ever known.'

'But less easy to kill, I hope.'

He tilted his head. No answer. I chewed eggs. They were good, I supposed. More importantly, they were fuel for a body that had spent its reserves recklessly.

My body fat was gone, and my blood sugar in the negative numbers. David's infusion of energy last night had kept me alive when my mortal flesh tried to shut down, but now it was up to me to get things back in order.

'The Sentinels,' he said. 'Did you get anything from them? Anything that could help us?'

I dropped my fork and stared at him. *'I didn't tell you?'*

'Tell me what?'

'Oh my *God*!' Of course I hadn't. I'd been busy trying not to die, and then I'd been completely consumed by the novelty of still being alive. Until he'd asked the question, the knowledge had been lurking somewhere in the back of my mind, waiting for the right moment. 'I know where he is! The – the anchor, the leader, whatever! Well, where he was, anyway.'

'Where?' David was already up and on his feet, and looking more Djinn than he ought to. *'Where?'*

I picked up my fork and gobbled down mouthfuls of egg as fast as I could, grimly intent on getting my strength back. 'The Florida Keys,' I said. 'Key West, or somewhere close to it. The bastard is our *neighbor.'*

Chapter Nine

I rested for a couple of days. My appetite returned with a vengeance on the second day out from the attack, and David was at first amused, then a little appalled at my lust for calories. 'Are you sure that's wise?' he asked when I opened up the fourth bag of barbecue chips. 'There's such a thing as overdoing it . . .'

I knew there was, but the food and the sleep were recharging my body, and I wanted to hasten the process. Impatient, that was me. And scared. I knew the Sentinels now, in aetheric form if not in actual physical shape, I knew how much power they were packing, and it was terrifying indeed. I wanted my body back and balanced, fast.

I knew that bags of chips weren't the way to go, but they tasted so *good*.

David distracted me from the chips by proposing

an outing: shopping. 'You,' I said, gazing at him approvingly, 'are getting to know me way too well.'

He raised his eyebrows. 'I plan to research you in the biblical sense later.'

'Mmmmm, maybe shopping can wait.' Those words were a sign of just how much that invitation really meant. I hardly ever delayed shopping.

'No, I want us out and visible,' he said. 'If the Sentinels are watching, I want them to see that you're alive, well, and strong. I don't think they'll try that again. You surprised them, and you scared them.'

'I did?'

'If you hadn't,' David said, 'they'd have come back for you already.'

Dressing took on a whole girding-for-battle significance now that I knew my enemies were going to be watching me. I bathed, scrubbed, exfoliated, shampooed, shaved, tweezed, moisturized. I spent half an hour on my hair, and another half an hour on makeup. Choosing the right sundress required another long stretch of time. When I finally appeared in the doorway, David was stretched out on the couch, feet crossed at the ankles, reading a battered paperback, which he dropped on his chest at the sight of me.

'Yeah?' I twirled for him, just fast enough that the floating hem of the light floral sundress showed my thighs. 'Healthy enough?'

He pressed his lips together and struggled to sit up. 'That's one word for it.'

'What's another?'

'Seductive.' That note in his voice made me shiver, but I put my shoulders back and shook my finger at him anyway.

'*You* said we needed to get out. So out we get, Mister.'

He sighed, stood up, and slipped into his coat.

'David?' I hated to say it, because this was a kind of dividing line, and I wasn't even sure why. 'The coat. If you want to be taken for human, only flashers wear coats in Fort Lauderdale in the summer.'

He seemed honestly surprised. 'But – ah. Yes. Right.' He took it off and put it back on the chair, petting its olive-drab surface as he did, like a favorite pet he was sorry to leave behind. 'Everything else OK?'

I gave him the walkaround. 'Not bad,' I said, 'but we can do better.'

'Oh no,' he said.

'That's right. We're shopping for *you*, buster.'

I knew all the good places to shop, but if I hadn't, even JCPenney would have been able to supply a decent alternative to the ever-present checked shirt that David seemed to think was the height of fashion. But I wasn't going for *better*, I was going for *make women stop and stare;* though with David, that wasn't exactly difficult.

He was made for Versace.

The salespeople thought so too; David was bemused by the whole affair, clearly wondering what the hell he'd gotten himself into, but as always, he was willing to experiment with the most trivial of human pursuits. I conspired with the lead saleswoman to do before and after digital pictures. Going in, David was a good-looking man, a bit conservative with his blue-and-white checked shirt and jeans.

Going out, he was so attractive that he was a menace to passing traffic. He wore a black, skin-tight Versace knit shirt, long-sleeved to give him sleekness, and his black Diesel jeans that hugged his ass and thighs, and flared out at the ends just enough. Because we were in Florida, I gave him a bit of a surfer fashion sensibility, and it suited him brilliantly. The coppery tan could have been stoked by days paddling in the surf. I added a very fine Hugo Boss sports coat, in midnight blue, and when he put it on, the salespeople gave a collective sigh and snapped pictures. He turned toward me, eyebrows raised, a slight flush in his cheeks.

I've made a Djinn blush, I thought. There was a weird satisfaction in that. Also, I planned to try to make him blush more, in private, later.

Some part of me, during all this public play-acting, kept monitoring the aetheric for any signs of Sentinel activity. Nothing. It was dead quiet, weirdly so. Maybe I really had given them a shock with not dying on cue.

I started to pay for the clothes, but David slipped a wallet from his pocket and pulled out a jet-black American Express card. I caught a look at the name as he handed it over.

DAVID CYRUS PRINCE.

David knew what I was thinking, and he met my eyes briefly, then smiled at the sales clerk and signed the credit card receipt. We left the store with his old clothes and shoes in a bag. I couldn't stop stealing glances at him, darkly gorgeous as he was; every woman we passed, young or old, plain or model-in-training, gave him an involuntary stare.

'That,' he said, 'was a waste of time. I could have just manifested the clothes, if you'd shown me what you wanted me to wear.'

'The point is to be seen,' I reminded him. 'Besides, buying clothes is something humans do. You want to be human, right?'

'Right.' His lips quirked, and he tried to suppress a smile. 'That's the first time I've ever purchased clothing, you know. For myself.'

'It's good to stretch,' I assured him. 'Mr Prince.'

The two of us strolled through the warm, humid

morning. My dress rippled and flowed in the ocean breezes, my hair looked fantastic, my shoes were kicking ass, and I had the most beautiful man I'd ever seen on my arm.

Still, I was constantly looking for a knife headed for my back. *Our* backs.

Nothing.

We shopped all morning, then ate lunch in a cafe next to the ocean. I could see that David was settling into his new look, which pleased me; I had the feeling that Djinn changed styles reluctantly. He couldn't help but notice the attention he was attracting, and unless Djinn were a whole lot less like humans than I suspected, attention wasn't unwelcome.

Otherwise, he wouldn't choose to be so gorgeous to start with.

Over chicken salad and iced teas, he asked me about our afternoon plans. I proposed more shopping. He counterproposed other things, which I confess sounded more interesting, but I'd pledged to keep to my timeline.

I really needed to find that wedding dress.

So after lunch, we went to Zola Keller, and I started the arduous task of trying on thousand-dollar-and-up couture. Which is not nearly as much of a hardship as you might think. I went through twelve styles, none of them quite right, and then . . .

And then it happened.

The moment the clerk unzipped the bag, I just *knew*. As the weight of the Italian silk settled around me, I knew even more. When she laced the back and prepped me for the mirror, I knew I'd found *exactly* what would drive David wild.

Unlike most wedding gowns, this was no Disney princess knockoff; it was sophisticated, subtle, sexy. Layers of silk dropped in subtle angles from the low-cut bodice, but it in no way resembled any kind of wedding cake. The fabric rippled in silk waves, layer upon layer, sweeping into a fantastic train.

But the back was what did it – a laced corset, fitted to show a deep, sexy V of skin down the spine beneath the lacings. It was demure enough, but I could sense, like a vibration on the aetheric, that it would drive him absolutely mad.

'I'll take it,' I said. The clerk raised both eyebrows.

'Don't you want to know—'

'If you tell me the price, I'll chicken out, so no. I don't want to know. Just ring it up.'

She cleared her throat. 'I really think I should warn you about the cost—'

'You really shouldn't,' I sighed.

The Warden AmEx was about to get a serious workout. Even though she was undoubtedly making a commission, my saleslady looked concerned for the state of my financial future. As well she should. If it cost anywhere near what it looked, I was going to be paying approximately the cost of a new car.

She fussed around with the dress, looking for necessary alterations and marking them. A thorough professional. We discussed indoor versus outdoor, potential hazards of having a court train to manage, and other things that I couldn't imagine ever discussing again in my entire life.

But it was done. I had a dress. And it was *the* dress.

I walked out of the dressing room feeling happier than I had in weeks, trailing the salesclerk like a lady's maid. I was smiling widely, anticipating the pleasant shock of seeing David in his still-new finery, and I wasn't disappointed; he was sitting sprawled on a velvet couch, looking ready for a fashion shoot. Women were finding reasons to shop in his vicinity. I couldn't really blame them.

'Done,' I said serenely.

'Really? That was fast.' It wasn't, but he was being kind. He kissed me, and that was *very* nice, especially when, as he pulled back, he whispered in my ear, 'I want to take you home now.'

'Let me mortgage my future first.'

I don't think a sale ever went through faster. In fact, I didn't even notice the total amount as I signed the slip.

And then, of course, everything went wrong.

David sensed it first, by a couple of seconds; he

looked up sharply, all the ease and humor draining away from him, and his hand closed around mine in an iron grip. He wasn't letting us be separated again, not this time.

'What is it?' I asked, or tried to. I never got to the last word. David pointed to the world beyond the glass windows.

The clouds were thickening so fast overhead that it looked like special effects from the most expensive disaster movie ever made.

I turned my focus out to sea, out to that calm and tranquil sea. There were no hurricanes brewing there, only the normal cycle of thunderstorms that needed no Warden regulation.

But someone was tampering with the clouds, forcing energy into a stable system – taking a standard garden-variety thunderstorm, which hadn't even really been threatening rain until later, and packing it with energy until it was a mesocyclone. I'd seen it done, but never this fast, never with so little to work with. The Sentinels were creating an emergency, and doing it so quickly that it made my whole body shiver with the corona effect of the power. Lightning ripped through the sky, blue-white and purple, and struck three times that I could see, blowing up transformers, destroying a metal light pole, stabbing into the lightning attractors on a building only two blocks away.

People began to react nervously.

Outside the windows, I saw the classic formation take shape: anvil cloud, hard and gray as lead; cloud striations below, showing the shredding forces at work; wall cloud pushing rapidly toward us, forming and hardening as it came.

An occlusion downdraft was taking shape, leading the forces into a spinning, fatal vortex.

I felt the forces coalescing, and turned my face upward as I rose into the aetheric.

Yep. Tornado. Right over the store.

David was right with me. We rose up into the boiling storm of opposing forces. I couldn't see the perpetrator; there was too much confusion, too much random energy masking his presence, but I sensed he was here, watching. Waiting.

The tornado was a trap, but it was one I couldn't help but spring. It was dipping down out of the clouds, heading for the crowded street. Heading for the bridal store.

Heading for *my dress.*

I took a deep breath, tightened my grip on David's hand, and prepared for battle.

'I'm with you,' he said. 'I'll give you what I can.' I understood, in that second, that the Mother had cut his circuits again, stranded him from the core of his power. He had whatever was in him, and no more.

Just as I did. *Why was she on the side of the Sentinels?* Or maybe it was simpler than that: maybe she didn't want the Djinn interfering in our internal struggles anymore.

I could understand that. It did seem a massive waste of resources.

'Watch our backs,' I told him, and focused on the glittering, complex, deadly snake of the tornado that was dropping toward us with the speed of a freight train.

It wasn't the classic rope-style tornado; this one was a brutal wedge of power. That was not necessarily a bad thing; the intensity of a tornado doesn't depend on its width. But if it was an F4 or F5, being a wedge tornado would make things that much worse.

Luckily, it wasn't quite that bad. An F2 at most, with wind speeds of about a hundred miles per hour – not bad, and not nearly as bad as it could have been. The Sentinels know how to make it look nasty, but that wasn't the same thing as truly building it right in the first place. I needed to reduce the core temperatures inside of the vortex, and I needed to do it fast. But as I reached out for it, the Sentinels sprang the trap.

A *second* tornado – this one a slender rope, and definitely built to the most exacting specifications – shot down out of the cloud beside the wedge I was focused on, and this one packed deadly, razor-edged debris. Metal, all kinds of metal junk and scraps. It was also spinning at a rate of more than two hundred miles per hour: F4.

One of them was going to hit. I could handle only one at a time, and I had no choice but to go for the worst. I abandoned the wedge and went for the rope, ripping into it with desperate force, drawing heat out of it as quickly as I could.

Not fast enough. I heard it hit the roof, which shuddered and groaned, and then heard the rising roar of the wind as it drilled through steel and wood and concrete.

People were screaming, running, looking for cover. They wouldn't find it, not in the store. 'Outside!' I grabbed my sales clerk, who'd thrown my dress to one side, and pushed her to the door. David was grabbing everyone else he could find and shoving them that way as well. 'Run! Get to cover! Go now!'

I'd succeeded in weakening the vortex down to an F2, but just then, the slower-moving wedge slammed down like a clenched fist, and the whole building shivered and began to come apart.

The two tornadoes, too close together for even the Sentinels to fully control, began to merge and feed off each other. The metal inside the smaller vortex spread out wider, slashing and cutting like the edges of knives as it whirled. Nobody had been hit yet, but they would be.

This had to stop. Now.

'David!' I screamed his name over the roar of the wind as the roof ripped off, disintegrated into a million tiny fragments of blowing chaos, and I felt the eye of the storm focus directly on me.

David put his arms around me from behind, anchoring me, and we faced it together. The power that flowed out of him was rich and strong, golden. It was easy to direct, capable of the finest touch and control.

Nobody did tornadoes better than me. I knew that without conceit; it was a gift, and one I'd had since childhood. For all their fury and force, they were fragile constructs, held together by finite forces. Like everything else, they had keystones. Change that one joint, you could change everything.

This tornado's keystone was hard to find, hard to get my hands around, but once I found the specific area I needed to affect, I poured David's power into it, added my own, and the weight of oxygen and nitrogen pooled, slowing the tornado's spin, shattering the forces that held it in form.

It blew apart in a confusion of winds, pelting down debris like deadly, sharp rain. I yelped and ducked, and David formed a shield above us. Good thing he did. The Sentinels took one last, spiteful swipe at me, arrowing a metal girder directly for me, but it met the shield and bounced off . . . and slammed into the bag that held my dress, shredding plastic and fabric as the girder was driven a foot into the concrete below.

I stayed where I was, sucking in deep breaths, until

it was over and the rain started to fall in a drenching downpour.

I'd just destroyed a second bridal shop.

David helped me up. He was keeping the rain off – a minor task, after the shield that had saved us – and I felt the subtle change in him as the Mother opened the flow again, connecting him back to his power base. His whole body brightened, as well as the light in his eyes.

'Did you see them?' he asked. I shook my head, frustrated and furious. 'I think I might have.'

'Still in Key West?'

'No. Kissimmee. But they're staying close. Maybe they can't do this at too great a distance.' He looked around, an odd expression on his face. 'Nobody hurt. They'll call it a miracle.'

I glared at the ruined wedding dress. 'Some miracle,' I said. 'My credit card charge already went through.'

I checked in with Lewis. He'd gotten word from Rahel that Kevin had been approached by the Sentinels, but it was early days; they were checking him out pretty thoroughly, asking around. No problems there. I doubted anybody had unreserved approval for Kevin; he simply didn't invite people to like him. He was respected because he was strong, not because he was in any way a team player.

The Sentinels wouldn't find anything that would put them off. Kevin was an arrogant little shit most of the time, and he could give drug dealers lessons in insensitivity. I'd seen him do murder. Granted, it had been well-deserved murder, but his reaction to it had been disturbingly vacant.

Still, Lewis believed the kid was redeemable, and I had to agree. I'd seen firsthand the horror his stepmother had made out of his life, and while I couldn't really *like* him, I felt for him.

If Kevin held it together, I was going to owe him big-time.

Not a pleasant thought, really.

My sundress, amazingly, had survived the freak tornado incident, and my shoes weren't too bad. My hair had a bit of a windblown do, but all in all, I'd gotten off lucky for a change.

Or so I thought.

When David and I emerged from the store and waved away the unnecessary medical attention, we headed back toward where we'd left the car, several blocks away. David was doing some subtle work to keep the rain off, so we were relatively dry. The effect became less subtle when a van pulled up at the curb next to us, launching a wave of dirty water waist-high; it hit David's shield and rolled off, leaving us dry.

Then I saw the camera in the window, and realised that it was a news van.

'Oh *crap*,' I breathed. 'Drop the shield. Drop it *now!*'

Too late, I realised. They couldn't have missed it. In fact, they'd counted on it, and they'd gotten it on tape.

I saw it in the triumphant smirk on the reporter's face as the van door slid open. 'Hi, Ms Baldwin,' she said. 'Want to talk to us about why you're once again at the scene of a disaster? And how exactly you are staying dry in the middle of a thunderstorm? Who's your friend?' She gave David a special twice-over, which burnt me even more than the fact I'd been caught on tape. 'What exactly happened back there?'

I realised I was clenching my fists, and tried to relax. The rain was plastering my hair to my face, and my dress was becoming a soggy, ill-fitting mess. I tried not to think about the shoes. 'Tornado,' I said briefly. 'At least, that's what they tell me.' I took David's arm and pulled him along.

'Reporters?' he whispered.

'Vultures. Keep going, no matter what. They can smell fear.'

His voice turned warm with amusement. 'Not really afraid of reporters, given what just happened, but I'll keep that in mind.'

'Shhhhh!'

The reporter donned a transparent raincoat, complete with a cute little hood to protect her hair, and climbed out of the van. Her camera guy and boom guy came after. The equipment was better protected from the weather than they were. 'Ms Baldwin, wait! We want to talk to you about the Wardens! Was this the work of the Wardens? If so, why was there so much damage? Weren't you supposed to contain that kind of thing? Was anyone killed or injured?'

'No one was hurt,' David said. I made a frantic shushing motion and kept him walking. It didn't matter. They kept pace, and now the camera guy had his portable light glaring on us in the downpour.

'How do you know that? Sir? Sir?'

'No comment,' I snapped, and tried to get between David and the camera. I must not have been as photogenic, because they broke off. I toyed with the idea of sabotaging the equipment, but I had the feeling somehow that was a bad move this time. Then I spotted it: across the street, another news team was following, photographing separately. They were trying to provoke me into a response.

Great. As if I hadn't had enough trauma in the past few days to last a lifetime.

'Look, this will be a lot easier on you if you talk to us now, rather than force us to run without your side of the story—'

'Run it,' I said. 'Somehow, I can't see you guys having a lot of credibility left once everybody asks you what brand of crack you were smoking. Now, leave us alone.'

They dropped back, mainly because we'd reached

the car and were already getting in. I was sure the videographer had a great shot of me getting into the car, looking pissed off; the only thing missing from a humiliating fleeing-the-cameras exposé was me shoving the cameraman or giving him the finger. Not that I wasn't tempted.

Once we were inside the car, I tried calming, deep breaths. It didn't really work, but it made me feel as if at least I was making an effort. David wasted no time exerting a pulse of power to dry out our clothes, hair, and shoes, not to mention the seats, even as he locked the doors in case they decided to try one more time. I hastily got the car in drive and pulled away into traffic, leaving the reporters behind.

I distinctly saw a high five behind me in their van.

'That,' I said, 'was not the plan.'

'What, the tornado? Or the reporters?'

'Both. Either. Not the plan.' I chewed my lip; too late to worry about my lipstick at this point. My carefully applied makeup, not to mention my hairdo, was long gone. 'Right. Enough making like a target for the day. Let's give the Sentinels some time to chew over their options while we go home and . . .'

'And?'

'Do whatever comes naturally.'

'I can think of a few things that aren't *quite* that natural. Are they off the table?'

'Depends.' My heart rate was slowly declining

from the triple digits, but I still felt jittery. Too many shocks, too close together. 'I think I'll have to ask for a massage first. I'm a bundle of nerves right now.'

He put his hand atop mine on the gear shift, and a slow warm pulse moved through my body, steadying me. 'I would like that,' he said. 'And if you want to take the phone off the hook and turn off that damn cell phone . . .'

'We'd have Lewis and a bunch of paratroopers storming the apartment,' I said. 'Being out of contact, not really an option right now. You know, since we're bait.'

He sighed. 'Yes. Bait.' Beat. 'I'm sorry about the dress. You seemed very happy.'

'Yes.' I bit my lip, unreasonably distressed, and was glad he sent another pulse of energy through my nerves to counteract my ridiculously out-of-proportion reactions. 'It was gorgeous. Well, I'm sure I'll find another one.' Maybe.

'We can look tomorrow.'

I couldn't help it; I laughed. He'd said it in all seriousness, as if our little outing hadn't netted a significant and near-fatal attack. As if that was just par for the course, an everyday hazard of going to the store.

'Yes,' I said, when I was able to speak around the chuckles. 'Oh, absolutely. Shopping tomorrow. But maybe we should try to pick someplace easier on bystanders.'

He nodded soberly. 'Internet.'

'Internet.'

'I hear there's pornography on the Internet.'

'Filthy pervert.'

His eyebrows quirked, then settled into a severe line. 'I take exception. I'm quite clean, actually.'

'Too bad. I like a scruffy man.'

'I can be scruffy.' His tone changed. 'Pull over.'

'What?'

'Pull over *now*.'

Oh. Not part of the banter, then. I looked in the rearview mirror but saw nothing out of the ordinary. Still, David wasn't exactly one to overreact. I took the next left and found a shopping center parking space, right between a nail salon and a Spanish-language video rental store. 'What is it?'

'We're being followed,' David said.

'I didn't see—'

'By a Djinn.' He was already opening his door. 'Stay here.'

'David! No, you can't—' I was having flashbacks to the horrible scene in my apartment, David on his knees and helpless at the hands of his fellow Djinn. I didn't trust any of them now, certainly not any of them who felt compelled to follow us in secret.

'I have to.' No point in arguing, because I'd be arguing with the rain; he was already gone, and even though I hurriedly scrambled out after, I saw no trace of him.

And then I did, in the deep shadows at the side of the building. David was in conversation with a very tall man – Djinn – with hair too long to stand up in the nearly pompadour style he was wearing. Thin, intense, and entirely unfamiliar to me. He was wearing retro clothes, circa the mid-1950s, but he didn't seem at all *Father Knows Best* to me; he radiated an unfocused kind of don't-mess-with-me menace.

The Djinn's gaze fixed on me, and I saw his eyes flare into a bright crimson. He bent his head and said something else to David, and blew apart into mist and was gone.

David came back in no particular hurry, hands in his pants pockets, lost in thought.

We both got back into the car at the same time, and I dried us off, a flick of power that felt satisfyingly productive for a change. He hardly noticed.

'Who was that?' I asked. David stirred, glanced at me, and looked surprised.

'Roy,' he said.

'Who's Roy?'

'One of mine,' he said. 'You don't need to have him over for drinks. He's not polite company. In fact, I'd rather you never met him. But he's very useful for some things.'

'Such as?'

'Such as keeping an eye on Kevin and Rahel.' He

cocked an eyebrow at my expression. 'You didn't seriously think I would let them do this without some kind of backup plan?'

Oh. Actually, I'd thought *Rahel* was the backup plan, but I could see his point. 'So what did Roy have to say?'

'Kevin was taken from his apartment a half hour ago, along with Rahel disguised as Cherise. It was efficient. He fought, but he was contained with a minimum of effort.'

If you knew Kevin, this was ominously impressive. 'Sentinels?'

'I can't think of anyone else with the strength and the motivation,' David said. 'The thing is, they did this *while* they were hitting us. Which implies—'

'A whole lot of organisation,' I finished. 'Not to mention power to burn.'

We looked at each other for a long moment, and I finally started up the car again. 'It's too late to change our minds, isn't it?'

'I'm afraid so. The game's in motion now, and we have to follow the play. I dispatched Roy to follow at a safe distance; he should report back when Kevin and Cherise reach a final destination. I don't think they'll be taken far.'

'Meanwhile?'

He reached out and traced his thumb over my lips. 'Meanwhile, we should find a place to stay that's far from innocent bystanders, and be prepared for another attack. Any ideas?'

'Yep.' I put the Mustang in gear and pulled out of the parking lot, merging with the rain and traffic. 'But you're not going to like it.'

I'd been right, and wrong. David wasn't wild about the beach house – which belonged to the Wardens, and was normally used to host visiting dignitaries – because it was long on ocean views and short on actual security. He also wasn't crazy about staying in a location where most of the Wardens would guess we'd go, but I wanted to continue to provide some kind of attractive target for the Sentinels. Anything to give Kevin time.

At least here, the beach was private, we were nowhere close to neighbors, and if the Sentinels decided to lower the boom on us, they'd do a minimum of collateral damage.

The rain stopped about the time I pulled up in the private drive, opened the massive metal gates with a pulse of Fire Warden power, and drove inside. The entrance was heavily landscaped, mainly with palms and leafy bushes to conceal the grounds from prying eyes. It looked like the sort of place a mid-level, once-all-powerful Hollywood player would stay to get away from it all.

I made sure the gates shut behind us, and followed

the winding narrow road around the curves until the white beach house emerged at the end. It was a neat little bungalow, big enough for a few people to stay out of each other's way, but not a place for massive entertainments unless you wanted to get full-body contact. I'd last been here back in my former boss Bad Bob Biringanine's time; he'd used it to house visitors to the Florida territory, and it was, in fact, the very place he'd performed his historic act of heroism in shaving vital strength out of Hurricane Andrew. If he hadn't, I doubted most of the state would have survived its landfall.

I hadn't thought of Bad Bob in a long time, but it seemed like his ghost walked over my grave at that moment; I almost felt his presence, strong and astringent, charming and bad tempered. Corrupt, but hiding it well. Of all the things I couldn't forgive Bad Bob for – and one of them had led to massive damages, once upon a time – I thought the worst was that he'd known what Kevin's stepmother was, what kind of perversions she enjoyed, and he'd allowed her to continue.

Worst of all, he'd given her David to play with as her own personal sex toy.

David sat in silence, looking at the beach house. If I hadn't known him so well, I'd have thought he had no reaction at all. I reached over and took his hand, and his gaze shifted toward mine.

'I know,' I said. 'I'm sorry, it's the best place. All right?'

'I'm fine,' he said. He wasn't, but he also wasn't ready to let me see that wound. He was all courtesy, opening my car door for me, handing me out, walking me up the steps to the front door. 'Keys?'

It didn't need one. I extended my hand, the one with the Warden symbol invisibly etched into the skin, and heard the lock click over. I opened the door, and the smell of the place washed over me, bringing with it another rush of memories as I stepped inside. Bad Bob hadn't been gone long enough for his imprint to completely fade from this place; I swore I smelt the ghost of his cigar smoke, before the more powerful odor of musty carpeting and furniture took over. The house needed a full-scale cleaning. Something to keep me busy, I supposed.

David hadn't followed me inside. I turned toward him and saw that he'd put out a palm, which was spread flat against an invisible barrier. As I watched, he moved his hand from side to side. I could see his skin flattening as it came into contact with . . . something.

'What is it?' I moved back to the threshold and waved my hand through the air. No barrier. I could even make contact with David's hands, but I couldn't pull him through. 'What the hell . . . ?'

'Wards,' he said. 'Set to keep Djinn out. You'll have to take them down before I can come inside.'

Wards – magical boundaries – were an exclusive specialty of Earth Wardens, and they were usually fiendishly difficult to unravel. They could be set to exclude anything the Warden designed it to exclude – Djinn, in this case, but I'd seen them engineered to hold out humans, and even specific individuals.

I was, theoretically, an Earth Warden, but I hadn't exactly been trained in the finer points. It was on the to-do list, but from all that I understood, breaking wards was definitely a graduate-level course. Maybe even postdoctoral. 'Any idea who put this up?' I asked. Not Bad Bob, at least; he was purely and completely a Weather Warden. But he'd had a lot of friends, and most of them had been . . . questionable.

'Yes, but it won't do you any good. He's dead. Bad Bob had me kill him.'

The matter-of-fact way that David said it made me freeze for a second, and not just in the not-moving sense. 'You . . . killed for him.'

'I had no choice at the time.'

'I know that. I just didn't know—' I shook my head. 'I'm so sorry, David. He had no right.'

David said nothing to that; he clearly wanted to drop the subject, and I obliged by focusing on the structure of the wards holding him outside the door. They were strongly made, and if they'd survived the death of their maker, they were independently fueled by some source. If I could locate the source, I could disable the wards – like pulling the battery. Problem was, a good Earth Warden (and this one had been very, very good) could imbue nearly anything with aetheric energy and set it on a slow, steady discharge. It could be something as innocuous as a teacup hidden in the back of the pantry, or as obvious as a big switch labeled TURN OFF WARDS HERE.

I systematically examined the house and its contents on the aetheric, looking for any telltale sparks, but nothing became obvious. David was unable to give me any pointers; the Earth Warden who'd created the wards had also done a damn fine job of erasing any tracks the Djinn could use to identify the control mechanism.

This left us at a standstill, ultimately. I couldn't break the wards. David couldn't enter.

'OK, bad idea,' I sighed, then shut the front door and sat down with David on the steps. A cool breeze was blowing in off the ocean, and we sat for a while watching the surf roll in. 'Maybe it's a good thing we couldn't get you inside. I know there must be – echoes.'

'Not as many as there were at Yvette's house, but yes, the history's very close to the surface here,' David said. He sounded remote and cool, as if he'd withdrawn into himself for protection. 'I'd rather not stay, if we can find somewhere else to go.'

I'd always liked the beach house; it had been my

favorite of the Warden properties in this part of the country. But that had been before I'd known the truth, and the depth of all the cruelty that the people I'd trusted were capable of inflicting on others. 'That Earth Warden. Was he the only one Bad Bob made you . . . ?'

'No,' David said, and got up. He looked down at me with dark, impenetrable eyes, and offered me his hand. 'Still trust me?'

I took it and let him pull me to my feet. 'I will always trust you,' I said. 'Thank you for trusting me.'

He kissed me, just a gentle brush of lips. Something about this place turned him cautious, opened old wounds, and I could tell that even if I'd found a way to break the wards, it would have been hard for him to stay inside these walls. 'Do you mind if I choose the next stop?' he asked.

'Hey, you're the guy with the black AmEx and unlimited credit line,' I said. 'Speaking of which, you know that humans pay their debts, right?'

He didn't look at me. He was staring at the beach house, with a shadow in his eyes that I'd never seen before. 'So do Djinn,' he said. 'When they can.'

Chapter Ten

David's choice for our temporary refuge was just outside of Miami: another beach house, but if the Warden retreat was one that would comfortably fit a B-movie lead actor, this was A-list all the way. A Mediterranean-style villa, probably large enough to hold twenty people in comfort on a long stay, it had a gracious, sweeping stretch of grounds, a sculptural waterscaped pool, and its own white-sand private beach, a near-impossibility in Miami. I shuddered to think what the place would cost to maintain, much less buy.

'You're kidding,' I said. David came around to the driver's side and opened my door. 'David, really. You've got to be kidding. Rich people don't find this kind of thing very amusing when they come home to find us performing *Goldilocks and the*

Three Bears in their bajillion-dollar mansion.'

'It's all right,' he said. 'It belongs to a friend.'

'A friend?'

'A very good friend,' he clarified, and flashed me a smile. 'We'll stay in the guesthouse, if it makes you feel any better.'

We made it only about three steps from the car when two huge, evil-looking Rottweilers came bounding out of the darkness, silent and intent on ripping our limbs off one at a time, but both dogs came to a fast, skidding halt when they came within five feet of us, or, more accurately, of David.

'Hello, boys,' David said, went down on one knee, and petted the two ferocious attack beasts. They licked his face and rolled over to have their tummies patted. 'See? It's fine.'

'It would be fine if you'd let me know when you were going to show up. By the way, you're ruining my guard dogs,' said a voice from the grand marble sweep of the stairs leading up to the house. Lights blazed on, bright enough to land aircraft, and I squinted against the glare. A man came down the steps, moving lightly despite the fact he was past his athletic days. In his fifties, with a pleasant, interesting face and secretive dark eyes, he was dressed in blue jeans and a comfortable old T-shirt that had DON'T PANIC, along with the little green guy from Douglas Adams's *Hitchhiker* series as a graphic.

The jeans were expensive. So were the deck shoes. I couldn't decide if he was a well-paid caretaker or a slumming owner.

'Good to see you, too, Ortega,' David said, and gestured toward me. 'Joanne Baldwin.'

There was something about Ortega that felt just slightly off to me . . . not the clothes, not the way he looked, not the smile he gave me. I couldn't define it, not immediately, and then I realised that the feeling was familiar. It was the indefinable sense that I'd had around David, when I'd first met him – a vibration that I'd grown used to now.

I nodded to Ortega. 'How exactly does a Djinn come to own a place like this?' I asked. He laughed, and his eyes flashed lime green, then faded back to plain brown. 'Very good,' he said. 'But then, I expected no less. So, this is the one causing all the trouble? The one you intend to marry?'

David nodded. Ortega gave me a benevolent sort of smile.

'Charming,' he said. 'And dangerous. But I suppose you know we're attracted to that. Well, then, how may I be of service to my lord and master?'

Ortega was New Djinn, thank God, but then again, that had pretty much been a given; I couldn't picture any of the Old Djinn reading Douglas Adams, much less wearing any kind of a T-shirt with a graphic. Well, maybe Venna, but it'd be a unicorn or a rainbow.

'Need a place to stay,' David said. 'Guesthouse?'

Ortega bowed his head slightly, and in the gesture I got a sense of antique gentility. It went oddly with the jeans and T-shirt. 'As always, what I have is yours. Just let me move the cartons. I haven't gotten around to sorting through things quite yet.'

'Thank you.' David gave the adoring Rottweilers one last pat and stood up to take my arm. 'We're not here, by the way,'

Ortega smiled. 'You never are.' My Mustang faded out. 'I put your car in the garage. Slot five, next to the Harley. Seemed appropriate.'

I looked at David, baffled. He shrugged. 'Ortega collects things,' he said. 'You'll see.'

I knew that some of the Djinn lived among humans, but I hadn't known it could be so *public* . . . Ortega owned some of the biggest, splashiest real estate in a big, splashy, highly visible community. Granted, the rich were different, but I was willing to bet his neighbors had never guessed just *how* different. It worked in his favor that the exceptionally well-off tended to isolate themselves in these luxurious fortresses, and only moved in their own particular social circles.

David took my arm and walked me down the wide, flawless drive toward what I could only assume was the guesthouse – big enough to qualify as multifamily housing, and fancy enough to satisfy even the pickiest of pampered Hollywood stars looking to slum it. He must have seen from the bemusement of my expression what I was thinking, because he laughed softly. 'We're safe here,' he said. 'Ortega's known as a recluse – it's not just as a disguise for humans; it's true among his fellow Djinn as well. The few of us he allows to visit here are carefully chosen.'

'He's . . . not what I would have expected.' The Djinn had always had a touch of the eldritch about them, but Ortega seemed . . . normal. His eccentricities were more like what you'd expect from a dot-com genius who'd cashed out of the Internet game early and sailed away on his golden parachute.

The door to the guesthouse swung silently open for us as we walked up the steps. Night-blooming flowers poured perfume out into the air, and I stopped to drink it all in. The cool ocean breeze. The clear night air. Rolling surf.

David, gilded silver by the moonlight.

'What are you thinking?' he asked me, and stepped close. Our hands entwined, and I crossed the small, aching distance between us. Our bodies fit together, curves and planes. He let out a slow breath and closed his eyes. 'Oh. *That's* what you're thinking.'

I put my arms around his neck. 'I'd be crazy if I wasn't,' I said. 'Look, it's been driven home to me today that we're living in a bubble. If it's not the damn reporters sneaking hidden-camera footage, it's the Sentinels trying to wipe us out. If we have even a second of safety and solitude, I don't think we should waste it.'

'I've been wanting to get you out of that dress all day.' His voice dropped low and quiet, barely a murmur in my ear. I felt my pulse jump and my skin heat in response. 'Jo, I don't want to go on like this. I can't stand knowing that at any moment they could come for you again. If I lose you—' His hands moved through my hair, urgent and possessive. 'If I lose you—' He couldn't finish the sentence.

We both knew that he was going to lose me, in the end. But it was the fullness of time, the *richness* of time, from now until then that would make that pain of parting something worth bearing.

'I love you,' I said, and his mouth found mine. He tasted of tears, but I saw no trace of them in his eyes or on his face. 'No more mourning. I'm here. While I'm here, we're together.'

'Yes.' Another soul-deep kiss that left my knees weak and every nerve tingling. 'We'd better go inside. Security cameras. Wouldn't want to shock the guards.'

'Mmmmmm.' He'd destroyed my ability to form words that didn't include adjectives, such as *faster* and *more*.

David picked me up and carried me across the threshold . . . and stopped. He had no choice. The entire room was filled with cartons, floor to ceiling, rows and rows and rows of them.

And each one was neatly labeled *misc.*

'Ortega!' he bellowed, and let me down. 'Dammit—'

The other Djinn popped in with an audible displacement of air, standing outside the door. He looked past us, at the makeshift warehouse, and seemed a little embarrassed. Just a little. 'Well,' he said, 'I did warn you that I needed to clean up.'

That wasn't messy; it was obsessive-compulsive. I'd met a Djinn with a behavioral disorder. Now *that* was new.

Ortega did something I couldn't quite follow, and two columns of boxes disappeared – probably moved into the mansion, I guessed. He gave David a questioning look, then sighed and repeated the maneuver with all the boxes in view.

'Any other rooms?' he asked.

'Bedroom,' David and I said together. Ortega's eyebrows rose. 'Please,' I added. 'Umm – bathroom. And kitchen.'

'Done.'

And it was. The areas I could see, at least; I had no doubt that if I opened up a closet (or for that matter, a drawer) I'd see more of Ortega's collecting fetish, but right now, the only things that mattered to me were open space and privacy.

Ortega was waiting for something, watching David, and once again I caught a hint of something otherworldly in him, something not quite in sync with the harmless human exterior he projected. 'I have what you asked me to find,' he said. 'When you're ready to see it.'

David had been looking at me, but now his gaze cut sharply toward the other Djinn. 'You have it? Here?'

'In the main house. It's warded. I can't open it myself.'

'What is it?' I asked. If I'd only left it alone, we might have been able to ignore the tempting, dangling bait and go on to a fevered night of fulfilling every delicious, decadent fantasy, but noooooo. I just had to ask.

Ortega's face brightened. 'The Ancestor Scriptures.'

David went very still. I sensed whatever chance we had to forget all this and hit the sheets vanishing like mist in sunlight. 'You persuaded the Air Oracle to give it up?'

'No.' The Djinn's smile widened, inviting us to join him, but David didn't, and I had no idea what we were smiling about. 'I persuaded the Air Oracle to let me make a copy. You have no idea what I had to give up for that.'

I'd met the Air Oracle once; it wasn't one of my most treasured memories. I'd had lots of scary encounters, but the Air Oracle had been one of the strangest, most remote, most malevolent creatures I'd ever met.

The fact that Ortega had charmed something out of him/her was fairly damn impressive.

David glanced at me, and I saw the frustrated apology in his expression before he said, 'I have to take a look. This could be important.'

My hormones were not understanding, but my brain tried to be. 'I know. Mind if I look, too?'

'I want you with me,' David said, and he meant it on a whole lot of levels. I smiled, and he turned his attention back to Ortega, who was waiting with a polite, attentive smile. 'Main house, you said?'

Ortega nodded and blipped out, then almost immediately blipped back, looking chagrined. 'You can't travel so quickly, can you?' he said to me. 'I do apologize. We'll walk.'

The stroll back to the main house was just as lovely as the first time, only with less anticipation of fun to come. Still, the destination was certainly interesting; when Ortega led us through the front door, I was struck once again by the incredible *scale* of the place. The massive chandelier overhead, loaded down with an entire year's production of Swarovski crystals, glittered like a captured galaxy. The ceiling was as tall as any respectable opera house lobby, and the foyer was just about big enough to stage a road-show production of *Aida,* complete with elephants. There was a sweeping grand staircase, of course, with all the usual marble and mahogany features.

What didn't quite fit in this oh-so-upscale setting was the clutter. Boxes piled randomly against walls, paintings (nice ones, at that, to my relatively untutored eye) leaning against the boxes, knick-knacks, and gadgets strewn over every flat surface. It was like walking into one of those clutter stores, crammed with bargains and cool finds, if only you can contain your sense of claustrophobia long enough to find them. My eyes couldn't focus for long on any one thing.

If every room was like the foyer . . .

'Sorry.' Ortega shrugged. 'There's never enough room. This way. Watch your step.'

There were boxes on the staircases, too, all labeled, unilluminatingly, *misc*. I wondered if they were the ones he'd banished from the guesthouse, but I was more afraid they weren't, actually. At the top of the stairs he took a right, edging around another bulwark of stacked cardboard, and led us into what should have been a spacious – no, gracious – room. It was a library, old style, with floor-to-high-ceiling shelves. An honest-to-God rotunda, and a sliding ladder on rails.

He kept books in the library, but it was about five times more books than could safely fit on the shelves. The stacks teetered and leant everywhere, and of course there were the inevitable boxes. These were labeled, not very helpfully, *books*.

Ortega blazed a trail through the maze and brought us to what must have been one of the few open spaces in the entire house. There was a massive podium, all of carved black wood, decorated with leaves and vines, and on it lay a closed, massive book with an iron latch, secured with a simple iron peg. No title was on the worn, pale leather cover.

Ortega stood back and indicated it with one graceful wave. David stepped up to the podium, studying it, and reached out to touch the latch.

It knocked his hand back with a sharp, sizzling zap of power.

'I thought you said it was a copy,' David said, rubbing his fingers against his jeans.

'It is. An exact copy. And I believe I did say it was warded.' Arms folded, Ortega watched with half-closed eyes, looking like nothing so much as an eccentric Buddha.

David nodded, never taking his eyes off the book, and touched the spine. There was no zap this time, but as he moved his fingers toward the pages themselves, I felt the surge of energy building up. He quickly moved back to safer territory.

'Jo,' he said, 'give me your hand.'

I did, and he guided it slowly over the leather toward the latch.

No response. I heard Ortega let out a low, quiet breath and say something in a language that might have been an antique form of Spanish, something last heard when the Aztecs were still running their own kingdom.

'I'm OK,' I said when David hesitated, and went the last bit of the way to lay my fingers on the metal.

No shock. The Oracle had protected the book against Djinn, but had never anticipated a human getting hold of it. It reminded me of something, this book. Something . . .

The memory snapped back into focus with an almost physical shock. I'd seen a book like this before, minus the latch, in a bookstore in Oklahoma.

It had possessed the power – or the knowledge, which was the same thing – to enslave Djinn.

I looked at David in alarm. 'It's like Star's book,' I said. 'Right?'

Star had been an old friend of mine, one who'd been badly damaged in the course of duty as a Fire Warden. I hadn't known how badly damaged, for a long while. She'd had something like this in her possession.

David nodded, confirming my suspicions. There were cinders of gold and bronze in his eyes, sparking and flaring. His skin had gone a darker shade of warm metal at least two shades off from anything human.

'Open it,' he said.

'You're sure?'

He was. I eased the iron peg out of the loop and folded back the black metal hinged piece, and then it was just a matter of opening the book itself. 'What now?' I kept both hands on the book, as if it might try to get away. Ortega, I saw, had moved back, but not far; he had an expression on his face that was half dread, half fascination.

'Open it,' David said. 'Turn pages until I tell you to stop, and whatever you do, don't focus on anything.'

Easier said than done. Like the book that my old friend Star had used – it seemed so long ago – this one seemed to *want* to be read. The symbols were incomprehensible, densely printed on the page; I was tempted to look at the thing on the aetheric, but I was also afraid. I had, in my hands, power that was off the scale as humans understood it. It was something that I was never meant to have in my possession; I felt that weight in every cell of my body. It made me wonder why it hadn't been warded against humans, but then again, it had been the possession of an Oracle . . . Humans didn't even figure in their equations. They'd been concerned about the Djinn.

I turned pages, trying to keep my gaze unfocused as I did. The symbols kept attracting me, trying to come clear into focus. I ran lyrics to popular songs through my head, the more annoying the better. I knew – I remembered – that the last version of this thing I'd seen had possessed an eerie kind of pull, and this copy had that in full measure.

After about twenty pages, the book began to whisper. *Turn pages. Don't listen,* I told myself. David's eyes were focused on the book, dark bronze with sparks and flares of gold. He looked completely alien in that moment, more severely lovely than anything in human form had any right to be.

I felt my mouth trying to speak, and I ground my teeth together to keep the words – if they were words – inside. I had no idea what was in this book, but I knew it was raw, undiluted power, and not meant for humans to channel. If the Oracles wouldn't even let the Djinn have it, it must have been deadly dangerous.

This made me wonder with a prickly unease why the Air Oracle had let Ortega have it. Unless maybe the Air Oracle had an ulterior motive of his own.

'Stop,' David said, and I froze. The page slowly flattened, revealing dense lines of text, all carefully scribed in a language that bore no resemblance to anything I'd ever seen in human writing. 'Ortega. Read.'

Ortega took a look, frowning, and his eyes widened. Unlike David's, they stayed firmly in the range of human colors, and he quickly backed away. 'What the hell is *that*?'

'I think that's what the Sentinels have found,' David replied, never taking his eyes off the text, as if it were a poisonous serpent poised to strike. 'I think it's the source of their power, and how they plan to strike at us.'

Ortega looked pale now, and deeply troubled. 'But – if that's true, we have no defense.'

'Then we have to come up with one.' David took a thick felt bookmark from a drawer in the podium and slipped it in place between the pages, then nodded for me to close it, which I did, feeling a massive rush of relief. I wasn't sure how much longer I could have resisted focusing on those words, and repeating the whispered sounds that echoed in my head.

'So, I guess you know that the Sentinels must have a copy,' I said, staring at the closed volume. I carefully flipped the latch back into place and slotted in the iron peg to secure it.

Clearly, it wasn't what David and Ortega expected me to say, and from their expressions, it hadn't occurred to them. 'Impossible!' Ortega blurted. David didn't try to deny it; he was already thinking along the same lines I had followed.

'Star had one.' I glanced at David for confirmation, and he gave an unwilling nod. 'Do you know what happened to it when she died?'

'I thought it was destroyed,' David said. He looked very troubled. 'If it wasn't . . .'

Ortega was looking, if anything, even more horrified. My voice ran down as I noticed his distress, and I watched as he staggered to a dusty velvet wing chair and dropped into it, rocking back and forth, head in his hands.

David and I exchanged glances, and David went to the other Djinn and crouched down, laying a hand on the man's knee. 'Ortega,' he said, 'what is it?'

'It's my fault,' he said. His voice sounded weak and sick, and pressed thin under the weight of emotion. 'I swear to you, I never meant – I thought – I was only curious, you see. You know how curious I am. It's always been a curse—'

A curse, indeed. David froze for a moment, then bowed his head. His hair brushed forward, hiding his expression in shadow, and he said in an ominously soft voice, 'You had it. The other book.'

Ortega nodded convulsively.

'Whom did you trade the book to?'

'A Warden,' Ortega said. His voice was muffled by the hands pressed to his eyes. 'He never knew I was Djinn. I swear to you, I never meant – I lied, I didn't get it from the Air Oracle. I created a copy of the original book—'

'I need this Warden's name,' David said.

'I never meant for any harm to—'

'The name, Ortega.' I shivered at the tone in his voice; he didn't often sound like that, but when he did, there was no possibility of argument. He was invoking his right as the Conduit, the Mother's representative to the Djinn, and it rang in every syllable.

Ortega took in a deep breath, lowered his hands, and looked David in the eyes. 'Robert Biringanine.'

'Bad Bob,' I said blankly. 'But he's dead!'

Ortega shook his head. 'I saw him,' he said. 'Two weeks ago. On the beach. And he's been around for a while now.'

Chapter Eleven

To say that was a shock would be an understatement. A shock implied a jolt, like sticking your finger in a light socket; this was more like grabbing the third rail of the subway.

I'd *killed* Bad Bob Biringanine – well, at least, seen him die. I'd always staked a lot of certainties on that fact; I'd been told his body was found, and nobody ever seemed to have any doubt that Bad Bob was pushing up daisies. They'd certainly gone after me with enough vengeance to sell the concept of murder.

As his last act prior to dying had been to infect me with a Demon Mark, ensuring my enslavement and eventual death, I didn't feel too good about his miraculous reappearance. Of all the people I would pick to claw their way out of a grave, he'd be the dead last – pun intended – I ever wanted to see.

Partly it was because he'd so successfully hidden his capacity for cruelty and corruption from me – from most Wardens – for so long. Partly it was that I still had nightmares about that horrible day, about the helpless fury I'd felt and the slick, gagging feel of the Demon sliding down my throat.

It couldn't have pleasant associations for David, either. He'd been the Djinn who'd held me down. *Rape*, he'd called it later, and he'd been right, in an aetheric kind of way if not a physical one. But it had been a rape of both of us – he hadn't wanted to do it any more than I had.

I'd taken three steps back from Ortega, an involuntary retreat that had nothing to do with him and everything to do with the monster that had just leapt out of the closet to roar in my face. David must have sensed my reaction, but he stayed fixed on Ortega.

'When?' he asked. 'When did you give him the book?'

'A few months ago.' Ortega struggled not so much to remember – Djinn didn't forget – but to order his mind so things were clear. 'The day of mourning. He came – he had something I was looking for. He said he'd trade. He wanted the book.'

By *the day of mourning*, Ortega meant the day Ashan had killed our daughter, Imara, or at least destroyed her physical body. Imara had become the

Earth Oracle, but on that very black day, we thought we'd lost her forever.

Oh, and I'd died, too. Kind of. I'd ended up split, amnesiac, and wandering naked in the forest. Yeah, good times.

That day had seen the expending of a lot of power. A *lot*. Some of it was from the Wardens, some a product of the Djinn, some from the Earth herself. And there'd been a Demon in the mix, fouling the well of power . . . Anything could have happened, out of that bloody mess.

Apparently, anything *had* happened. Somehow, Bad Bob had managed to come back.

If he'd ever really been gone at all.

Suddenly, the appearance and rise of the Sentinels was beginning to make sick, deadly sense. Bad Bob was a player; he wanted power, and he'd do anything to anyone to get it. I'd cheated him the first time.

He'd make damn sure that David and I weren't in any position to do it again.

By separating the Wardens from the Djinn, then destroying the Djinn, he could ensure that no one had the resources and strength to fight him when he made his final move. Divide and conquer. A timeless classic.

'He's in Florida,' I said. I was sure of it, as sure as I'd ever been of anything in my life. 'The bastard's not even hiding, really. This is his old stomping ground. He's got networks of friends and supporters; he feels safe here. That's why we traced the signature to the Keys, and Kissimmee—'

'The beach house.' David snapped to his feet.

'What?'

'The beach house. I sensed him. I thought it was just a memory, but—' A pulse of light went through his eyes, turning them pure white. 'The signature of the power fits his.'

'He's been at the goddamn *beach house*?' I'd gone inside. I'd searched the house looking for the focus of the wards. Bad Bob must have been out picking up his latest issue of *Megalomaniacs Weekly*, which was damn lucky for me, because if he'd been there, I'd have been trapped inside the house, with David outside, and Bob could have done anything to me, anything at all . . .

I couldn't think about that. Not without shaking. I'd been through a lot of trauma in my life, but there was something so slick and calculated about Bad Bob's use of me . . . It was worse than betrayal. He'd cultivated and trained me specifically to transfer the Demon Mark to me, a cold long-term plan that I'd spoilt by not being quite as weak as he'd anticipated.

You're stronger now, I told myself. But I also remembered the moment in my apartment when Bob had focused all the power of the Sentinels on me, and I'd realised that I wasn't going to be strong enough, in the end.

None of us was going to be strong enough, not alone.

'If he's still at the beach house,' David was saying, as if he couldn't see I was melting down, 'he won't be there for long. We need to get word to Lewis.'

I shook my near-panic off with what I hoped wasn't a visible effort, and focused on the problem at hand. 'Contact Rahel. Tell her to get Kevin out of there. I don't want him caught in the middle if we spring a trap. We're screwed if Bad Bob has the contacts in the Wardens that I think he does. He was too well liked, even after the facts started coming out. Too many good people still like him. They wouldn't even think of it as betraying us to do a little under-the-table heads-up to him.'

David nodded. 'Ortega. I need for you to go to Rahel and give her the message. Tell her to extract Kevin. I don't care what she has to do. I don't care how noisy it is. Just tell the two of them to get out.'

'Me?' Ortega looked completely thrown. 'But I—'

'It's an emergency,' David said, and again, I felt that pulse of command and control. 'I'm sorry, I know you don't like to leave this place, but it has to be done.'

Ortega looked utterly miserable now. 'Can't you go? She won't listen to me. She doesn't even *like* me—'

'No,' David said. 'I can't.' He didn't explain. Ortega heaved a great sigh, nodded, and blipped away.

David didn't relax. He looked grim and angry, and avoided my eyes.

'Why didn't you go?' I asked. 'I mean, I'm grateful. I'm just surprised.'

'Because if you're right, and if they have what I think they have, they will be setting a trap,' he said. 'A trap designed specifically for me. They want to lure me in. I hope that they haven't managed to get everything together yet to spring it. That's why I'm sending Ortega.'

'Because they'd be planning to get you.'

'The Conduit,' he said. 'If they can destroy me, they can destroy the structure and power of the Djinn. You were right, Jo. I didn't believe it, but you were right. They've found our one true weakness, and I don't know how we're going to defend against them. Maybe Ashan was right. Maybe the only way to win is to withdraw.'

'And leave us to fight alone.'

He turned toward me, and I saw the fury and frustration in his eyes. 'Yes.' His hands clenched and unclenched. 'The book. We need to get it to his vault. I don't want it out where anyone can stumble across it.' He forced some of his anger back with a visible effort; it wasn't directed at me, but at the world. At Bad Bob. 'I'm sorry, Jo. I can't touch it. Can you carry it?'

I picked up the weight reluctantly, afraid that even

latched it might still have the power to seduce me, but it was quiet. Just leather, paper, ink, and iron.

Just a book that held the secrets to destroying an entire race.

No wonder it felt heavy.

The vault – of course a mansion like this would have one, along with a genuine, honest-to-God panic room – was crammed with stuff. Valuable stuff, to be sure. I was no expert, but I knew that early comics were worth money, and he had shelves full of them, each carefully bagged and labeled. Coin collections. Stamp collections. Toys. Rugs. Artifacts. I edged into the big steel-cased room and waited while David reorganized the collections enough for me to put the book down in an open space on a table. 'Does he ever sell any of this stuff?' I asked.

'No,' he said, moving a collection of what looked like vintage one-sheet posters. 'But he buys a lot on eBay. Put it down here.'

I did, gratefully, and stepped back from it. So did David, letting out a slow breath.

'Ortega,' I said. 'Is he going to be OK?'

David didn't answer. I understood a lot in that moment – his frustration, his anger. There was a good deal of self-loathing in there. David was not Jonathan, who'd held the position of Djinn Conduit before him; he wasn't naturally the kind of man who could make ruthless, cold decisions and sacrifice his friends and family when necessary. *Lewis* was like that. David was more like me – more willing to throw himself in front of the bus than push someone else, even if it was the tactically right thing to do.

'He'll be OK,' I said, and took his hand. 'It's a simple enough job, and they won't be looking for Ortega. Hell, I'd never have had a clue he was a Djinn if I'd met him in any other context.'

'I know,' David said. 'I just wish I'd told him that I didn't blame him for trading the other copy of the book. I don't. His obsession is to collect things. Ortega has always been an innocent when it comes to humans; he could never see the potential for evil in them. That's why Bad Bob took advantage of him.'

'He doesn't seem very . . . Djinn.'

David led the way back out of the vault and swung the massive door shut, then spun the lock. 'No,' he agreed. 'Ashan wanted to destroy him completely. I wouldn't allow it. Ortega doesn't have much power, for a Djinn – barely more than a human. He's never been able to really become what he was meant to be.'

'Which is?'

'Cold,' David said. 'Like the rest of us.'

I kissed his hand. 'You're not cold.'

He looked at me, and I saw the shadow of what he'd done haunting him. 'I can be,' he said. 'When I have to be.'

We went back downstairs, edging through the boxes, trying to find empty space. Ortega had left himself a small nest, a room filled with the most beautiful things of his collection . . . exquisite crystal, breathtaking art, blindingly lovely furniture. I hated to sully it with my human presence, but my feet were tired, and the Victorian fainting couch was exquisitely comfortable.

David didn't sit. He paced. None of the beauty touched him; he was focused elsewhere, on things far less lovely. I used the time to make calls; Lewis had been maneuvering Wardens slowly into position in Florida, using his most trusted people as well as the Ma'at, who still were outside the Warden system and therefore would be more trustworthy in something like this, if less powerful. I broke the news about Bad Bob – which was met with a suspiciously long silence, as if he'd already known and had hoped to keep it from me. That would have been par for the course.

I also gave him the update about the book, and realised midway through that I didn't actually *know* what it was David had read that had so unnerved him. It didn't tactically matter to Lewis, but it mattered to me, so after I finished the call, I asked.

'The Unmaking,' David said. 'I didn't think – until I read it in the book, I didn't think what you were describing could be true. The Unmaking is the opposite of creation.'

'Antimatter.'

He nodded slightly. 'You see it as science; we can't see it at all, but the Ancestor Scriptures tell us that if it can be brought forth, it will feed on and destroy all Djinn, and we won't be able to see it. It's been thought to be nothing but a ghost. A boogeyman.'

'But it's real,' I said. 'It's the black shard, the one we found in the dead Djinn. That *was* a dead Djinn.'

'It's how they grew more of the Unmaking,' David said. I saw his throat work as he swallowed. 'It feeds and grows inside a Djinn. What you found was just the husk, discarded and left behind. The Unmaking itself is far, far more powerful. That's how the Sentinels are able to wield so much power; they steal the energy that pours from the Unmaking's destruction of the world around it.' He closed his eyes briefly. 'I sent Rahel to them without any idea of the danger.'

'You couldn't have known!'

He ignored my attempt to mitigate things. 'Ortega should have been back by now.'

'Maybe he's having trouble finding them—'

'No.' His eyes unfocused into the distance. 'No, that's not it.'

I felt a sick lurch. 'David?'

'He's—' David reeled, as if he'd been slapped, and crashed into a table that held a glittering display of crystal. He went down amid a shower of glass like falling stars. I threw myself onto my knees next to him, trying to think what kind of first aid I could do for a Djinn, and saw a sickening blackness bloom along the right side of his face, like fast-growing mold. His mouth stretched in a silent scream, and his eyes flared a muddy red. 'Ortega,' he gasped. 'Help him. I'll hold on to him as long as I can, but you have to *help him*!'

Ortega was under direct attack, and it was manifesting in David. Of course it was; he was the Conduit. Until he severed the connection, and left Ortega to die alone, he would suffer along with him.

I launched myself up on the aetheric, burning through the six inches of steel roof like mist, all the way up until the entire Florida coastline was below me, sparking and burning with psychic energy. It wasn't hard to identify the trouble spot; it was a huge red dome of boiling, smoky power, and as I plunged down toward it, I felt the turbulence of the ongoing battle batter me, threatening to rip me apart. I couldn't spot Djinn on the aetheric; they were like ghosts, flitting out of the corners of my eyes. But I could see the destruction.

Oversight isn't ideal to seeing the details of an event, but it is useful for watching the ebb and flow of power. Ortega was an elusive sparkling shadow, dodging between thick threads of power that formed psychic nets; the Sentinels were trying to trap him. They'd already hurt him. I could see the darkness in him, just as it had been manifesting in David back in the real world.

I could sense his fury and despair. He couldn't get free. There was something holding him here, something—

I needed to get to him. Quickly. But instant transportation was a Djinn thing, and mostly fatal to humans; the only Djinn I'd ever known who could carry a human from one point to another without leaving pieces behind was Venna.

I slammed back down into my skin, a disorienting shock that I ignored because I didn't have time for it. David was writhing amid the broken glass, fighting for control. My hands hovered over him, but I didn't want to try to touch him. I wasn't sure what was happening, but it was beyond my capacity to fight.

'Trying – trying to hold him,' David gasped. 'Have to—'

David was *choosing* this. Ortega was in trouble, and David was trying to anchor him, send him power. That left David open to attack, just as Ortega was.

'Let go!' I shook David by the shoulders with as much violence as I could. 'David, *let him go*! You have to! If they get to you, it's over. *That's why you sent him*!'

'Can't let him die,' David panted.

'What can I *do*?' Why didn't the Sentinels come after me again, the bastards? At least then, I'd feel less helpless . . .

'The vault,' David gasped. 'The book. Use the book.'

No. There was power in that thing, sure, but it was raw and untamed and all too easy to misuse. There had to be another way to—

David's hand became a skeletal claw. His skin was turning the color of clay.

I had no time to think about it. I jumped to my feet and ran, threading through the maze of boxes, shoving over obstructions, hurdling what I could and climbing what I couldn't to make the most direct route back to the vault. I was trembling with fear by the time I arrived, because precious seconds were ticking away, and upstairs David was *dying . . .*

The vault was locked. I remembered David closing it and spinning the dial. *Christ, no, please—*

I had no choice. I reached out with all the Earth power at my disposal, ripped the locking mechanism to pieces, and slammed the heavy metal door aside like so much cardboard. It ripped loose of the hinges and tipped, hitting the concrete with enough force to shatter stone.

I scrambled over it into the vault.

I lunged for the book, opened the latch, and began flipping pages. *I need something to save him*, I was thinking hard, trying to direct the book to meet my desperate need. *Anything. Show me how to save him*!

A page flipped and settled, and my eyes focused on

symbols. I heard the whispers again, felt them rushing through me like wind, and had time to wonder if this was the right thing to do, the *smart* thing . . .

But then it was too late. I felt my lips shaping sounds, heard my voice speak without my understanding what it was saying. On the page, each symbol lit up in fire as it was spoken, burning like miniature suns until I could barely see the rest of the scripture.

Midway through, I felt dry, aching, drained body and soul. It was taking my power to fuel itself, and I still didn't know what it was designed to do. *Doesn't matter*, I told the part of my self that was screaming, the part that was in charge of self-preservation. *If I don't, he's gone.*

I had to take the chance.

As I spoke the last word, the entire book flared hot and white, and the force leapt from the pages into the center of my chest, knocking me down in a heap. I felt a sickening, sideways motion, as if the world had been twisted into a rubbery pretzel around me, and when I opened my eyes, I was lying facedown on industrial looped carpet, smelling dust and mold. I rolled over, gasping, and felt every muscle and nerve in my body shriek in protest.

I had no idea where I was, but it seemed that I was all alone. Nothing moved in the shadows around me, as far as I could see. The room looked like a deserted hotel ballroom, but one that had seen its last happy dances long ago. The carpet I was draped across was old and filthy, and the remaining furniture was a drunken muddle of broken chairs, listing tables, and fouled linens.

My brain was racing frantically, but my body was slow to follow. I managed to force muscles into enough order to get me to my hands and knees, and then to my feet, though I had to keep a hand on the dusty wall to brace myself. Apparently, Djinn spell books weren't the most comfortable way to travel, or the most accurate, since I'd been trying to arrive at the place where the Sentinels were hiding out . . .

I heard voices outside, in a shadowed hallway. I quickly crouched behind a table as a flashlight speared sharply through the dark, sweeping the room. It was a casual check, but I heard footsteps coming farther into the room, and risked a look. There were two people, one with the heavy flashlight in hand. I knew their faces in the backwash of light: one was Emily, Earth Warden, and an occasional adversary; the other was even less comforting – Janette de Winter. I'd last seen her in the Denny's, after the first earthquake in Fort Lauderdale; she looked just as polished, perfect, and diamond-hard as ever.

And just by being here, she was proving out my suspicion that she was a Sentinel.

'Do you feel anything?' Janette asked. I concentrated on concealing myself, aetherically speaking; minimising the blaze of power around me, drawing in all my senses until I was nothing but simple human flesh. If they were looking for a Warden, they'd miss me.

The flashlight played slowly around the room again in a methodical progression, counterclockwise. I was at the nine o'clock position, and I concentrated harder as the light crawled over the detritus in the room, heading my way.

It illuminated something strange; then there was a flash of movement, and then all hell broke loose.

They hadn't been looking for me. They'd been looking for *Kevin,* and he was on the offensive.

Fire streaked out of his hand in a flat plane, slammed into the two women, and knocked them back. Emily shrieked, but Janette reacted quickly, damping down the flames before they were injured and setting up a glittering shield that splashed Kevin's assault away in a rolling orange stream. It ignited dry carpeting, brittle walls, and broken furniture in an instant bonfire.

Emily, who could control wood and metal, grabbed an entire tractor's worth of furniture and slammed it toward Kevin with shocking violence and power. I knew her; she hadn't been nearly that strong before. Kevin tried to dodge, but there was no way he could win; Janette was lining him up in the crosshairs for her own assault, and he had no way to stop Emily at all.

As Kevin backed toward the wall, he tripped and

went down, rolled into a crouch, and instinctively covered his head with both arms as the wall of furniture tumbled toward him.

I put up a wall of power around him, and both Emily's flood tide of furniture and Janette's flaming wave broke against it at the same time. Again, I was shocked by the force of what they were wielding; it was all out of proportion to what most Wardens would have used, even in extremity. Kevin was strong, but he couldn't have equaled even one of them, much less two in direct conflict.

I could. Barely.

I stepped out from behind the table. I considered a snappy announcement of my presence, but really, it wasn't necessary; both the other Wardens – no, Sentinels – were already turning and looking for me. I felt them lock on and acquire the target, and I shook my hands lightly to loosen myself up.

'One chance to live,' I said. 'Where's Ortega?'

I couldn't really tell their expressions, not from across the room, but their body language suggested my sudden appearance wasn't just a surprise; it was a real shock. If I'd been hoping that would throw them off balance, though, the surprise was mine; Janette hesitated for barely a second before I sensed a surge of power traveling invisibly through the wall next to me, and the paneling around me burst into white-hot flame. I ignored it. Playing their game was a sucker bet, and I needed to get to Kevin before they could separate us and use us against each other.

I gathered up the heat vortex being generated by Janette's flames and sent it spinning toward both the Sentinels. Neither of them were Weather Wardens, and they weren't trained on how to defuse such things; instead, they scattered to get out of its way. I kicked off my shoes, picked them up, and did a broken-field sprint across the ballroom toward Kevin. When I reached him, I grabbed him by the collar and yanked him out of the tangle of burning chairs and tables surrounding him. 'Where's the Djinn?' I shouted. Kevin coughed, spat up black, and jerked his chin toward the doorway. 'Ortega! Have you seen him?'

'Yeah,' he said, and coughed again, with deep wracking spasms that made my chest hurt to hear them. 'Outside. They had him.'

Janette and Emily were standing between me and my goal. Not a good place to be. I began throwing flaming furniture together and rolling it toward them in unwieldy balls, and not even their combined powers could catch it all. One ball got past Janette and plowed into them head-on. They went flying. *Strike!*

'Come on,' I snapped to Kevin, and went to the first downed Sentinel. Emily. I straddled her as she lay on the floor, and put her down for the count by encasing her in a thick layer of ice, pulling all the water out of the air to do it. The heat would set her free, but not for a while. Maybe not even in time. Gosh, I was going to lose sleep over that one. I have no idea what Kevin did to Janette, but it wasn't likely to be as merciful. Seeing his smudged, grim face, I had the feeling it was well deserved, too.

We left the ballroom. At the last minute, I damped the fires behind us. Kevin shot me a glance, and I shrugged; I had the desire for bloodshed, but somebody had to set a good example. I knew it wouldn't be him.

'Where's Rahel?' I asked. The hallway outside was more of the same – dim, cluttered, deserted, smelling of age and mildew.

Kevin coughed again, wiped his mouth on his shirt, and said, 'They figured it out. They have her, too. I couldn't get to her.'

'Do they know—'

'Fuck *yes*, they know! We were sold out. They were buying it right up until about an hour ago, and then everything went crazy . . .'

I wanted to hear it, but the anxiety building in me wouldn't stop clanging its warning bell. 'We've got to find Ortega, *now*. Go that way. If you spot him, yell.'

But in the end, I was the one who found him.

They'd posed him carefully, the Sentinels, just as they had the Djinn I'd helped discover before. Someone – one of the Earth Wardens – had looped whorls of living wood, thick and stronger than iron, around his arms and legs, pinning him in mid-air against the wall.

He'd been helpless. However they'd managed it, they'd taken away his defenses, and they'd done it so fast, so horribly fast . . .

'Jo?' Kevin's hoarse pant came from behind me. I was standing very still, not blinking, not looking away. '*Jesus.*'

We couldn't get to him. There were too many Sentinels between us and Ortega. Six at least that I could see.

I'd expected to see Bad Bob Biringanine, so the sight of him shocked me less than it had a right to.

He looked exactly as I remembered him – white hair, fair Irish skin turned ruddy on the cheeks and nose, fierce blue eyes.

He smiled when he saw me. It was the same cynical, sweet expression that I remembered so well.

And then he turned to the man standing next to him and said something. The man's back was to me, but I knew already, before he turned. Before I saw his face and knew how badly screwed we were.

Paul Giancarlo, my trusted friend, was *with the Sentinels.*

I saw the terrible guilt in his eyes, but there was something else, too. A fanatical light that I'd never truly recognised before. *He was hurt,* I thought. *He was hurt by the Djinn. He was in charge while they destroyed the Warden headquarters. He saw people die, people he liked. People he loved.*

Bad Bob had preyed on him as surely as he had all these others. He'd made them victims all over again. Worse – he'd made them victimisers.

'Jo,' Paul said. 'Christ, what are you *doing* here? Get out!'

'You want me to send David instead?' I glared at him. 'Paul, there's not enough *what the hell* in the world for this!'

He clenched his fists, and I saw the muscles in his jaw tense and jump. He'd always looked a bit thuggish, but never more than when he was truly angry. 'If we get David, it's over. It's done. No more bloodshed,' he said. 'If we have to go through all the Djinn, how much suffering is that? Come on, Jo. You know they can't be trusted. You *know*!'

'Apparently I can trust them more than I can trust you,' I said.

'Ah, reunions,' Bad Bob said. He reached down and flipped open the lid on a black box on the floor, something like what Heather the scientist had used to carry her radioactive materials when she'd done her show-and-tell at Warden HQ. 'Stop it, you two. You're making me all teary-eyed. Next thing you know we'll all be group-hugging and braiding each others' hair.'

Nothing seemed very real to me, and yet was

simultaneously very, very clear. I could see every single line of wood grain, every strand of Ortega's hair where it drifted in the subtle breezes of the hallway.

I could see everything.

A black spear rose of its own accord from the box that Bad Bob had opened. This was no shard; it must have been at least six feet long, glittering and lethal. It slowly turned, and I had the horrifying idea that it was *aware,* that it was seeking out its victim. It was nothing on the aetheric, an absence of all things around it, just a black hole that could never be filled.

'Too bad your boyfriend couldn't be persuaded to make an appearance,' Bad Bob said. 'I suppose we'll just have to perform a small demonstration instead with this unlucky fellow.'

Paul caught sight of the hovering spear, and his face went an ugly, ragged shade of pale. 'No,' he said, 'No, you agreed, only if we could get—'

The spear oriented itself and launched itself with sudden, horrific violence at Ortega.

I screamed and tried to form a shield in front of him, but the spear – the Unmaking – tore right through as if my power was completely meaningless to it, and buried itself in Ortega's chest.

The sound he made was like nothing I had ever heard, something I couldn't bear to hear. It was sheer torment, the sound of a Djinn being pulled apart and feeling every hard second of the process.

Oh God no no no.

I was watching Ortega, but I was picturing David writhing on the floor of that room amid the shattered crystal, and dying along with him.

The Unmaking was *burrowing* into him. I could feel it eating at him, could see the color leaching from his skin.

And as it ate him, it grew *larger*.

'Oh God,' Kevin said, and I'd never heard him sound like that, so utterly blank and young. As if he'd never seen anything terrible in his life.

On the other side, Paul Giancarlo and most of the others winced and turned away. Some covered their ears. Some looked sick.

Bad Bob continued to smile, utterly unmoved, and all my hate focused to a red pinpoint, right between his crazy blue eyes.

My power wouldn't work against the Unmaking, but it would damn sure make a dent in *him*.

I called up everything, *everything*, and balled it into a single bright lance of light in my right hand, and slammed it toward Bad Bob Biringanine.

Who kept smiling.

Paul Giancarlo stepped in the way – no, not stepped. *Lurched.* I don't think he meant to; I don't think that it was his choice at all. Bad Bob owned the Sentinels, body and soul, and even they probably didn't understand just how much his creatures they'd become. They'd opened the door to hate and revenge, and the darkness had claimed them. Lee Antonelli had shown me that.

Bad Bob used him as a human shield, because he knew it would hurt me the worst of all.

I didn't scream, but the anguish must have shown in my face; Paul must have seen it, in that instant before the force I released hit him squarely in the chest.

It was fast, so fast he never blinked as the light hit him and blew out his nervous system, destroyed his brain stem, and dropped him lifeless to the floor. I'd just *killed my friend*.

Kevin paused, just for a second, eyes wide, and then he attacked when he realised that I wasn't capable of doing anything else at that moment, too frozen in shock to move or even defend myself. The Sentinels were in confusion; Bad Bob was smiling at me, oblivious to anything but my horror, and the rest of them had no idea what they were supposed to do. Like the Ma'at, they were a collective mass of power, and without a guiding force, they fell apart.

Even so, if it had been just Kevin and me, we'd have been lost. Each of the Sentinels had more power than we did, drawn from that black well of energy the Unmaking created when it destroyed things; they'd have killed us on their own, given time.

They didn't have time.

An explosion rattled the entire building from outside. I saw a flaming car roll by the doors at the far end of the hall.

The cavalry had arrived with a bang.

I felt the aetheric popping and crackling with the arrival of more Wardens – some on the scene, some pouring power in from remote locations. I heard the sound of fighting from outside, and then something massive crashed against the outer wall, smashing a hole the size of a Buick in the brick, and through it I saw . . . the Apocalypse, or at least, as much as could fit in the parking lot of a condemned motel.

A tornado skimmed past the opening, sucking and howling, sparking lightning against every metallic surface. Cars rolled and disintegrated under the assault, then caught fire as Weather Wardens clashed with Fire. I couldn't tell the good guys from the bad guys, at least until the rest of the wall came down with a heavy slam, and Lewis walked in over the rubble, leading a small but heavily kick-ass army, and joined me and Kevin.

'Surrender,' he said flatly to the group of Sentinels at the end of the hall. 'Do it now and we'll let you live to see a trial. Otherwise, you get buried today.'

He meant exactly what he said. Lewis was giving no quarter today, if they pushed him into a showdown. There was no trace of hesitation in him at all.

Bad Bob must have known it. He winked, jolly as a leprechaun, and blew me a kiss. Then he went to Ortega and wrenched the black spear out of him with his bare hands.

As it came out, it grew, adding inches more to its length. With every death it was fed, it grew more malevolently, horribly powerful.

Ortega was a dessicated corpse. A husk.

Bad Bob reached down and yanked up a small female form that lay huddled at his feet, tied with glittering black ropes. Cherise's big blue eyes were wide under the confusion of blond hair, but the fury in her was all Rahel.

'You don't want to risk this one, do you?' Bad Bob asked, and yanked hard on her hair. 'Come on, Lewis. I know you better than that. You're one of the good guys!'

Lewis's expression didn't alter by a flicker. 'She's human. Humans get hurt when Wardens clash; you know that. It's on your head, not mine.'

'My son, you've really learnt how to operate in the subzero, haven't you? Well, very fine, but we both know that despite this very pretty shell, what's inside is no more human than that.' He jerked his head toward Ortega's body. 'Probably a whole lot less human, actually. She's a wild one, isn't she?'

Rahel was playing Cherise for all she was worth, and it broke my heart to see my friend so scared, shaking, and crying. 'Please,' she choked, 'I don't know who you think I am, but I'm not—'

'You're a Djinn,' Bad Bob cut in. 'Show me. *Show me now,* or I use this.' He still had the spear in his other hand, and he raised it, prepared to thrust it into her guts.

Lewis let out a low, almost inaudible moan.

Rahel flowed out of her disguise, dark and commanding and imperious, but still restrained by the black ropes. Her eyes snapped violent yellow sparks as she struggled to get free. She subsided, panting, dreadlocks wild around her hawk-sharp face.

'That's better,' Bad Bob said. 'Do tell David that we'll be in touch, Jo. If he wants to stop me from continuing to kill his people, he should consider giving himself up to us. Very soon.'

The Sentinels crowded around him. Bad Bob grabbed Rahel, and each of them touched the black surface . . . and vanished. All of them together, Rahel included.

He'd taken her.

Kevin collapsed against one of the left-standing structural walls, gagging for breath. He looked terrible.

I must have looked a hell of a lot worse, because Lewis took one look at me, gestured, and suddenly there were two Earth Wardens at my side, pouring warm, sticky power into me like syrup.

I felt a rush of *presence* around me as I started to fall, and David's arms caught me and held me close. 'Oh God,' he whispered against my hair. 'Are you *crazy*? What were you trying to do?'

'Save you,' I whispered back. 'Always.' I wanted to tell him that everything was all right here, too, in this warm, soft place I'd reached where nothing hurt. But I couldn't stay in that place, even though it was so tempting to just give up and let shock take over.

Instead, I forced my legs to stiffen, and I pulled away from him. David let me go. He saw what was in my face, and he let me go.

I walked toward Ortega. When Lewis tried to stop me, I shook him off. When he tried again, I hit him with a lightning bolt. I was insane, but not quite that insane; I pulled the charge at the last moment, feeding just enough through him to knock him back a step.

Ortega was dead. His eyes had gone black, burnt and lifeless, and his skin was a dull, dusty gray, as if he'd turned to stone. David joined me, standing close but not touching.

'It's not your fault,' I told David. I could only

imagine that he was thinking about ordering Ortega to come here, because he'd known there was a chance . . .

But that wasn't what he was thinking at all. David cocked his head slowly to one side, staring at the dead Djinn, and asked, very quietly, 'Who is he?'

Chapter Twelve

None of the Djinn knew him, not even Venna, when I insisted that she be summoned from whatever beach resort Ashan had decided to take his people to for the duration of the crisis. I wasn't sure that Venna would come, but she'd always been her own master, and that hadn't changed just because Ashan thought it had. He might be her Conduit, but he'd never own her.

Venna, dressed in her vintage Alice outfit, paced slowly in front of the wall and Ortega's body, studying him closely. It was eerie, seeing that kind of detachment packaged in the body of a little girl who almost radiated innocence.

She and David were the only ones allowed near the body at all. The entire room had been cordoned off in space-age-looking shielding, and all of the rest of us were being thoroughly checked out by a radiation team. Not surprisingly, we'd all gotten a dose. 'Not that it's as unusual as people think it is,' said the chatty Cathy in the hazmat suit who was drawing my blood. 'The average American gets about three hundred fifty millirems a year, just from the environment. Hey, want to know the weird part? Forty millirems of that comes out of our own bodies. We're little fusion reactors, you know. Potassium-40 in the brain, Carbon-14 in the liver.' She was chatty because she was scared, though her hands were steady enough. She must have realised it, because she sent me an apologetic glance through the plastic visor of her space suit. 'Sorry. I jabber when I'm nervous. This is just – well. They don't exactly train you for this at NEST school.'

I wondered what the government had been told, or was telling them; the whole thing was founded on need-to-know, and I doubted even this woman had a clue. There were some FBI agents stalking the scene in their trademark dark windbreakers, talking into cell phones. Lots of cops. Fire department.

And reporters. *Lots* of reporters, a cresting wave of them held back by a sandbar of uniformed police around the perimeter. I could hear the dull thud of news helicopters overhead. No doubt we were in heavy rotation on all the news channels.

In the shielded room, Alice finished her inspection of Ortega and came out. The NEST doctor working on me muttered something under her breath, but she kept her eyes down and focused on what she was doing. *Keep on living in denial,* I thought. *Safer that way, lady.*

Venna came up to my side and stared at the needle in my arm. 'What is she doing?'

'Taking blood.'

'Is she going to give it back?'

'Venna, what did you sense in there?'

'He is not a Djinn,' she said. There was no doubt in her voice at all. 'I don't know what he is. Or was.'

'He was a Djinn,' I said. Venna slowly shook her head. 'Venna, that was Ortega. You know Ortega; you remember him—'

Another slow shake of her head. It was exactly the same response I'd gotten from David, and from two other Djinn he'd summoned. None of them recognised Ortega at all. They didn't classify him as *human*; they didn't classify him as anything. Certainly, not anyone.

I thought with a sudden hot pang of the Miami estate, all that fascinating, rich chaos that Ortega had surrounded himself with. I'd barely met him, but I was the only one who could mourn him.

'Never mind. Thanks for the help,' I sighed to Venna, who cut her eyes sharply toward the doctor, who was withdrawing the needle and applying a bandage to the bend of my arm. 'You know about Rahel?'

'That your enemies have her? Yes.' Venna continued to stare at the doctor, to the extent that the poor woman fumbled the tube she was holding, but caught it on the way to the floor. 'I do care, you know. But this is a mess humans made, and humans must correct. Ashan won't interfere. He won't want me to interfere, either.'

'Venna,' I said, 'that's Bad Bob Biringanine in charge of the Sentinels. You know what he did to Djinn before. You think he's going to be any better now? Any kinder? You can't stick your heads in the sand and pretend like you don't live here, too, as if you're not at risk. Rahel's proof of that.'

No answer. She transferred her unblinking stare to me, which at least enabled the doc to make a confused, nervous getaway.

'There's a book,' I said. 'The kind of book Star had. You know the one. And Bad Bob has it.'

Her eyes went black. Storm black. She didn't move, but there was something entirely different about her, suddenly.

I held myself very, very still.

'A book of the Ancestors?' she asked. I nodded. I was very careful about that, too. 'Then he has power he should not have. Like Star.'

'Does that change anything?'

She never blinked, and her eyes stayed black. 'I don't know,' she said. 'I will find out.'

That sounded ominous. She blipped away before I could ask how she intended to go about doing that,

and I didn't think any amount of calling her name was
going to get her back. Not now.

David was still in the shielded room. He
was studying Ortega, the way someone might a
fascinating abstract sculpture, trying to find meaning
in random patterns. I tapped on the window and got
his attention; he shook his head, as if he was trying to
clear it, and came through the decontamination door.
One of the NEST members tried to lecture him about
procedures, but he ignored it and came directly to
me.

'Radiation,' I reminded him.

'I shed it in the room,' he said. 'How about you?
How do you feel?' Oh, the joys of being Djinn . . . I
wondered how much of the toxic stuff I had crawling
through my cells right now. Too much, almost
certainly. The Earth Wardens had done their work, so
I was probably going to feel sick, but not drop dead.

Probably.

'Fantastic,' I said sourly. 'Do you recognise him at
all?'

David's head shake was just as certain, and just
as regretful about it, as Venna's had been. I could see
how frustrated he was, how baffled by his inability to
comprehend what was in front of him, and it scared
me, too. He was one of the most powerful entities on
the face of the Earth. He shouldn't have this kind of
blind spot.

I was trying not to think about it as an Achilles' heel, but that was getting more difficult all the time, especially when the whole thing ran through my head and the person imprisoned on that wall and impaled by the black spear was David, not Ortega.

They wouldn't know him, I thought, with a sickening drop of my stomach. *Venna, Rahel, all the Djinn – they'd just stare at his body and not know who the hell they were looking at. They wouldn't even remember him at all.*

Of all the possible ways to destroy someone, that had to be the worst.

It reminded me, with a sudden snap, of how Ashan had tried to destroy me, not so long ago – on the day that my daughter had died. He'd tried to strip away not just my life, but the *memory* of my life. He'd been stopped midslaughter, which was why I was still around, but there was something fundamentally similar about what Ashan had done, and what was happening now, to the Djinn.

The Mother had intervened to stop him – but, I thought, that had mostly been because he'd done it on the grounds of the chapel in Sedona, on what was, for them, holy ground. The same kind of protection might not apply for David out here.

The answer was in the book. It *had* to be in the book.

'David—' I chose my words very carefully,

remembering Venna's extreme reaction. 'The book, the one that we looked at earlier—'

He raised his eyes to meet mine, and I saw surprise in them. 'The Ancestor Scriptures.'

'You remember them.'

'Of course I remember them.'

'And what about where we left them?'

'In a vault,' he said promptly. 'Locked up.'

'Where was the vault?'

He opened his mouth, but nothing came out. For a second be looked baffled, then angry, then blank. 'I don't know,' he said. 'How can I not know?'

'David, what did the book say about Unmaking?'

His pupils expanded, black devouring bronze.

'Don't say that.' His words had the ring of command, but I was no Djinn.

'You have to listen to me. I think that all this is connected to—'

He grabbed me by the arm. 'Don't say it. Don't.'

'David, stop it!' I yanked free. He hadn't used Djinn strength on me, but plain old human strength was enough to piss me off. I didn't like being grabbed, not in that way, and he knew it. 'It's connected to what Ashan did when he messed with our reality, to try to erase me from the world. Bad Bob reappeared about the same time. This weapon, the thing they're using, it's a tool of Unmaking; that's what they're calling it—'

His eyes flared black, like Venna's. 'Stop,' he growled.

'It's killing you, and you can't even *see* it. You can't see those you lose. It's just *destroying* you.'

He spun around and stalked away, fury in every sinuous movement. He knew, somewhere deep down, but there was something in Djinn DNA that kept him from acknowledging any of it.

The secret was in that damned book, which I couldn't read without major consequences. I knew I wouldn't be able to resist its pull.

Lewis was watching us from the back of the room, having completed his own blood donations; he looked tired, but alert. 'Everything OK?' he asked.

'Do you think Rahel is OK?' I shot back, and saw the flinch. 'Sorry. I know you – care for her.' I wasn't exactly sure what that entailed, between Lewis and Rahel; I wouldn't have been surprised if they'd been casual lovers. Rahel wasn't the type to fall in love, and Lewis . . . Lewis already had, with the wrong person.

'He hasn't hurt her yet,' David said. He had his back to us, but he was listening. 'They're hiding their tracks, but the connection is still there. I can trace her as long as they hold her.'

Was that a good thing, or a bad thing? I thought about the trap Bad Bob had laid this time around. He'd known – because of Paul, oh God, Paul, you *fool* – that Kevin and Rahel had been planted to spy on him. Surely he was assuming that David could sense and track Rahel's position, too.

Surely he would just lay another trap.

Depressing as that was, we'd won a kind of victory here. Yes, Ortega was dead, but so was Paul; not only that, but the Sentinels had been forced to regroup and retreat. The current count was twelve dead in total.

Problem was, all of them were Wardens. And it was impossible to tell which of them had been Sentinels, except for anecdotal information about which side they'd been fighting for. I was sure about Paul, Emily, and Janette. The rest . . .

Once again, we just didn't know who our enemies really were.

Lewis stood up and walked to where David was standing, facing the window. Facing Ortega's desiccated body. 'We can't follow them,' he said. 'They've got weapons that can destroy the Djinn, and we don't know what they're planning. Let's talk to Kevin. Maybe he's got some information we don't.'

That was coolly logical, something that neither David nor I seemed capable of being at the moment. David nodded, and the three of us left the treatment area.

Or tried, anyway. An FBI agent got in our way. She was a tall woman, curved but in that I-work-out kind of way. Feathered dark hair around a heart-shaped face. Cool, impartial green eyes.

'Sorry,' she said. 'Nobody moves. We haven't finished our interrogations yet.'

David was likely to just walk over her, in the mood he was in, and that would at the very least lead to a confrontation we didn't need. I looked over at Lewis, who sighed and dug something out of the back pocket of his jeans. 'Right,' he said. 'All-access pass.'

He held it up. I couldn't see what it said, but the woman's eyes widened, and she took a step back. I got the impression she hadn't done *that* in a while.

'Yes, sir,' she said. 'Sorry. And they are—'

'With me,' Lewis said. 'Thanks for your vigilance, but it's not necessary, Agent. We're the good guys.'

She looked as if she sincerely doubted that, but she didn't say anything, just moved out of the way with a be-my-guest motion. Then she went to tell her boss, a tall gray-haired man. Cover your ass. It was the absolute code of any governmental agency, no matter how well-intentioned.

'This,' Lewis said, 'is a cluster fuck.' He was looking at the parking lot, which was littered with burnt-out, crushed vehicles, downed trees, fragments of glass and metal. The hotel, which had luckily been scheduled for demolition anyway, was partially destroyed, whether by us or by the Sentinels it was impossible to say. At a certain point, it really didn't much matter.

The news media was out in a huge, baying pack. I

tried to count the number of satellite trucks, but my head hurt. I was sure that a fair number of those photo and video lenses were being pointed in our direction, though, and remembered the reporter from Fort Lauderdale. Man, wouldn't she feel vindicated? She now officially had a scoop.

'How much did they get?' I asked.

'Oh, everything. Tornadoes forming out of nowhere. Cars bursting into flame and exploding. Trees getting thrown. Buildings disintegrating.' Lewis's shoulders twitched, then straightened. 'The FBI wants me to give a statement. Something along the lines of, we're a secret government agency; we'd tell you but we'd have to kill you, blah blah. They'd like me to tie it to terrorists.'

I stared at him. 'And what are you going to do?'

He shrugged. 'Don't know yet.'

'You really think this is a good time to lie?'

'Well, I don't think it's exactly a good time to tell the truth.' He glanced at David, whose eyes seemed to be fading back to a more normal color. 'I'll leave the Djinn out of it, if you'd like.'

'That's kind of you, but I think we'd better tell everything if we tell anything,' David said. 'Let's talk to Kevin. We don't have a lot of time.'

Kevin was sitting with his least favorite people. Well, that probably wasn't fair; he didn't like anybody, so *most* people were his least favorite people, but he reserved a special kind of dislike for the Ma'at. I wasn't really sure why, except that in general, the leadership of the Ma'at was pretty unlikable.

Two of them were flanking him: Charles Spenser Ashworth II and Myron Lazlo. Talk about the Old Boy Network . . . they weren't just in it, they'd laid the original cable. Lazlo had dressed down for his public appearance; he normally liked subtle, tailored suits that reeked old money, but he'd deigned to wear what I supposed was his 'field outfit' – khaki slacks, a cotton shirt open at the neck, and a sport coat that undoubtedly cost nearly as much as the sports car he'd probably arrived in.

Even so, Charles Ashworth's outfit made Lazlo look cheap.

Both of them were older than the pharaohs, and twice as stern, both in looks and in attitude. Yeah, I liked them just as much as Kevin did.

I thought it was just about the first time I'd ever seen actual relief on the kid's face as he spotted me. 'About time,' he said. 'Who put me in fucking detention with the Mummy Twins?'

I had to admit, that made me smile. The Ma'at had taken a lot of their iconography for their organisation from the Egyptians, and it was no accident they'd made their headquarters at the Luxor in Las Vegas. I suppose they could have made a case for Memphis as well, but where else do you get a real live pyramid for a clubhouse?

'I did,' Lewis said. 'Thanks, gentlemen.'

The gentlemen in question glared and, in Lazlo's case, gave him a well-I-never patrician huff. 'We are not your *staff*,' Ashworth snapped. 'Do you have any idea what kind of imbalance this little fracas has caused? Oh, of course you do. You're supposed to be preventing this kind of thing, you know. Protecting people, not putting them in danger. Isn't that the Warden credo?'

He said *Warden* as if it were an epithet, which it practically was, for the Ma'at. They looked on themselves as the accountants of the aetheric; they were concerned about balance, always balance. Important, yes, but even supernatural double-entry bookkeeping was still bookkeeping, and I couldn't work up much enthusiasm for their way of doing things.

'The credo of every one of us is to stop Bad Bob Biringanine from screwing things up any worse than he already has,' Lewis said. 'I'll expect your support.'

He sent them on their way with a jerk of his head. He was probably the only person in the world they'd have taken that kind of treatment from, another mystery of Lewis Levander Orwell. He had an impressive presence, but not *that* impressive – generally. And yet we all jumped when he snapped his fingers.

Kevin stayed where he was, slouched in the plastic

chair, as the two older men vacated. I settled in on one side, Lewis on the other. David paced. It was what David did, at times like these. He looked preoccupied, and I knew that he was tracking Rahel, trying to find out everything about what the Sentinels were doing.

'You saw Paul, right?' Kevin asked. He kept his head down, and addressed the question toward the tops of his dirty Nikes. 'Bastard sold us out.'

'I know,' I said. My whole heart hurt, and I hadn't allowed myself to really feel it yet, the depth of Paul's betrayal. Things he'd said came back to me – his refusal to disagree with the Sentinels, his reluctance about my relationship with David, and the wedding. For Paul, it had been a matter of us versus them. He had never really understood, deep down, that Djinn and the Wardens were the same. Different points on the same scale.

Sometimes I despaired for the human race.

'I think they bought the cover at first,' Kevin was saying. 'They had us in a room for almost a day, talking to us. All about how the Djinn had always been dangerous, and we'd been stupid to ever open ourselves up to them.' His bitter eyes followed David. 'Can't say I ever really disagreed with that. Made a lot of sense to me.'

'That's why you were perfect,' Lewis said. 'How'd Rahel do?'

'Fine. If I hadn't known she wasn't human, I'd

never have figured it out. She was—' Kevin's throat worked nervously, his prominent Adam's apple bobbing. 'She was really good at being Cherise.' And I couldn't imagine Kevin had been able to really play along too well, but that might have been OK. After all, he was socially awkward at the best of times.

'When did Paul show up?' I asked.

'About an hour ago,' Kevin said. 'That was when they cut us off. Tried to make it seem like they were just testing us, but Rahel knew Paul was in the building, she told me. She knew he'd sell us out.'

'Didn't she try to get the two of you out?'

'Yeah.' Kevin's voice faltered, 'I made her stop.'

Silence. I looked at Kevin's hands. They were tightly bound up together, trembling.

'Why?' Lewis asked the question I wanted to, in a voice far more gentle than I could have. 'What happened?'

'There was this girl. I didn't know – she might have been one of them, I don't know. But they said – they said they were going to kill her if we tried to leave. I had to—' Kevin squeezed his eyes shut. '*Christ.* I should have just let Rahel get out of here.'

'Trust me, if Rahel hadn't thought it was important to stay, you'd have been yanked out whether you wanted it or not.' Lewis glanced at David, who was still pacing, but listening to every word. 'Then what happened?'

'They had this stuff. Black stuff, I guess it was like – like the stuff you found.' Antimatter. I nodded. 'They tied Rahel up with it, and she couldn't move. I know she tried to get away, but she couldn't; she was able to make enough noise that I could run. I was looking for a way out when you showed up.' He nodded at me. 'I should have—'

Kevin stopped. I knew that feeling all too well. I wanted to help him, but I knew it was something that he had to deal with himself. No platitude was going to help, no matter how sincere.

'Kevin.' I took one of his hands and drew it out of its tight ball; it stayed tense in mine, trembling, ready to yank away at a second's notice. 'Before Paul showed up, they may have told you some things. Something that could help us.'

He was already shaking his head. 'I'd have said if they spilt their guts, OK? But they didn't. They just talked about what a bitch you were, and how you were willing to fuck over the Wardens for your boyfriend . . .'

'Finally, someone you could agree with,' I said. He shot me a covert look, almost hidden by his dangling, shaggy hair.

'No,' he said, 'I don't. Not after I saw what they wanted to do.'

I felt a shiver crawl hand-over-hand up the bones of my spine. 'What did you see?'

'They were going to torture him,' Kevin said, glancing up at David, then away. 'Make him tell everything about the Djinn. About the Oracles. About how to destroy them.'

'They really are crazy,' Lewis said grimly. 'Destroying the Djinn and the Oracles would destroy *us*. There's no way humanity, or anything else alive on this planet, would survive a catastrophe like that.'

We thought of it at the same time, our gazes locking over the top of Kevin's bowed head. David must have as well, because he spun toward us.

'He knows that,' I said. 'Bad Bob knows that. He's not stupid enough to assume anything else. So why would he *want* to destroy the human race?'

'You know,' David said.

'It's not Bad Bob,' I said. 'Is it?'

'No,' Lewis agreed. 'I think it's a Demon wearing his skin.'

Unfortunately, I had way too much personal experience with Demons. Most recently, I'd seen the damage they could do once they took on a human form. I thought the Wardens had been pretty successful about purging anyone from their ranks who carried a Demon Mark – a larval form of a Demon that granted the carrier more-than-normal strength and energy, almost like having a secret Djinn under your control. But you could carry a Demon Mark only so long before it began to corrupt you from within, and if you wanted to survive, you had to get rid of it by passing it to someone else.

Someone else more powerful, because the Demon Mark was only attracted to power. It traded up.

I'd been the unfortunate recipient of such a thing, at Bad Bob's hands. I hadn't understood, at the time, that he'd been paying me a kind of backhanded compliment . . . I hadn't known, then, how really strong I was.

He had. He'd chosen me for just that reason.

It had killed him in leaving his body – he'd waited too long, hung on to his power until it was nested deep inside. I thought about his cold body lying in a grave somewhere, and wondered if his flesh was still there, peaceful and empty. Maybe what was walking around right now was Bad Bob reanimated; maybe it was just a semblance, like the one Rahel had worn to play Cherise. Either way, it wasn't Bad Bob on the inside. Couldn't be. But if it was a full-grown, fully formed Demon, it had powers I couldn't begin to understand.

'The antimatter,' I said. 'The Demon produces it, secretes it, something like that. That's why there's no machinery, no plant they've had to set up. That's why we couldn't find any kind of permanent base for the Sentinels – they don't need a plant, not even a hidden one. Because he just . . . makes it.' Like sweat, or blood, or other bodily fluids. It was the very essence of why the Demon didn't belong here; it literally destroyed the world around it, just by being. The human shell kept it contained, like a space suit insulating an astronaut from the cold of space.

If it left that shell . . .

I remembered what Jerome Silverton had said about the black shard we'd found embedded in the dead Djinn. *One kilogram of antimatter annihilating itself is supposed to produce about 180 petajoules of energy.* The spear I'd seen Bad Bob use to kill Ortega had been at least five times the size of the shard we'd originally found. *Catastrophic would be charitable.*

The Demon was hunting us. Hunting Djinn, using the Djinn to power the growth of the antimatter weapon. Once it was strong enough, what would he do with it? Where would he—

'The Oracles,' I said. 'What if he goes after the Oracles?'

David was already gone when I turned toward him; a blurred motion was all that was left. *Imara.* My daughter was in Sedona, locked for all time in one location. Unable to flee.

I sat with Lewis, holding Kevin's shaking hand, and waiting for the end of the world.

The end of the world didn't come before dinner, anyway.

As the hours went by, the FBI decided they'd have

a better chance of containing the situation – ha! – if they ejected those of us not wearing three letters or badges on our outfits. That went for the Wardens, the Ma'at, and would have gone for the Djinn, had any been present. I'd stood witness to the FBI forensic team taking Ortega down from the wall, then interring him in a metal casket that was marked with all kinds of warning signs. Somehow, I felt someone should watch. He'd been a kind man, a peculiar sort of Djinn, and he hadn't deserved this kind of ending.

Lewis, Kevin and I were bundled into an FBI helicopter – not my favorite form of transportation – and flown to the Miami field office, where we were left in a severe-looking room for a few more hours.

Dinner was served, and apart from its being warm and edible, I don't remember much about it. We barely talked. There didn't seem to be all that much to say.

When David reappeared, he came with reinforcements – six Djinn. One of them was Venna, which made me smile in relief; one was the tough-looking specimen David had identified to me as Roy, when we'd seen him earlier – he'd been Rahel's hypothetical backup. I wondered where he'd been when he was needed the most.

Zenaya was the third. I didn't know the other three, but they all had the otherworldly grace and glitter that I associated with the most powerful of the Djinn, Old or New.

'The Oracles are protected,' David said. 'Ashan's taking care of it, and Wardens we trust have been assigned alongside them as backup.'

'He won't like that,' I noted.

'He doesn't have to like it. I've explained the necessity.' There was a cold, angry shimmer in David's eyes, and I wondered exactly how civil *that* discussion had been. 'We intend to go and get Rahel.'

'You can't,' I said. I was calm about it, and authoritative, but all too aware that David might not be in any mood to listen to reason. 'She's bait. You go charging in there, that's exactly what they want – especially you, Conduit Boy.'

He didn't answer me, but he didn't argue, either. He was biding his time. I knew I couldn't get him to just stand by and risk Rahel's life, not under these circumstances. Time was running out. If I wanted to avoid watching David throw his life away, I needed a plan, and a damn good one.

And all of a sudden, looking at him, I had one. Granted, I was operating on little sleep, too much adrenaline, and next to coma-levels of caffeine imbalance, but it *sounded* good. I bit my lip, running it over in my head, and made a *hold on* gesture to David as I beckoned Lewis toward a convenient corner of the room.

'What is it?' he asked. He sounded just as stressed as I felt.

'I think I know what will bring them out in the open. We need to get the Sentinels to come after us again, not the other way around. If we allow them to choose the ground—'

'Yeah, I get it. The Djinn don't even know how much of a disadvantage they have.' Lewis leant closer. 'It's crazy, isn't it? Your idea?'

'Pretty damn crazy.'

'Tell.'

I did. *Crazy* didn't really exactly cover it, as I listened to the words tumble out of my mouth. *Insane,* that was closer. Also, *stupidly suicidal,* but that was par for the course with me. At least it would be consistent.

Lewis stared at me as if he couldn't quite believe what I'd said, and in truth, I wasn't sure if I was believing it, either. Then he said, slowly, 'It could work. It allows us to assemble all the Wardens in one place, choose the ground, protect the Djinn, offer the Sentinels a target they can't afford to pass up . . .'

Oh God, it actually *was* a good plan. Damn. I'd been half hoping he'd shoot it out of the air. Instead, it looked as if I was going to have to kick my shopping into high gear.

'Right,' I said, and turned to David. 'How do you feel about getting married tomorrow?'

I had no idea Djinn could look so blank. Venna turned to David and said, with the perfect blend of alarm and puzzlement, 'Are you sure she isn't insane?'

David continued with the blank look for a few more seconds, and then the light dawned warm in his eyes, and he slowly smiled.

'Actually,' he said, 'I'm fairly certain she is, and that is exactly why I'm marrying her.'

Chapter Thirteen

Chapter Thirteen

One nice thing about having the Djinn Conduit on your side was receiving no arguments from the rank and file – no arguments of any substance, anyway. The other Djinn still thought we were crazy, but generally decided that was our personal business.

What they weren't so wild about was the idea that we weren't going to charge off to Rahel's rescue, but I knew they weren't tactically inept; they knew if we played the game the Sentinels had set in motion, we would all pay the price.

I also knew how hard it was going to be for them to stand by and sacrifice Rahel for a tactical point. I was hoping it wouldn't come to that. I knew David, and I knew that making those choices was just as impossibly hard for him as it was for me.

Part of what we planned was, again, complete

insanity. Lewis carried out the first part of it at four o'clock, on the steps of the Miami FBI field office.

We called a press conference. To say it was well attended would be to say that the hottest club in LA had a bit of a wait to get in. I'd expected to draw attention, but as we walked through the lobby with a flying escort of FBI agents, Homeland Security, and anxiously hovering, nameless other governmental representatives, I could hear the roar of the crowd outside.

One of the no-name governmental types, nattily turned out in a nicely tailored suit and a two-hundred-dollar haircut, pushed in front of us and physically threw himself against the glass doors leading out, facing us down. 'Wait!' he blurted. The parade trickled to a halt, and Lewis and I glanced at each other. We'd had bets on how long it would take for the cold feet to manifest. I was about to make a cool twenty bucks. Sweet. 'Are you sure about this? You're sure there's no other way? The chaos – the fear—'

'Let me put it this way,' Lewis said. 'You had half the news media covering the meltdown out at the motel earlier today, and every phone line to every possible agency has been jammed ever since, demanding an explanation. Do you want to try to coordinate some big lie that won't get found out, at this point? Because I'd be happy to put your name forward as the guy in charge.'

No-Name Nice Suit Guy swallowed and lowered his arms. He straightened his lapels with an unconscious gesture and stepped out of the way.

'Damn,' Lewis said. 'Kind of hoped he'd go for it, actually.'

Fat chance. This wasn't a hot potato; it was the entire state of Idaho, fresh out of the microwave.

'Here goes,' Lewis said, and opened the door.

The noise washed over us in a wave, and we walked out into a whiteout of flashbulbs and video spotlights. It was like hitting a psychic wall, and if I'd been on my own, I'd have caved fast and hard. *God.* I couldn't focus on anything; the crowd was a faceless mass of shouting faces, all blurring into a snarling, hostile entity. I transferred my probably shell-shocked stare to the buildings on the far side of the street. Somebody was in an office, backlit, looking out at us. Nice to have that kind of distance.

The FBI special agent in charge stepped up to the bank of hastily taped-together microphones and made some brief remarks, nothing incriminating for the agency, and introduced Lewis by name, adding that he was with 'a special branch of the United Nations known as the Wardens.' That was it. He got out of the way, ignoring the shouted avalanche of questions.

Lewis took a deep breath and stepped up. He was tall, imposing, and had the kind of personal aura that made people take notice, when he deigned to use it.

He used it now. I saw ripples of quiet move through the crowd, and reporters lean forward to catch every word he had to say.

'Earlier today some of you witnessed a battle between two opposing sides in a conflict,' he said. 'As you reported, there were casualties on both sides. I'm here to explain to you what that conflict is, what it's about, and how you can help.'

I expected a torrent of questions, but the crowd stayed still in the pause. Maybe they were stunned that they were actually going to be given information. Or maybe Lewis had sneakily exerted some Earth Warden influence on them. I used some myself, *on* myself, to slow my racing pulse and get myself ready for the inevitable.

'The Wardens are part of the United Nations,' Lewis said, 'in the sense that we are a worldwide organisation, independent of governments but working in cooperation with them whenever possible. There is a world around you, a world you see every day without knowing the truth behind it. At its most basic level, the forces at work in the universe, or at least on this planet, are real and tangible.' He paused again and took the leap. 'We are the ones who help control and shape that world. Without the Wardens, the disasters you report on, the floods and hurricanes, forest fires and earthquakes – all these things would be far, far worse.'

Somebody laughed. A few others took it up, and it grew in a ripple through the crowd. 'You're kidding. This is what you have to tell us?' somebody shouted from beneath the glare of a video spotlight. 'Where's Gandalf?'

That was pretty much my cue, although I would have preferred Galadriel. I stepped forward. The FBI had furnished me with a change of wardrobe – not my normal style, but workable. It included a navy blue pencil skirt, a severely cut jacket, a white shirt and serviceable granny pumps. I'd put my hair up in a bun, to complete the image of competence and authority, sexy schoolteacher style.

I pointed up at the sky, which was full of lightly scudding altocumulus clouds – nothing out of the ordinary for Miami.

Lewis waited, patient as a stone, giving them absolutely no indication what was going to happen. We'd agreed that it needed to be big, spectacular, and easily captured on videotape.

I slowed the progress of the clouds and began packing energy into the system, careful to balance the forces as I went. I knew the Ma'at were standing by in case I screwed it up, but it was a point of pride not to need them to clean up after me. The shape of the clouds began to change, from sheer and wispy to solid white, then gray as the moisture condensed. Altocumulus.

Then nimbocumulus.

Once I had the system packed as full as I dared, while still remaining in control, I opened both my hands, palms up. I could feel the dawning sentience in the clouds above, as the energy accumulation granted it some very basic level of awareness, of hunger. Of *anger.*

What I was about to do was dangerous, and not just to me. If I got it wrong, there could be a lot of collateral damage.

Easy, I heard David whisper on the aetheric. *I'm here.*

I called the lightning.

Florida is the lightning capital of the US. With the daily, constant interaction of wind, water, sandy soil, and marshland, every reporter in the crowd had probably seen close lightning strikes.

None of them had ever seen *this.*

The bolt streaked down out of the clouds, long and purple, crackling with energy, and broke into two jagged prongs. It hit my outstretched palms exactly on target, and for a long, long second, I kept it there as the video cameras and photographers documented the event.

Then I clapped my palms together, and the lightning vanished. Thunder rolled loud enough to rattle windows, but there was no other visible damage, apart from a slight reddening on my skin. I'd deliberately kept the lightning to the bare minimum voltage necessary to stage a visible demonstration – about forty kiloamperes.

But *damn*, it ached inside me. I kept my smile in place with an effort, and hoped I wasn't sweating too much under the lights.

Lewis said, in the same dry, calm tone, 'This is Joanne Baldwin. She is a Weather Warden. The demonstration you've just seen is one of several we'll conduct for you over the next few days. The rest will be under controlled conditions, and you can provide your own scientific experts if you'd care to do so, to document and question the experiments. But ultimately, you're going to find that what we're telling you is the real thing. We can control the weather. We can control the land. We can control fire. The problem is, all these things *fight back*.'

Nobody seemed to know what kind of questions to ask, exactly. Already, they were scrambling to find a logical explanation for what they'd seen – some kind of magic trick would be the most likely one they'd land on. I was sure whoever was the most outrageous street magician *du jour* would be calling in to debunk what I'd already done.

But what gave it weight was the silent presence of the FBI behind me, and the fact that we were standing on the steps of a government building.

Eventually, somebody found a question that made enough sense to voice. 'How do you control the

RACHEL CAINE

weather? Is it some kind of machine, or . . . ?' He sounded as if he couldn't quite believe he was even asking the question. I understood that, too. An entire street full of very logical people had just been tipped over the edge of a cliff, and were still trying to figure out which way was up.

'That's the other part of the story,' Lewis said. 'The simple answer is magic. The more complicated answer is that the world around you is not how you imagine it to be – it's deeper and stranger than you know. For many thousands of years, the Wardens have guarded humanity, and we've done it in silence, in secret. But it's time to come out in the open, because now we have a very serious threat to deal with.'

'What kind of threat? Does this have anything to do with what happened at the motel?'

I wondered if the question was a plant. Lewis wasn't exactly above that kind of thing, bless his soul. He wasn't particularly worried about our impartial image.

'Let me tell you,' Lewis said, 'about the Djinn, and the Sentinels.'

David and his strike team misted into view at the bottom of the steps, right in front of the cameras.

All hell broke loose.

We'd intended to grab the world stage, and we did. The feverish speculation occupied every news channel, every broadcast on the local level. Experts talked about a massive hoax; scientists sneered; magicians explained how all we'd shown on television could have been done by mirrors and illusion.

But it didn't matter. We'd taken the Sentinels by surprise. They'd expected us to hide, and we weren't hiding. Instead, we'd thrown their name into the public awareness, and we'd given them the one thing I knew they didn't want: notoriety.

I was the lucky one. Exhausted by the efforts of the day, not to mention the lightning strike and the management of the storm I'd leveled over Miami, I collapsed on a cot and slept for six hours of blissfully ignorant darkness. Lewis didn't sleep at all. When I woke up, he'd already issued three more press statements, and a whole packet of information about Bad Bob, including his photograph.

The Sentinels could *not* be happy about that. They were even less happy, I imagined, over the announcement that David and I planned to celebrate our marriage in public, in front of all the cameras we could gather to document the affair. It was a trap, a perfectly obvious one, and one I didn't think they dared pass up. The Sentinels had gathered membership on the idea that the Djinn were toxic to us; they couldn't allow the two of us to make such a public commitment without striking. Hell, they'd already ruined two wedding dresses.

Pulling together a last-minute affair is surprisingly easier than planning something more formal. Once I gave up the idea of catering and open bar and invitations, things simplified dramatically. All I really needed was a minister, a dress, and of course, as much security as possible so that we all survived the happy day.

My cell phone was ringing off the hook. Mostly, it was Wardens who hadn't been given the heads-up about going public, and were blistering my ears off. One or two said they were going to complain to Paul, which stabbed me deep and hard all over again. Paul had been a part of my life for so, so long, and now . . . now all that was tainted. I couldn't even begin to imagine how much it would hurt, when I had time to actually feel again.

One of the few welcome calls was from Cherise, who had checked herself out of Warden witness protection and was boarding a flight for Miami, 'because you're *so* not getting married without me, bitch. Where else am I going to wear that dress?'

One major side benefit of becoming instantly famous – or infamous – was that I no longer had to shop. Instead, I was under siege from local bridal stores all trying to throw dresses my way, under the theory that a little discreet promotion never hurt anybody. I never thought I'd have a *sponsored by* wedding, but I had more to worry about than my ethical standards.

Principally, I had to find a dress in my size in less than twelve hours that didn't suck.

That, it turned out, was far easier than it seemed. Instant organisation . . . just add Cherise.

'I booked the Palms,' Cherise said after bursting into the FBI offices, giving me a fast, fierce hug, and giving Lewis a warm peck on the cheek.

'You – wait, what?' I blinked, and so did he. I was barely out of the coffee-zombie stage, and Lewis was well into his must-have-sleep cycle. 'When did you get in?'

'Exactly forty-eight minutes ago,' she said. 'Gotta love that executive car service. By the way, I charged it to the Warden card, so don't go all budget-conscious on me. Talking to *you*, Lewis.' He blinked, again. Cherise must have had extra coffee on the plane; it was like being hit by a pink hurricane. 'So, I made some calls,' she continued. 'You didn't get a hotel, right? I booked the Palms. Royal Palm Room for the reception, outdoor gazebo for the ceremony. They're used to celebrity weddings, no problem on the security, although I went ahead and called a couple of other firms. I guess you'll have the FBI, too, huh?' Cherise paused long enough to wink at Mr No-Name Nice Suit, who still looked fresh and well tailored. 'Mmmm, I feel safer already.'

'Cher—'

'OK, I'm going to let the Palms handle all the catering and flowers and crap – it's going to be expensive, but there you go. If you want to make a media circus out of the whole thing, you have to pay for the big top and the clowns.'

'Cherise.'

'I think we should head over there now. I got you the bridal suite, naturally. Five of the couture bridal shops are coming in an hour with their best stuff. They'll want credit on the official press statement, but they're doing it for the publicity. No charge. They'll want the dress back, though, unless you get blood or something all over it, in which case, you break it, you buy it—'

'Cherise!'

She stopped, blue eyes wide, staring at me. I covered my face with both hands, fighting for control between hysterical giggles and the shakes.

'It's not a joke,' I said finally. 'We could all be killed. We could get a lot of other people killed. I can't have this at the Palms. The Sentinels *will* attack. I can't put all those innocent lives at risk!'

Cher sat down next to me on the hard, narrow cot, and took both my hands in hers. Her manicure was fresh, her hair glossy, her makeup perfect. I looked like I'd rolled out of the bad side of Satan's bed, and forgotten to brush my hair, but there was real love in her eyes. Real friendship.

'Honey,' she said, 'this isn't about you anymore. This is about ideas. Those innocent people, they live with risk. You need to quit thinking that all us regular folks can't handle the truth.'

I didn't think she understood what she was saying, but I gave her a cautious nod.

'You want to stick it to those bastards who think David and all the other Djinn need to die, right?'

Another wordless nod.

'When you hide, when you call things off because you're afraid of getting hurt, that's when people like this win. Live loud, Jo. It's the only way to win. No fear.'

She tucked a stray lock of hair behind my ear and cocked her head.

'Besides,' she said, 'I cannot *wait* to see David in a tuxedo. My God, Jo. How can you even think of depriving the world of that?'

Well, she had a point. Across the room, David was deep in conversation with Zenaya. He caught my look and smiled, and I felt the connection between us snap taut and thrum like a guitar string.

'Suck it up, girlfriend,' Cher said. 'All you have to do is stand there, look pretty, and say the right things. Let us do the rest. You,' – she turned and stabbed a perfectly polished fingernail toward Lewis – 'you need to get some sleep. Best man, right? I am *so* not having the bags under the eyes. Lie down, *now*. And I'm bringing in a stylist, because *God.*'

I moved off the cot, fast, to make room for Lewis.

* * *

Cherise set to work. It helped that Lewis granted her autonomy for all wedding-related decisions, including open credit, and that the Feds, who didn't know the players in the Warden world, anyway, just assumed she was 'one of us.' Which I guess she was, in the greater sense. She cheerfully commandeered everything and everyone she needed, and appointed a subcommittee – my wedding had *subcommittees*! – to handle security services.

An hour later, I was in a smoked-glass limo – not a stretch, but one of the anonymous, though perfectly well-appointed Town Car varieties – clutching a bottle of mineral water and watching chaos on the tiny built-in television screen in the back of the seat. CNN was running Talking Head Theater; the Wardens were staging additional demonstrations, including Fire and Earth, and people were starting to actually pay attention. I wondered if anybody had considered the legal implications. Talk about malpractice insurance . . .

'Paul's dead,' I said, out of absolutely nowhere. I turned the cold glass bottle in my hands, remembering that moment so vividly it hurt, that moment when Paul turned to face me, guilt and anger in his face. 'I killed him, Cher. He got in my way, and I killed him.'

Nobody had told her. I watched a tremor run through her, and she bowed her head for a second. When she raised it, her eyes were clear and bright. 'I knew he was the walking wounded,' she said. 'You didn't see him like I did, when he thought nobody was watching. He was scared all the time. And angry. And he never really stopped hurting. He shouldn't have been in charge. All those people dead under his watch – he couldn't take it, Jo. It wasn't his fault, and it's not yours, either.'

It definitely was my fault that I'd killed him, but I didn't argue the point. I was going to have the rest of my life to reconcile myself with that, although I wasn't sure how much time that would be – maybe no more than a couple of hours, in which case I'd be one of those tragic tales for the ages, slain by the bad guys at the altar and taking a couple hundred innocent lives with me because I was arrogant enough to think my life was somehow so important, such a beacon for change . . .

No, Cher was right. Hiding was wrong. Reacting the way the Sentinels wanted us to was wrong.

This might be wrong, but at least it was wrong in the right direction. Somebody had to be the symbol. I was just filling the dress.

I looked in the rearview mirror. We were being followed by black chase cars, probably federal or private security. There was a helicopter overhead, sleek and military looking, that kept the chubbier news choppers at bay by its mere presence. I couldn't see the paparazzi, but I knew they were out there. Waiting.

'Hey,' Cher said. 'You with me?'

'I'm getting married,' I said. 'Jesus Christ, Cher, I'm getting married to a *Djinn*. What the hell am I thinking?'

She smiled. 'Oh, good. You're with me.'

The Palms was a blur: smiling faces, people saying kind things, Cherise running interference. She ensconced me in a penthouse the size of most houses, with a breathtaking ocean view, and I sat numbly on the couch, worrying. I know, most brides worry, but I had considerably more to worry about than whether or not I was going to trip over the hem of the dress I didn't yet have.

I was worried about Rahel, first and foremost. I'd been trying hard not to think about her. I knew that David was focused on her; how could he not be? She was a friend. She was in trouble. And I felt as though I was horribly betraying her, even though I knew that tactically, we were doing the right thing.

He'll hurt her, part of me said. *He knows we'll come if he hurts her.*

It was kind of odd, actually, that he hadn't done it yet. *What if he has? What if David is hiding it from you?* That wouldn't be too hard for him to do, because I hadn't seen him since before we'd left the FBI building. *No. He'd tell you.* Unless he thought I couldn't handle the pressure.

Or unless he tore off to do something crazy, which was entirely possible.

'Hey!' Cherise snapped her fingers in front of my face. 'Fashion show. Here. Have some coffee. Nod when you see something you like.'

Thus began the most surreal experience of my life, and with my life, that's saying something. How she'd done it I have no idea, but apparently my current CNN celebrity status had upgraded me to the temporary level of an A-list star. The bridal shops hadn't just sent dresses; they'd sent *teams,* with models who were fresh off Paris runways, apparently, far prettier and sleeker than I'd ever be. I felt dull and slightly nuts, even with the freshly brewed coffee sipped from a delicate china cup. The dresses ranged from something Cinderella would find too ruffly to something better suited to the wedding night than the glare of the spotlight. I mean, I'm daring, but I'm not *that* daring.

In the middle of the parade, a model who bore a striking resemblance to Heidi Klum (couldn't really *be* Heidi Klum, could she?) entered, and for a second, I just stared, shocked. I shot Cherise a look; her mouth was curved in a triumphant smile. She'd requested that one specially, I could immediately see that.

And she was right. It was *The* Dress. The one that I'd bought, the one that had been ripped apart in the Sentinels' last public attack on me.

Maybe-Heidi-Klum swept to a graceful stop in

front of me, and the silk fluttered to perfect layers, slightly angled and draping to that gorgeous, dramatic train in the back. When she turned, the corseted back displayed the deep V of skin that had so entranced me the first time. Sexy, yet demure. Sophisticated, yet still startlingly innocent. Hopeful.

'Yes,' I said. Bridal Shop Team Number Three – I'd forgotten the names; Cherise had been keeping track – high-fived one another. Maybe-Klum gave me a cool smile and rustled out, back straight, chin high. If I could look half that good in the thing . . .

Well, that took care of the dress.

Cherise did all the work, reassuring the runners-up that we still liked them and would mention them fondly. She signed a just-in-case-of-damage credit card slip, discreetly proffered by the winning team, and slipped the copy into a black leather binder.

'How much?' I asked. She shook her head sadly.

'Really, you don't want to be asking that today,' she said. 'Just go with it. Besides, we can return it unless, you know. Now. You go take a shower. We've got the stylist coming in forty-five minutes.'

Stylists made house calls. I was learning a lot today.

I cried in the shower, where it didn't show. I cried about all the doubt, all the craziness. Cherise was doing a good job of keeping me moving, but this was like standing on the train tracks, watching the Heartbreak

Express rocket toward you. I was in the crosshairs, and I'd given up my safety to other people. Worse, I'd given up Rahel's life to the gods of chance and fate.

I arrived on time for the stylist, who was a temperamental, gorgeous young woman with not one but *two* assistants, one of whom took charge of my nails while the others waded into the misery that was my hair. I closed my eyes and focused on the weather, moving in slow, peaceful waves outside the thick window. The aetheric was almost artificially calm; the Wardens were keeping their heads down, and the Ma'at had done a fantastic job of smoothing out the ups and downs of the day.

Whatever problems came about, they wouldn't be rain-related.

I'll skip the rest of the rituals. By four o'clock, I was laced into the dress, staring at myself in the floor-length mirror of the Palms penthouse, balanced on shoes rushed to us from one of the most exclusive boutiques.

I was seeing a stranger. My hair was up, piled in loose, sexy, complicated layers, secured with diamond pins and a veil as soft as fog. My face was my own, only perfected with expert cosmetics. The dress was, as I'd thought, exactly right.

My eyes were the only things that gave the lie to the whole illusion. They were wide, dark blue, starkly terrified.

Cherise squeezed my hand and stood next to me, sharing mirror time. She looked absolutely, deliciously adorable. 'You should see Lewis,' she said. 'That man was born for formal wear. I'd totally be all over him, except he's way too tall. I have a fear of heights.'

'Thank you,' I said.

'For complimenting Lewis? Trust me, that's a freebie.'

'No, for – for all this. For keeping me sane. I couldn't—' My hands were shaking again. I closed my eyes and concentrated on calm. 'Whatever happens, thank you. I couldn't ask for a better friend. I love you.'

'Love you too, sweetie, but I'm not marrying you.' Cherise cocked a perfect eyebrow. 'You notice I didn't mention what David looked like.'

No, she hadn't. That wasn't exactly like her.

'You'll see,' she said smugly.

There was a discreet knock on the door, and one of the incredibly intimidating security gentlemen stuck his head in to nod at Cherise.

Time to go.

'I don't think we should do this,' I said.

But I let her lead me out, anyway.

I was taken through deserted hallways, feeling more and more isolated and surreal with every moment. Was this how most brides felt, or only those with

targets painted on their chests? Hard to say. I just
tried to swallow the growing, acrid lump of dread
in my throat, and followed the confident shimmy of
Cherise's stride.

Holding open doors, hotel staff smiled at me as I
passed. I had no idea where we were going, so it was a
surprise when the last set of doors opened on blinding
sunlight. The strains of a highly accomplished string
quartet – good enough to overcome the barrier of surf
noise, conversation, and humidity's effect on wood
and strings – hung luminously in the air. It was an
absolutely perfect day. The sky was a breathtaking
ceramic blue, washed clean of all imperfections.

I felt so much dread that I was afraid my knees
would collapse underneath me. *They'll hit us. They
can't* not *hit us.* And there were so many people to
protect. So many people I couldn't swear wouldn't be
hurt in this.

Cherise squeezed my hand one last time and said,
'Stay fierce, Jo. We'll get through this.' And then she
moved through the rose-covered archway, taking the
arm of a tall, elegant man who I only after the fact
realised was Lewis. A drastically different Lewis.
Smoking hot, in fact. She was right: he was made for
formal wear. The severe black-and-white tailoring
made him look extraordinary.

I fidgeted slightly, clutching the small, perfect
bouquet of ivory roses that Cherise had handed me,

and the security men on either side of me scanned the perimeters for any threats. I spotted Wardens, Wardens everywhere, waiting. If the Sentinels were coming, they were coming into the teeth of the buzz saw.

If the Wardens watching me aren't undercover Sentinels . . . I had to leave that terrifying thought behind. It was too much.

I knew mere security wouldn't stop Bad Bob, or the thing that was wearing his face. The bigger the clash, the bigger the boom; he'd love to smash us here, in this most public of settings.

The string quartet shifted into the traditional bridal march, and the security man offered me his arm. He looked good in a tux, too. A little beefy, but you really wanted that in a quality bodyguard.

We passed under the arch and began the long, long walk down the rose-petal-strewn path to the graceful, arched gazebo.

For some reason, I hadn't thought about who'd be here. Mostly Wardens, of course, mostly friends. Cherise had even managed to get some of our old TV station colleagues here at the last minute, including some of the crew, who were looking highly uncomfortable in their suits and jackets, but were beaming at me in universal accord.

In the front row was my sister. Sarah looked elegant, perfectly coiffed, and terribly pissed off. She was glaring hard at Cherise, and if looks could kill, there would have been a warrant out for her arrest. In fact, now that I thought about it, I was a little surprised there *wasn't* a warrant out for Sarah. She'd scammed a lot of money, and if her old boyfriend (psycho but strangely honest) was to be believed, she'd been one step short of Master Criminal status. I hadn't planned on inviting her, but in retrospect, I guess I shouldn't have been surprised that she'd shown up anyway. If there was any chance of notoriety coming from the day, she'd be right in front to tell her story to the cameras about growing up with the Freak.

I forgot all about that momentary stab of distraction, because Lewis moved aside, and David turned to look at me, and the world just . . . stopped.

I knew why Cherise hadn't said anything about how David looked. There simply weren't words in the human language to describe his vividness, his presence, his – his *beauty*. He was wearing a tuxedo, very much like the one Lewis was modeling so effectively, but no matter how flattering the clothes, it was David, and David's essence, that blazed forth in that moment.

I saw it clearly: all his love, all his hope, all his commitment. He was immortal, and this was no act for him, no temporary amusement. I'd been told Djinn loved intensely, but in that single, crystalline moment, I *knew*.

It felt like a dream. I extended my hand – no longer trembling – and his fingers closed around it, drawing me to his side. I felt the aura fold around me, warmer than sunlight, and the euphoria was like nothing I had ever felt.

Somewhere, the minister was speaking. I had no idea what kind of service Cherise had cobbled together on the spur of the moment, and I didn't care; the words didn't matter. I understood why David had asked this of me now; I understood so much more than I'd ever thought I would. It wasn't just words.

It was a *vow*. And vows among the Djinn were law, immutable as physics. I could feel the forces gathering, as the words progressed; I could see the shimmer spreading through the aetheric.

The minister had gotten to the heart of the matter. 'Do you, David, take this woman as your only true lover, now and for her lifetime, forsaking all others, in sickness and in health, in wealth and in poverty, in hardship and in joy?'

I saw the aetheric flare hot gold, so much power gathering, more than I'd ever seen, and David opened his mouth to reply . . .

'No,' said a new voice, before he could reply. 'He doesn't.'

Ashan had crashed our wedding.

Chapter Fourteen

The power on the aetheric went wild, currents flowing around us like whirlpools, lashing and foaming in distress. David and I turned together and saw Ashan standing behind us. From the forbidding expression on his face, I was guessing he hadn't brought us any wedding gifts, or at least none that wouldn't explode.

'I can't allow this folly,' Ashan said. 'Maybe you truly believe this is right, but we can't take the chance. You expose us all to slavery, David, not just yourself. No.'

The minister looked justifiably bewildered, and not just by the sudden popping in of supernatural guests. I was thinking his brain had skipped right over that part. The human race was absolutely stellar at plausible deniability. 'But I haven't asked for any objections,' he said faintly. 'We don't do that anymore. Really, this is most—'

Ashan ignored him. Ignored me, too. He was focused only on David, and if David was a glorious bright star, burning with potential, Ashan was his polar opposite: leached of color; pale as an undertaker; grim as impending death. He was even wearing black – a severe suit, with a black tie paired with a white shirt. His idea of formal attire, I guessed. It might have even passed, if it hadn't been for the bitter expression and the cold, cold fire in his teal-blue eyes.

'You have no place here,' David said. I felt the power of the Earth rising up in him, rich and thick and irresistible; Ashan was a Conduit, yes, but this was David's territory, David's home ground, in a sense. Ashan was an intruder, uninvited and unwelcome. 'Leave us.'

Ashan slowly shook his head. 'I don't come for myself,' he said. 'I come for all of us, to *ask*. Don't do this, David. Don't destroy us again, for your personal satisfaction.'

I'd expected assault, not a plea, and especially not a plea that had the ring of sincerity to it.

David didn't respond. He gazed at Ashan, fire in his eyes, but he didn't lash out.

Ashan said, even more quietly, 'I also didn't come alone.' He didn't move, not even his gaze, but I felt the shocking flare on the aetheric, and suddenly there was a *presence* beside him. It was human in shape, but not human at all – a wild power, barely contained by flesh. His skin was hot red, shifting with patterns of color, and his eyes were the pure white of the hottest flame. I'd never seen him take human form before, but I knew him.

The Fire Oracle had left his protected home in a crypt in Seacasket. I hadn't even known he *could*.

With a whisper, rather than a flare, another presence shaped itself out of the air on Ashan's other side. Milk-glass skin, a vessel containing fog and ice. The Air Oracle was only barely human as well, and androgynous in form. *Two of them*. The Air Oracle had no fixed abode that I knew of, but still, it took a major event for it to manifest so publicly.

I knew, without even asking, that it had never happened before. Not in all the history of the Djinn.

Another surge of power, this one familiar, so bitterly and sweetly familiar. My daughter, Imara – human and far more than human, beautiful and unreachable and remote. She looked sad, but sure of herself – a mirror of my face and form, but with a totally individual core she'd inherited from both me and her father.

She was standing with the others, against us.

David closed his eyes, and I knew it hurt him as much as it did me. When he opened them, his eyes had gone dark, almost human. 'You're sure,' he said. 'Imara?'

I thought for a few heartbeats that she might defect, might throw her support to us, but then she bowed her head. 'I'm sure,' she whispered. 'Too dangerous. So much at risk. You can't, Dad. You just . . . can't.'

Silence. The audience was whispering. I couldn't imagine what they were making out of this. Lewis had moved Cherise out of the line of fire, in case there was going to be any, but somehow I knew this wasn't going to come to fireworks. Not this time.

David slowly turned back to me and said, very simply, 'I do.'

My mind went blank for a second, and I felt the seductive flow of power wash over me. *Half done.* This was an exchange of vows; his was powerful, but not complete without my consent. The minister nervously cleared his throat, eyes darting from David, to me, to Ashan, to the three Oracles.

'Do you, Joanne—' His clerical voice was about half an octave higher than it ought to have been. He cleared his throat and tried again. 'Do you, Joanne, take this man—'

'Wait,' I said.

All of the Djinn – even Ashan – let out a sigh, and David's grip on my hand tightened painfully. His eyes went wide, and his skin bone-pale. 'Jo—'

'Just wait,' I repeated. 'Ashan, the Oracles – you admitted yourself that you don't know what will

happen, David. How can we do this? How can we change the rules like this when we don't even know what's coming for us?' My voice broke. My *heart* broke. I was watching the fire die in him, and it hurt. 'It isn't about us. It's about *them,* all of the people who depend on us!'

'I'm willing to take the risk,' he whispered. 'Believe in us, Jo. Please. *Believe.*'

His hand came up to trace my cheek, and I felt tears well up in my eyes and burn trails down my cheeks. His fingertips came away wet from my face, and he raised them to his lips.

Please.

I might have changed my mind. I can't swear that I would have, or I wouldn't; the fracture between my head and my heart ran right down to my soul.

I didn't have time to find out.

The aetheric caught fire. At first I thought it was David, erupting in frustration and anger at me for what I'd done, but then I realised it wasn't him at all.

We were under attack.

David spun away from me. So did the other Djinn, all facing outward, blindly seeking the threat. 'You know what to do,' David shouted to Ashan. 'Protect the Oracles!'

A silver scar formed on David's right cheek, then darkened, and the infection I'd seen earlier at Ortega's house began to spread its tendrils again under his skin, moving frighteningly fast.

'David!' I grabbed for him, but he spun away, avoiding me. Doing his job. Dispatching his waiting Djinn according to some plan he hadn't shared with me . . . Lewis was moving, too, shouting at the Wardens. *Everybody* had a plan, it seemed, except for me.

I felt the black wave sweep over me. It wasn't meant for me; it was centered on David, but even the edges of it made me feel faint and sick.

He collapsed against me, shuddering, and I felt a scream trying to rip loose from him. I was the only thing holding him up, the only defense he had left.

The Oracles vanished, leaving gusts of hot wind in their place that fluttered the pale layers of my gown. David's weight pulled me down. It seemed as though he was growing heavier with every passing second.

Ashan stood there, immobile, impassive, *perfect*.

'Help!' I screamed at him, and grabbed his hand. It felt like cold marble. 'Damn you, *he's your brother*. Do something!' The two of them were the same, united by purpose and power, if not by the ties of blood that humans understood.

Ashan pulled free of my grip. 'If you want him,' he said, 'save him. He won't save himself. He could, if he wished.'

I couldn't hold David up. Lewis lunged forward and tried to help take his weight, but there was something strange happening here, something worse than anything I'd expected.

'God,' Lewis muttered. 'Hold on, we're trying to put up the shield. Hold on—'

The Sentinels attacked from all around us, on every front. I heard some physical confrontations, and saw a bloom of fire erupt somewhere off to the side, followed by shouts and screams. Security piled on top of me and began hustling me away; I gathered up my train with both hands, clutching it out of the way of traffic. Lewis had arranged our forces in teams, but even so, the assault was shocking in its suddenness and force. I grabbed Lewis's arm as he pushed past and shook it fiercely. 'They're using Rahel to get to him! If you're going to counter, it has to be *now. Right* now! *Go!*'

'Already on it,' Lewis snapped, and spun away. 'Stay here. Draw them if you can.'

David was down on the ground, surrounded by fierce-eyed Djinn protectors ready to fight anything that came for him, but they let me through. I sank down at his side in a flutter of silk and held him. He was gasping and trembling, eyes molten gold but with ominous sparks of darkness flying through them. The gray mottling on his face was taking on a shocking life of its own, moving dark tendrils beneath his skin. Seeking out the aetheric pipeline that made David the Conduit. Once it had that . . .

'Let her go!' I shouted, and grabbed him by the lapels. 'David, you have to let Rahel go, please!'

He shook his head. His hand grabbed for mine and clenched tightly. 'Say it,' he said. His voice was raw in his throat, almost primal. 'Say the words. *Say it*!'

I felt tears trembling in my eyes. The whole world was coming apart. I heard the crack of gunfire somewhere off to the side, and more screaming. Someone was shouting about a Warden down; someone else was warning of a Sentinel attack coming in the form of a tidal wave from the ocean.

This couldn't be right. It couldn't be.

I squeezed my eyes shut, felt the tears burn down my cheeks, and whispered, 'Oh God help me, I do. I do.'

There was an eerie second of utter silence, not even the wind moving. Conflicts stopped, pinned on the instant, and I felt something inside me shifting, aligning like a puzzle box.

And a wave of pure golden power flowed into me, through me, and out.

I opened my eyes and saw David watching my face with a look I could think of only as awed relief. The gray faded from his face, back to a silvery scar. Gone.

And I felt the echoing power between us build, and build, and build, waves on the beach, pounding and ceaseless, cascading out into the other Djinn, enhancing their raw power and refining it into surgical weapons.

I'd just made the New Djinn a quantum leap more powerful, by giving them a second anchor into the aetheric.

I'd also just gotten married, even if the minister hadn't quite gotten around to saying the words before he'd fled to the hills, along with most of the others.

The Djinn snapped a glowing shield of power over us, brilliant as shimmering gold. It covered not just the two of us, but all of the Palms – hell, it went so far out that it might have been covering all of Florida. Whatever the Sentinels were doing, they quit doing it, fast, rightly recognising that they had just been dealt a very serious blow. It would take them time to figure out exactly what had happened.

'Did you know?' I felt giddy, halfway to heaven. Endorphins kicking in. 'Did you plan that?'

David grabbed me and kissed me, long and hard, with a good deal less restraint than most bridegrooms would have shown under similar circumstances. His hands roamed, stroking down the silk, crushing it to my hips, his fingertips brushing over the skin left exposed by the open V of the corset at my back.

'Absolutely,' he said, deadpan, when he pulled back.

'You had no idea.'

'I knew.'

'You liar. You *guessed*!'

He laughed and buried his face against my neck, picked me up, and whirled me around in the deserted gazebo. A storm wind lashed surf against the rocks, and a wild cascade of lightning slashed out of the sky and grounded spectacularly out at sea. It was the joy of the Djinn, made real.

David sobered, but the light stayed in him, burning fiercely. He kissed me again, this time more gently, with a promise of things to come, and I felt the curling smile on his lips. 'I need to go,' he said. 'Things to do.'

'Same here,' I said. 'They'll be looking for an explanation of what just happened.'

He stepped back, and his gaze raked me from head to toe, ravenous and warm. 'Don't change,' he said. 'I'll be back. I want to take that off you.'

I shivered, nodded, and watched my lover – no, I supposed I was going to have to get used to the idea of *husband* – mist away on the hot, humid breeze.

I couldn't see any other Djinn, but there were plenty of hired security, all looking grim and efficient as they herded guests to cover. I had a whole contingent of them stationed near me, all facing outward. I reached up and tapped the nearest one on the shoulder. 'Hey!'

'Ma'am?' He angled in my direction a huge ear that looked as though it had been badly mangled in some

kind of sculpting accident, but didn't turn to face me.
'You ready to go?'

'Guess so. Looks like the wedding's over!'

He snorted. 'Right. Let's get you to the safe zone!'

'Sure,' I said. I felt giddy. Almost invincible, actually,
but even if bullets might bounce off me, I was pretty
sure they wouldn't do the dress any good. Priorities.
'Hey, didn't you notice all the cool stuff going on?
Supernatural stuff all over the place?'

'Lady,' he said wearily, 'I've guarded the Rolling
Stones. Trust me, you guys are amateurs.'

When the phalanx of guards closed in around me,
it was like being in a moving tank of body armor; I
clutched the train of my dress well out of reach of
their boots, and hustled along down the path, up the
steps, and into the narrow hallways I'd come through
before. No staff were smiling at me this time; they
were probably busy totting up the damage charges. I
hoped David's black AmEx was up to the job.

My security detail arrowed me straight past Lewis
and a group of Wardens all huddled together; I tried
to bail out to talk to them, but clearly that wasn't in
the plans. No matter how loud I yelled, we continued
moving straight for the elevators. The guards broke
up there, facing outward in an arc while the guy in
charge – Mr Squishy Ear – took my elbow in one
massive, scarred hand and escorted me firmly across
the threshold and into one of the lifts. He punched in

a key card, and away we went, just the two of us.

'Where's Cherise? My maid of honor?' I asked.

'Cute little thing? 'Bout this high?' He marked off a height just above the waistband of his ripstop pants. 'Blond?'

'That's the one.'

'Yeah, she's already upstairs. We got her out ASAP. She wasn't any too happy about it. Said she wanted to see you kick some ass.' He sent me a sideways look that doubted my ass-kicking abilities. Sucker.

I smiled sweetly. 'Not in these shoes. They're rentals.'

The elevator lurched and came to a stop, and when my bodyguard came to alert, I held out a hand and launched myself up into the aetheric, searching for trouble. A Sentinel was in the woodwork, trying to short-circuit the brakes and snap the cable. Nice. I didn't even have to act; the Wardens and the Djinn swarmed in a golden blur, smothering the unfortunate enemy combatant. I smiled serenely at the guard, who looked tense and prone to frowns, and leant against the polished wood of the elevator wall. 'So,' I said, as the lift trembled and started up again. 'Roiling Stones, eh? Crazy?'

'Hard to believe, I know' – he shrugged – 'but I gotta say, lady, in the crazy sweepstakes, you and your wedding are coming up fast.'

'I wouldn't bet against us.'

The doors dinged at the penthouse level, and I strolled majestically out into the foyer. More bodyguards, equally grim and serious looking. I wasn't asked for ID; apparently, the dress was a big tip-off.

I went into the suite, walked straight to the bar, and poured myself a stiff, two-fingered shot of tequila. No lime, no salt, none of the party trappings. This was about serious alcohol, delivered in its purest form at maximum impact. It was like getting slapped with an agave cactus; I gasped and bent over the bar, tingling all over.

'Wow,' Cherise said, watching me. 'It's like Brides Gone Wild. Impressive.'

I held out my arms, she ran into them, and we hugged. 'Glad you're OK,' she whispered. 'I was so scared . . .'

'I wasn't,' Kevin said. He was stretched out on my nice beige jacquard sofa, ruining a perfectly good tuxedo and getting his nicely polished shoes all over the fabric. Unlike Lewis and David, he wasn't improved by formal wear. He looked like a hoodlum who'd mugged a groomsman. 'I was betting you'd be barbecued.'

'Asshole,' Cherise said. It sounded like she meant it for a change, and Kevin's perpetual slouch straightened a little. 'Her wedding just got blown all to hell. You could at least not be a total wad about it. For once.'

He sat up completely, brushed the hair out of his

eyes, and looked a little less smug, 'Sorry,' he said, and almost meant it. 'I mean, I knew it was going to come out the way you wanted it to. You wanted to draw the Sentinels out; you did it. Most of them got obliterated, right?'

'I don't know,' I said. 'The plan was to force them out in the open so we could identify them. That seems to be working pretty well.'

'It wasn't just the wedding,' Kevin said. 'All the shiny pieces were here, right? Ashan? The Oracles?'

Yeah, as if I'd actually planned that part. 'Sure. The better to get them to step out and show themselves.'

'So you got him. The old guy.' He meant Bad Bob, I didn't answer. I poured another shot glass of tequila and downed it.

'You might want to leave,' I said. 'Because this isn't over.'

Both Kevin and Cherise looked taken aback, looking around at the calm, orderly luxury of the penthouse. Out at sea, the storms were dissipating; there was still tension in the tectonic plates, but it was being bled off in harmless ways by the Earth Wardens. The Ma'at were all over the whole balancing problem. It all looked . . . calm.

'Leave,' I said, even more softly. I poured two shot glasses and put the bottle asid. 'Go now.'

Kevin grabbed Cherise's hand and dragged her, still protesting, toward the door. I didn't raise my head to watch them go. I stayed focused on the silvery glitter of the alcohol in crystal, and when I heard the door click shut, I said, 'You might as well show yourself. I know you're here.' I could feel his presence now. I couldn't believe how it felt – how cold, how *empty*.

I heard the chuckle, and it was so familiar, so damned familiar it burnt. I tried hard not to shudder, tried to keep my head up and my back straight. 'Tequila,' Bad Bob said. 'Always thought you were a scotch girl, Jo.'

'I am,' I said. 'But I remember you always had a taste for the stuff.' I took a shot glass and turned, holding it out.

Sure enough, on the other side of the room, Bad Bob stood watching me. He was wearing a tuxedo, too, or half of one, anyway; the pants were formal, the shirt untucked, the tie loosened. No coat. His suspenders were in a garish rainbow that brought to mind the early oeuvre of Robin Williams.

'Like it?' He snapped the suspenders with his thumbs. 'Thought I'd help you celebrate the happy day. And it's a happy day, isn't it? You and David, all cozy and bound up together, *till death do you part.*' Bad Bob grinned, all teeth and crazy blue eyes. 'I'll take that drink now.'

I levitated it across to him. He laughed and snatched it out of the air, threw it back, and blew the shot glass into powder in midair with a random burst of power.

'You know what I am, don't you?' he asked. He

continued to grin, relentless as a shark, and ambled slowly around the room, poking and touching things at random. 'You know why I'm so set on getting you.'

'I know,' I said. 'I've killed three of you so far.'

That snapped his head around fast, and the grin turned bloody in its intensity. 'Don't flatter yourself,' he said. 'You used our own against us twice. That doesn't even count. Any fool Warden could have done it. But the last – ah, the last one was special. She was *mine*.'

'I didn't think the Demons had family.'

'I didn't say she was family; I said she was mine. I created her; I cultivated her. I set her on you. And you stood there and watched her die.' His smile twitched insanely. 'Poetic justice, I suppose, your Djinn pouring poison down her throat the way I did it to you in the first place. Never been much for poetry, myself.' He stretched out a hand. The bottle of tequila left the bar and arrowed across the room to smack into his palm. He swallowed one mouthful, then two, and licked his lips. 'Down to us, isn't it?'

'Is it?' I cocked my head and smiled back at him, trying to be as winter cold as he. 'So what're you going to do, Bob? The Djinn have twice the power they did an hour ago, and none of the restraints they used to have. You can't command them. You can't trick them. And you damn sure can't scare them anymore. The Wardens know you now, and the ones who thought the idea of the Sentinels made sense are learning better, fast. You can't threaten to go public. What's left?'

'Same thing that's always left, girly-girl.' He shrugged. 'Death, horror, destruction. No matter how good you are, you can't stop it all. I'll push you until you break, you, the Wardens, the Djinn. Until you make a mistake and I come for you.'

'You don't think coming here was a mistake?' I asked. ''Cause I have to admit, ballsy. Not real smart, but ballsy.'

'Oh, I'll be gone well before help arrives,' he said. 'Might surprise you, but I can do the Djinn thing now – blip around through the aetheric. Handy when you want to visit old, suspicious friends.'

I felt the atmosphere shift, slide toward the darker spectrums. 'OK. Nice to see you, Bob. Now, fuck off.'

'I always did love your sharp tongue,' he said. 'I'm not going to fight you today. Be a shame to destroy that dress.' The bastard *winked* at me. 'No, I'll just go home, play with my new friends. You know them, I'll bet: Rahel, that rascal, pretending to be all soft and human like that. Oh, and my *new* friend. Someone very special.'

He reached into the shadows, and he pulled out my daughter.

Imara stumbled and fell to her knees, the brick-red dress she normally wore now fluttering and writhing around her. He'd bound her up with black ropes of twisting, glittering power, and where they touched her, they burnt. *No,* I thought numbly. *Impossible. She was safe; she was taken back to the chapel; Ashan was guarding her . . .*

'Ashan never did like this one,' he said. 'Figures on appointing a new Earth Oracle in short order. Nice friends you have. Maybe you ought to reconsider which side of this you're on, girl; what do you think?'

I lunged for Imara and slammed into a barrier, one that blew me back across the room to slam full force into the glass tiles of the bar. I saw stars and darkness, and sank to an awkward sitting position on the floor, surrounded by fallen shards of mirror.

'Oh, don't fuss. She's not really here. Just thought I'd give you fair warning, because it's going to hurt you a whole lot worse than it hurts me when I *do* get around to taking your kid.'

'Stop,' I said. I felt light-headed, sick, hot. I no longer felt in the least invulnerable. 'What do you want?'

'I want to make a deal,' Bad Bob said. 'Your daughter's life for David's. Fair trade.'

'No.' I snarled it. 'You don't even have her, you bastard; you already said so!'

'I said I don't have her *now*. Not that I wouldn't have her by the time your little rescue party fails to take me out. Sorry, kid,' he said to Imara's image.

'Mommy doesn't love you all that well, looks like. Too bad, you're a cutie.'

He showed me what he was going to do to her, to my child, and I didn't look away. I wanted to, desperately, but something in me that was far colder, far wiser than my heart made me stay strong.

'When I'm finished,' he said, in a whisper as black as the Unmaking itself, 'then I'll reach through her to destroy you. But not before. I want you to feel every moment of it, Joanne. Every . . . single . . . moment.'

The Wardens and the Djinn had finally arrived, no doubt summoned by Kevin and Cherise. I felt the flare of power outside the doors; they were out there, but Bad Bob was keeping them shut out. He could do that. He had power to burn . . . but he wasn't doing it alone. I recognised the signature behind it.

Ashan. Ashan was still interfering, throwing up barriers, trying to get me killed. He'd consider his problems solved, if I just disappeared from the face of the earth. After all, the vows David and I had exchanged had elevated the New Djinn in power – made them, I suspected, a match for the Old Djinn. Maybe even more than a match.

'You don't have my daughter, and you're not going to have her,' I said, with an icy calm that I was far from feeling. 'The Djinn would be all over you right now if you'd harmed a hair on an Oracle's head. You're a fool if you think anything else – and that includes

Ashan, by the way. He might be using you, but he'll never stand with you.'

Bad Bob stared at me for a second. The grisly vision of Imara vanished into mist. Gone. He lifted the tequila bottle to his lips and drank. Drank it dry. Then he tossed the bottle back to me, and I snatched it out of the air.

'You come on, princess,' he said. 'You find out what I've got. Call my bluff.'

I didn't blink. 'All right,' I said. 'I call.' Anything, *anything* to buy time. My backup didn't dare come at him unprepared, any more than I dared a direct assault against him; they had to be sure he was cut off from his support, and that they could get to him before he got me. Bad Bob had it in him to slaughter me, right here, right now. I felt it in the air. David needed to counter Ashan's influence first.

We'd wanted this. We'd asked for it. I only hoped that we were prepared to actually deal with it, now that the moment was staring us in the face.

'Good girl.' That smile, that evil, dark smile, grew wider still. 'So give me your expert opinion: do you think this is just another illusion?' He reached aside, into the shadows, and this time he pulled out a book: *the* book, a twin to the one, bound in leather and wrapped in iron, that I'd last seen in the vault in Ortega's Miami mansion.

I felt the pull of it from here, and the whisper of

power. Nope, that was not an illusion. And our time was running out. I reached through the golden thread that welded me fast to David and whispered, *It's here; he has it here,* and felt the Djinn surge in response.

They slammed hard into a black shell of crackling power that Bad Bob threw up so fast it made me shudder. The Wardens backed off, and the Djinn melted away, circling, looking for weakness.

I was trapped.

Bad Bob took the iron peg out of the latch with a flick of his finger, opened the book, and flipped pages. 'You have any idea what's in here, sweetheart?' he asked. 'What kind of havoc I can wreak? Ah, here's a good one . . .' Words spilt out of his mouth, strange and liquid, and something in my brain trembled and screamed an alarm.

I froze as the last syllable left his lips, and felt something seize control of me, and a burning sensation high on my right shoulder blade, like a brand being pressed deep into the flesh. I couldn't flinch. Couldn't scream. I smelt my own skin burning, and couldn't so much as cry.

This shouldn't happen. This can't *happen!*

'Hush,' Bob murmured. 'Sooner done, soonest over. There. Now I own you, sweet little Jo. The way it was meant to be.' He snapped the book shut and dropped it; it vanished into mist before it hit the floor. He was storing it in a pocket universe, somewhere in the aetheric. No way to get to it without knowing exactly where, without having the keys he'd crafted to hide it.

I still couldn't move. I stayed stiff and silent as Bad Bob walked toward me. He was a short, bandy-legged old man, but none of that mattered. I was looking at him on the aetheric, and he was no longer troubling to hide himself at all. He was a morass of boiling black, tentacles whipping and tangling, razor edges slashing at everything around him, and where he touched it, the aetheric *bled*.

I couldn't even close my eyes. *You son of a bitch,* I thought. *How dare you do this. How dare you . . .*

I felt the power of the Wardens and the Djinn beyond the room flare up into one white-hot unity, burning through the black shield he'd put up.

Not quickly enough.

'You know, you cost me,' Bad Bob said. 'I spent a while cultivating all that hate, all that fear from the Sentinels. And you had to go put on a public show and get all the fanatics to wriggle out of the woodwork, whether I wanted them to or not.' He leant very close to me, lips lover-close, and whispered, 'That's why I need you, Joanne. Be thou bound to my service.'

That made no sense. I was no Djinn. The Rule of Three didn't work on me, and in any case the agreement between the Warden and the Djinn had ended; it was just words. It meant nothing.

It had to be a bluff.

And I couldn't help a surge of pure fear, because there was so much visceral delight in his face.

'Be thou bound to my service.' His eyes were bloodshot, not entirely human anymore. His breath smelt foul and ancient, something ages in the ground.

Stop, I wanted to say. I couldn't. He wasn't even letting me breathe, and my lungs were crying out for air. I couldn't even wield the power necessary to supply a trickle of oxygen. *Stop this.*

'Be . . . thou . . . bound . . . to . . . my . . .' He whispered each word separately, eyes drifting half closed in pleasure, and then smiled. 'Service. Ahhhh.'

I felt the white-hot force of the united Wardens and Djinn break apart into a million spinning pieces. The thread between me and David held, but only barely. Things were changing, terribly changing, and I couldn't see the edges of the wave that was rippling out from this moment. I didn't know what he'd done, or how, but it was flooding the world, drowning everything.

And when the flood receded, there was an ominous silence. The aetheric felt clean and very empty.

I drew in a whooping, gasping breath and sobbed it out, then breathed in again. Some of the black spots dancing in front of my eyes started to recede . . . not all, by any means. I felt one half step from unconscious, but I kept myself on my feet, facing Bad Bob.

'There,' he said. 'That's better.' He chucked me

under the chin, as if I were his favorite niece who'd just performed a cute trick. Or a puppy. 'Oh, you have questions, don't you?'

I managed to get enough breath to gasp, 'What – did – you—'

'You had a Demon Mark, once upon a time,' he said. 'You may have gotten rid of the Mark, but it left you stained. Vulnerable. *Mine.*'

The Wardens burnt through the shield and launched their assault, with or without the Djinn, and the doors of the penthouse blew off the hinges. Lewis strode in, surrounded by a barely visible nimbus of red light, and behind him came a grim-faced phalanx of my friends: Marion Bearheart, walking with a cane; Kevin, scared but determined; Luis Rocha, the Earth Warden I'd first met during the original Fort Lauderdale event. Dozens more, people I knew and liked, people I hadn't even known would put themselves at risk for me.

David stepped out of the center of the group.

'Whoops, Daddy's home,' Bob said. 'Time for me to be leaving. You will come see me, won't you? I'll expect you around sunset. Love that bloody color on the water.'

My muscles were working again. I shakily reached for power and pulled it down, pulled it from all around me, every surface. The room lit up with miniature lightning strikes, all bleeding toward me.

'Bride of Frankenstein,' Bad Bob said. 'All right, all right, I'm going. Don't set your hair on fire.'

He crooked his little finger and vanished with an audible pop of air. I stared at the spot in the aetheric; the writhing black tentacles took longer to leave, finally slipping through a raw wound in the world.

I didn't drop, though I'm sure everybody expected me to. Instead, I turned to David and asked in what seemed like a very normal tone of voice, 'How badly are we screwed?'

He should have rushed to me, taken me in his arms. It was what he always did – what I *expected* him to do.

But he stayed where he was, watching me, and I no longer understood what I saw in his bright, burning-penny eyes.

He said, 'Ashan was right. The vow we exchanged has made the New Djinn vulnerable again to the Rule of Three. My people are at risk now. From yours. We did this, the two of us.'

He sounded . . . distant. Almost cold. I couldn't control a shiver. *Go to him,* I told myself, but I couldn't seem to move. If I moved, I'd fall down.

'He's already turned Rahel to his cause,' he continued. 'She belongs to him. You can't trust her anymore. Remember that.'

He sounded so *alone.* I got myself steadied, a little, and took a step toward him.

He stepped *back*. Keeping plenty of space between us.

'I can't,' he said. 'I'm sorry. I have to see to the safety of my people now.'

'David—'

For an instant, I saw the torment inside him, and it stopped whatever I was going to say dead in my throat. 'I can't,' he whispered. 'He's destroying her. He's taking great pleasure in it. How many more of my people have to die, Jo? *We're not mortal.* This shouldn't be happening to us. It should never have happened.' He blinked, and the metallic shine came back in his eyes. 'I'm sorry.'

The Djinn left. Just . . . left. All of the Djinn, gone without a sound, including David.

He hadn't even said goodbye.

I collapsed to my knees. Someone – I didn't even see who – helped me up. I told everyone to get out, but they wouldn't. Understandable, I supposed.

I went into the bathroom, slammed and locked the door, and skinned down the fabric of the dress to get a look at my right shoulder blade.

Bad Bob had branded me, the same way he'd branded his Sentinels. It was a mark in the shape of a torch. The old stains left from the Demon Mark I'd once carried had given him a gateway . . . like a cut letting in bacteria. And now I was infected.

The proof was right there on my skin.

I stared into the mirror at the black mark, hideously reminded of the Demon Mark that had once grown inside me, and how that had felt.

How *good* that had felt.

I flinched at a hesitant knock on the door.

'You OK in there?' Lewis asked.

My eyes, in the mirror, were wide and empty. *He can have me, any time he wants me.* I couldn't allow that. If David wasn't going to fight Bad Bob . . .

Then I had to.

We settled up damages with the Palms; nobody acquainted me with a final figure, for which I was very grateful. I hoped the Wardens' bank account wouldn't snap under the strain. I changed out of the lovely wedding dress alone, not daring to let anybody – especially Cherise – catch a look at the brand-new black tattoo I was sporting. When I came out of the bedroom dressed in jeans and a purple knit shirt, the entire crowded roomful of Wardens stopped talking.

'What?' I snapped. 'Never saw anybody left at the altar before?' Wow. Being dumped made me bitchy, which was, of course, a brave front. I didn't feel bitchy; I felt . . . alone. I felt as if my whole world had gone the dead, burnt color of the torch on my shoulder.

Looks were exchanged among my friends. I wanted to kick and punch something, preferably Bad Bob, until the sun burnt out, but I'd have settled for anyone who said something flippant right at that moment.

Nobody did. Cherise finally stood up and said, 'Let me take that.'

Oh. The dress. It was draped over my arm like a limp silk corpse. I held it out to her, and she zipped it safely back in its protective plastic cocoon.

'Probably should get that back to the store,' I said. I was trying to disconnect, trying to shut off all my emotions. I was being pretty successful at it, too.

Cherise looked devastated, as if I'd admitted defeat. 'No,' she said. 'Um – can't return it. There was a smudge.' She put on her determined face, which was just cute, and dared me to say otherwise. 'You'll have to keep it.'

'What for?' I asked. 'Not like we're going to get a do-over on the wedding.' And that nearly broke me. I wanted David. I wanted him to manifest out of the thin air and sweep me up in his arms and carry me off. I wanted Bad Bob to be gone and all to be right with the world, for *once*.

That wasn't going to happen. At least, it wasn't going to happen unless I *made* it happen. *All that is necessary for evil to triumph is for good men to do nothing.* I supposed old Edmund Burke had meant to include women in that. And if he hadn't, well, screw him.

'What's the plan?' I asked Lewis. Lewis seemed

lost in thought, but that was probably because, in his typical fashion, he was manipulating a dozen different things at once. Now, he looked up, met my eyes, and I had a second of icy doubt. Could he see what Bad Bob had done to me? *No.* If he could have, Paul would have been busted for a Sentinel the second Lewis laid eyes on him. Whatever Bad Bob had done to me, it was invisible to the Wardens. *And the Djinn,* I reminded myself. David hadn't tipped to Paul's betrayal, either.

I knew I should say something, but if I did, I'd be making it real.

I'd be admitting defeat.

'We have to go after him,' Lewis said. 'We got most of his support, I think; he's isolated, maybe even alone. We need to get him before he can recruit more followers.'

'He's going to go after the Oracles,' I said. 'After my daughter, Lewis. I can't let that happen.'

He didn't argue the point. 'He won't go after anybody if we don't give him the time.'

'Do we have *anything* that can counter what he's got?' Meaning, the Unmaking. And his sheer, horrible power.

'Maybe,' Lewis said. 'But I think this is going to be more a matter of wearing him down until we can strike. More of a siege than a blitz attack.'

The light dawned. 'You know where he is.'

'He's at the Wardens' safe house, on the beach,' he

said. 'He didn't try to hide it. He's inviting us to come get him.'

'Which means it's a trap.'

Lewis nodded. 'But what are our options? We've lost the Djinn, but if we don't go for him now, he'll have time to build up his organisation again. Even if Bad Bob's got control of Rahel, we may never have a better opportunity.'

No, I didn't like it. This was Bad Bob's version of our wedding – an obvious, juicy target, just waiting for us to strike it. 'We can wait him out.'

'He can move through the aetheric, like a Djinn. How do you propose we seal him off, without the Djinn's cooperation?'

Lewis had a point. We needed to get Bad Bob to fight us on our terms, and that meant letting him think he was winning.

That meant walking into the trap – but being ready to turn the trap to our advantage.

Lewis was thinking of something I hadn't, but then, he usually was. 'Your link to David. It's still holding?'

I went still, listening. It was – slender as a silk thread, but strong as steel. I couldn't reach him, because he was blocking me, but I could feel him. I nodded.

'Can you draw power from it?' Lewis asked.

I concentrated, and felt a tingle of energy creep along the link from David to me. Then more. I held up my hand, and a golden, unfocused glow formed in my palm.

Lewis didn't look happy with the outcome, which surprised me until he said, 'Then you're the one who has the best chance. He'll send you energy to keep you alive, and as the Conduit, he's got access to more energy than any other Djinn except Ashan. That could give you the edge you need to defeat Rahel, if it comes to that. And Bad Bob.'

I needed to tell him, couldn't avoid the embarrassing and fatal truth any longer. I shook the glow out like a match and opened my mouth to explain about the mark Bad Bob had burnt into my back – about my vulnerability to him.

I couldn't. Not a single word.

'Jo?'

I focused past him, to the delicate, antique desk in the corner. There was creamy, expensive hotel stationery and a Montblanc pen right there, just waiting for me to scribble out a warning if I couldn't force my voice box to cooperate.

Except I couldn't so much as make a move toward it.

Dammit. Bad Bob had installed safeguards.

'Nothing,' I heard myself say. 'I think you're right. Send me in. I think I'm your best bet.'

Lewis didn't seem happy with it, but I knew he'd do it. 'Not alone,' he said. 'I've already got teams surrounding the compound. I'll go with you.'

'No, you won't,' I said, and I meant it. 'Lewis, one of us at risk is enough. The Wardens need a leader, and like it or not, you're it. I'm expendable.'

'Don't say that,' he said. Not, I noticed, a denial, just an avoidance. Lewis was far too practical not to realise that I was right about that. 'I said you had the best chance, but we can do this another way, Jo. All you have to do is say the word, and we'll—'

'Lose? Yeah, that works great. Good plan.' I felt tears sting my eyes. 'Come on. Have I ever backed off from certain death? Ever? Even when I had something to live for?'

He flinched at that one, but he didn't look away. 'No,' he said. 'Bad Bob knows that, too. He's going to count on it. Don't let him push you into a corner, or you'll die for nothing. I don't think I can stand that. You mean too much to me, Jo.'

It was the closest he'd come to admitting how he felt about me, and he'd done it right out in public. The room – full of Wardens – was deathly still, though whether they were waiting for more revelations or for me to reject him, I couldn't tell. 'I know,' I said softly. 'I won't.'

Cherise cleared her throat. 'If you need somebody to, you know, ride along and—'

'No,' I said flatly. 'Not this time. This is no job for anyone who can't throw a lightning bolt, a car, or a ball of fire the size of Cleveland. I don't want you anywhere near Bad Bob.'

She looked disappointed, but not really surprised. Despite the chaos of the day, there wasn't a smudge on her. Kevin put his arm around her and looked down; elfin and lovely and entirely human, she looked up into his face. The smile they exchanged made my heart ache.

'You're going?' she asked him. Kevin shrugged.

'Might as well,' he said. 'Got nothing else planned for the day. My Nintendo's busted.'

'Watch your ass,' she told him.

Ah, young love.

'Ready?' Lewis asked me. I nodded. I still wished I could live a normal life, have what I wanted, be at peace. *I should have taken all of my vacation.* I was just now starting to see the wisdom of waiting for trouble, instead of courting it. 'Can you get David to help at all?'

I shook my head. 'No. He's – staying away.'

Lewis looked very, very grim. 'You mean, he's walled himself off on the aetheric. The way Jonathan used to do.'

'I can't be sure. He's not giving me anything back about where he is, but it would make sense.' David could save himself, and his people, by shutting himself off like that for as long as necessary. Ages, if need be.

Lewis pulled in breath to say something, then decided that discretion was the better part of valor; he held up his hands and walked away to confer with the others.

He didn't have to say it. I'd already figured out that if David had really withdrawn into his stronghold on the aetheric, I might never see him again.

Not even to say goodbye.

To say that there was a military operation at work on the beach when we arrived was an understatement. One handy thing about the Wardens coming out in public was that we no longer had to make do with covert ops-style equipment. No, this time we had cops, FBI, air surveillance, coast guard boats . . . everything but the dancing bear and big top.

I was pretty sure that none of it was going to mean a damn thing to Bad Bob, in the end. Mortal firepower was beyond insignificant to him, except as an inconvenience, and with the Djinn off the board, we had very little left to counter him.

Just me, the battered and damaged white queen, with a little fleck of black to betray her true allegiances.

Lewis and I sat in a surveillance van, the tricked-out kind, watching monitors in all different spectrums. There was no movement from the beach house. SWAT teams had gone into position, stealthily moving from cover to cover inside the overgrown estate grounds. It wouldn't help them. Bad Bob knew they were there; he had to know. He probably just didn't damn well care. Humans weren't his thing, and in fact they mattered very little to him except as window dressing.

'Nothing on any of the monitors or sensors,' one of the Wardens reported. 'Maybe he's not there.'

'He's there,' I said. I was watching the house itself. I couldn't sense or see anything, and I had absolutely no basis for believing what I'd said, but somehow, I knew. I just knew. 'He's got ways to conceal himself. Probably using Rahel.'

'We need physical recon,' Lewis said.

'I think that's my cue.' I didn't wait for them to approve; I didn't wait for the protests. I just jumped down onto the road and walked up to the gates. I looked up at the perimeter camera, and felt Bad Bob's smile like a fetid ghost all around me.

'Jo, *wait*!' That was Lewis, trying to order me back.

'For what?' I asked him, and he had absolutely no answer to that. I read it in his eyes, though.

He wanted me to say something, anything, to make this easier. But I didn't have it, and neither did he.

So I went on.

The gates creaked open, and I walked alone, shadowed by the SWAT commandos and FBI tactical units, up the winding path. I remembered walking it with David, in happier times; Ortega was still alive then, still delighting in all his lovely things. I hadn't feared Bad Bob, except as a ghost safely sealed in my memories.

The night was cool, and there were clouds blowing

up at the horizon. A natural front, nothing sinister about it. Overhead, the stars were chips of ice, sharp enough to cut.

If I'd been walking with my lover, with my *husband*, it would have been magical. *I love you,* I whispered to him, along the bond between us. *I will always love you. I'm sorry.*

I felt nothing in response.

I walked up the steps, moving steadily and without hesitation. I reached for the knob, and opened the front door. It was unlocked. I'd known it would be.

Bad Bob was sitting in a leather wing chair next to the fireplace, feet up, puffing on a cigar. He had a bottle of liquor next to him – scotch, this time. He raised the bottle, and I levitated it to me. The taste of liquid gold burnt the roof of my mouth, then poured down my throat and started a sickening burn in the cold pit of my stomach.

'It's not poisoned,' I noted, and sent it back. He caught it effortlessly out of the air and chugged a few mouthfuls, then put it aside.

'Wouldn't waste good scotch. Or good poison,' he said. 'Wouldn't kill you, anyway, would it? Nothing kills you. Goddamn cockroach, you are. You'll survive a nuclear winter.'

'Look who's talking,' I said. I sat down on the edge of the couch across from him. There were a few lights burning, not many, and the whole effect was ghostly.

Outside the windows, the beach was dark, the water slick and almost flat – a calm sea. 'You've been dead a few times, I hear.'

He chuckled. 'Hurricane Andrew should've killed me,' he said. 'Came damn close, actually. But there was always just one more damn challenge, one more thing to do. One more life to save. You know how it is.'

'That's your story? That you were in the business of saving lives?' I leant back and folded my arms. 'Oh, come on.'

'I'll put my scores up against anybody's. Including yours.'

'You *killed* people!'

'How many collateral goddamn damages have you had over the past few years, girl? *What the fuck makes you the hero of the story*? No, more to the point: what makes me the villain?'

I stared at him, not exactly sure what he was doing. I'd come here intending to make him kill me, or to destroy him in the process, if that was possible; to wound him badly enough that Lewis could finish him off. I hadn't expected him to be so damn defensive about, of all things, his record as a *good guy*.

'Your hands aren't clean,' he pointed out. 'Hell, you've stood by and *let* people die, if nothing else. How come I'm the bad guy?'

'Because—' I ground my teeth together. 'Because

nobody ever became evil overnight. Because the bad guys don't see what they do as evil; they see it as their own personal good. Sound familiar?'

He took another slug, straight from the bottle. 'Joanne Baldwin, big-time hero. If I hadn't given you that Demon Mark, you'd still be paddling around the shallow-personality pool, wondering if you could destroy a tornado fast enough to make the shoe sale at Macy's. Not good, not evil. Not anything.'

'I don't understand.'

'Yes, you do.' He leant forward, resting his elbows on his knees, hands clasped. 'I've made you strong. I'm going to make you stronger. Stronger than any goddamn Warden in history. And I'm going to do that by changing the whole ecosystem of the planet – by destroying the Djinn. Makes humans the *real* apex predators of this little ball of rock. And I'm putting you in charge of it.'

It hit me what he was trying to say. 'You – you think this is a good thing for me. For the Wardens.'

'I don't give a shit if it's good or bad. It's what's necessary. I always do what's necessary.' Bob's grin flashed. 'Sometimes that's also fun, though.'

I didn't want to hear any more. Outside the windows, the seas began to chop as the wind moved faster, as temperatures shifted and swirled. He was playing with the weather. Taunting us. Sending temperatures into a downward spiral out near Cuba, creating an imbalance that would surely force intervention.

'I'm going to kill you,' I said. 'Demon or not. Dead or not. You're not walking away today, not if it costs me every last breath I have. If you made me what I am, then what I am is coming after you.'

He sighed. 'Ah, Jo. Wave a red flag, and you run at it like a bull, every time. You think I didn't know that?'

Which was exactly how I wanted him to think. My gaze had fixed on something black and glittering, mounted like some exotic trophy weapon on the back wall of the house, right out in the open, almost as a taunt.

The whole house was lethally radioactive. I was, in effect, already dead. Even as an Earth Warden, I couldn't diffuse that much radiation through my system without damaging my own cells. Maybe Lewis could, but not me. My daughter had cut herself off from me – had been forced to.

The power I was drawing from David in a steady stream was keeping me alive, but it wouldn't save me over the long haul. It was a treatment, not a cure.

I turned away from Bad Bob and walked to the Unmaking. It was glimmering with its own black aura, sending its poisonous tendrils deep into the house, into the aetheric.

'You don't want to do that, honey,' he said. 'It's suicide.'

I picked it up.

The outside of it felt shockingly hot. A slightly rough texture when I ran my fingers lightly down, finding the balance point. The horrible thing was heavier than I'd expected, and my muscles began to shake, trying to rid me of the burden.

Bad Bob hadn't moved. He raised the cigar to his mouth and puffed, eyes half closed. 'You got the wrong idea, Jo. You can't kill me this way.'

'You're probably right,' I panted. I fought, but lost, the battle for control of the weather system that was rotating in past Cuba, moving high and fast and wild. It collided with warmer air, and the clouds built walls of thick, heavy gray. Lightning burnt inside it, living and dying in rapid-fire flares. 'But I'll bet it slows you down for the others to finish.'

'They'll have their hands full trying to keep half of Florida alive by nightfall. If I make things bad enough, the Djinn will have to show their faces just to keep the balance, and once that happens . . . they're mine.' His pale blue eyes focused on me. 'Put it down, kid. You're just killing yourself faster.'

I shook my head. Sweat dripped down my face, matted my hair. 'No. Make me. I know you can.'

'Why should I?' he asked. 'You want to kill me, kill me. Do it, Maybe you'll be right. Maybe it'll just be that easy.'

I lunged, both hands barely able to keep hold of

the black spear, and as I did I had an involuntary flash of sense-memory, of Jerome Silverton digging that black shard from a dead Djinn, and of my dream of David lying dead in the street, pierced just like this.

I dragged myself to a wild, panting halt, flat-footed, staring at Bad Bob's blue eyes. The tip of the Unmaking trembled just an inch from his chest. He made no effort to get away.

'Do it,' he said. 'Maybe I'm not your enemy after all. You ever think of that?'

Sweat burnt down my face, in my eyes, and I felt my hands spasming, trying to drop this thing that was already killing me. It wouldn't do any good, but you couldn't blame my body for trying to save itself.

He was trying to tell me something. There was a message under all this, a message unknown and beyond translation, but somehow, one I was receiving.

Bad Bob had expected me. He wasn't the type to go in for self-sacrifice, and he knew how to set the hook firmly.

How to use the best possible bait . . . himself.

He had the power to stop me, if he wanted. *Why wasn't he?*

He'd taunted me. He'd threatened my daughter. He'd done everything he could to drive me to this moment. He'd used my vows with David to open the Djinn up to the Rule of Three. We knew he had

Rahel. And Rahel had a gift . . . for mimicry.

The last piece fell into place with a physical shock. *This wasn't Bad Bob.*

It was Rahel. It had to be Rahel, forced to take on his shape, be his puppet, his sacrificial goat.

I felt a pulse of power in the black torch on my back. Bad Bob was getting impatient with me. I wasn't following the script.

I closed my eyes and reached for the cord that bound me to David. Energy was flowing through the connection, thick and golden, a torrent that was racing through my body in a frantic effort to keep me alive. It wasn't working anymore. *I need you to show me,* I whispered. *I need to see. Help me see.*

I went up into the aetheric. It was hard, so very hard that it was like ripping off my own skin; I barely made it into the lowest levels, and my Oversight revealed the room in dull reds and blacks.

It wasn't Rahel in the chair after all. Rahel was outside, *heading to the van.* Bad Bob was holding me here, and going after our flank by attacking Lewis. I needed to act. If Rahel was out there, that meant that Bad Bob was in front of me. *Had* to be. I just had to strike that last inch . . .

I saw a bright copper flash, just a flash, with the last fading strength of Oversight before I fell back into my skin, and I knew. I knew the truth.

David hadn't gone to the aetheric. Bad Bob had

used Rahel to lure him here, and he'd bound him, just as he'd bound Rahel.

David was sitting in the chair in front of me, and I was an inch away from taking his life. I'd come so close, so horribly close, to making the wrong choice. One more inch, just one, and my life would have been over, even if I'd survived this day.

David had been trying to warn me all along. *Maybe I'm not your enemy.*

Oh God.

I tried to keep my expression the same, except for a slight involuntary widening of my eyes. I was barely hanging on; subtleties would be lost, if Bad Bob was – and I knew he would be – watching.

He wouldn't want to miss seeing me make such a catastrophic mistake.

I know it's you, I tried to say to David, through our locked stare. *Trust me.* If Bad Bob had put him in thrall, he wouldn't have much room to maneuver, and no room to give me any real assistance. All I could hope was that Bad Bob, clever and cruel as he was, hadn't thought of everything.

And of course, that I had, which wasn't too damn likely.

'Where?' I shaped the word only with my lips, burning my question into Bad Bob's eyes, trying to get across one simple, impossible message. For a second I thought I'd guessed wrong, that I'd just destroyed myself for nothing and missed my only chance, but then those blue eyes darted quickly away, to a point just behind me and to my right.

The doorway. Of course. Bad Bob would want to see this up close.

One thing about the Unmaking; it was pointed on both ends. I didn't have enough strength and control left to turn, so I lunged backward, angling toward the doorway. One step, two, fast and hard, letting my own exhausted weight do the work as I drove the weapon in reverse, straight for the real enemy.

I felt the end of the spear slam home, and felt the whole thing vibrate like a struck bell. It shook my hands off its heated surface, and my whole body threw itself into an uncontrollable spasm, every muscle sparking and spasming and driving me hard to the floor.

In the chair next to the window, the fake Bad Bob continued to sit, watching me – unable to move, because he *couldn't* move.

I writhed over on my back. Sweaty hair clung to my face, obscuring my vision, but as I swiped it away I saw Bad Bob – the real one – standing over me, staring down at the black rod that had punched completely through his stomach and emerged glittering and bloody from the other side.

He laughed. 'Good thinking,' he said, and blood fountained out over his chin and bubbled in his mouth. 'Damn, girl. Still got an arm.'

He fell heavily to his knees, face draining white, and gripped the Unmaking with both hands. I wriggled backward away from him as he began to pull it free of his body, one torturous inch at a time. His hands were shaking, turning gray, but he kept at it with single-minded intensity.

And what he pulled out of his body was *thicker*. He was creating more of it, generating it from his own body.

But it looked as if it hurt like a son of a bitch.

I crab-crawled back until I bumped into the legs of the man sitting in the chair, and looked up at him. I saw a single flare of Djinn fire break free of the disguise.

'David,' I whispered. I got no response, of course. There was a container somewhere; there had to be if Bad Bob had bound a Djinn – something glass, something breakable. But even though the beach house was relatively uncluttered, I didn't have time or strength to search. Bottles in the kitchen, the refrigerator, hidden in cupboards, forgotten in the attic – it could be anywhere.

Bad Bob grunted with effort as he pulled, one convulsive jerk after another. The Unmaking was sliding slowly out of him. I watched the sharp end disappear into his back. Another two or three pulls, and he'd have it out, bigger and more powerful than ever.

I'd bought us some time, but it was running out.

Outside, I heard explosions, and felt the ground tremble under my feet. Rahel had reached the van, and she was going after Lewis. It was a free-for-all outside.

I closed my eyes and found what little small, still pool of Earth power I had. I'd never had time for real training, real control, but for this, I didn't need it. It's always easier to destroy than to create.

I attuned myself to the specific frequencies of glass, crystal, and porcelain, and sent out a pulse of power that rippled out from me like a sonic boom.

It hit the bottles in the bar and exploded them in a mist of silica. Crystal decanters and tumblers vibrated apart. The wave reached the windows and blew them out in sprays of glitter. It rolled over Bad Bob, past him, and shattered everything that could be shattered, continuing relentlessly through the entire house, as far as I could push it.

He *could* have hidden his bottles somewhere else, but he'd want to keep them close. Warden instinct. I pushed the wave front as far as I could, but my strength failed before I reached the gates of the estate.

'Bitch,' Bad Bob whispered, and with one convulsive jerk, pulled the spear completely out of his body. The gaping wound crisped black at the edges, then began to knit itself closed.

In the chair, the false image of Bad Bob flinched, and I felt the timbre of power in the room shift and flow as the force that had been holding David apart from me cut off.

I'd destroyed the bottle.

David was free.

The golden thread between us vibrated and snapped tight again.

In a second, he had his hands around me and was pulling me up, preparing to carry me through the open window.

'No you don't,' Bad Bob gasped, and pointed his finger at us. I froze, off balance, unable to control my muscles. *Dammit*! I'd forgotten about the torch mark on my shoulder blade. It wasn't only David he'd been able to manipulate.

'If you won't play, you pay,' Bad Bob said, and grinned with bloody teeth. He reversed his grip on the Unmaking, found the balance point . . . and drove it straight down, into the floor – through the floor, into the concrete.

Through the concrete, into the bedrock of the earth.

I felt the sentience of the planet cry out, a wave of horror and emotion that overrode every synapse in my body. I *felt* her agony. She hadn't been hurt so badly in a long, long time. David cried out, and I felt his hands slide away. He lunged past me, heading for Bad Bob, but after one step he pitched onto his side, convulsing.

Conduit to the aetheric and Mother Earth, he was also the most vulnerable to her pain.

The earthquake hit with the force of a bomb, shattering steel and wood and concrete as if it were so much glass. I sensed the perimeter troops, Warden and human alike, being tossed around like dice outside. I heard explosions, cracks, the sound of trees groaning in agony and breaking off in lethally heavy pieces.

I couldn't move. Bad Bob didn't move, either; he stood staring at me, one hand still outstretched, the other gripping the shaft of the Unmaking still sticking out of the ground.

Walls roared, cracked, and shattered. The floor rippled like liquid, then, the carpet shredding, it broke into jagged fragments. Dust became a mist, then a storm.

The roof joists snapped, and the entire thing inverted into a V, crashing toward us.

Bad Bob never stopped grinning. He waved merrily, ripped the Unmaking out of the ground in a single mighty pull, and vanished.

I dropped like a discarded puppet, rolled into a ball, and felt the first heavy piece of debris hit me. It was the wing chair, tipping on top of me. I curled underneath it for protection and screamed as the entire house came down in a rush of smoke, sparks, and crushing chaos.

The chair might as well have been made of plastic.

* * *

Breathe.

I couldn't. Something was on my chest. I couldn't get enough room to allow my lungs to expand. My diaphragm fluttered, trying vainly to pull in air. I choked and tried to reach for power, but it felt slippery, greasy, elusive. All my strength was gone.

You have to stay calm. Master your panic.

I had a house on top of me. Not that easy to stay calm.

You're alive.

And dying fast.

David—

I heard the distant groan of wood being moved. Rising noise, scrapes, the tortured scream of metal.

Can't breathe. I concentrated on putting my body into a state of meditation, to minimise oxygen burn. *Stow and steady, wait, wait . . .*

Something shifted, and I felt a piece of debris as heavy as the fist of God slam down on my lower chest. Ribs snapped in hot little starry snaps. I heard myself whimper, and then the weight shifted again, vanishing in a cloud of dust, and the pressure against me was gone.

'Oh Christ,' someone said. It sounded like Lewis. I tried to open my eyes, but it was too much of an effort. 'We're losing her.'

A warm hand was under my head, cradling it. I felt a strangely comforting sense of cold creeping through my limbs, tunneling through me toward my heart. Energy cascaded through me, trying to fight the chill, but the chill was stronger. Harder. More determined.

'No.' It was David's voice, choked and despairing. 'No, *no*. Jo, hold on—'

I pulled in a delicious breath and let it out, one last time. I wished I could open my eyes and see him, but in my mind I saw him as he'd been at the wedding, alight and golden and perfect.

I hadn't wanted to hurt him this way.

It didn't hurt at all, slipping away on a tide of darkness. It felt . . . peaceful. *Hello again,* I said to death. I was resigned, if not ready.

And then I was caught by a sharp, red-hot hook. The tide tried to pull me, but the hook – burning through my body, back to front, on my right shoulder blade – held fast. Heat flared and blazed – not the gentle healing of Earth power, something else. Something wild and dark and harsh, burning black in every nerve.

The next breath I took I let out in a raw, thin scream. I opened my eyes, and saw Lewis leaning over me, and David, and Marion Bearheart. Kevin was standing in the background, looking helpless and oddly vulnerable. Dozens of others were behind him. The sky ripped open with lightning, and rain began to fall in a cold silver curtain.

I laughed. My body put itself back together in hot,

agonising snaps and jerks, every nerve carrying every second of the pain to my brain.

And the pain felt so *good*.

Lewis let go of me, staring in bafflement that was turning fast to grim horror.

David didn't move, but I saw the same thing in his face – the same revulsion and sickness.

'You think I'd let her go that easy?' It was Bad Bob's voice, but coming raw from my own throat. 'You think I'd let *any* of you go that easy? She's the future, boys. *My* future.'

The laughter that exploded out of me was like a black, nauseating cloud, and this time even David flinched away from it. I rolled up to my hands and knees, covered in fine dust like flour where I wasn't streaked in blood.

Alive. Whole. Even the radiation sickness had been flushed out of me.

The torch on my back burnt, burnt so hot . . .

'So who's the bad guy now?' I taunted. *He* taunted.

There wasn't any difference now.

I turned my face up to the rain, and laughed, and for the first time, I understood why he was as he was, what about this was so intoxicating. No ties. No worries. No burdens. Just power, as pure as it came. People didn't matter. All that mattered was *winning*.

I didn't care about David, or Lewis, or any miserable

little collection of cells walking the planet. They were all just meat and fuel for the engine.

And it was so . . . *beautiful.*

Then Bad Bob let me go, once he'd shown me the world as he saw it, a landscape where flesh and blood were as meaningless and desolate as sand and rock: I felt the fire gutter and die on my back, and my whole body jerked and folded in on itself.

Mourning for what I'd just lost.

I felt tears burning in my eyes and knew that the worst thing of all this was that I couldn't be sure anymore that if he offered me the choice to feel that again, of my own free will, that I wouldn't take it.

So who's the bad guy now?

The circle of people around me waited tensely. I lifted my face again, and said, 'He's gone.' My words were almost lost in a blast of wind flying in from the ocean, blowing dust and debris and tattered palm leaves into the air. 'I have to go after him.'

The Wardens shifted, looking at each other, at Lewis. He slowly shook his head. 'We're not doing that,' he said. 'Christ, Jo. What just happened to you?'

David knew. He reached around and pulled the back of my shirt down, and I saw Lewis's face turn a sick shade of white. 'Oh God,' he said. 'We need to get it off you.'

'I don't think laser removal is going to cut it,' I said. I felt hollow, cored out. Beyond anything but gallows humor. 'It's deep. I don't know how to shut him out.'

'Then you can't go,' Lewis said. 'We need to keep you safe. If he can use you—'

'He can use me *here*. Against *you*. I need to – I need to finish this.' I swallowed hard. 'He's still got a Djinn. Rahel. And he's going to use her to make that thing he has even stronger. The next time he puts the Unmaking into the Earth, do you really think any of us is going to survive it?'

I turned and looked at the night sky. Impossible to see how much damage had been done, but I saw fires, heard sirens in the distance.

'I can block him,' David said. 'If you'll let me. But it will hurt.'

He hadn't said a word about being bound, about my almost killing him in the beach house; I supposed there would be plenty of time for that later. But for now, I nodded.

David put his hand flat against my bare skin on my back, and I felt power surge up from beneath me, racing through my body, concentrating in a red-hot ball around the torch tattoo. Burning. I trembled and felt David's other hand close around mine, sending me strength and support.

'I'm here,' he whispered. 'I'm here, my love.'

I stood it for as long as I could, and then turned with a cry and threw myself into his arms. The white-hot pain in my back faded slowly, but it didn't go away. I couldn't see what he'd done, but it felt as if the mark had been overlaid by something else. Contained.

Masked.

'It won't last,' David said, and stroked my hair. 'I'll have to renew the block when it weakens.'

Joy. 'How often?'

'That depends on how hard he's trying to reach you.' His arms tightened around me. 'I'm so sorry.'

That covered . . . everything. For now. I took a deep breath and stepped back, smiling despite the continuing low sizzle of pain. 'Can you stay?'

'I'll try,' he said. 'You're right. My people have to try to stop him. We don't have a choice. He's hurting the Mother directly now. We're her only defense.'

'Not the only one,' Ashan said, striding out of the darkness. Behind him stretched all of the Old Djinn, hundreds of them. The mightiest Djinn force I'd ever seen in one place – maybe the mightiest ever assembled.

On David's side, the New Djinn began to take shape out of the shadows – maybe just out of self-defense. The Wardens, caught in the middle, looked understandably worried. These two clans had been in cold-war status for ages, but the war had heated up, and I wasn't sure what Ashan would consider *defense* these days.

His cold, teal-blue eyes turned on me. I felt him considering whether or not to strike.

'Try and I'll destroy *you*,' David said, low in his throat. Lightning ripped the sky again, breaking into dozens of streams of light.

'Amusing as that contest would be, you're probably right,' Ashan said, and his smile was as cold as the rain. 'She's our guide into the abyss. We can use her to track our enemy. And to tempt him into the open.'

'Wait,' Lewis said. 'What are you saying? You're all going after him? All of you?'

'The New Djinn are vulnerable. The Old Djinn aren't – at least, not yet. Besides, we have no choice now,' David replied. 'We can't let him go. He may actually be able to destroy the Djinn.' He paused, and looked at the Wardens. 'This isn't your fight anymore. Go home.'

'Hell with that,' Kevin said. 'I'm not taking orders from you.'

'Tell him,' David said, spearing Lewis with a glare. 'Tell them all.'

Lewis looked around at the Wardens, taking his time. When he spoke, he had the unmistakable ring of command in his voice. 'He's right. I make the decisions for the Wardens. You'll all follow my orders.' He paused for deliberate effect. 'And my orders are that the Wardens will send a support team with Joanne and the Djinn.'

'And where exactly are we planning to send them?' Marion asked.

I looked up at the clouds, then out to sea.

'He's gone where he thinks we can't follow,' I said. 'To the Cradle of Storms.' As far as I knew, no Warden had ever ventured out to sea in that area and made it back to shore alive. The storms out there were sentient, and they were *vicious*. And a Warden, any Warden, became a Jonah. Any ship they were on became prey.

And I was about to lead a whole team of them into the jaws of death.

This was *not* the way I'd planned to take a honeymoon cruise to Bermuda.

Sunrise came. Sunrise always comes, no matter how dark the night – it's one of those tired truths of life, one you can take as either positive or negative as the situation calls for.

For me, this morning, it was just the morning after the night before. No change, except that there was more light to see the damage.

The burning sensation on my back had faded into a dull buzz, but the whole area still felt warm and tender to the touch. I still felt hollow and empty, and I ached for . . . something – something to feel; something to make this morning worth living through the night.

I felt too disconnected from the others, who had things to do. I wandered away – not too far, watched constantly by an FBI surveillance team – and sat alone on the beach, a blanket around my shoulders. I watched the sun gild the rolling waves and thought about Hurricane Andrew rolling in over these waters; about a Warden named Bob Biringanine wading out into the pounding surf and giving up his soul.

'Can I join you?'

I shaded my eyes and looked up. David was standing next to me, looking out at the ocean. Sunrise looked good on him, but he seemed remote and guarded.

'Sure. Pull up some sand,' I said. He folded himself down with raw, beautiful grace, and put his arm around my shoulders. I let my head rest against his chest, and felt a little of the darkness bleed out of me – just a little.

'I should go help,' I said dully. 'There's so much to do. So many people hurt—'

'And you're one of them,' David said, and pulled me into his lap, cradling me in his arms so he could look at me at close range. He gave me the distant Djinn X-ray stare for a second, and then the distance faded away. 'So much pain, Jo. You can't hold that much pain. You have to let it go.'

'It's all my fault,' I said. 'I could have—'

'You could have done a million things differently, and Bad Bob would have been the same creature,' David said. 'He's no longer human, Jo. He hasn't been human for a long time. You're not to blame for what he does.'

'Only for what I do. I should have said no. If I'd said no to you, none of this—'

'If you'd said no to me, Bad Bob would have found another way to control the Djinn. Maybe just by taking you away from me.' His lips found mine, gentle and sweet and salted from the sea spray. 'You make me vulnerable, yes, but you also make me strong. Jonathan knew that. He knew this was coming, and that he wasn't capable of fighting it, not alone. He knew the two of us would be together. I love you. I will always love you. With or without a vow, a ring, a wedding. Yes?'

'Yes,' I whispered. Our lips were still touching. 'I – yes.' There didn't seem to be anything else to say. We understood each other completely in that moment.

The sun cleared the waves, burning through the clouds in bands of hot gold and orange, and in its warmth, in his arms, I got my wish.

However brief the moment, whatever would come, we had peace.

DON'T MISS THE NEXT BOOK IN THE

The Weather Warden series

'The forecast calls for . . . a fun read'
Jim Butcher, author of the Dresden Files

'Another powerhouse urban fantasy'
SFRevu

'This is one that fans won't want to miss'
Darque Reviews

ALSO BY RACHEL CAINE

The Morganville Vampires series

Check out our website for free tasters and exclusive discounts, competitions and giveaways, and sign up to our monthly newsletter to keep up-to-date on our latest releases, news and upcoming events.

www.allisonandbusby.com